PRAISE FOR
WORLD WITHOUT END

"You can't keep track of the psychopaths without a score-card in Mooney's second nonstop action thriller . . ."

—*Publishers Weekly*

"Mooney's second novel is an espionage thriller that rings alarmingly true, especially in depicting the ways technology can be perverted to deadly uses. . . . Timely and thoughtprovoking."

—*Booklist*

"Chris Mooney's second novel, following on from the superb *Deviant Ways*, is a 21st century techno-thriller par excellence, where the line between the good guys and the bad is as ephemeral as a chalk mark on a rainy road. Not to be missed under any circumstances. And believe me, you'll be looking at fish tanks in a totally different way in future. Don't ask. Get the book."

—*Independent on Sunday* (London)

PRAISE FOR
DEVIANT WAYS

"This book has it all—a great thriller. . . . Polished writing, outstanding characterization, and superb plotting."

—*Tulsa World* (OK)

"A really, really exciting story. . . . A most thrilling manhunt. . . . The Sandman is pure evil, pure genius, pure killer, and brilliantly portrayed. . . . *Deviant Ways* is a terrific novel by a new author. . . . This guy is good."

—*Times Record News* (Wichita Falls, TX)

"Move over, Hannibal Lecter. The Sandman is coming, and he's going to knock you off your perch as the world's creepiest and smartest serial killer. . . . [A] nailbiting, scarifying debut thriller. . . . Grab this bloody, violent, and mesmerizing study of psychological terror and the redemptive power of love. . . . Just don't read it on a stormy night when you're home alone."

—Amazon.com

"Mooney develops the key players almost as if he has plausible real-life people to copy their traits. Placing these individuals into a community inside an action-packed story line turns *Deviant Ways* into a brilliant thriller that will gain much fan and critical acclaim for a rising author."

—*Book Browser Review*

ALSO BY CHRIS MOONEY

Deviant Ways

WORLD WITHOUT END

A THRILLER

CHRIS MOONEY

POCKET BOOKS
New York   London   Toronto   Sydney   Singapore

This book is a work of fiction. Names, characters, places and incidents are products of the author's imagination or are used fictitiously. Any resemblance to actual events or locales or persons, living or dead, is entirely coincidental.

 POCKET BOOKS, a division of Simon & Schuster, Inc.
1230 Avenue of the Americas, New York, NY 10020

Copyright © 2001 by Chris Mooney

Originally published in hardcover in 2001 by Pocket Books

All rights reserved, including the right to reproduce this book or portions thereof in any form whatsoever. For information address Pocket Books, 1230 Avenue of the Americas, New York, NY 10020

ISBN: 0-671-04064-2

First Pocket Books paperback printing November 2002

10 9 8 7 6 5 4 3 2 1

POCKET and colophon are registered trademarks of Simon & Schuster, Inc.

For information regarding special discounts for bulk purchases, please contact Simon & Schuster Special Sales at 1-800-456-6798 or business@simonandschuster.com

Cover design by Jesse Sanchez

Printed in the U.S.A.

Mike Hauptman
Ted Castonguay
John Amirsakis

Three good friends.

NIGHT FALLS FAST

Stephen Conway sits alone in the cold, semidark office that is full of the sound of heavy rain drilling into the window so hard he wonders if the glass will shatter. He has no idea why he has been summoned here. He worked late into the night installing the audio bugs inside a working laser-rifle prototype, the only one in existence, and then went to bed, thinking his work was done. The phone call came a few hours later, at the ungodly hour of 4:00 A.M., the caller on the other end giving him the address and telling him to book it over here quick, no explanation, and hung up. As Conway waits, he guzzles coffee from a large paper cup. Sweat rolls down his back, gathering under the arms of his dark-blue shirt, his head pounding, his eyes puffy and bloodshot from being torn from sleep. He needs to stay awake and alert. Something is going down.

The door to the office bursts open and in walks the imposing figure of Raymond Bouchard, Section Chief, CIA Special Operations. He is widely known for being the type of guy you call when you need to get a job done quick and clean, no fingerprints, no mess. The man is a legend in CIA operations circles. He inspires loyalty, is fiercely protective of his people, and is extremely picky in his selection of Gold Team mem-

bers, those operatives who are on the outside, working in the line of fire. Conway's time in special operations has been spent on the technical side. This is Conway's first one-on-one meeting with the man.

Despite the early hour, the man's eyes are bright and free of fatigue; his gray hair is perfectly combed, his black suit and modern monochrome tie-and-shirt combination give him a stylish, contemporary edge not usually seen within the Agency.

Bouchard is not here on CIA business—at least, not in the official sense of the word. This meeting, this operation and its players do not exist.

Unofficially, their group is called the Information Warfare Analysis Center, or IWAC. Raymond Bouchard is Team Leader for this top-secret unit of select people that deals strictly with technology proliferation and, when needed, steals technology from other countries that could pose a threat to the national security of the United States. The IWAC group works on the fringes of the law, using whatever means necessary to combat potential terrorists. Its members cannot be traced back to the CIA and cannot depend on the Agency to bail them out if caught or captured.

Raymond Bouchard sits down at the head of the table, crosses his legs as he opens up a folder on his lap, and then looks up at Conway over his bifocals. As always, Bouchard's face is still, his eyes expressionless, the way a bear studies you to determine not only who and what you are, but if you pose a threat. The effect is unsettling, as if he is staring through you and finding nothing of merit.

"Chris Haug had a heart attack three hours ago," Bouchard says.

An IWAC operative, the forty-six-year-old Chris Haug is the man responsible for establishing a relationship with Armand. Armand and his group—all of whom are known to the IWAC team after months of surveillance—have been trying to purchase a blinding laser rifle that is being developed by a New York company. For the past eight months, Haug has been posing as Mr. Paul Elliot, a vice president of the company who is looking to sell the only working prototype of the rifle to Armand. Haug was to bring the case containing the weapon to Armand this morning. In less than two hours.

"Haug's listed in critical condition. Needless to say, he won't be there to make the exchange," Bouchard says. "You worked as Haug's assistant. Armand has met you."

"Twice, only in passing."

"I want you to be the one to give Armand the weapon and close the deal."

The words hang in the cold air, the void filled with the pounding rain. Cars and taxis race up New York's Madison Avenue, the world outside dark and wet.

"All I need you to do is carry the case into the house, give it to Armand, let him inspect the weapon and answer any questions he may have," Bouchard says. "Take the money and leave. The other team members will take it from there. Can you do that?"

"Yes." Steve Conway is twenty-nine, ambitious, and hungry for recognition.

"Now listen to me: Armand is itching to test this weapon out. Don't let him test it on you. The battery pack remains in the car. If he doesn't want to deal, then walk out of there. Don't try to be clever and don't lie. You know what happened to the last guy who tried to lie his way out of a situation."

Conway is all too familiar with the story about the man from Armand's inner circle, the man named Mitchell, who tried to line up a side deal with another buyer for the laser rifle. Armand found out about it and personally performed and videotaped the torture session that lasted over a twenty-

four-hour period. Conway recalls the autopsy pictures of the guy forced to put his hand inside a garbage disposal unit.

"You don't think Haug's absence is going to make Armand suspicious?" Conway asks.

"Armand's suspicious of everything. If Armand wants to know why Haug—Elliot—isn't there, tell him the truth. If he doubts you, have him call the hospital and ask for Room 226. You've got nothing to hide.

"Pasha will be listening to you through your watch." Bouchard points with two fingers to Conway's diver's watch. The watch's depth sensor is actually a sophisticated microphone that allows the IWAC team to overhear conversations. "If the deal goes sour—if Pasha even thinks you're in danger, she'll move her Hazard Team in. The car's waiting for you downstairs. The driver will fill you in on the rest. Any questions?"

"No."

"Good. Get going."

Inside the back of the limo is a dark navy-blue Armani suit, white shirt, a tie, and black shoes. While Conway changes, the driver, an IWAC member who has been working closely with Chris Haug, gives Conway the script: Be confident; act as if you belong there; don't let Armand or his asshole assistants try to intimidate you; if he does, give it back to him, show him you're equals, that with one phone call you can fuck up his world.

Conway asks a few questions, then the talking stops and they are driving across the rain-whipped highway, Conway alone with his thoughts in the back seat, listening to the windshield-wiper blades working overtime. An hour later, when the limo pulls up to a sad white ranch house with chipped paint in White Plains, New York, Conway has immersed himself in his character.

The driver, holding an umbrella, opens the back door. The

lawn is covered with colorful leaves; it is early fall and the days are still warm. A black, beat-up Honda Accord sits in the driveway. Conway grabs the bulky black case that holds the laser rifle, steps out of the limo, and, grabbing the umbrella from the driver, walks up the cracked concrete walkway, steps onto the porch, and rings the doorbell.

The man who opens the door is Blake Mattenson, Armand's computer expert. Blake, wearing a gray muscle shirt under a black suit jacket, is a pretty boy with pouty lips and the soft, feminine eyes of a doe. His thick, shoulder-length brown hair is pushed back over his scalp and falls over to one side like a girl's. On the surveillance tapes Conway has watched him inject steroids into his ass and then work out in his home gym wearing nothing but his Calvin Klein knit boxers, surrounded by mirrors, admiring himself as he works his muscles. If the guy put the same effort into his computer work, he might have found the sniffer program that monitored and tracked Armand's every e-mail.

"Mr. Mattenson, my name is——"

"David Klein, Elliot's assistant, yeah, I know who you are." *Blake, annoyed, looks out at the limo and says,* "Where's Elliot?"

"Mr. Elliot suffered a heart attack early this morning." *Conway's voice is strong and firm.* "He's in critical condition, but stable."

Pretty Boy Blake tilts his head to the side and eyes the case, his lips at full pout, and Conway gets a glimpse of the shoulder holster with the nine millimeter under the suit jacket. Blake is mulling over the situation. Conway thinks the meeting is about to get canceled when Blake jerks his head toward the inside of the house. Conway enters.

The ceilings are low, the rooms small and packed with old furniture and a worn, tan carpet that smells of mildew and wet dog. Blake opens a door and Conway follows him down the stairs and walks into a basement littered with stacked boxes, Christmas decorations, and the kind of discarded junk that belongs in a dump.

A table with a banker's lamp has been set up near the hot-water heater and furnace. Sitting in a chair in the drowsy yellow light is Armand, late fifties, balding, with a dark-brown mustache and beard that matches his dingy brown suit. His brown eyes stalk Conway.

Conway puts the case on the table. Blake pats Conway down for a weapon, Armand sitting there, his gaze still, unblinking. The man is small but compact and wears High Karate cologne—the only guy left in the world who owns the stuff—which only intensifies his body odor. His comical appearance is disarming, but Armand's people are too familiar with his violent, unpredictable mood swings that can, like a tornado, wreak havoc at a moment's notice.

Blake explains the situation to Armand. Conway doesn't wait for an invitation; he reaches over the table, unlocks the case, and flips the top open.

Lying inside the case's sculpted foam is a bulky weapon that looks like a movie prop from one of Arnold Schwarzenegger's Terminator movies. The laser rifle can cause a brief period of blindness or, at it's highest setting, can burst the capillaries in the eyes and cause permanent and irreversible blindness.

"Where's the battery pack?" Armand asks in broken English.

"You hand me the money, I transfer it into the case, and then I give you the battery pack and schematics so you can start production," Conway says. "That's how it works."

"How do I know this works? It could be a toy."

"You've seen the test results."

"On video. But I haven't seen it used on a real person. This could be a fake."

Conway smiles. "Are you suggesting that my boss is trying to cheat you?"

"Go outside and bring me back the battery pack. I want to test it now."

"No."

"What did you say?"

"Mr. Elliot's instructions were very specific. You know how the deal is supposed to go down, so stop trying to jerk me around."

"You stupid—"

"If you don't like it, I walk out of here with the weapon. Now, do you want to complete the deal or not?"

Armand's face is red. The air feels warm, too close with Armand's body odor and cheap cologne and the smell of the rain on his clothes. Behind the man is a door leading out into the backyard. Through the panes of glass inside the door Conway can see mud puddles dancing with raindrops.

Armand places the rifle back inside the foam, shuts the box, locks it. Then he reaches down for something on the floor. Blake moves a step closer to the table. Pretty Boy is grinning, acting tough and cocky the way all juice heads do, thinking that muscles and size win the fight. Conway is glad for the close proximity; it will make his job easier if he has to take the guy down or, better yet, use him as a shield.

Conway, his face neutral, watches as Armand's hand comes up. Conway's body is tense, ready to react.

Armand is holding a green L.L. Bean duffel bag. He places it on the table, unzips it. The bag is full of one-hundred-dollar bills.

"It's all there," Armand says. "Count it."

"I trust you."

Armand reaches inside the bag and comes back with a nine-millimeter Glock, raises the weapon to Conway and pulls the trigger.

The round slams into Conway's left shoulder, right above his heart, the intended target, and Conway is hurled back against the concrete wall, knocking over boxes and falling backward until the floor breaks his fall.

Blake grabs the case and runs up the stairs. Armand should have left with him. He should have taken the money and bolted out the back door. Instead he walks over to Conway. Armand's deeply tanned face glows in the pale light, his face a blank stare, his eyes so far, far away.

Conway writhes on the floor, his right hand grabbing the wound, his shoulder a throbbing mess of pain and blood; he can feel it pouring through his fingers and spurting on his chin and dropping on his face like red rain. He's losing blood—fast.

Armand gets down on one knee and places the gun in the center of Conway's head and clicks back the hammer. This close Conway knows how to disarm Armand—an easy kenpo maneuver. But he can't move. He feels weak and light-headed and it triggers a memory from his childhood: himself at age ten, lying in a fetal position on the freshly mowed grass in the backyard of his foster parents' house with two broken ribs, every breath being drawn into the lungs like air laced with acid. That doesn't stop Todd Merrill, the fifteen-year-old punk with the thick, rugged build of a bouncer, from kicking. With eyes as lifeless as stone, he winds his foot back, his mouth twisted in an odd, erotic grimace, the expression of a boy relishing the taste of a dark gift that promises to deliver him the most intense orgasm of his life, and kicks the back of Conway's head like it's a football. Todd winds up again and this time kicks him in the spine, wham-wham-wham. Blinding white stars of pain explode behind Conway's eyes like fireworks while Merrill's younger brother Jarrod sits in a lawn chair, eating from a bag of Fritos, Conway helpless and unable to end it.

Armand licks his lips and then smiles, his brown and yellow teeth like a row of crooked tombstones, his breath reeking of rotten eggs and coffee and nicotine.

"You think you can trick me? You don't think I know what you're up to?" Armand says. From upstairs comes the sound of gunfire, bodies dropping to the floor, car doors slamming.

"Fuck you," Armand says and presses the trigger.

The weapon jams.

Armand stares at the gun before he tosses it away. Conway hears it skid across the floor, and from upstairs, he hears men screaming. One of the voices is familiar. Paul Devincent. Hazard Team member. He's hit, he's down, he's . . . what? Conway can't hear. Everything sounds distant now. He's starting to slide down that black hole, his eyes barely registering Armand as he removes the knife from the sheath tied around his ankle and then raises the weapon in the air.

The back door explodes open. A rush of footsteps followed by the soft puff from a silencer and Armand's head bursts apart like a dropped melon. Gunshots are being fired upstairs, furniture is being overturned; there is shouting, more gunfire, Conway can barely hear it. He is losing consciousness.

A black-clothed figure dressed in combat gear and dripping wet from the rain kneels down and takes off her head gear. It's Pasha Romanov.

"Man down in the cellar, quick," Pasha says into her chest microphone. She doesn't shout; her voice is even and focused. But when she leans over him and starts to work the wound, Conway catches the sad expression in her blue eyes, the growing knowledge of a mounting loss that cannot be altered.

I'm dying.

His world is fading. He sees blood—his blood—splash

against the pale skin of her face and mouth. She calls again for help. But he can no longer hear. Conway already has surrendered himself to a darkness that promises to deliver him to a new world that never ends, a place that holds the answers to the questions he has sought his entire life.

1

Conway woke with a start. He lay on his stomach, sweating, the white bed sheet tangled around him like a vine and sticking to his bare skin, his heart pumping with a frantic energy, as if it were mustering all of its strength to ward off a familiar and powerful enemy.

The window fan was on; cool air blew across his damp, fevered skin. Outside, the Texas sun had just started to rise, the stars still visible in the dark blue sky. Dull red and gold slivers of light glowed across the cream-colored bedroom walls of the condo. The clock on the nightstand read 4:30 A.M.

Going back to sleep was useless. He had to get up in another hour and a half. He rolled over onto his back and stared at the ceiling.

The specifics of the dream didn't bother him. Over the past five years, the shooting had visited him dozens of times during odd moments—and always in his sleep, the rational part of his mind replayed the specific events of that day in a desperate attempt to glean some hidden truth that, once discovered, would somehow prevent him from future harm. Fairytale bullshit. Life, he knew, didn't work that way. Shit happens. What you did was bottle the incident, give it a label, shelve it away, and ignore it. His experience at St. Anthony's Group Home had taught him that.

What *did* bother him was the feeling the dream always left in its wake: an indescribable sensation of debilitating loneliness. The feeling was not new to him; it had been with him as long as he could remember, coming and going, varying in its intensity, and in his thirty-four years of life he could still not explain to himself or any friend or priest the cause of its origin.

"Bad dream?" Pasha asked, her English flawless. She lay in bed with her back facing him, her voice clear and strong, always strong.

"I'm good."

Pasha rolled over onto her stomach and placed her head against the pillow, her thick, dirty-blond hair strewn about her face and shoulders. She wore white panties and one of his white tank top undershirts. Her normally pale skin had a slight tan from the hours spent under the harsh Texas sun and her long body was firm and strong from her training in sambo, the martial-arts system used to train Russia's Special Forces. Middle age had given her a slightly feminine softness that he found attractive. That didn't mean she wasn't dangerous. Conway had seen her go up against the big boys many times. Pasha always won.

"The thing with Armand was a fluke. An accident," Pasha said. "You survived it."

Barely, a voice reminded him. But even now, in his semiawake state, he knew the dream had little to do with Armand and more to do with his irrational need to have the power to control and alter his surroundings.

"There's a lot riding on today," Conway said. "Two years of work. I want to make sure it goes down right. Make sure all the team members are in place and know what to do."

"We're prepared, Stephen. You're not in this alone."

"I realize that."

Pasha waited for the rest of it. She stared at him, her blue eyes filled with that constant expression of wariness and guard, the vigilant hunter staring down the scope of a rifle searching for the next target.

Conway looked away from her hard gaze. Her left ear was missing; what remained was a molten blob that, even when they were alone in the bedroom, she carefully hid behind her shoulder-length hair. No one knew what had caused the deformity. Her private life was as vaulted as her emotions.

Pasha Romanov was nine years older than he—had turned forty-three two days ago—and in the five years they had worked together, and even when their professional relationship had turned private, she had rarely opened up about her life. It was as if all of her memories and their affixed emotions were stored in vials only to be examined in private.

Conway propped himself up and rubbed the fatigue out of his face. "I'm going to go out for a run," he said. "Want to come?"

Pasha's full lips were clamped together, pouting.

"What?" he asked.

Pasha pushed herself up to her knees. Conway watched as she climbed up on top of him, her breasts swelling against the tightness of his white tank top. The first time he saw her breasts, he had been taken aback by their size and fullness. Pasha wore modern Armani business suits to work. She never wore clothes generally worn by most women and eschewed any style that accented her femininity.

Without a word or sound, Pasha yanked his boxers down his legs and then took him into her mouth. Behind her thick locks, her blue eyes stared up at him, her gaze serious and intense, the way one stared down an adversary. Conway surrendered himself to the smooth texture of her mouth, and the dream and the hollow feeling of loneliness that had haunted him just moments ago began to drift away.

Several minutes later, his knees grew weak. His body started to jerk. Pasha sensed what was about to happen and stopped. She slid out of her underwear, removed her tank top, then moved on top of him and guided him deep inside her. Pasha always had to be on top—she didn't like sex any other way—and he wasn't surprised when she grabbed his wrists, moved them over his head, and pinned them hard against the mattress with a surprising strength. Pasha needed to dominate him like she did everything else in her life; she controlled how they fucked, set the pace and tempo—she even controlled where he touched her by guiding his hands to certain areas, watching him the entire time.

Pasha leaned forward, her back arched, until her breasts rubbed against the upper part of his chest and the whiskers along his face, and then rocked back and forth, slowly, in full control, and stared down at him through her hair. Other women in his life had required constant foreplay before actual intercourse. Sex was a production. Not with Pasha. She fucked like a man, got right down to it without any pretense, no moaning, no change in expression, just greedy, give me what I need and absolutely no talking, her eyes always open and watching, her intense gaze reminding Conway of the way a jewel thief prizes a rare, priceless stone locked behind glass.

What a pair we make, Conway thought.

A moment later Conway felt the pressure build again. Without a sound or a change in expression,

Pasha rocked her hips even quicker while keeping his hands pinned above his head, her strength amazing. His body jerked and shuddered and a moment later it was over, both of them quiet, breathing hard and sweating.

Pasha lay on top of his chest, her breasts damp with perspiration, sliding against his already wet skin. She still held his hands in place and then rested her chin on his shoulder, near his scar, her hair covering his face and eyes. It was like he was looking at the world from a jail cell.

"I'll always be here for you," Pasha whispered, her words a low, drowsy hum against his ear. Conway could hear her labored breaths, could smell the sleepiness and sweat lingering on her skin.

"I know."

"I'll keep you safe," she said. "I promise."

Conway pried his hands away from her grasp, wrapped his arms around her back, and hugged her close to him. He felt the hard, rubbery stump of her left ear press against his cheek, a grim reminder that love and the whispered promises of solace and protection were no match against the chaotic agenda of the outside world.

2

According to the glossy sales brochures and slick advertising materials, Delburn Systems specialized in helping companies develop successful e-business solutions
for their Web sites. Delburn's twenty-odd employees,
the overwhelming majority of them in their late twenties to early thirties, had their own business cards
printed with their names, phone numbers, and job
titles, listing their areas of expertise. They hustled
about the city of Austin, Texas, playing the part of eager
young professionals looking to cash in on the exploding
potential of the Internet.

In reality, Delburn was a CIA front, the temporary
base of operations for the Information Warfare
Analysis Center. The five-floor, nondescript brick
building that housed them was owned and operated by
the CIA and used the latest technological advances in
biometric security to keep the true activities of the
company safe from prying eyes and ears.

The conference room was painted a pale yellow and
had floor-to-ceiling windows that offered a partial aerial view of the bustling activity of downtown Austin's
sprawling University of Texas campus. Steve Conway
was alone, the dream still clinging to him. He looked
away from the window, went over to the coffeemaker,
and poured himself another cup. Mounted on the

opposite wall was a flat-screen TV hooked up to a desktop computer.

Conway finished pouring his coffee and then drew the blinds. He picked up the remote from the long table, sat down, leaned back in the comfortable leather executive chair and hit the MENU button. Using the remote, he moved the arrow down until the word ROMULAN was highlighted and then hit the PLAY button.

The TV screen came to life with the crisp, vivid picture of a man dressed head-to-toe in what looked like futuristic combat gear. The black, lightweight outfit and attached motorcycle-style helmet was, in reality, a working prototype of a high-tech military-combat suit being developed by the Army's Future Warrior combat system.

The narrator began a Discovery Channel–type overview of the military suit. The two small boxes attached to the back of the utility belt contained a power supply fueled by liquid hydrogen, the other a climate-conditioning system that provided either warm or cool air to the soldier wearing the suit. The weapon's pod mounted on the soldier's wrist responded to voice commands, which, when activated, would fire either rounds of bullets or launch one of the four projectiles that could take down a car, even a helicopter. Mounted on the opposite wrist was a small, rectangular box containing a keypad and computer rolled into one unit, the heart and brain of the suit.

On the screen the soldier ran across an open field. Out of nowhere came a pistol shot, its sound erupting over the conference room's ceiling-mounted speakers. Conway watched as the soldier collapsed to the ground. The soldier was not hurt; the suit's outer shell consisted of a layer of body armor. Microsensors attached to the soldier's skin relayed his life signs to the nearby base camp; orders were relayed back to him through the receiver placed inside the helmet. The enemy could not hear the encrypted voices speaking over the helmet.

The soldier made a hand gesture to signal he was okay. No one was around to see it. The sensors placed inside the fingertips of his gloves relayed the gesture through microprocessors and then simultaneously transmitted the data back to base camp and across the visors of the other soldiers.

The helmet itself was a technological marvel; it offered night vision, could pick up thermal heat signatures given off by any living creature, and allowed a soldier to zoom in on a target and then transmit the image and its coordinates to both base camp and onto the visors of other soldiers. The carbon nanotubes installed in the helmet's visor protected the soldier from an attack from a new and potentially lethal technology: blinding laser weapons.

The next demonstration was the reason why Conway was in Austin.

The soldier stood up. For the purposes of the video, the soldier typed the five-digit code into the keyboard instead of whispering the voice-activated command. When he was done, the soldier faced the camera.

Conway leaned forward in his chair and stared at the screen. This was his favorite part.

Blink and you'll miss it.

The soldier waved to the camera . . .

And then vanished.

"Jesus," Conway mumbled under his breath. The transition was so fast, so fluid, that the first time he saw a demonstration, his mind couldn't process what had just happened—had, in fact, refused to believe what it had just witnessed.

This wasn't some Hollywood special effect. The technology used to make the soldier vanish was called optical camouflage. The wrist-mounted computer took pictures of the soldier's surroundings and using real-time pixel replication "painted" the images on the suit through thousands of fiber-optic cameras. Thanks to recent advances in computer microprocessors, the cloaking happened so fast, the transition so fluid, that it looked like the soldier had vanished into thin air. With the suit's power supply, a soldier could stay cloaked for more than eight hours.

Invisibility was now a reality.

A soldier could sneak into an enemy camp and kill everyone in their sleep, could sneak across enemy lines and plant a bomb, day or night, it didn't matter. Wearing this suit, you could walk up to a terrorist target and blow the back of his head off and no one would be able to see you.

The possible scenarios—and potential applications—were endless.

Which was why Angel Eyes was willing to pay cash for the working prototype.

Angel Eyes was the code name given to the man who, over a six-year period, had stolen several high-tech weapons from U.S. companies, most of them working prototypes. The stolen weapons never appeared on any black markets; they were never used to wage a battle on U.S. soil or against a foreign company. It was as if the weapons had simply vanished.

The true identity of Angel Eyes, his race and age, what he did for a living—all of it was unknown. The IWAC team believed he had a group of professionals who worked for him. The team didn't know if Angel Eyes was operating out of the U.S. or, more disturbing, what the man's true agenda was. Was he going to use the weapons for some sinister purpose whose agenda would one day announce itself to the world like the Oklahoma bombing? Theories abounded.

What IWAC *did* know was the name of Angel Eyes's last two victims.

A sticky foam spray used as a nonlethal means of riot control had been around for several years. You sprayed the target, the foam formed and then hardened, and the person was stuck to the floor or street, immobilized. No one died. A great, nonlethal weapon.

The problem was clean-up. It was a time-consuming, pain-in-the-ass process that was very, very expensive. Massive police departments like Los Angeles and prisons, where the sticky foam would be the most useful, wanted to wait until the technology was more refined. A twenty-two-year-old brainiac chemist from Berkeley named Jonathan King stepped in and developed a foam that, when sprayed with a certain chemical compound, turned into dust.

The working prototype and design schematics for the spray gun, along with all the backup information on the chemical compounds that made the foam work, disappeared from the Berkeley-based lab. Three days later, at a junkyard in St. Paul, Minnesota, a man and his four-year-old son were looking at a part on a 1987 Buick Century when the boy heard what sounded like someone crying. The father pressed his ear against the trunk and heard a dry, tired voice just barely stronger than a whisper crying for help.

King had been beaten unconscious, and someone had poured Drano down his throat. He was airlifted to the hospital and by the time he arrived had slipped into a coma.

Six weeks passed and then on a cold March morning King woke up. The police came by for questioning, but the problem was that King had suffered severe brain damage. He couldn't talk, but he could write, and when asked the name or a description of the man who had done this to him, all King could (or would) write were the words *Angel Eyes*. King suffered a heart attack later that night and died.

The major break came two years ago, with thirty-four-year-old Alan Matthews, an MIT graduate who was developing for the government a portable spying device that could pick up the magnetic signals from any unshielded computer monitor or laptop screen—any CRT screen. Using a specialized antenna, a person sitting inside a car could stare at the device's screen and watch as you typed your PIN number into the ATM machine to access your account; could read your e-mail or document as you were typing it; could even watch you perform business transactions that ranged from the simple credit-card order on the Internet to buying and trading stocks. Unlike its predecessors, this device had been designed to resemble a laptop, making it inconspicuous. The device's spying implications were endless.

Angel Eyes, posing as Mr. George Winston, the name of the main character from Orwell's *1984*, approached Matthews with an offer of half a million dollars for the device. It was not known how Angel Eyes discovered the device or how he found out the name of the Cambridge, Massachusetts, company developing it. What was known was that Matthews accepted the offer.

Matthews was a bitter man, insecure, a brilliant loner

who craved a glamorous lifestyle. On the day of the exchange, Matthews did not bring the schematics for the spy device called Tempest. He told Winston the device was worth more than half a million. The new deal required Winston to double the purchase price or the deal was off.

Mr. Winston accepted. Matthews, who had full access to the company and its lab, arranged a break-in.

A week later, on a Saturday evening, the spying device was stolen from the company's lab. A fire broke out sometime after midnight. By the time firemen arrived on the scene, the raging blaze had already decimated half the building. Matthews's charred body was found in the ashes. The device wasn't recovered.

The fire was front page news for both the *Boston Globe* and the *Herald*, but the theft of the spying device was never made public. The FBI was called in to investigate. One of the agents was a CIA liaison; the information was forwarded to Raymond Bouchard.

Matthews's condo was broken into the same night as the fire. The thief stole every item that could be easily fenced, including Matthews's computer equipment, discs, answering and fax machines, cell phone, pager and his Palm Pilot electronic organizer. What the thief didn't know about was the floor safe under the rug inside the walk-in closet.

Stored in the fireproof safe was a microcassette recorder that Matthews had used to keep a running verbal diary on his meetings with a man named George Winston. The tapes were mostly full of Matthews's ramblings about how smart he was and how he was going to retire off the money. He also boasted that if George Winston tried to double-cross him, Matthews would threaten Winston with the tapes.

While the tapes didn't contain an actual recording of Angel Eyes's voice or any in-depth descriptions of the man, they did contain one gem, the golden key the IWAC team needed to possibly infiltrate Angel Eyes's covert group: the name of Matthews's friend who was working on a highly advanced military combat suit that used a technology called optical camouflage.

Winston was very interested in this cloaking technology and offered Matthews an additional $200,000 for the information. Matthews refused, saying that he wouldn't accept an offer less than two million. Winston agreed and deposited the money in a Cayman Islands account that could be accessed only by Matthews, and only after the business was completed. Matthews handed over the name of his friend, Major Dixon—that was actually the guy's God-given name— and the name of the company developing the technology: Praxis, based in Austin, Texas. The money in the Cayman account was withdrawn just two hours before Matthews was killed. Had Matthews checked his account, he might have known that Angel Eyes had had a change of heart.

By the time Angel Eyes, still posing as Mr. Winston, contacted Dixon, Conway and the IWAC team were already in place. Conway worked as the company's network security administrator, a position that granted him access to all the company's servers, including the one that stored all the information on the project code-named ROMULAN.

It took the better part of a year for Conway to form a bond with the slightly aloof Dixon. During that time, Dix opened up and told Conway that a man named George Winston had contacted him via e-mail and then by phone and offered half a million dollars for detailed information, preferably testing footage, of the military suit and its applications. An additional 4.5 million would be paid to Dixon in cash should he decide to sell the prototype.

It took Conway only a few months to convince Dix to sell the information to Angel Eyes. Conway was in the perfect position to help Dixon. As the company's network security administrator, he could doctor the audit logs to show that Dixon had never accessed or downloaded the highly protected schematics or the more prized video footage showing the stunning cloaking technology in action.

Dix agreed to sell the video.

Today, after skydiving, at one o'clock, Major Dixon would walk through the Austin-Bergstrom International Airport to Terminal D, where he would wait for Winston and then hand over a compact disc containing video footage of the stunning optical camouflage technology. Dixon would walk away with half a mil in cash, the advance for the compact disc. Angel Eyes would walk away with video footage that contained a computer virus that would infect all of his system and registry files, decrypt his e-mail, and send all of the information, along with his location, to Delburn Systems. A microscopic transmitter inserted in the CD would allow the IWAC team to track the disc's location within a two-mile radius.

The door to the conference room opened. Conway turned around expecting to see Pasha. Instead he saw Raymond Bouchard, the team leader of the IWAC group, walk into the room.

3

"Stephen." Raymond Bouchard reached across the table with an extended hand. Conway shook it, feeling the power in Bouchard's long fingers as they wrapped his own. "Nice to see you."

"You too. You look good." The guy always did. With his deeply tanned face, his thick gray hair cut short, and his sharp, modern dark-blue suit with matching shirt and tie, Raymond Bouchard had the commanding, confident look of a powerful Hollywood agent about to ink the kind of deal that made national headlines. As always, his eyes were bright and clear, and he looked well-rested, as if just moments ago he had returned from a long and satisfying Caribbean vacation.

Bouchard pulled out the chair, eased back into the soft black leather and then crossed his legs, the cool air scented with coffee and a whiff of the man's cologne and shampoo. He scratched his chin—a sure sign he was about to deliver an unpleasant piece of news.

Conway sat back down. "What's up?" he asked, reaching for his coffee cup.

"Last night Echelon picked up a transmission."

Echelon was the name given to the U.S.-owned global surveillance network whose existence had, until recently, been kept secret. Monitoring stations placed around the world used computer-programmed dictionaries and voice-recognition systems to covertly intercept telephone calls, mobile phones, faxes, and e-mails. It was rumored that the U.S. had used the system for economic spying on other countries. With the Cold War over, the name of the game now was obtaining information on new and upcoming technologies to gain a competitive—and economic—edge.

"As you know, Echelon has the ability to lock on to key words or phrases," Bouchard said. "The male caller used the words *optical camouflage*, so Echelon recorded the conversation. The caller said, 'I can't wait to see this optical camouflage stuff in action. Everything's in place. Don't worry. It's all going to go down according to plan.' Then the call ended."

"You run the voice through the computers?"

"Same voice that called Dixon months ago, that's it. We traced the call to a pay phone about a block away from Dixon's condo."

Conway's mind jumped into overdrive, his imagination conjuring possible scenarios, none of them new. These scenarios—and how he would respond to them—had visited him in his sleep in one form or another over the past two years.

"You thinking Angel Eyes is going to make a run on the suit?" Conway said.

"Today, in broad daylight?" Bouchard shook his head. "Too risky. Besides, the Praxis lab employs some of the latest advances in biometric security—voice and fingerprint authentication, microchip-encoded badges. If he or anyone else tried to set foot in there without a properly encoded badge, the lab's alarm would sound and he'd be locked inside the lab."

"Not unless he uses Dixon. He's the only one who can gain access to the lab and the suit without tripping the alarm system. If he kidnapped Dixon and, say, arranged a bomb scare or a fire—something to get everyone out of the company—then Dix could walk inside the lab and take the suit."

"That's an interesting scenario."

"We need to be prepared for the possibility."

"We are prepared. Pasha's at the Austin airport right now with a surveillance team and two Hazard Teams. Two other teams will follow you and Dixon to the skydiving school, and we've got Randy Scott inside Praxis. And Dixon's wired. Everything the man says or does, no matter where he goes, the surveillance teams will have a lock on him and we'll be ready. For the scenario that you just described to happen, Angel Eyes would have to kill off every member of the IWAC group."

"Maybe that's the plan the caller was referring to."

Bouchard was about to say something when he saw the look on Conway's face.

"You're serious," Bouchard said.

"This guy . . . it's like he's made of vapor. He walks into an army base and somehow manages to disappear with a Blackhawk helicopter with the optical camouflage technology. We still don't know how the hell he pulled that off—unless there's something I don't know."

"We came in on that in the end, after the chopper was stolen. That one was strange, I'll give you that much, but this time, we're involved right from the beginning. Angel Eyes doesn't even know we're here."

"That suit offers total invisibility. Wearing it, being invisible—you would be a god. He could walk in and out of any company he wanted, steal whatever he wanted. Shit, the guy could walk straight into the White House

and assassinate the President." Conway twirled his coffee cup on the desk, stopped, and then said, "A man
would go to great lengths to have that kind of power."

Bouchard propped his elbows up on the chair's arm,
spread his fingers wide and then stared at his fingertips
as he bounced them together. "You really believe the
shit's going to hit the fan today."

"The truth is we've studied what little intel we've
got on this guy, and we're not any closer to discovering
what makes him tick. He has an uncanny ability to stay
off the radar screen. He reminds me of a bolt of lightning—just pops out of the sky, strikes its target and
then disappears."

"Does Dixon's sudden need to go skydiving have
anything to do with why you're spooked?"

Late yesterday evening, Dixon called Conway at
home and with a voice bursting with enthusiasm said
that they were going skydiving first thing tomorrow
morning. Conway, an experienced skydiver, had tried
to talk him out of it, but Dix said no, he was going to
do it—with or without Conway.

"You've got to admit, it's odd," Conway said. "Dix
said he *had* to do it. Today."

"So?"

"So you don't know Dixon. This isn't his style. The
guy suffers from panic attacks and he suddenly has the
need to go skydiving? Come on. It doesn't fit."

"You're suggesting that someone might have put
him up to this."

It was a possibility, sure, but highly unlikely. Dixon's
life was monitored around the clock. Every phone call,
e-mail, fax, therapy session—everything that the man
had said or done for the past two years had been
recorded and analyzed. If someone had contacted

Dixon, the IWAC team would have known and would have immediately reported it to Conway.

That hadn't happened, of course. So why was that sick feeling still twisting inside his gut, telling him something was wrong?

It's Psychology 101, my friend. You're afraid that what happened with Armand is going to be repeated today, so what are you trying to do? Control the outcome by minimizing the risks.

"I'm saying it doesn't fit," Conway said.

"I'll admit it's odd," Bouchard said. "But Dixon's an odd duck. I talked it over with Pasha. Everything checks out."

In a flash, Conway recalled the day of Paul Devincent's funeral. His wife had died three years before of cancer, and now that he was gone, his two small boys, ages eight and six, would go to live with an uncle in San Francisco. Conway would never forget the haunted look on the boys' faces as they watched their father's coffin being lowered into the ground.

Paul Devincent shouldn't have died. If I had done my goddamn job, then those kids wouldn't be orphans.

"What do you want me to do, Stephen? Cancel the meeting and blow our one clear shot at taking this guy off the board?" Bouchard opened his hands in an inviting motion, his tone so patient, so understanding, that it grated on Conway.

Conway looked out the window. It was mid-October, about two weeks away from Halloween, the blue sky cloudless. Back home in Boston, the air would be cool and filled with the pleasant aroma of leaves and wood-burning smoke blowing from chimneys. But here in Austin, it was going to be another scorcher full of humidity.

"Stephen?"

"I voiced my concerns," Conway said.

"Do you find your team members talented?"

"Of course."

"Intelligent? Dependable?"

"You know I do."

"Do you trust them?"

Conway looked back and shot Bouchard a hard look. "With my life."

"Then have faith in me when I tell you all the bases are covered. Go skydiving, go to a movie, get him laid—go wherever Dixon wants to go today. I want him nice and relaxed when he walks inside the airport with the CD. Dixon's the key to this operation."

"Understood," Conway said.

Bouchard leaned forward in his chair. "Hindsight's great after the shit's hit the fan," he said. "Hindsight loves to tell you what you should have done. I'm here to tell you that there was nothing, Stephen, nothing you or I or anyone else could have done that morning that would have prevented the Armand gig from turning sour. You're lucky you didn't die."

But two team members—two of my friends—did die, and we also lost the laser rifle. Conway drank some of his coffee. The whole operation had turned FUBAR—Fucked Up Beyond All Recognition.

"I have confidence that it will go smoothly," Bouchard said, and stood up. "You should, too. Just focus on Dixon."

"I won't let you down."

"You didn't let me down the first time, Stephen." Bouchard opened the door and then shut it behind him, leaving Conway alone in the quiet air-conditioned room.

Conway went to take a swig of coffee and saw a tiny clump of cream that had settled on the top. He thought of the evasive rat that once again, despite all the intense planning, had managed to thwart the trap and escape with the prized cheese.

4

The architectural plans for the penthouse suite were so odd, so unusual, that the condo association, naturally, had balked. But when it was explained that the owner suffered from a compromised immune system, the condo association, fearing a discrimination lawsuit, decided to let it go through. It certainly helped matters that each of the board members had received a handsome cash gift for their assistance.

The contractor who oversaw the construction had made a copy of the plans and had them framed. The two pictures had hung on the wall inside his home office until a burglar, for reasons unknown, stole them. The contractor died shortly thereafter, in his sleep, the victim of a heart attack.

The penthouse consists of three floors. The first and second floors are made up of wide, airy rooms with high ceilings and magnificent windows that offer sweeping, breathtaking views of the city of Austin, Texas. The floor is a seam-sealed white laminate called Mepalam; the corners of the room are rounded and leave no crevices, allowing for easier cleaning. Most of the third floor is uninhabitable; it is packed with bulky HEPA air-purification equipment and temperature controls that keep the air inside the suite cool, even during the winter months. The refrigerated air and the

Vesphene/Spor-Klenz cleaning solution keeps any bacteria or germs from incubating. At least, that's what his mind believes to be true.

Beyond the front door is what can only be called a two-room changing chamber. The first part has a floor made of white marble and a set of four lockers, two on each wall, for the three-man cleaning team. They work solely for the owner and have been handpicked for their discretion. They are well paid and must submit to blood tests at the beginning of each month. In this age of technology, disease runs rampant—a man in his position needs to be careful. When the owner is in Austin, as he has been for the past few months, they come to clean the condo every two weeks. If you are granted the rare opportunity to meet the man inside, this is what you must do:

Strip out of your clothes and hang them neatly inside the locker. Now face the long, rectangular monitor. The owner will want to check your skin for sores or lesions. Exposed cuts, even ones that are in the process of healing, are cause for rejection. Make sure your nails are trimmed. And do not try to hide anything. Security cameras placed in the corners watch your every move.

The stainless-steel shower has two doors that operate on locks controlled by the owner. Enter. The door will shut and lock itself, and the water will be turned on for you. It is hot. Pick up the bottle of PhisoHex and the scrub brush and then face the monitor. Start scrubbing your skin, paying particular attention to your fingernails, a known breeding ground for bacteria. If the owner is satisfied with the manner in which you have washed, the water will be shut off and the lock on the shower's second door will be released. Step out into the second room and begin the elaborate process of suiting up.

The regimen is specific. Do not deviate from it for any reason.

Towel yourself off and then toss the towel inside the biohazard bag. Use the iso-foam alcohol on your skin. Make sure you cover each part of your skin; the camera is watching you, and you will be told about the areas you've missed. Tyvek suits, folded and sealed inside plastic bags, are stacked in a stainless-steel container next to the shower. Rip open the bag and place the provided sterile Tyvek strip on the floor. Place one foot on the strip and then put the bootie on your other foot. Now step down with the booted foot and place the second bootie on your exposed foot. Slip into the Tyvek body suit and secure the hood around your head. The Tyvek body suit will keep your body hair and any remaining dead skin cells from contaminating the condo.

The glove process is elaborate and time-consuming. Two pairs of gloves are required. Again, rub your hands with the iso-foam alcohol and then put one glove on, rolling the cuff down. Repeat with the other. Now rub more iso-foam alcohol on your gloved hands and repeat with the second set, making sure that the gloves are sealed under the cuffs of your Tyvek suit. Secure the breathing filtration system across your mouth and nose, and then put on your goggles. If the owner is satisfied by the procedure, you are granted access.

The lock on the door clicks open. Come inside.

The HVAC unit is a constant, low rumble. The air-conditioning units give the rooms a cold, refrigerated feel. As always, the owner is alone.

Outside, the morning temperature has already

reached ninety degrees. The man's breath fogs the air and then disappears. If he is bothered by the cold, he doesn't show it. He stares out the window, the sunlight bright and warm against his pale face. He can stand like this for hours and stare. Thinking. Meditating. Right now, he is thinking about the origin of the name the CIA has given him: Angel Eyes.

The man's real name is Amon Faust. The CIA doesn't know this, of course. They know nothing about him. But Faust knew about them, about the trap waiting for him at the airport.

This morning, Faust was dressed in white linen pants and an off-white sweater. When inside, he preferred wearing white, the only color that could be bleached. His head recently had been shaved. Faust detested body hair. Each morning, he shaved his head and the few patches of skin on his body that were not horribly scarred by the burn. Only his eyebrows remained. Removing them would only draw attention when traveling outside. His line of work demanded anonymity.

Faust walked across the hardwood floor in his bare feet to the living area. Clipped to the waistband of his pants was a phone with a wire running to the headset and microphone. He would be on the phone a large part of the day.

It was safe to talk. The windows were multiple-pane glass with a Mylar film inside. If someone outside was using a laser listening device to pick up vibrations off the glass, they wouldn't be able to hear anything. The phone he used had state-of-the-art digital encryption that Raymond Bouchard and his private group of twenty-first-century warriors couldn't crack. The condo's walls were lined with copper and for added security he had devices that prevented phone calls, conversations, and emissions from TV and computer screens from being picked up by any outside monitoring devices.

Mounted on the wall was an audio system along with a single row of neatly stacked titles of rare vinyl records that dated back to the early fifties. He preferred vinyl records over audio tapes and compact discs, or the more popular MP3 music files, which could be pirated from any number of Internet sites. Faust found the weight and feel of the cardboard sleeve in his hands comforting, the way the needle sounded when it first hit the record, implying a shared intimacy between the singer and listener.

He was in the mood for something soulful. He scanned the titles . . . Dinah Washington. Perfect. He removed the cardboard with his bare hands and then slid out the record, catching a whiff of the aged, moldy cardboard. The man who brought him these records, Gunther, the boy Faust had raised himself, used a special cleaning process to disinfect the record. Ultraviolet light killed lingering germs on the cardboard sleeve.

Faust played one of his favorite songs: "TV Is the Thing This Year." As Dinah sang over the ceiling-mounted speakers, he walked into the kitchen, rubbing his hands over the cool, smooth surface of the Corian counters. He preferred the look of granite but couldn't risk possible infection. Granite was notorious for holding germs and lethal bacteria deep in the microscopic crevices, places that not even the cleaning solutions could reach. He opened the Sub-Zero refrigerator and removed a glass bottle of water. Faust had the water imported from Iceland, where the water came from a glacier that was over one thousand years old. He did not drink water from the United States, and avoided drink-

ing any fluid stored in plastic. The chemical used to
form plastic, Bisphenol-A2, was a carcinogen known to
leach its way into bottled water. The world was in such
a deplorable state, plagued with viral diseases that had
no cure and cancers and toxins that lived in the very air
we breathed, the food and water we ate. Faust knew his
measures were extreme, but they would help to ensure
his health. He had to live in order to carry out his personal vision.

The phone rang. Faust pressed the TALK button.
"Yes, Gunther."

"Conway and Dixon are on their way to the skydiving school."

"How many following?"

"A surveillance unit and two vans containing their
Hazard Teams."

Since Major Dixon wouldn't make it to the airport,
there was no need to direct any resources to the IWAC
members lurking about the terminal—or the CIA's base
of operations, Delburn Systems. The exchange of the
disc, no doubt laced with a computer virus, was not
going to occur today.

"And how is Major Dixon?"

"Nervous. At breakfast Conway tried to talk Dixon
out of skydiving."

"Obviously. And?"

"Dixon wouldn't back down. He wants to go
through with it."

"Good for him. It's about time the boy came into his
own." And over time Faust would show him how—the
same way he had taught Gunther.

"The equipment's all set up. You'll be able to watch
everything in your office," Gunther said. "I'll call you
when we're ready to move."

"Gunther?"

"Yes?"

"Be careful."

"You worry too much."

"You can't replace the things you love deeply."

"I'll be careful," Gunther said and hung up.

Faust's mouth was still tingling from the special mouthwash he used to neutralize any lingering bacteria. He slid his tongue across the smooth texture of his upper lip and looked out the window. To pass the time, he imagined Raymond Bouchard lying crumpled at his feet, naked and trembling as he begged for his life, terrified to turn around and stare down at the yawning valley of bones.

5

Major Dixon was throwing up again. This time he was doing it outside, around the corner of the Snack Shack so the skydiving instructors wouldn't see him. His painfully thin body was hunched forward, one hand splayed against the chipped blue paint, the other fiercely gripping the rim of a stainless-steel water bubbler. His sweating face turned an unnatural shade of deep crimson as he hurled more undigested remnants of his breakfast against the ground and sprinkled his sneakers and the yellow pant legs of his jumper's suit.

"A minute," Dixon wheezed when he stopped gagging. His nasal voice was pure Texas and had a slight, high-pitched whine to it. "Just give me a minute and I'll be fine, I promise."

Conway didn't say a word, just drank his coffee, his fourth cup. He was awake now, wired; behind it, he could feel his anger building, the way a car slowly warms up on a frigid New England winter morning.

He had tried talking Dix out of this skydiving nonsense at breakfast, but Dix didn't want to hear it. They were going—today. End of discussion.

Very unlike Dixon.

Conway looked across the wide, sprawling burnt-green field. An hour and a half drive out of Austin, and now they were standing in some town that didn't deserve to have a name. The skydiving school and the Snack Shack were the only signs of civilization on the lonely stretch of highway. As Conway looked around his remote setting, the air hot and smelling of baked dirt and dead grass, he was gripped with an overwhelming feeling of isolation. Somewhere beyond that deep, hard blue sky a satellite was locked on them, watching and listening.

Come on, Pasha, call and tell me what the hell's going on.

"You were right, I shouldn't have had that big breakfast," Dixon said, and then straightened up, slowly. He took a mouthful of water, gargled and spit. When he was done, he placed his head in the bubbler. Cold water sluiced off his face and hair.

At five foot six, Dixon was a good six inches shorter than Conway, and had a shallow chest with thin arms and legs that carried no muscle tone—the kind of body more suited to a twelve-year-old boy than a thirty-two-year-old computer genius. His eyes were set deep in his skull and close together and wide, giving him a look of perpetual wonder. The cheerful demeanor he projected to the outside world masked the sadness of a man who realized he was invisible through no fault of his own.

Dixon used his sleeve to wipe down his face. He had become a pro at blowing his lunch. Conway had seen the surveillance tapes of Dixon throwing up at the office, at his condo—Conway even knew about the most recent development, the blood. Dix had an ulcer.

Which made the job of trying to keep him sedated next to impossible.

Dix had suffered from panic attacks for a good part of his adult life, but it was only over the last few weeks, as today's meeting date drew closer, that the attacks intensified, becoming a daily occurrence that seemed to be inching him closer to having a nervous breakdown. Dixon usually kept it together at work, where his mind was focused on some bit of code or technical problem, but later, when he went home alone to his small condo, some disturbing word or image would worm its way into his mind and disrupt the normal, rational flow of his thoughts. He would stare off into space at an adversary only he could see, and within a matter of minutes his entire body would shake with fear, the alien voice that had taken over his mind convincing him that he was worthless and stupid—that was why he had never had a girlfriend, why everyone laughed at him and made fun of him behind his back, and why his whole life would come apart at the seams the day he handed over the compact disc at the airport. He would be arrested and sentenced to a life in prison, being gang-raped in showers. The panic attacks only lasted several minutes, but the irrational thoughts lingered in his mind for hours. Conway had witnessed it firsthand.

Dixon's therapist wanted to put him on the antianxiety drug Paxil. Dix refused. Meds were for sickos, the sort of thing a loser used to keep it together. Besides, he did *not* have a problem. It was stress, that's all, nothing to worry about, it would all pass. He was in total control and had everything together.

Dixon removed his glasses from his pocket, put them on, and looked over at the Cessna parked on the runway. The oval lenses magnified the nervous intensity of his small, birdlike eyes.

"You throw up your first time?" he asked.

"No, but I thought I would." Conway saw an opening and tried again. "Dix, if you're throwing up now, you'll do it again once we're in the plane."

"I'll be fine."

"A guy with a stomach condition shouldn't be going skydiving."

"A stomach condition?" Dixon snorted. "I don't have a stomach condition, I just ate too much food, that's all. Indigestion and a little stress. No big deal."

"I've seen the empty bottles of Maalox, Dix."

Dixon's face tightened.

"I know about all those trips to the bathroom, I've smelled the mouthwash. You've been throwing up for weeks now."

Dixon scratched the corner of his eye, his tongue working the back of his molars. "You saying I can't pull this off?"

"I'm not saying that," Conway said, choosing his tone and words with care. "What I am saying is on the biggest day of your life, you don't suddenly decide to do something as risky as skydiving without a specific reason."

"You didn't have one."

"What are you talking about?"

"On the morning of your twenty-first birthday, your friend John Riley picked you up and didn't tell you where you were going. He just pulled right into the skydiving school. You had no idea."

Conway didn't remember telling Dix the story.

"Don't you remember? Last year, when Riley was in town, he told—"

"Why do you have to do this today?" Conway asked, again.

Dix rubbed the corner of his mouth with his thumb, his eyes focused on the runway where the pilot was loading gear into the plane.

"I'm your friend," Conway said. "You can trust me."

"Your first time out? You told me when you jumped

it was the most exhilarating experience you ever had. That when your feet hit the ground you felt like you were painted with magic, all confident, like you had the world by the balls." Dixon's gaze dropped to the ground, but he wouldn't look over at Conway. "I never felt that way in my entire life."

Conway had his words ready. *Don't. Let him have his moment or you'll push him away.* He drank his coffee and waited.

"That's how I want to feel today," Dixon said. "I want to jump out of that plane and shed my old skin."

"Then let's go tomorrow. Let's go to a bar and relax, and then we'll go to the airport and—"

"No," Dixon said. Something in Dixon's face changed. "It has to be today."

Again with the urgency. Why?

"Dix, if something happens to you in the air and you can't make it to the airport, you can't call up our man and ask him to reschedule." Conway could feel the anger creeping into his voice and didn't care. "The deal will be off and then where will we be?"

"You know, I thought you, of all people, would be happy that I decided to do something like this." He had the wounded look of a man who had shared a deeply held secret only to have it ridiculed.

"Dixon, listen to me."

"No, you listen to *me*, Steve. *I'm* going to do this. You can stay here if you want, but I'm going to do this. Understand?"

"Dixon, look at the ground. You're throwing up *blood*."

"This conversation is over."

"No, it's not. You're going to listen—"

"End of discussion, Steve."

"Goddammit, Dixon, you're not making any sense."

"*I said end of discussion!*" Dixon stormed off to the bubbler.

The pilot and one of the jump instructors, Chris Evans, looked up in their direction, both of them staring.

Something's wrong.

What are you hiding, Dix?

Conway's pager vibrated against his belt. Had to be Pasha. Good. Maybe she had figured out what the fuck was going on.

6

Conway left Dixon and walked behind the back of the Snack Shack and kicked open the bathroom door. Soft yellow blades of early morning sunlight poured in from the window on his left, reflecting off the scuffed gray-linoleum floor that was peeling in the corners and the chipped white walls decorated with graffiti, crudely drawn images of male and female genitalia, and names with phone numbers advertising blow jobs. He checked under the stall, found no one, and locked the door.

His pager, the cell phone that was in reality hooked up to a satellite, his Palm Pilot—all of it was strapped to his belt under his yellow jumpsuit. He yanked the zipper down, removed the phone and then dialed the number displayed on the pager's screen. While he waited for the encryption technology to engage, he looked outside the screen window above the urinals and watched Dixon pace with his head down.

A beep as the encryption engaged, and then Pasha's voice burst on the line: "Back off. You're getting him worked up."

Dixon's Citizen's diver's watch, a gift from Conway, not only contained a transmitter and a hidden microphone that listened in on all of Dixon's conversations, the microsensors placed in the watchband measured his pulse, which could be read by the IWAC surveillance team.

"Crank up his heartbeat any more and you'll launch him into a panic attack," Pasha said. "Ease up. Now."

Conway kept his voice low and his eyes on the window. "He's hiding something."

"Raymond went over this with you."

"And we're about to go over it again. I know Dixon. The guy calls in sick when he wakes up with a headache. Now he's outside throwing up blood and wants to go skydiving? Come on. We're missing a piece of the picture."

"Stephen, everyone at the school checks out. Name, pictures, everything. We ran Dixon's voice through the machines. He's not lying to you, he's not keeping anything from you."

"Then what's this stuff about him getting the idea for skydiving—"

"From your friend John Riley. I pulled the tape. The whole conversation is there, only you were too drunk to remember."

"I'm not buying it."

Pasha sighed. "It's an easy read, Stephen. Dixon's father had dreams that his only offspring was going to be a big football star—that's why he stuck Dixon with that ridiculous name, Major. Only genetics had a different agenda. Dixon grew into this frail, awkward-looking weakling who has no interest or talent for football or any other sport, but what he *does* have is a brain that operates on a different plane than everyone else's. So what does the father do? Washes his hands of his son. Classic family drama.

"Now you step into his life, you develop a friendship, Dixon starts to confide in you. He can't measure up in his father's eyes, so what does he do? Tries to measure up in your eyes, the only guy who's taken an interest in him, the only person who accepts him for who he really is and doesn't judge him.

"The problem is, Dixon can't compete. You're good-looking, you're in shape, you're social, and women find you interesting—you're everything Dixon wants to be and can't. He's not going to back down because he doesn't want to look like a failure in your eyes. It's basic psychology, Stephen."

"You're giving me too much credit."

"Explain this: You come into Dixon's life and suddenly he's going to UT football games with you, taking an interest in the sport responsible for most of the pain in his early life. Why do you think that is? So he can patch up things between him and his father?"

"It's not that simple. Look—"

"Human behavior *is* simple. Take yourself. After the shooting you got back into the game. Why? To prove yourself to the team. And to me."

It was the second time today someone had questioned his professional judgment; the fact that it was now Pasha, his lover and confidante, who was testing him sparked his anger. "I'm getting tired of the cheap analysis," he said. "This gig is going south. Mark my words."

"I'm tired of baby-sitting. Go and do your job," Pasha said and hung up.

Conway pulled the phone away from his ear. His face burned. He ran his tongue over the edges of his bottom teeth and stared at the wad of chewing tobacco that someone had recently left in the sink.

The morning air was suddenly splintered by the sound of the Cessna's engines coming to life.

Conway walked to the window and looked outside.

A thin, wiry man with spiked blond hair and a lit cigarette dangling from the corner of his mouth was jogging over to them: Chris Evans, Dixon's jump instructor and partner.

Conway went back outside and rejoined Dixon, who refused to look at him.

"Time for takeoff," Chris Evans said in that long, trademark Texas drawl. His eyes shifted down to the breakfast splatter on the ground. A grin tugged on the corner of his mouth. "You boys sure you're up for this?" he asked.

"*I* am," Dixon said and moved past Conway without a glance or word and trotted down the slope of grass that led to the runway. Evans watched after him, taking a long drag off his cigarette.

"Puking always happens the first time out," Evans said. "Better he got it out now than when he's falling through the air. I can't tell you how many times that I've had jumpers spew all over me." Evans turned to Conway. "But I guess you've seen all that, since you've done this before. I see you packed your own chute."

"I had it in the car," Conway said, not really hearing himself. Unconsciously, he scratched the scar on his collarbone.

Dix couldn't stay mad. Once he got to the plane's door, he turned around and, typical Dix, he smiled and motioned for Conway to join him.

Evans said, "Time's ticking, my brother. We got a full docket today. You joining us or bowing out?"

Not right, it still doesn't feel right, goddammit.

Decision time, yes or no?

Conway boarded the plane.

7

Deep in the woods, less than half a mile away from the runway, Gunther Prad sat with his back against a tree, his hands folded across his lap, his entire body covered by a blanket that was in turn covered with actual leaves and tree branches. The blanket was critical in another way; it prevented a satellite from picking up his heat signature. As long as Gunther stayed under it, the CIA wouldn't know he was here.

Strapped across his shaved head was a pair of Viper binoculars. They were hooked into a specialized computer—part of the army's M.A.R.S. system. The computer took what Gunther saw on his headset and transmitted the real-time images directly to the computer screen in Faust's Austin condo. From the open hole in the blanket, Gunther watched as Steve Conway, lead team member of the secret CIA unit called IWAC, boarded the small Cessna.

Gunther had wanted to break into Delburn, the fictitious consulting company back in Austin. All those computers hooked directly into the CIA; man, the place was a gold mine just waiting to be tapped. It wouldn't take much to figure out a way to bypass the building's security. Once inside he could hack his way inside the company's computer network. Gunther was no script kiddie; he was a professional hacker. Bypassing the security and then raiding the databases to see what the CIA had on Angel Eyes, Gunther could do it blindfolded. After that, he would plant a sniffer program on the line that would record the group's passwords, activities, you name it, and then encrypt the info and bounce it all over the Internet so it couldn't be traced. A simple process, he had done it hundreds of times and not once had he got caught.

Faust wasn't interested.

Faust listened—he always listened—and sometimes paused to ask questions, but in the end had said no. Gunther knew better than to press for an explanation. He figured Faust already had someone working on the inside, maybe a mole within the CIA, someone with access to IWAC. Faust, Gunther knew, had contacts in all the major agencies.

Faust never mentioned who this CIA contact might be—or if this person did, in fact, exist. That didn't mean he was trying to hide the truth. He had been very up front with his reasons behind stealing the technology: "It's up to people like us to protect the good and the innocent. That's who we are, Gunther. That's what we're about. Always remember that."

Gunther trusted Faust. His debt to the man was a large one.

Gunther had been fourteen and homeless, forced to live on the streets of Prague after being kicked out of the house by his cunt of a mother, a goddamn *whore*. She was pretty for her age and always had a man in her bed. Sometimes late at night, when the groans cut his sleep, he would walk over to her bedroom and in the space between the opened door he would look inside the room full of candlelight and see his naked mother being straddled by a man, usually an older teenage boy (and sometimes, but not often, it was someone Gunther knew). Gunther's attention always drifted toward the men. He liked men. At least he thought he did.

Gunther sought refuge in the local gym around the corner from his house. The gym was this musty-smelling basement of gray paint and mirrors and pounding techno music and a locker room with showers that offered no privacy. Gunther begged the owner for a job and finally got one: working after school as a sort of janitor to keep the place clean. The money was horrible, but it gave him a free membership and allowed him to stay out of the house and away from his mother. More importantly, it allowed him to be close to the older crowd of teenage bodybuilders. Gunther liked to watch them work out, their muscles gorging with blood, sweat running off their brows and backs. When their workouts were done, he would find a reason to wander inside the locker room, the steamed air packed with sweat and testosterone, and through the pockets in the steam Gunther would drink in the sight of the hot water sluicing off their hard bodies and feel a sexual urge that he knew once validated would condemn him to a lifetime of rejection and hate.

But that knowledge didn't stop him from experimenting. When one of the boys approached him and offered sex, Gunther made the mistake of inviting him back to his house. His mother worked the bar on Wednesday nights and never came home until late. But for some reason, she came home early that night, drunk as always, and when she opened his bedroom door and saw what was going on, she threw him out and told him that she wasn't going to live with a faggot, that from this day on her son was dead. Gunther would never forget the look of relief on her face, as if she had suddenly been given the perfect reason to torpedo him from her life. Word got around. Friends wrote him off. Gunther was alone.

Living on the streets was manageable. But when the free food and scraps stolen from garbage pails dried up, the hunger gnawed at him until he grew desperate. Gunther had heard of the places where a boy's flesh could bring money.

It was about survival. It was just sex, that's it, no big deal. The men he was forced to transact with were often older, in their late forties to mid-fifties, some of them married, all of them out of shape and flabby, their bodies overgrown with untamed weeds of hair, their greedy hands gentle at first as they removed his clothes and then working his skin with a desperate and often violent hunger. Gunther didn't care about the temporary discomfort or the occasional beating. As long as he didn't have to look into their eyes and see the way they glowed with a perverse sexual energy that always made him feel like they had torn away chunks of his soul, Gunther knew he would survive. All he had to do was close his eyes and he could transport himself inside the dream world he had built, a place of constant blue skies and oceans and streets that didn't reek of dog shit, a warm sun, and a house with the kind of parents who could see the love inside the heart of a fourteen-year-old boy. The dream would die in the morning's harsh gray light.

The defining moment came on a winter evening. The man was a well-dressed foreigner from the United States who had been gentle, even loving, in bed. The man was buckling up his pants when his hands started shaking and he broke down and cried. Gunther had recognized his torment. He put a hand on the man's shoulder and told him it was okay to be gay, that he understood. The man's face twisted, and he turned around so fast that Gunther couldn't prevent the storm of fists from hailing down on him.

The air was cold, the wind biting into his skin like nails when Gunther bolted outside. He turned into an alley and found a stairwell that was out of the wind. He sat down and wrapped his coat around him and cried more out of anger than from the throbbing mess of welts and cuts. He touched his nose. It was bleeding.

"Don't worry, Gunther. It's not broken. Tilt your head back and the bleeding will stop."

Gunther looked up. An older man in what looked like a blue suit under a long black cashmere coat stood with his hands folded behind his back. His head was shaved, his skin pale and stretched close to the bone.

"What do you hate more, Gunther? Your mother or the fact that you're a whore just like her?"

The man's deep voice was pleasant, though oddly flat, with a distinct monotone quality that reminded Gunther of the space ship's voice from that movie *2001: A Space Odyssey*. The man came toward him, speaking.

"How would you like to start your life over? Leave all of this behind?"

"Who are you?" Gunther asked.

"The person who can make it happen. I can give you the world you dream about."

Gunther tried to see the angle, couldn't. "In exchange for what?"

"Loyalty."

"Loyalty," Gunther repeated.

"That and one other item, by far the most important." The man knelt down and handed him a handkerchief. His blue eyes were as bright and clear and as warm as the morning sky from Gunther's dreams. "Under no circumstances do I tolerate lying," the man said. "Always tell me the truth, even to the most personal and sometimes embarrassing questions."

Loyalty and don't lie? It couldn't be that simple.

"And I have to do what, blow you once a day?"

"No need to be crude, Gunther. You're a good-looking boy, but I don't view you in that way. I never will."

"What are you, like some sort of good Samaritan?"

The man grinned. "I've watched you on the street. You're cunning. Very adaptive. And you have other qualities I admire. I hate to see talent go to waste."

Gunther watched the man's face carefully when he spoke next. "I'm gay."

The man's eyes, his face, did not change.

"Did you hear what I said? I'm a faggot, I get off on sucking—"

"Thank you for enlightening me on the proclivities of homosexual men." The man reached inside his jacket and handed Gunther a sealed white envelope. "Inside is the name of my hotel, my room number, and a passport. You'll find enough money to buy a good meal and some nice clothes. The name and address of my tailor are in there."

Gunther ripped open the envelope. American money and a first-class plane ticket to New York.

"My flight leaves tonight. If you want to join me, come to my hotel no later than eight. The choice belongs to you, Gunther. It always will."

In the United States, Amon Faust provided him with unlimited educational opportunities, introduced him to culture, fine dining, showed him how to dress and act and walk so people would stop and take notice. But what Gunther prized the most were the personal gifts Faust had shared with him: the ability to sharpen one's mental clarity and to move through life fearlessly, and, most importantly, to never be ashamed of the dark range of desires and fantasies that ran through his blood. Some of the visions were so powerful, so real, he would wake up in the middle of the night covered in sweat, his heart exploding inside his chest, an intense heat building inside his loins that ached for release.

He decided to tell Faust about the visions. When Gunther was done, his eyes dropped to the floor, feeling ashamed and vulnerable and dirty for reasons he couldn't quite form into words.

"There's no need to be embarrassed. The visions are quite normal," Faust said, his eyes free and clear of judgment. "The key is to act against those people who can hurt or injure the good and the weak."

People like Raymond Bouchard and his IWAC team. People who intended to harm Faust.

The plane's engines climbed, getting ready for take-off. It was about to begin.

8

The plane's engines were warming up, the steady, rumbling sound vibrating inside the cabin packed with four bodies that were, thankfully, not very tall or wide. Conway had only been expecting three people: himself, Dix, and the jump instructor, Evans. The fourth guy, Paul something—Conway hadn't caught his last name—was clearly the cameraman; a small video camera was mounted on the top of his helmet.

Videotaping the jump was extra. Conway, having no use for it, didn't check it off on his registration form. It must have been Dixon's idea. Apparently Dixon was sparing no expense today.

Conway sat in the rear of the plane, next to the cameraman. Directly across from Conway and seated right next to the jump door was Dixon, wearing a helmet and clear wind goggles strapped across his glasses. He stared out the window at the ground, his attention turned inward to the business of psyching himself up for the jump.

The plane lurched forward. Dixon gripped the edge of his seat with both hands and kept swallowing, his eyes focused outside the plane, on the ground. The plane gained speed, bouncing over the bumpy runway of packed dirt and stone, the cabin shaking so violently it made him wonder if the plane would suddenly burst apart at the seams. The cameraman stared passively out his window while eating carrots out of a plastic Baggie. Evans blinked one eye at Conway in a gesture of shared conspiracy and then blew out a long pink bubble. Dix looked like he was about to blow his breakfast again.

Then the plane lifted off the ground and the cabin stopped shaking, the windows filling with blue sky as the ground faded fast. Conway's mind rolled back to that beautiful, warm October morning he first jumped, the day of his twenty-first birthday. He had sat in a plane not unlike this one, listening to its engines straining and leveling as it climbed higher into the sky, the engines sputtering, sometimes stalling, as if they were undecided about their job and without warning might suddenly quit. At that moment his heart had seized with an icy shudder that left him wondering why he had yet again listened to John Riley—the son of a bitch was always doing crazy shit like this—and had willingly strapped himself inside this badly constructed and amateurish machine that would at any moment give up and plummet to earth, killing them both.

Of course that didn't happen. The plane's engines had leveled off and everything was fine, and, just like now, the Cessna sailed straight up into the sky, nice and smooth. Conway felt that wonderful adrenaline-filled mix of fear and excitement burst deep inside his loins, electrifying his skin, and washing away his exhaustion and earlier paranoia.

Dix was no longer looking out the window. His head was bent forward and he was taking in quick breaths, his eyes locked on the altimeter strapped across the center of his small chest, watching for the magic number: 10,000 feet, the altitude at which they would jump. It would take the plane roughly twenty minutes to reach that height.

"Hey, Dix," Conway said calmly, like everything was great. His voice carried over the headset, catching the attention of Evans and the cameraman. "Take in deep, controlled breaths, Dix. In and out, nice and slow."

"I'm fine," Dixon replied, his voice cracking. His head was bent over the altimeter.

Evans clamped his hand on Dixon's shoulder in a show of camaraderie. "It's okay to be nervous. My first time, hell, I thought I was going to *shit* myself." Evans and the cameraman laughed. "Do the deep breathing and you'll be fine."

Dixon nodded and then went to work on his breathing, taking slow and steady deep breaths. After a few minutes, the wired energy in his eyes abated. The tension melted out of his shoulders and his grip on the seat loosened. His face didn't look as pale. He seemed relaxed. Now all Conway had to do was to get Dixon through the next hurdle.

Twenty minutes later, the plane leveled off. Conway looked at his altimeter. 10,000 feet. Time to jump.

"Show time," Evans said, unbuckling his seat belt.

Dixon would be performing a tandem jump. With Evans attached to Dixon's back, they would jump out of the plane together and free fall. Using his headset Evans would talk to Dixon, telling him how to tuck in his legs and where to place his arms to increase wind resistance. At roughly 6,000 feet, Evans would pull the cord and deploy the chute.

The tandem jump was the way to go. You had the built-in security of having a professional jumper attached to your back. If Dix got sick or blacked out, Evans would be in total control. This was a much more appealing route than what Conway had performed for his first jump, the static line jump. With only a line attached to his chute, he stood at the jump door, his knees turning to jelly, the harness wrapped around his chest that had felt so tight on the ground now feeling loose and flimsy, his twenty-one years of life in control of what seemed like a piece of string. Conway couldn't remember how he had managed to jump, but when he did, he had blacked out for a good three seconds. The next thing he knew, the parachute had deployed, *whoosh!*, and with a hard yank he was sent back up into the sky where he finally leveled off and then sailed toward the ground. When his feet hit the grass, the adrenaline rush flooded his brain with such a high that he felt invincible, in full control of his life and thoughts, like one of those maniacal Tony Robbins disciples who walk barefoot over a bed of hot coals and emerge unscathed at the other side, jubilant and victorious.

With any luck, that's how Dix would feel today, and the disc exchange at the Austin airport would go smoothly.

Evans talked as he made the final attachments to Dixon's harness. "Let's go through our checklist. When you jump, what's the first thing you're going to do?"

"Tuck my legs back like I'm trying to touch my butt with my feet. Keep my body loose and relaxed, like Gumby," Dixon said.

"Right. Now for the most important question: If you're in the air and have to blow chunks, what are you going to do?"

"I'm not going to puke."

"But if you have to, what's the plan?"

"Tuck my chin under my armpit."

"My man. How you feeling?"

"Nervous. A little light-headed."

"That's the adrenaline. It's going to make everything seem really vivid and intense. This is going to be the biggest rush of your life."

The pilot signaled Evans.

"Time to rock and roll. You ready?"

Dixon swallowed hard, nodded.

"Okay then, let's do it," Evans said, and then reached across Dixon's waist and slid the door open.

Air filled with the roar of the plane's engines rushed into the cabin, pushing Dixon away from the door. He grabbed each side of the door frame and steadied himself, his elbows bent, his eyes wide and unblinking behind the goggles as he stared past the infinite blue sky at the world below.

The cameraman reached up and turned on the camera, ready to record the moment, and moved behind Evans.

"All you've got to do is tumble forward, just like we talked about on the ground," Evans yelled over the headset.

Dixon didn't say anything. His body was frozen, his eyes wide and staring at an adversary only he could see.

"Nothing can happen," Evans said. "I do this every day. You're golden."

Dixon's arms were shaking. At first Conway thought it was from the wind. Then he saw that Dixon's mouth was moving, his words inaudible, his head shaking, *No*.

"I can't," Dixon said, his voice small under the plane's engines.

"What did you say?" Evans yelled back.

"I can't, I—I can't do this." His tone had a fevered pitch to it, each word growing louder.

"Dude, you *can* do this," Evans said.

"I can't."

"You going to puss out right here in front of your friend?"

Conway said, "Back off."

"Hey, once we turn around, no refunds," Evans replied. "That's the deal."

Dixon pushed himself away from the door, knocking Evans back. Dixon looked over to Conway for a sign of support. When Conway didn't answer right away, Dixon's face turned red, his eyes shining with venom, the look of a man cornered and prepared to come out swinging. *"You were right, Steve, I didn't have the balls to do it! You fucking won! I'm a fucking pussy!"*

Oh shit, he's having a panic attack. Conway said, "Dix, you're not a pussy."

"It's what you're thinking—it's what you're all thinking!" Dixon spat through his clenched teeth. *"I can see it on your faces!"*

"Dix, listen to me. It's no big deal. You're beating yourself up for nothing. It's all—"

A force like a brick wall slammed into Conway's chest and knocked him back against his seat. His body slumped to the floor. His head came to rest with a hard thump against the side of the plane.

Conway felt dazed. He tried to move and found he couldn't. His muscles weren't listening. They were limp and useless, and his eyes felt heavy. He could see Dixon clearly, could see the perplexed look on Dixon's face, Dix, unaware of the syringe in Evans's hand.

Dix, turn around, the guy's got a needle. Conway could hear the words clearly in his head, could feel the fear and urgency behind them. He wanted to push them out, but his throat wouldn't work.

"Steve, what's going on?" Dixon asked, frightened.

Evans sunk the needle deep into Dixon's neck and pressed down on the plunger. By the time Dixon felt the sting and moved his hand up to touch his neck, the needle was gone.

"Steve. . . . Help me, please."

Then Dixon's head slumped forward and the rest of his body went limp. Evans jumped out of the plane with Dixon attached to him. Conway sat there, powerless to stop it. Dixon was gone.

The cameraman placed the end of the stun baton just inches from Conway's eyes. The charge dancing between the two metal prongs looked like an electric blue and white snake.

"When I'm through with you, they won't even be able to donate your organs," the cameraman said, smiling, and hit Conway in the waist with the charge. Conway's body writhed until his mind turned off and everything went black.

9

*His own kidnapping—that seemed the appropriate word—
came when he was only five weeks into a six-month planned
vacation—a sabbatical, really. Conway was entitled to the
time, he had earned it. Christ, he had been going nonstop
since he graduated from college and that was . . . God, that
was coming up on nine years ago. Time seemed to be moving
at the speed of light. He blinked and the next thing he knew
he was eight months away from turning thirty. The pull of
his own mortality consumed his thoughts. He was coming to
grips with the fact that his life was nothing more than a finite
line held together moment to moment by chance and luck.*

*Of course the shooting had something to do with all of this.
How could it not? Every time he closed his eyes he could see
Armand's shaking hand, with its yellow nails and nicotine-
stained fingers, reach into his briefcase and instead of pulling
out the money, pulling out a nine-millimeter Glock and
boom, it was over.*

*The operation went fine. There had been a good deal of
blood loss, shattered fragments of bone that needed to be
mended, but overall it was a clean wound, the doctor had
said. You're in great shape, Steve, all that muscle helped save
your life. You're very lucky to be alive.*

*Lucky. The word was a constant echo in his mind, even
in his sleep. That's what life really came down to: people.
Everyone's a victim of someone else's decisions. I suddenly*

don't like the look of your face and boom, you're bleeding to death on a cold basement floor, the pain is excruciating, and upstairs, two teammates from the Hazard Team, guys who you consider friends, John Murphy and Paul Devincent, men you respect and admire—guys who have families and girlfriends and wives and kids—have rushed in to save your life only to be ambushed, and guess what, Steve? There's not one fucking thing you can do to stop it. And the truth of the matter? The goddamn kicker? You should have died with them. Want to know why you didn't, Steve? Pure luck.

That's right, ladies and gentlemen. It was pure luck *that Armand's gun jammed on the second shot,* pure luck *that Pasha came rushing in at just the right moment with her drawn handgun,* pure luck *that it took only one shot for her to cancel Armand's ticket before he got the chance to use the knife. Pure luck, ladies and gentlemen, no grand design or scheme, no divine intervention. It was simply* pure luck.

The rehabilitation for the shoulder went fine. The physical therapist kept saying the word over and over again: Everything's *fine.* You're doing *fine, Steve, that's it, keep moving, the shoulder's doing just* fine. *The scar's healing nicely, don't you think? Conway knew that the worst scars are always the ones you can't see.*

All he wanted was to be left alone. That landscape was very familiar, the mental geography well defined. Safe. A mental harbor. When the physical therapy ended, he turned in his cell phone and pager and left no forwarding address, promising to wear the watch with the GPS transmitter at all times, pay for everything in cash and use the alias. Conway knew the drill. Thank you, good-bye, and please don't call.

He rented a nice, small house in Vail, Colorado. A little expensive, sure, but he had some money put aside and man, it was worth every cent. Mornings were spent mountain biking, a sport that had always bored him, but he couldn't pass up the scenery: steep cliffs holding rolling fields of green, snowcapped mountains everywhere he looked, the air so clean and crisp that when it filled his lungs he felt a renewed sense of energy, of rebirth. Maybe a short run later in the evening if he was full of that peculiar energy that had no place to go—or better, some reading. Dennis Lehane's excellent novels got him through most of those long nights when he couldn't sleep. Sometimes he would look up from a book, the fire crackling behind him, and just watch the sunset, marveling at the way the sky would turn shades of magenta and red and orange, casting the world below in a soft, warm glow. His mind would grip it and carry it with him to sleep. The next morning the same routine was repeated. He craved routine the way a junkie hurts for a fix. Routine kept him from thinking about the shooting, kept him from hearing his two teammates screaming, begging for it to stop.

For five weeks he had spoken to no one. He had no family—not in the biological sense—but what he did have was two close friends from college, two people he could trust who both lived in downtown Boston. Booker and Riley didn't know about the shooting or how close to death he had really come, and they had no idea what he really did for a living. He had been pretending all his life, trying on different lives, seeing how they fit under his skin. Now he got paid to do it professionally. Funny how life prescribes exactly what you need.

A voice above him, far away, said, "Get rid of his watch."

A second voice, this one familiar

The cameraman. The stun baton. Dixon, he's gone.

responded, "I fried it. No way can they hear us."

"We have to make this look authentic. Hurry up and get the syringe ready. We'll be at the drop zone any minute."

Conway's thoughts seemed disjointed, the torn pieces of a picture he felt he should have recognized. He was aware of someone touching his wrist. Then he remembered.

Friday night, late October, and a whopper of a storm blanketed Vail with ten inches of powder. The following morning he went skiing and came back to the house around six. Samantha Richardson, a twenty-six-year-old investment planner from Boston, blond hair with a plain face and thin, tight lips, pretty in that waspy New England way, was here on vacation. She knew him as Jeff Cotton, a Web designer from Los Angeles. Conway checked his watch. She would be over in less than an hour.

When he opened the door, he saw at least nine men moving about the living room, dining room, and part of the kitchen, their hands covered in latex, all of them packing boxes and wiping down counters with an electrified urgency. Standing in front of the lit fireplace was Pasha, dressed in a solid-black suit, cut with the kind of sharp lines and curves that made Conway think of the sleek, powerful elegance of a Mercedes. A phone was pressed against her good ear, her right.

Pasha looked up and saw him, put the phone away and picked up the briefcase next to her leg. "Downstairs, right now."

The gray basement was cold and bare and smelled faintly of mildew. It was lit by two bare lightbulbs hanging from the ceiling. A dining room chair had been brought down; standing next to it was a bearded man with a blond crewcut drawing clear fluid into a syringe. When he finished, he placed the syringe on a silver tray full of needles and shiny surgical instruments that was set up on a TV tray stand.

"Strip," Pasha said to Conway. She wasn't smiling—she never did—but it was the way her expression changed when she looked at her watch, like an invasion was imminent, that

*made him rip off his clothing without question. When he had
stripped down to his boxers, Pasha kicked the clothes away.*

"Get rid of the underwear," she said.

"This is about Armand, isn't it?"

*"The woman you invited over for dinner is bringing
along two friends who plan to peel back your skin with pliers.
Their buyer wants pictures, so this has to look authentic.
Hurry, we're running out of time."*

*Conway slid out of his underwear. Pasha put her hands—
very strong, masculine almost—on his shoulders and turned
him around. "The scar's still visible," she said. "Perfect.
Stand still."*

*Behind him, Conway heard a briefcase snap open, followed
by the sound of latex snapping over skin. Next he felt something cool and wet, like hard jelly, wrap around his throat.
Pasha pressed it against the skin, making sure it stuck.*

*"It's a fake gash to make it look like your throat was slit.
Now get on your stomach," she said, and when he was lying
facedown on the cold floor she bound his hands and feet with
plastic flex-cuffs. "Turn your face to the left side, just stare.
You'll feel something cold. Don't move, just lie there and keep
still or you'll ruin the effect."*

*Cold liquid was splashed around his throat first and then
poured over his wrists and feet. A small red river ran across
his cheek and dribbled onto the floor: blood—or at least it
looked like blood. His mind rushed back to the memory from
not that long ago, that of himself writhing on the floor, the
blood real, the pain real. Pasha rubbed the fake blood into
Conway's hair, streaked it across his back and then rubbed
her gloved hand across the floor in a wide, flat streak to make
it look like Conway's body had been dragged.*

*"Stare off into space, keeping your eyes still. . . . Like that.
Good."*

A flash went off, followed by the small whine of the cam-

era as the flash recharged. Upstairs were the sounds of loud, urgent footsteps. This comfortable, quiet slice of life, with its luscious winter landscapes and clean, soothing air was being taken from him.

"Take a piss," Pasha said. "It will look more authentic."

Conway didn't ask, just did what he was told. He relaxed himself and urinated, feeling its warmth spread across his legs, his embarrassment overshadowed by the panicked tone in Pasha's voice. More pictures. Still bound, Pasha and the agent picked him up and threw him on the chair. More pictures. Pasha cut the flex-cuffs and tossed Conway a bath towel. Clean clothes were folded neatly in the corner, near the furnace.

A phone rang. The man grabbed a cell phone from the silver tray.

"Targets are moving," he said. "One van is following her, the other just broke off."

Pasha said, "Time to leave, Stephen."

As the van pulled out of the driveway, the last image Conway had was that of gloved men drawing the shades.

It was snowing at a good clip. They drove through the snow-packed roads, the ride bumpy. Conway listened to the van's tires crunching over the packed powder, his mind numb, unable to process the thoughts playing behind his eyes. Pasha sat across the table from him, leaning against the van's window. The moonlight highlighted the smooth texture of her full lips, but her eyes were hidden by shadows. The computer screens and the surveillance equipment were turned off, the back of the van dark and cut only by the bursts of moonlight that filtered in from the gaps between the trees.

"The woman you met on the slopes is Armand's second in command," Pasha said. "We think she may have formed her own group. We don't know how she found you. One of our informants provided us with her name two days ago. We've been watching her ever since. We got lucky."

Conway turned and looked out the window and watched the rolling banks of snow glowing in the moonlight.

"I'll find out the rest of the details later," Pasha said. "The pictures are to be left at a locker at the airport. We'll stake it out, follow the person who picks it up tomorrow morning and take it from there. Hopefully, they'll lead to the laser rifle."

"How long have you been following me?"

Pasha drummed her fingers across the table. She was never at a loss for words, even in times of crisis. Pasha was like Spock in that way: the vigilant, logical stoic; every problem had a solution. And she never, under any circumstances, let her emotions interfere with her job or her personal life—whatever personal life she had. No one had been invited to her island.

"Watch this," *Pasha said, and then handed him a pair of bulky goggles with earphones and a wire running into a virtual reality machine. Conway put the goggles on.*

A brief period of darkness followed, and the next thing he knew he was standing in a desert, watching a tank moving across the horizon. It was dusk. The sky was dark blue and full of rolling clouds. He didn't feel the wind but could hear it blowing around him. The effect was very real. It was like he was actually standing in the desert watching the sun's dying gold color reflecting off the tank's armor and—

Hundreds of dots appeared on the tank's armor, showing the area behind the tank, as if holes had suddenly burrowed through to the other side, and with almost lightning quickness the dots exploded into paint spills, bleeding into each other until the tank was gone, replaced now by desert and sky. The tank was there—it had to be, it couldn't just vanish—but Conway couldn't find any shadows or outlines.

"The technology is called optical camouflage," *Pasha said.* "Thousands of fiber-optic cameras are mounted on the tank's *armor. A computer takes pictures of the surroundings and, using pixel replication, paints a picture across the tank. Any missing information is filled in through an interpolation algorithm and within the blink of an eye, you're invisible. The U.S. Army's battle lab in Colorado has been trying to develop and integrate high-tech equipment for battle situations involving troops. It's called JEDI—the Joint Expeditionary Digital Information program. They're in the process of finishing a working prototype of a combat suit that uses this optical camouflage technology. You climb inside, press or speak the code, and within the blink of an eye, you're invisible.*

"The military, just like the FBI and CIA, can't afford the top-drawer technical talent, so they've turned to the companies that can. The advancements in this optical camouflage technology are due to the work of one individual: Major Dixon. Dixon works for a company called Praxis, based out of Austin, Texas. The project is code-named ROMULAN, based on the cloaking technology from Star Trek. I'm sure you've seen an episode."

An assignment was coming. Excitement bubbled through him and then a voice screamed out NO, *this was* his *time, he had earned it, the deal was that he would be left alone. Let someone else deal with it.*

Then another voice piped in and asked, What's the problem, Steve? Are you afraid to get back into the game, or are you afraid you've lost your edge? Which is it?

"Dixon was offered half a million dollars for information on the suit," Pasha said. "He hasn't accepted yet, but he's thinking."

"Who's the buyer?"

"We're calling him Angel Eyes. We've been tracking his movements for the past three years. Ten months ago, he stole this working prototype from an army base in New Mexico."

The desert disappeared and now Conway was standing on the floor of a high-rise office building. A Blackhawk attack helicopter was hovering just outside the window, the sound of its blades muted. The Blackhawk turned to fly away and suddenly the image of the helicopter melted, as if caught behind ribbons of intense heat, and then vanished. Amazing.

"What we know is that someone placed several remote-controlled devices inside the ventilation system that, once activated, delivered a drug that knocked everyone out inside the building," Pasha said. "Angel Eyes and his group—he would have to have a group to pull something like this off—managed to bypass all the security, got inside the helicopter and flew away. We've never been able to recover the chopper."

"What about the blueprints?"

"The databases were raided, and then a computer virus wiped out anything left. The paper files, which were stored inside a safe, were also stolen. All of it's gone, including the tape backup copies. Angel Eyes is extremely thorough."

"If Angel Eyes has the helicopter, then he has the optical camouflage technology. Why does he need Dixon?"

"The helicopter is a solid structure. It can't change shape or run or jump. Dixon is modifying the technology for a man. It's much different."

"Tell me more about Angel Eyes."

"We know he steals cutting edge technology—weapons mostly—and that the inventors disappear without a trace. So do the prototypes and every blueprint, backup copy—all of it disappears. We know he's left only two victims, and we know that he wants this military combat suit bad. I'll debrief you when we get to Austin."

"I haven't said yes."

Pasha removed his goggles. It took Conway a moment for his eyes to adjust to the van's semidarkness. "There's going to be an opening at Dixon's company, Praxis, for a network security specialist," Pasha said. "LAN management and all that. I want you to get friendly with Dixon. Guide him. We want him to sell it to Angel Eyes."

Pasha handed him an envelope. Inside was a one-way plane ticket to Austin, a license and credit card under the name Peter Miller, and a thousand dollars in cash. "Use the Miller identity until all this is settled," she said. "Then you'll be using your real identity."

This was happening too fast. He couldn't process it. He was quiet for a moment, thinking about the Armand gig, how it had turned sour and what he could have done to prevent the outcome.

"The shooting just happened," Pasha said. "You can't control every moment of your life. Let it go and move on."

"And Bouchard?"

"He handpicked you for this."

That surprised Conway. The last time he had seen Bouchard was at the funerals for the two team members, both of whom grew up in Maryland. At the last funeral, the one for Murph, Bouchard had been quiet, aloof from the rest of the group and not wanting to talk. Conway had tried to approach him after the crowds started to drift, but Bouchard had already walked down the grassy slope, sprinting almost, and was in his car. As he watched Bouchard drive away, Conway had the distinct feeling that he had let the man down. That feeling grew as the days stretched into weeks without a call from Bouchard, Pasha—no call from any of the other team members. It was as if Conway had been ostracized, a potential cancer that could infect the rest of the group.

And now here was Pasha with an offer to play in the starting lineup.

"Okay," Conway said. "I'm in."

"Good. Now I need you to—"

The window next to them splintered. Conway jumped back. Gunshots rained across the van, rounds ricocheting off the bullet-proof armor. The driver killed the headlights and floored the gas. The van started fishtailing over the ice. Under the bright full moon the winter landscape glowed in an electric neon white and blue light.

"Don't worry," Pasha said, nonplussed. "The whole van's protected, even the tires."

A phone rang. Pasha removed a phone from a console, pressed it against her good ear, listened, and then hung up without a word. She reached into a cabinet, removed a nine-millimeter Glock and handed it to Conway.

"Stay away from the airport, Stephen. Use the Miller credit card to rent a car. That way I'll be able to track you." Pasha got up and slid the van's side door open. "Get ready. . . . Now."

Conway jumped out of the van. He dove headfirst through a snowbank, tumbled over ice, and then came to a stop. He scrambled onto his back, his scalp, arms, and legs groaning from the fall, his exposed skin tingling from the snow and ice. Far away he heard the van's tires skidding. More shots rang out. He held the Glock and waited, his breath fogging around him.

The image faded away. Conway was coming out of his daze. He could hear the plane's engines and the voice yelling over it:

"Remember to inject him behind the ear so it won't show up in the autopsy."

"So it looks like he had a heart attack in the air, yeah, I know what to do," the cameraman said.

"Then hurry up and kill him. We've got to dump his body."

Conway's eyes fluttered open. He was lying on his back, that much he knew. His head was tilted to the side, pointed at the opened door with the roaring wind rushing over his face. He wiggled his fingers, felt them move, good, but still felt strange, a little dazed. He blinked, the heaviness in his eyelids dissipating, the world coming into sharper focus.

Hurry up and kill him, the voice had said. Conway was alert now. Ready.

Something made of glass hit the floor. *Clink*, it was a vial. Conway saw it roll past his head. Someone was straddling him. It was the cameraman, Paul, and he was holding a syringe. He looked at Conway, who was awake.

"Oh shit," Paul said.

Paul shifted the syringe in his right hand so it was now pointed like a dagger, his thumb on the plunger, bringing the needle down fast. Conway planted his knee hard in the man's scrotum. Paul's body went rigid; the plan that had been so firmly planted in his eyes evaporated and gave way to the god-awful bolt of nauseous pain exploding deep in his loins. He still tried to bring the needle down, but his strength was gone. Conway's left arm came up, blocking Paul's forearm, and using his momentum sent Paul's balled fist crashing against the floor, snapping the needle. Conway brought up his right arm, swiping his elbow hard across the man's face and shattering his nose. The cameraman tumbled off him and buried his bleeding face in his hands.

Conway scrambled to his knees. The disorientation was still with him; he had to grab the edge of the seat to keep from falling. The stun baton was on the floor. With his left hand Conway picked the stun baton up, turned it on and shoved the dancing electric spark right into the guy's scrotum. He watched Paul quiver until he slumped into unconsciousness, and then moved the baton away and turned toward the pilot's cabin.

The plane banked hard right; the floor tilted back and Conway lost his balance. He let go of the stun baton and tried to grab the pilot's headrest, missed it, and then tried to grab on to something, anything. He slid out the door like trash being spit from a chute. The last thing Conway saw before being swallowed by the sky was the altimeter reading: 9,500 feet.

On his back with his arms and legs outstretched, the wind roaring past his ears, Conway twirled and twirled and twirled through the blue sea of sky. Everything was spinning.

Get your bearings, quick.

He closed his eyes. A moment later the world stopped spinning. The wind pushed against his back and roared past his ears. He tucked his knees into his chest and then wrapped his arms around his legs so that he looked like a meteor hurtling toward the earth. Using his weight, Conway rolled forward onto his stomach and in one motion stretched out his arms and straightened out his legs, tucking his feet back. Through his wind goggles he saw the stretches of dead green fields. He pulled the cord and with a loud *whoosh!* and a hard yank was pulled back into the air. Conway was floating now.

The Cessna flew away from him, heading east back to the skydiving school, the building looking as small as a Monopoly piece. Conway navigated his way toward the school.

Dixon's fine, he told himself. By now, the IWAC surveillance team knew something had gone wrong with the operation and had moved the Hazard Team into position to rescue Dixon—probably had the goddamn school secured. The IWAC team could pinpoint Dixon's location anywhere on the planet through the GPS transmitter placed inside his watch.

And what if Angel Eyes has removed the watch?

There were the transmitters placed inside Dixon's shoes, belt, and wallet. His location could be pinpointed; he couldn't just vanish.

And what if IWAC doesn't know Dixon is in trouble?

Conway felt a cold wave of panic move through him.

You said it yourself. This guy has a habit of making things disappear. What if he—

No. The IWAC team *had* to know.

And what if they don't, Steve? You heard what the pilot said: "Get rid of his watch." Then the cameraman Paul responded, "I fried it. No way can they hear us." Angel Eyes knows about you, Steve, and he knows about IWAC and the teams—that's why his men removed your watch. The fact that he kidnapped Dixon means one thing.

Angel Eyes was going to use Dixon to break into Praxis and steal the military suit.

Pasha.

Conway felt his body grow still, his mind replaying what had just happened in the plane.

If they knew about me, then they know about her. About the rest of us.

Conway needed to land. Quick.

11

Two hundred miles away from the skydiving school, Martin Spader, dressed in a white T-shirt and jeans, sat at a circular table at a coffee shop inside the Austin-Bergstrom International Airport. A blueberry scone lay uneaten on a white plate and a copy of the *Wall Street Journal* lay spread across the table. Spader pushed the eyeglasses back up his nose, his ears covered by a pair of headphones attached to the Walkman clipped to his belt, and drank his coffee while he read the newspaper. Every once in a while he would look up from his reading and scan the area around Terminal D, the inconspicuous camera installed inside the glass frames transmitting the images to the white telephone-repair van parked in the airport lot.

Pasha's voice came over the headphones: "Martin, turn your head to the left—right there, stop."

A short, burly Portuguese man with black hair combed straight back on his skull, early thirties, sat hunched forward on a chair, reading a copy of the local newspaper, the *Austin American Statesman*. He wore pleated khaki pants and a dark-blue, silk short-sleeve shirt printed with dozens of white figures of big-breasted women riding surfboards. The man scratched the day-old growth along his chin, the brown eyes beneath his uni-brow shifting back and forth over the people in his personal space as if they were about to perform a lewd act.

Inside the back of the news van, Pasha Romanov leaned back in her chair, her attention focused on a monitor. The guy looked like a dark little . . .

Elf, a voice said.

Pasha propped her left elbow up on the chair arm and massaged her bottom lip with her index finger and thumb, her eyes locked on the monitor. Three men, all part of the airport surveillance team, sat with her.

"What is it?" Rick Bernard asked. He sat next to her, staring at the same screen but watching her out of the corner of his eye. He enjoyed watching Pasha—enjoyed thinking about what it would be like to be pressed against her bare skin, how she would taste. The ways he could make her moan. She wasn't classically beautiful, but banging her, he knew, would be a blast.

Pasha had sensed this, of course. She could smell Bernard's mouthwash and the expensive cologne he wore, not a hair out of place, not a blemish or wrinkle or scar on him. He probably detested sweating and getting dirty—the kind of guy who should have played Ken and lived with Barbie in their dream house.

Pasha said into the microphone, "Martin, the dark little guy in the blue Hawaiian shirt who looks like a reject from *The Sopranos* . . . yes, him. Keep your eye on him." Then Pasha turned to Bernard and said, "Zoom in on the guy's face. When he looks up, take a picture and run it through the database."

"You know this dude?" Bernard said, working the controls.

Pasha's brain worked visually; memories, even ones dating back to her early childhood, were stored like filmstrips, bright and vivid. She was especially good with faces.

"I've seen him somewhere before," Pasha said.

"Where?"

Pasha's eyes never left the monitor. "He's CIA."

In the back of the van the three pairs of eyes turned to her. They waited for her to elaborate. She didn't.

On the monitor, the Elf looked up in Martin Spader's direction.

"Got it," Bernard said. *Click-click-click* and a snapshot of the man's face was loaded onto another monitor. The computer scanned the dark man's face and with the click of a mouse button Bernard sent it off through the air back to Praxis, where the computer would search a specialized CIA database for a match. Facial-recognition technology had been used at the last Super Bowl. Each person who entered the stadium had his or her face scanned and run against a database of terrorists. As usual, the technology had fueled the Big Brother paranoia of several privacy groups.

"Print me a copy of his picture," Pasha said.

The van filled with the whirring hum of the color printer spitting out paper. Pasha kept her attention on the monitor, watching the Elf. Where did she know him from? Her mind couldn't retrieve the connection, but it was there, she could feel it; all she needed to do was wrestle it free.

She needed air, needed to be moving.

Pasha reached across Bernard, getting a stronger whiff of his cologne, and grabbed the thick sheet from the paper tray.

"I'm going to take this to Hazard."

"That's at the other end of the lot," Bernard said. "Let me fax it to them."

"I want to hand deliver it. Fax a copy to Bouchard." He was at Delburn, monitoring the operation.

"You think something's going to go down, don't you?" Bernard asked.

"It's too early. Maybe when Stephen arrives with Dixon." Pasha looked at her watch; Stephen and Dix were probably jumping right now. "Call me on my phone if you get this man's face," she said and exited the van.

Outside now in the aching heat, blinding white sunlight beamed off the car roofs, hoods, and windshields. Pasha put on her sunglasses. The dark lenses cut the glare. Under her black blazer, a white silk shirt was already sticking to her skin.

Why is that little man's face familiar? Or was she just spooked from the conversation with Bouchard?

Tomorrow morning, in what was destined to be national headlines for weeks, the world would know the story of how FBI Special Agent and counterterrorism expert John McFadden sold devastating secrets on joint FBI and CIA operations to the Russians over a ten-year period. Even more chilling was that Bouchard believed that McFadden, using a high level and still unknown source within the CIA, had discovered the identity of the IWAC group and knew about its operations. It was quite possible, Bouchard had said, that they had been sold out years ago to Armand, who had high-ranking Russian contacts.

That part of the story wouldn't make it to the papers. And Bouchard was strict with his orders: This information was not to be shared with the other team members. It would only put them on the edge. God knew they were edgy enough today. Once this morning's mission was completed, they would be advised of this recent development during this evening's debriefing.

She thought about the Elf again. She knew better than to try to rush the answer. It would come to her. As she moved through the space between the rows and rows of parked cars, her eyes focused on the end of the lot where the FedEx truck was parked, she felt the sharp knock of the Glock housed in the shoulder holster bounce against her ribcage.

Pasha eschewed the usual garnishes of femininity; she did not wear makeup or paint her fingernails, wear perfume or jewelry; she did not wear dresses, shorts, or the kind of shoes women often enjoyed wearing. She opted for what was traditionally men's clothing, pants and suits, and favored stylish Kenneth Cole loafers, which were comfortable and, if need be, excellent for running. She had never played or dressed the role of the pretty, delicate Barbie doll. Barbie couldn't bench press two hundred pounds. Barbie didn't know how to snap a man's neck or, if necessary, line up the sight of a nine millimeter and blow an enemy's head off with one shot.

The men around her were often troubled by her appearance and demeanor. It didn't surprise her. Men were terrified of women they couldn't control or mold, let alone one who could with a single punch drop them to their knees.

But not Stephen.

Stephen Conway was different, one of the rare handful of men she had met who wasn't intimidated by her abilities or lack of feminine wiles. And unlike the majority of men around her, Stephen had no problem learning or taking criticism from a woman. Stephen looked at her as an equal.

The fact that he made her knees buckle when she saw him in those tight knit boxers didn't hurt either.

The man at the airport has something to do with black ops. Something to do with Raymond Bouchard.

Pasha stopped walking.

At Bouchard's . . . was it his house? No. An assignment. Something to do with—

Her phone rang and the thought swam away.

She unclipped the cell phone from her belt and pressed it against her good ear. Parked in the corner of the lot and looking like a toy was a FedEx truck housing the five members of Hazard Team Four. Unit Three was inside the airport. Hazard Team Two and a surveillance man watched Stephen and Major Dixon. Everyone was in place, ready.

"Spader just collapsed inside the airport," Bernard said, his voice excited but not panicking—an emotion she refused to tolerate.

"Walk me through it," Pasha said, her eyes fixed on the FedEx truck.

"He grabbed his chest and fell forward and tumbled over the table. The watch he's wearing that monitors his pulse, it just flat-lined."

The FedEx truck exploded.

Pasha felt the ground shake beneath her feet; she stumbled forward, off-balance, reached out with both hands and grabbed the trunk of a white Honda Accord. All of it happened so fast her brain could only digest video snapshots: the two surrounding cars pushed onto their sides, knocking against the other parked cars in a screech of buckling metal and shattering glass; the force of the blast expanding, blowing out hundreds of windows and car headlights; the torn fragments from the truck showering down across the parking lot and roofs and hoods of the parked cars, dozens of car alarms going off.

Pasha turned away from the wreckage, looked back toward the IWAC surveillance team's white telephone-repair van and brought the phone back up to her good ear.

A man wearing shorts, sneakers, and a white T-shirt was hunched over the gas cap of the surveillance van. The brim of his orange UT baseball hat covered his face. Then he turned and ran up the road, his eyes covered by cheap sunglasses.

Stuck against the metal right above the gas cap was a device the size of a pack of index cards.

"Pasha, Unit Three has . . ."

"Rick, there's an explosive on the van, get everyone out of there."

Pasha tossed the phone to the ground and then reached inside her jacket for the Glock. Over the rooftops of the parked cars, she saw the man stop running, open up the back door of a black BMW and throw himself inside. The car sped away in a squeal of rubber—too late to get a shot.

Her attention snapped back to the news van, the side door open now. She was a good distance away but close enough to make out the frightened expression on Rick Bernard's face as he stepped out into the parking lot.

Pasha blinked and the next image she had was that of Rick Bernard being torn apart.

The van exploded. *Too close*, she thought, *I'm too close.* Then the shock wave slammed into her body and knocked her up into the air so hard and fast she saw her shoes jump off the ground. Her arms stretched wide, her hands clutching at the air, she flew backward with dizzying speed to the row of cars parked behind her.

The last image she held in her mind before blacking out was that of her father sitting next to her at the kitchen table, his stern, cold voice telling her to shut her mouth as his meaty hand pressed the medicine-soaked rag against the freshly burnt stump on the side of her head.

12

Conway's hands were quick. He removed the harness and then worked himself out of the jumpsuit, the air hot and smelling of baked grass and dirt. He noticed that his phone and Palm Pilot were still attached to his belt. A wave of relief washed through him. He thought that while he was unconscious, Angel Eyes's men may have removed the devices.

First, the phone. He removed it from its leather case and dialed Pasha's number, each number beeping loudly in still air pounding with heat from the unrelenting Texas sun. He hit the SEND button and pressed the phone against his ear. High above, very faint, was the sound of the plane's engines, fading. Conway made a visor with his hands, and covering his eyes looked up and saw the Cessna, so far away it looked like one of those remote-controlled model flyers.

He listened to the phone ring . . . and ring . . .

Come on, Pasha, pick up.

The connection died.

Conway swallowed, his throat dry, and dialed the number again. The call wouldn't go through.

Either the satellite was down or sunspots were interfering with the signal.

Or Angel Eyes is jamming your signal. He knows you're alive, that you're going to try to call and warn the others. You think he's going to let you get away with that?

If they were jamming the signal—entirely possible—that meant Angel Eyes and his men had to be close by. That didn't help Conway with the more pressing problem: calling to warn Pasha.

Conway tried a third time. Nothing. He shoved the phone back into the leather case and snapped it shut. He started pacing.

You're pissed because Pasha and Bouchard didn't listen to you. Congratulations. You won the "I-Told-You-So" Ribbon. Go ahead and pin it on your chest. Feel better? Good. Now get to work and solve the problem.

I'm standing in the middle of a field, surrounded by trees, and I need to get back to the skydiving school.

Conway's Palm Pilot had been modified by the Information Fusion Lab, one of the many labs within the CIA's massive Office of Science and Technology. He removed it from his case, powered it on, and then pressed his thumb against the square pad area normally used for writing. His thumbprint was scanned and then accepted. In the bottom right was a whisper-sensitive microphone half the size of an eraser. Conway brought the Palm closer to his mouth.

"Global."

The voice-recognition technology kicked in; the global positioning system program loaded and within seconds Conway had a bird's-eye view of where he was standing, all of it in full, rich color on the active matrix screen. A red circle was drawn around Conway's figure; next to it were the letters: SC.

Conway's red Saab was also equipped with a GPS transponder. "Locate Saab."

The position on the screen pulled back and then stopped. Conway could see the rooftops of the school, and in the upper right-hand quadrant of the screen, parked in the dirt lot in front of the school, was his red Saab, looking no bigger than the tip of a match. Now Dixon.

Conway spoke Dixon's code-name into the microphone: "Locate Traveler."

A blue circle appeared in the field behind the school, not far from where the plane had taken off, the word TRAVELER glowing in blue letters.

Dixon's still at the school, and he's still bugged.

Conway removed the plastic stylus from the back of the Palm and drew a line from himself to Dixon. A red line linked the two circles together. Distance: 6.3 miles.

"Shit."

On a good day, dressed in shorts and running sneakers, and if he pushed himself to the limit, he could do a six-minute mile. At that rate, he could make it to the school in just under forty minutes. Factor in the heat and the aftereffects of the stun gun and the six-mile run seemed like a marathon.

Conway drew a box around Dixon and then said, "Magnify."

The satellite zoomed in. The image grew fuzzy until it reassembled—the image of a man dressed in a yellow jumpsuit lying on top of the front hood of an SUV, an old Ford Bronco by the looks of it. *Dixon's still knocked out by the drugs.* Two other men stood beside the vehicle. Conway looked at the bottom right-hand corner of the screen that listed Dixon's six transmitters. They were all on and working.

For now, a voice said. *If Angel Eyes knows about my watch and the group, then he knows Dixon's bugged and will remove the transmitters.*

What were the men waiting for? They should have

already stripped Dixon of his transmitters. They wouldn't want him wired. That would send the Hazard Team into action.

Unless Angel Eyes has taken care of them.

Conway felt his chest tighten.

The only thing we know for sure is that the guys in the plane know you're alive. They know you're on the ground, standing in the middle of nowhere. The only way out is your car. It's not like you can just jog over to another road and call a taxi. You have to go back to the school. It's your only escape route. They know that and are waiting for you.

And while we're playing the guessing game, chew on this: Don't you find it the slightest bit odd that while you were unconscious, they didn't remove your phone or your PDA? They knew about your watch—you heard the cameraman say so himself.

Conway looked up at the blue sky. The plane was barely visible but was beginning its descent. Once it landed, they would head to the next logical place: Praxis. He slid the Palm back into its holster. A six-mile sprint in this heat. Jesus.

Bitching about the distance isn't going to change the number of miles. If you want to save Pasha—if you want to save Dixon's life—then get moving.

Fear blooming inside his chest, Conway started sprinting.

At the age of three, one night after dinner Amon Faust's mother duct-taped his mouth and hands and feet, picked him up and carried him into the bathroom. She dropped him into a tub of scalding water, and while her three-year-old son thrashed and screamed, she walked to the front door, picked up the suitcase she had packed earlier that day, and headed out of their tiny San Francisco apartment to the taxi waiting for her downstairs.

An elderly neighbor had heard the commotion and ran upstairs. Fortunately, the door to the apartment was unlocked. Without hesitating, the old woman, who had grandchildren of her own, reached inside the water and rescued Amon from the tub, burning both her hands in the process. While Amon was at the hospital being sedated for pain, his mother was in Los Angeles, picking up her fake license, passport, and social security card. She then disappeared into a new life.

The burns were so severe that they required numerous and painful surgeries, all of them paid for by the state. He was lucky, the doctors had said. His face wasn't damaged, and his hands were healing nicely. Still, foster homes had been reluctant to take him. Nobody wanted to be responsible for a child who was constantly sick, his immune system having been weak-

ened from the burns. At the group homes, where children knew no mercy, Amon was ridiculed and avoided.
Nobody wanted to be around a freak whose entire body
was covered with thick, hard red coils and rubbery
patches of scars that resembled seaweed.

Amon had retreated into the world of literature and
art. He discovered that he had a talent for painting. He
preferred oils over watercolors, and in times of great
stress, he would pick up a brush and lose himself in a
blank canvas for hours. He was painting right now.

The human physique had always fascinated him. The
female body, while sexually appealing, seemed too soft.
It lacked strength. Amon preferred the male anatomy.
Maybe because he lacked a defining male physique of
his own, but the truth was that Amon preferred to be in
the company of men. He understood the male psyche's
vast complexity, its testosterone-filled drive to dominate
and shape its world, while women were, by their very
natures, slaves to their moods and hormonal storms,
irrational creatures who had difficulty grasping the most
basic tenets of logic and reason. As a result, Faust had
little use for them in his organization.

Faust was painting a portrait of Stephen Conway.
While he painted, he thought of the young man's troubled background. Like himself, Stephen had grown up
an orphan. Stephen had a strict moral code, was intelli-
gently gifted, adaptive, and, when needed, so very cunning. While Faust admired those traits, what fascinated
him most was the man's ability to get back into the
game after the Armand fiasco. Most people would have
shied away, but not Stephen. He was consumed with
proving himself, with proving his worth to his team
members. Stephen Conway was that rare twenty-first-
century gladiator willing to walk back inside the arena

to slay a new foe. If Stephen could be molded and shaped, Faust could turn him into quite a valuable asset. Granted, it would prove to be a difficult challenge, but it *could* be done. Faust had an idea, a way to turn him away from the rest of his pack.

His phone rang. The headset still attached, he hit the TALK button on the phone attached to his belt and then continued painting.

"Yes, Gunther."

"You in your office?" Gunther's low voice sounded troubled.

"No. Do you have Mr. Dixon?"

"You need to turn on your monitor."

Trouble.

Faust had programmed himself not to react. Anger disrupted the natural homeopathic stasis of his body and released toxins that would rob him of his strength and energy and, even worse, do irreversible damage to his heart.

"Just a moment, Gunther." Faust put his paintbrush down and then went into the kitchen and refilled his water glass. Dinah Washington's marvelous voice swam around him. Glass in hand, he moved into a sunlit room of hardwood and windows that offered a spectacular view of the University of Texas's sprawling campus.

Set up on a glass U-shaped desk were three twenty-one-inch flat-screen monitors, all of them pointed away from the window. Faust turned on the monitor showing the live video feed from Gunther's headset and sat down in the leather chair, leaned back and crossed his legs, his eyes focused on the screen now coming to life.

Through Gunther's Viper binoculars was a close-up of the computer prodigy, Major Dixon, splayed across the front hood of a rusted, battered Ford Bronco. Dixon was oblivious to the two men busily removing his clothing. Faust recognized one of them: Chris Evans. Evans removed Dixon's pants and stuffed them inside a blue laundry bag.

"They're stripping Dixon of his transmitters," Faust said, his tone and heartbeat normal. "Interesting."

"Who the fuck is doing this?"

"Language please."

Gunther sighed. Still young and still excitable. "You recognize these dudes?"

"I was told that Mr. Evans and the other members of the school were who they purported to be." *Obviously my inside source was misinformed,* Faust added privately.

"You think they're leftovers from Armand's group?"

"Armand didn't hire the intellectually gifted. We have audio, correct?"

"If Dixon is still wearing the watch the CIA gave him, yes. Ask Craven." John Craven was Faust's surveillance expert. Like the IWAC group, Faust had the frequency of Dixon's watch and could listen in on Dixon's conversations.

Line two was ringing.

"Speak of the devil, Mr. Craven's calling in," Faust said and hit line two, bringing the second caller into the conversation. John Craven told Faust to turn on his monitor.

Monitor two: a jarred imaged of an overturned Delburn Systems van engulfed in flames, its metal twisted from an explosion. Bodies on the ground, the screaming muted as Dinah Washington broke into "Evil Gal Blues," her voice strong and clear as it played over the office's wall-mounted speakers.

"The man I got monitoring the airport just called in with this," Craven said. "An improvised explosive device was placed on the first van and took down the Hazard Team. Then an unidentified man placed a second IED right above the gas cap on van number two, the surveillance van, and then jumped into a car and sped away."

Faust was quiet, his eyes locked on monitor two playing the carnage at the airport.

Craven continued. "The IWAC guys placed inside the airport are both dead. Whoever's behind this is making sure there are no survivors."

"What happened on the plane?"

"Dixon had a meltdown and then it got real quiet."

"What about Mr. Conway's watch?"

"Nothing. And the teams monitoring and covering Conway have got *real* quiet."

Faust turned his attention back to monitor one. Dixon now lay naked on top of the car hood, his watch and clothing with its transmitters stuffed inside the blue laundry bag that rested on the ground.

Gunther said, "Gunshots."

On the screen Faust saw through Gunther's eyes the back of the skydiving school through the gaps between the trees.

"I just heard two more," Gunther said, keeping his voice low and calm, the way he had been trained. He tried to zoom in on one of the windows. "I'm not in a good position. I can't see anything."

"Gunther, move your attention back to Mr. Dixon."

Chris Evans and his partner had finished putting on a new pair of pants and a white T-shirt on Dixon. They slid him off the roof, dumped him into the back seat of the Bronco, got inside and tore up to the school in a cloud of dust and dirt.

Gunther said, "You think these guys are going to make a run on the suit?"

"That would seem like the logical progression," Faust said. "Gunther, find out who our new friends are. To do that, I'll need fingerprints. Mr. Craven, move your team to the skydiving school. Concentrate your efforts on the registration office and the plane."

"Understood," Craven said.

Gunther said, "Lifting the prints and transmitting them to you will take time. I'll have to wait until these guys leave to get started."

"I understand," Faust said.

"Then you also understand that by doing this, it gives them a head start to Praxis. All of our resources are here—"

"Would you look at this," Craven said. "Conway just landed."

"Stephen's alive," Faust said, hopeful.

"Alive and running in Gunther's direction."

Gunther said, "By the time Conway gets here, these guys will be driving off with Major Dick. You want to head them off?"

"Let them go," Faust said. "They'll do our job for us. And Gunther?"

"Yes."

"I want Stephen protected at all costs."

"Understood."

Faust hung up and settled back in his chair. He folded his hands across his stomach, his throat dry as he stared at monitor two, firefighters at work dousing the burning wreck of a van. Inside the office, Dinah Washington sang "Lover Come Back to Me," and Faust was gripped with a sense of loss he wasn't ready to acknowledge.

Through the gaps between the trees in the woods Conway saw the plane's white wing shining in the sunlight and stopped running. He leaned his lower back against a tree and then hunched forward, placing his hands on his knees, his breath coming in sharp bursts. His clothes were soaked, his wet hair matted against his head, his heart pumping so fast that he saw white stars dance across his vision. Panting, he checked his watch.

It had taken a little over forty minutes to get here. Forty-five minutes. Shit, that was a long time. Twenty more minutes and Dixon would be at Praxis—if they had, in fact, left.

The Palm Pilot was wedged in his right hand; he had consulted it as he ran. He brought it up to his mouth and said, "Locate Traveler."

The satellite locked on what appeared to be a blue bag, maybe a pillowcase, sitting in a dirt-baked lot. Angel Eyes's men had stripped Dixon of his transmitters. Now Conway had no way of tracking him. Neither did the Hazard Team.

During his run, Conway had secretly hoped that by the time he arrived, the Hazard Team monitoring Dix would have moved in and rescued him, putting an end to this situation. The fact that Hazard was nowhere in sight meant only one thing: They were dead.

I can't assume that. I can't assume anything. Dixon could still be here—the last time I saw him he was sprawled on the Bronco, right? Well, the Bronco's still here. Maybe they're waiting for me to come out, take care of me and then head to Praxis.

Conway had to get to a phone. Going for the cell phone inside the Saab was out. The parking lot was too exposed. Angel Eyes's man or men—whoever was waiting around here—would be expecting Conway to make a run for the car.

Wait. The registration office had a phone, a cordless unit that hung on a wall near a window that overlooked the runway. Conway could see it in his mind, a white AT&T unit with an answering machine. Now to find a way to get inside the building undetected.

The advances in satellite imagery were astounding. Not only could a satellite zoom in on a golf ball and count the number of dimples, it could also pick up your heat signature using a technology called thermal imaging. It didn't matter if you were sitting inside a car or walking inside a building, the satellite could look through walls and steel and concrete, as if they were made of clear plastic food wrap, and watch as you moved.

Using the Palm's controls, Conway decreased magnification until he had what he wanted: an aerial shot of the parking lot with four vehicles. There was his red Saab, a black van, and what appeared to be another SUV, also black and—holy shit, the old Bronco he had seen earlier, only now it was parked right near the highway, looking like it was about to take a turn and speed away.

Conway brought the PDA mike close to his mouth. "Switch to thermal."

The screen turned a dark gray, taking away the crisp, vivid colors. A single, glowing, yellow blob of color appeared on the screen where the Bronco was parked. Using the stylus, Conway drew a box around it. The satellite zoomed in on the Bronco until he saw the blurred, glowing heat signature of the driver sitting behind the wheel. The ground around the van glowed a dull yellow—the result of the sun beating down on the dirt lot—and from the back of the van came glowing puffs of smoke that burned and faded.

The Bronco was running. The driver was waiting for someone.

The skydiving school was broken up into three small units, all attached: on the left, the registration office, followed by the bunker containing walls full of parachuting equipment, and on the right, the final building, call it the video room, where he and Dixon had watched the skydiving video, talked to the instructors about how the jump would take place, and then signed the waivers freeing the school of any liability in case either he or Dix were injured or killed.

Part of the bunker and video building's roof was covered by the shade of the trees. Without the harsh sun beating down on the roof, the satellite could pick up heat signatures nicely. Conway moved the controls and checked both areas. Clean, nobody inside.

The registration office was trickier. With no shade and the sun beating down on the roof for hours now, the shingles had absorbed the heat. The registration office was a glowing blob of color. The satellite only offered an aerial view; Conway had no way to tell if anyone was inside. He stared at the blob, looking for movement, an outline or a shadow. Shit. If he only had a pair of handheld thermal binoculars, he could from this position scan each floor and check to see where the driver's partner was—

A screen door banged against its frame.

Conway looked up. He couldn't see anyone, not from this distance. On the screen, right outside the registration office door, stood the glowing red and yellow and orange figure of a man.

"Switch off thermal."

On the screen the world stopped glowing. Using the stylus, Conway zoomed in on the man and saw the blond hair—had to be Chris Evans. He was fitting what had to be a handgun into the back waistband of his pants. Evans ran down the length of deck that separated the office from the bunker and across the dirt lot. With one hand he reached down and scooped up the pillowcase. The Bronco's passenger's side door opened and Evans got in. The Bronco skidded out of the lot, kicking up clouds of dust, hit the highway with a squeal of rubber and disappeared down the road on its way back to Austin. To Praxis. Conway doubted they were taking Dix to the bank, where the compact disc was waiting. Angel Eyes wouldn't have gone through all this elaborate planning to retrieve a CD.

Conway looked up from the screen. White plastic patio furniture was scattered across the concrete deck in front of the bunker. To the left of the bunker was the set of stairs that led up to a weathered deck, and then the final three steps that led up to the registration office, all of its windows open.

He was close enough to see part of the office's white walls—and a shadow.

The shadow moved.

Someone was in there.

Conway removed his phone and tried calling one

more time, hoping. Nothing but static. *Someone must be jamming my signal.*

You've got to get inside the registration office and call Pasha, now, before Angel Eyes's men get to Praxis, before they kill Dixon and this mess of an operation turns FUBAR.

To get to the office, he would have to step out of the woods and run across the wide open field, exposed. No more cover from the trees, no Hazard Team coming to his rescue, no last minute miracle. One shot and he would be down.

Time to roll the dice.

Conway bolted toward the building.

Conway ran past the white patio furniture, shot into the bunker and pressed his back against the wall, next to the door that led into the video room. One hand on the doorknob, ready to make an exit.

No gunshots.

No shouting.

No rush of footsteps running down the stairs after him—nothing except the sound of his blood pounding in his ears.

He pulled out his Palm Pilot. Drops of sweat as big as marbles splashed against the color screen. Staring at the Palm's screen, waiting for a man to appear . . . nothing. All quiet.

Conway moved out of the bunker and stepped back into the harsh Texas sun. A quick but careful jog across the concrete and then he skulked up the first set of stairs, blood pounding in a steady *thump-thump* sound in his ears. He cleared the first set of steps and stood on the landing. Still quiet. His eyes pinned on the window screen, his ears straining as they listened for sound, Conway crawled up the final set of steps, staying under the two windows. The screen door was less than a foot away and the only way to know if someone was inside was to stand up and look. Big risk.

They had to have left someone behind. They wouldn't leave knowing you're alive.

Then why the hell was it so damn quiet?

If someone's in there, you duck and get down the stairs and jump over the railing and book it into the woods. If not, get inside and get to the phone.

Conway wished he had his Glock. It was in a lock box under the car seat. So close.

Taking a deep breath, hold it . . . now.

Conway stood up and saw

(Armand pulling the gun out from the bag and then, boom!)

an empty office. The figure he had seen earlier was the shadow of a tree branch against the white wall. No one inside here, just a tree branch. The office was clear.

Conway was alone.

His heart slowed a little.

He was sure he had seen someone inside the office.

The kid's starting to lose it, a voice said, one that sounded a lot like Gil Santos, the Boston sports radio announcer for the New England Patriots. *Conway's made a bad call. The other team's got him running around in circles and the kid's wasting precious time.*

Conway opened the screen door and stepped inside the office with flooring made of the same scuffed gray linoleum as the bathroom. Boxes stuffed with old computer equipment, sneakers, and boxes of cheap white T-shirts lettered with the words PROFESSIONAL TEXAS SKYDIVER were stacked on the floor and on flimsy tables cluttered with knickknacks and pictures and reams of paper. Conway shut the door softly behind him. The cordless phone was mounted on the wall, behind the front desk. Above the phone was a sky-diving certificate with Chris Evans's name. Conway grabbed the phone, dialed the number, and pressed the receiver against his sweaty ear.

No dial tone.

Conway tried dialing again. Nothing.

They must have cut the lines.

Conway tried his own phone again. The call still wouldn't go through. He wanted to slam the phone—

You're wasting valuable time. Solve the problem.

The closest sign of life was about a half hour down the road, a Mobil or an Exxon, he wasn't sure; it was the last thing he had seen before being swallowed by this expanse of flat green fields. The station would have a phone, but by the time he got there, Pasha would be—

Something wet hit the back of his neck.

Conway reached up, touched his neck, and then examined his hand.

Blood. His eyes moved up.

Mounted in the ceiling was a set of pull-down attic stairs, the wood painted white like the ceiling so it didn't stand out. A small red pool no bigger than a quarter had formed in one of the corner seams. Another drop formed and splashed against the floor.

Conway positioned himself so that when he pulled down the stairs he wouldn't get soaked with blood. He reached up and grabbed the pull-string and with a hard yank pulled down the stairs.

Warm tongues of blood slid off the wood steps and splattered against the chair and desk and floor. He moved off to the side and looked through the windows, half expecting to see someone coming for him. Nobody did. Back inside the office bright red pools gleamed in the sunlight and continued to drip from the ceiling and splash against the floor like spilled paint.

No way to step around the blood. He reached up and unfolded the wooden steps that would lead him up to the attic. He could see the rafters, the trapped hot air above filled with a distinct buzzing sound. Conway's mind flashed with the image from moments ago: Chris Evans standing outside the registration office as he fitted the gun into his back waistband.

Conway knew what he was about to discover. He climbed the steps until his head peeked over the attic floor.

A chubby woman with dyed blond hair and dressed in a white T-shirt and jeans lay facedown in a pool of blood, the right side of her face pressed against the plywood floor while her left eye, wide open, stared at Conway as if waiting for an explanation. A fly sat near the bridge of her nose, licking her drying tears. Her mouth was gagged with a cloth and duct tape, her hands bound behind her back with plastic flex-cuffs; so were her feet.

Conway climbed the stairs and stepped up into the hot attic laced with the overpowering stench of copper and urine. Lying next to the woman and bound in the same manner were two other bodies, both white men. All three had been shot execution-style in the back of their heads.

Conway crouched down, balancing his weight on the tips of his feet, and checked their pockets, hoping to find a cell phone. No phones, wallets, or IDs. Their pockets had been stripped clean.

The crotch of the woman's jeans was stained with urine. Pasha's words from Colorado: *Take a piss, it will look more authentic.*

Conway looked up. Through the screen window he could see his car parked in the dirt lot. The tires hadn't been punctured, and they had left Dixon's cell phone.

They cut the phone lines but didn't leave anyone here to get rid of me?

Conway stood up. He looked back out the window at his car and had a strong idea of what was supposed to happen next.

Confident he was alone, Conway let the office door slam shut behind him and walked across the deck shaded partly by the bunker's wall to his right. He moved down the final set of stairs and stepped into the parking lot, his hiking boots kicking up clouds of dirt, and looked at his Saab. The sun reflected off the front windshield and hood so brightly it made him squint. The car windows were rolled down, just as he had left them.

Conway removed the Palm Pilot from his back pocket, brought it close to his mouth and said, "Locate Traveler."

On the color screen the satellite zoomed in on the Bronco. It was no longer moving; it had pulled off the highway and was now parked twenty-three miles away from the school.

Conway knew why they were waiting.

Give them what they want.

He jogged back to the steps leading up to the deck, turned the corner, and pressed his back up against the bunker wall. Facing the office now, he used his free hand to fish the keys out of his jeans pocket.

Attached to his key ring was a black plastic keypad that allowed him to engage and disengage the car security system, unlock the doors and the trunk—it even had a remote starter, a great feature if you lived in New England and wanted your car warmed up on a cold winter day. Living in Austin, where the temperature never dipped to such frigid temperatures, he never had a reason to use it.

Conway found the button for the remote starter and placed his thumb on it. He turned his hand around the corner of the bunker and pointed the keypad at the Saab, his muscles tense. He pressed his back even harder against the wall and secured his feet. The thought of what was about to happen might have depressed him if it weren't for the fact that another vehicle was in the lot, a black Nissan Pathfinder, no doubt belonging to one of the dead employees.

It's going to be loud, but you should be safe.

Conway pressed the button to start the car.

The Saab exploded.

It was louder than he had expected, a deafening boom so intense that it muted his hearing. The pressure wave shook the earth beneath his feet and vibrated through his bones. Torn fragments of metal and flaming bits of debris blew past him and hit the bunker and registration office roofs, *clunk-clunk-clunk*. The overhang of the bunker roof protected him from being hit by the hail of debris. The Saab's steering wheel bounced off the deck and then a moment later the air grew still again.

Conway looked at the Palm Pilot, angling the screen in the shade, and saw the blue case being tossed out the window as the Bronco tore out of the dirt in a cloud of dust, on the highway now and headed back to Austin.

Angel Eyes now thought he was dead.

Conway turned the corner and moved into the lot. Blasted fragments of his car, most of them engulfed in flames, were scattered across the dirt. The windows in the bunker and video building had been blown out, and some flaming piece of debris had penetrated the video room. Flames had started to devour the curtains and a section of the couch where he and Dixon had sat and watched the skydiving video. *Going to be a breeze*, Evans had told them, snapping his gum. *You're going to remember this day for the rest of your life.* Conway bolted over to the Pathfinder.

The SUV's windows had been blown out; the seats were covered with shards of glass that sparkled like diamonds in the sunlight. Conway opened the door, hoping to find the keys dangling from the ignition—not a farfetched idea since auto security wasn't going to be a big concern out here. No keys in the ignition, no keys in the glove compartment, visor, or under the seat or mat. And the bodies in the attic had been stripped clean. *Probably inside the pillowcase with Dixon's stuff.*

The Pathfinder was a brand new model—automatic locks and windows, a security system, the entire SUV dependent on the dashboard computer system. Perfect.

Conway brought the Palm Pilot's mike close to his mouth and said, "Access Midnight Exit."

The IWAC group had developed a program called Midnight Exit to assist operatives who might need to make a quick escape. As long as the vehicle was a new model, the program could turn the Palm Pilot into a remote starter. All he needed was the Pathfinder's vehicle identification number. Conway searched the Pathfinder for the VIN, found it, and then spoke the long series of numbers and letters into the mike.

To drive the car, he'd have to disengage the steering lock, which meant popping open the steering column. Conway searched the back and in the compartment where the spare tire was stored found a toolbox. He removed a screwdriver and used it to pop the column. The wheel turned freely. Then he used the screwdriver to brush away the shards of glass on the driver's seat and when he was done checked the Palm's screen. The Midnight Exit program loaded, he pressed the button on the Palm and the Pathfinder started.

Conway got himself settled behind the wheel. The Bronco had a good thirty-mile lead. Pursue or go to the gas station and use the pay phone? Conway checked the gas gauge. A quarter of a tank. Shit. He'd have to stop down the road and get gas and use the pay phone to call Pasha and Delburn.

Gearshift in hand, Conway drove out of the parking lot. The driver's side mirror had been miraculously spared by the explosion and when Conway looked into the cracked glass he saw the video building engulfed in flames that stretched up toward the sky. The place was burning to the ground.

17

Gunther had removed the blanket. He was out in the open, exposed if the satellite was focused on this area. He doubted it. The guys who had killed everyone in the school and had planted the bomb in Conway's car were long gone. And so was Conway. Shit. Gunther had had Conway locked in the crosshairs of his tranquilizer rifle but couldn't get off a clear shot. Then the dude was off and running in the hot-wired car.

Soaked to the bone, Gunther moved out of the woods, the Viper binoculars flipped up so he could see with his own eyes, and jogged up to the debris-scattered dirt lot. Flames were devouring the last building on the left, and he could see a fire that had started in the woods. In this heat, the ground dry, this place was going to be the world's biggest bonfire in a matter of minutes.

Gunther called Faust: "They planted a bomb in Conway's car," he said.

"And Stephen?"

"Conway figured it out and detonated the bomb. Our new friends think he's dead."

"Do you have him?"

"I couldn't get a clear shot. Conway hot-wired a black Nissan Pathfinder and is headed back to Austin."

"To Praxis, of course."

"You think he'll try to tackle these guys by himself?"

"Stephen would rather die than live a life staring at a coward in the mirror."

"That's suicide. If he rushes in there by himself and tries to stop them, they'll find him and kill him."

"Agreed. What are the chances of him stopping at the gas station?"

"Good. I saw him try to use the phone in the registration office and then slam it back on the cradle. They must have cut the lines."

"So Stephen's phone must not be working."

"Or is being jammed. The gas station's the closest thing out here. He'll stop and use the pay phone. Rigby's there, waiting for my call. When Conway pulls in, we'll grab him."

"Are you sure Mr. Rigby's up for the job?"

"You need to give him more credit."

"Stephen could kill Mr. Rigby if he's not careful."

"Understood. The plane is still in one piece. Where's Craven?"

"On his way to you. When Mr. Craven arrives, hand over the M.A.R.S. system and let him work on the plane."

"He better get here soon. It's going to get hot here—quick."

"I want those fingerprints," Faust said.

18

A half hour later Conway pulled into a gas station, one of the new Mobils that had a garage and an attached air-conditioned mini-mart stocked with soda, candy, and pre-made turkey and ham sandwiches that tasted like rubber. On the front seat was a blue pillowcase containing all of Dixon's clothes and gear. He had seen it lying on the side of the road where it had been dumped, and he had stopped and picked it up, hoping to find Dixon's cell phone. It was in there, along with the rest of his clothes and transmitters. They had stripped him clean.

The problem with the cell phone was signal strength. Out here, with no towers around, a call wouldn't go through. Conway would have to use the pay phone.

Inside the mini-mart, a heavy man with tan pants and a blue shirt ran a mop back and forth across the floor. The pay phone was thirty feet or so away from the pumps, next to the air hose and well out of view of the mini-mart. Conway pulled the SUV up next to the self-service pump that was the farthest away from the store, angling the car so the pumps hid the missing windows—no need to draw attention to the stolen Pathfinder that would later be traced back to the sky-diving school. His time in Austin, he knew, had just come to a close; he would be gone by nightfall and didn't need a police inquiry detaining his exit.

The pumps were shaded by the enclosed roof; over the speakers Britney Spears's grating voice hiccuped "Oops, I Did It Again." Paying cash for the gas involved interacting with the attendant. Conway had a special credit card with an alias, which could not be traced back to him, but would, with any luck, send the police on a wild chase for Stanley Peters, a thirty-five-year-old Maine native who existed only on paper.

Conway picked up the Palm Pilot from the passenger's seat, pressed a button and the car shut off. Palm in hand, he got out and shut the door. The dispenser for the fuel gloves was right next to the pump. He removed a pair and put them on—no need to leave any fingerprints—and then removed the card from his wallet, slid it inside the slot on the pump, and then started pumping gas. In the space between the pump and the pole, Conway could see that the attendant had stopped mopping and was now looking in his direction. *Just keep your fat ass in there*. A moment later, the attendant went back to mopping. Conway clicked the latch inside the pump's handle to keep the gas pumping and then jogged over to the pay phone.

The scrambling unit he needed to insert inside the pay phone's mouthpiece had been stored in the Saab's trunk. With no change in his pocket, he would have to use the calling card number—not a problem since Delburn could easily hack its way inside the phone company's database and erase any evidence of this phone call. He placed the Palm on the bottom lip of the pay phone's tray, right above the area where the phone book sat and in the shade so he could see the screen. He picked up the receiver and punched in his calling-card number first, then dialed Pasha's number and waited for the call to go through. He could feel the sun drilling into the back of his neck. The air was dry and filled with a throbbing, eerie emptiness.

The phone started ringing. Conway glanced over his shoulder. Fat man was still inside the mini-mart, and no other cars had pulled in.

The phone kept ringing . . . ringing . . .

"Come on, Pasha, pick up."

Eight rings and no answer.

She's gone. Conway felt a wave of sharp and sudden loss rise within him.

Talk to Bouchard and get an update. Conway called Delburn.

"Good morning, Delburn Systems."

Conway was talking over an unsecured line, so he used the code words: "Good morning, Carol, this is Foster."

A pause, then the woman said, "Yes, Mr. Foster, how can I help you?"

Conway cleared his throat, took in a deep breath and said, "I've lost the Traveler account."

"I'll have Mr. Jacobs call you back on your cell phone."

"It doesn't seem to be working. I'm calling you on a pay phone." Conway gave her the number.

"I'll page Mr. Jacobs and have him call you back."

Conway hung up. Page Bouchard? What did she mean by that? A blooming silence followed. He checked his watch. By now, Dixon was at Praxis. There was still a good chance to save the operation. Randy Scott, member of the IWAC team and Praxis's LAN manager, could trigger the building's alarm system and lock Angel Eyes and his men inside to prevent the suit from being stolen.

Conway's cell phone rang. *Sweet Jesus, yes.* He removed it from his leather case and said, "Go secure."

The encryption technology engaged, beeped, and then a deep male voice exploded over the line.

"Jesus Christ, Steve, we lost track of your life signs. I thought you and Dixon were dead," Raymond Bouchard said.

"The whole thing was a setup. Angel Eyes knew we were coming. They stripped Dix of his transmitters and stuffed them inside a pillowcase and used the transmitters to lure me out. He killed everyone at the skydiving school. The place is burning to the ground. They're going to make a run for the suit."

"So they don't know you're alive."

"They think I'm dead. That I died from the bomb they planted inside my car." Conway squeezed the receiver in his hand, his anger getting away from him and not caring, heat building in his voice. Sweat worked its way down his back. His heart climbed inside his chest when he asked the next question. "Where's Pasha?"

"About twenty minutes ago, we lost contact with all the team members at the Austin airport," Bouchard said, his voice flat. "Same thing happened with the surveillance and Hazard Team covering you and Dixon. The watches that monitored their life signs . . . they all flat-lined. People who witnessed the explosions at the airport called the police and fire departments. It doesn't look like there are any survivors, Stephen."

Conway felt a sharp pain twist inside his chest, like razor wire working its way through his heart. He stared across the empty field, white dots of light dancing and burning in front of his eyes. *That doesn't mean she's dead.*

"Stephen?"

You have to forget about Pasha—you have to forget about all of this and focus on Dix. He needs you. You're the only one who can save him.

Training took over. He compartmentalized his thoughts and feelings, pushed them to the side, and focused on solving the problem.

"I'm here," Conway said. "What do you want me to do?"

"The only bright spot in this mess is the Hazard Team I brought in."

"Wait. You brought in a separate Hazard Team?"

"Yes. One not connected with the IWAC group. I didn't tell you—I didn't tell anyone except Pasha. Tomorrow morning the news is going to break about John McFadden. He's CIA. He's been a Russian spy for almost twenty years. And we think McFadden knows about us."

Jesus Christ. "When did you find this out?"

"Last night. But his connection to us, I just found out about it an hour ago. The hole . . . it just keeps getting bigger and bigger. It's a disaster.

"Steve, I'm on a satellite phone in my car, on my way back to Delburn. I had to get files on McFadden. The Hazard Team at the airport, they're alive, but I can't get in touch with them."

"Angel Eyes must be jamming our signal. I couldn't call you from the school." Conway's voice was dry, separated from himself. "What about Randy Scott?"

"Last time I heard, no life signs." A pause, and then Bouchard added, "It doesn't look good."

"He might be in the lab. If he is, the lab's security would prevent us from monitoring him. Or calling." *Or he might be dead.*

A distinctive chirping noise came from his Palm

Pilot. It was the sound of an e-mail that had just come through.

"Hold on," Conway said. The color screen read: *Would you like to read it now? Yes or no.* Conway pressed *Yes* and the e-mail message opened. It was from one of the servers inside the Praxis lab.

Conway felt the muscles in his back and shoulders tense.

"Dixon's inside the lab," he said. Then, as expected, the security program he had coded in case of such a possibility launched a new window, this one showing an empty white bar that read 3 percent, the bar slowly filling as the files for the latest version of the optical camouflage software were downloaded into the suit. "He just accessed the server. He's downloading the new software into the suit."

"How long until he—"

"Twenty, twenty-five minutes tops and he's done."

"Can you shut him down?"

"Not without my laptop."

"How far away are you from Praxis?"

"I won't make it in time."

"We've got to shut him down." Fear had eaten through Bouchard's confident tone. "If Angel Eyes gets that suit—"

"Randy has the same security clearance as I do. He can bounce Dixon off the system and then activate the lab's alarm, and they'll be trapped." Conway glanced back down at the Palm's screen. Ten percent of the files had already been copied. "You need to find a way to move the Hazard Team to Praxis."

"I will. Keeping trying Randy. And get to Praxis. Do whatever it takes to contain the situation until I can get the Hazard Team there. We can't let Angel Eyes leave with that suit."

"Understood."

Conway hung up and dialed Randy's direct number. No answer. Not surprising, since Randy was always traveling around the company fixing various computer problems. Conway called Praxis's main number. The voice mail system immediately picked up.

The secretary should have answered the phone, not the company's voice-mail system.

Something's wrong.

Fifteen percent of the files had been downloaded.

Conway tried Randy's cell phone next. Two rings, three, come on, Randy—

"Hello?" Randy whispered.

Relief, as the opportunity Conway had hoped for suddenly presented itself. "What's going on? I just called the main number and the voice mail is picking up."

"We've got a bomb inside the building."

The receiver felt loose and wet in Conway's hand. Behind him came the ring of the phone from inside the mini-mart.

"I was in the lab working on Lankler's hard drive when the main fire alarm went off," Randy Scott said, his voice low, almost a whisper. "I'm thinking it's a routine drill, and I'm about to go down the stairs when Peter McCabe calls up and tells me to stick around because someone called in a bomb threat, that the firemen and bomb squad guys are downstairs evacuating everyone out of the building and they want to come up and take a look around the lab."

"The caller said the bomb was inside the lab?"

"No, but the caller *did* say it was on the fourth floor."

Right. Saying it was inside the lab would be too suspicious.

Conway looked across the field, beads of sweat sliding down his face and running into his eyes. *A bomb threat, how perfect. The call gets everyone out of the building and Angel Eyes's people move in disguised as bomb-squad technicians and firemen. No one suspects a thing.*

"You let them inside the lab?" Conway asked.

"No. I got the hell out of there. They're looking for me."

That meant Dixon was physically inside the lab—alone.

To get inside the lab, you placed your palm on the handprint scanner and then spoke your name into the voice-recognition system. If accepted, you entered your code and the lab doors slid open, allowing you access. To travel deeper inside to the staging area where Dixon worked, you needed to wear a special badge encoded with a microchip; otherwise, the lab's sensors would pick it up, trigger the alarm system and lock you inside the lab until the police arrived.

You got Dix and the suit inside the lab alone, all you need to do is have Randy trigger the alarm and you'll trap him—away from Angel Eyes and his men. Get back to the Pathfinder and get moving.

Conway turned around and saw that the attendant had moved behind the counter, the phone pressed against his ear.

"I'm hiding out on the third floor in Neil Joseph's office—that's why I'm whispering. They don't know I'm in here," Randy said. "I can't get through to Pasha. I just tried using the office phone here and the line is dead. I can't call out."

"Randy, I'm running out of time, so listen to me carefully." Conway picked up his Palm and jogged back to the Pathfinder. "Dixon's inside the lab right now, and he's downloading the latest version of the software into the suit. It's encrypted, and Dixon knows the decryption code. If the download happens, the suit will be operational and Angel Eyes will be able to use the cloaking technology."

"Where's Hazard? They should have moved in by now," Randy said.

"Dead. You and I are the only ones left."

Silence on the other end. Conway removed the gas pump, placed it back into the cradle and then walked around to the other side of the Pathfinder. The attendant was still inside. The phone was pressed against his ear, and he was looking in Conway's direction. *Shit.*

Conway opened the door and got behind the wheel. "Bouchard's trying to reroute a Hazard Team from the airport to Praxis but he's been unable to contact them. They may not make it there in time. They may not make it there at all," he said. "You'll have to shut them down."

"How can I—"

"Listen. Use the PC in the office and log on as the network administrator. Then you can shut the server down. WinNuke the whole thing, I don't care, just make sure you delay them for as long as you can. The suit is useless without the new software."

"They might have already blocked off my access."

"Then log on as me and use my passwords. They think I'm dead, I doubt they would have changed them."

"And if they did?"

"Trigger the lab's alarm."

"That's in the security office. They might have someone guarding it."

Conway looked at the Palm Pilot. Forty-five percent of the files had been downloaded.

"Another twenty minutes and he's done," Conway said. "You armed?"

"The Glock's in my office lock box." A sharp intake of air, Randy drawing confidence. Conway could picture the twenty-eight-year-old agent, a rookie and the youngest member of the IWAC group, his pale Scottish skin flushed the way it always did when he got nervous.

In the distance, Conway heard the wail of approaching fire engines. He looked up and through the bands of heat rising off the long stretch of highway he could see the tiny, red-blurred, flashing fire-engine lights growing larger and heading his way.

"I've got to get moving," Conway said. "Your phone has vibration mode, right?"

"They all do now." Randy's voice sounded detached. Uncertain.

"Set it to vibration mode, I'll make contact with you when I get there. Randy?"

"Yeah?"

"You can do this."

Conway hung up. Two fire engines were rushing toward the gas station, the wail of the sirens building. He ran back to his car and just got himself settled behind the wheel when the attendant opened up the mini-mart's glass door. The man ignored the commotion, his eyes locked on Conway.

"Your car's all busted up, and it looks like you're leaking oil," the Texan yelled. "Pop open your hood and let's take a look." The attendant, his face and voice nervous, reached behind his back as he walked, less than two feet away from the Pathfinder.

Get out of here.

Conway pressed the button on the Palm and the Pathfinder started just as the fire engines raced by, kicking up large clouds of dust and dirt across the gas station. Conway floored the gas and peeled a good two feet of rubber out of the station. When he hit the highway, he looked in the driver's-side mirror and saw the man standing in the middle of the road, his hand still behind his back as if guarding a shameful secret.

The gas station attendant stood in the dust and the aching heat, the tranquilizer pistol tucked into the back waistband of his work pants. He watched the Pathfinder until it disappeared.

His real name was Charles Rigby. The original plan was to abduct the computer wiz, Major Dixon—the father should have been arrested for child abuse for giving out such a stupid name—here at the gas station. On the way back from skydiving, both Major D and Conway would have to pass along this road, the only way back to Austin, and just as Conway was about to ride past another car would blast out of the gas station and hit his car. When Conway wasn't looking, Rigby would hit him with a tranquilizer dart. By the time he woke up, the man the CIA called Angel Eyes would have the highly coveted military combat suit from Praxis. That was the plan.

Rigby thought it would have been easier to try to take Dixon at night, while he was sleeping. Hit the two IWAC teams that were monitoring Major D—one IWAC team lived in the same apartment complex, the other was housed inside a van—and then take down Delburn. With the IWAC team gone, they could take the Major straight to Praxis, slip in and get the suit, then disappear. That was how Mr. Faust operated in the past.

The strange thing was that Mr. Faust wanted Dixon *and* Conway. Why Conway was wanted was unknown. Only Mr. Faust knew that, and the only one who had direct access to him was Gunther, who never talked about the man or the reasoning behind his decisions. You did what you were told, or you were let go. And never, under any circumstances, did you lie. Even if you fucked up. Like now.

Charles Rigby continued to stare down the highway. *Man, I should have come here earlier, when Conway was on the phone. Just walked up to him and asked him about his car and then popped him with a dart.* But it didn't feel right. When you dealt with guys like Conway, guys who could snap you in half without breaking a sweat, you had to make sure you could pull it off, otherwise you were in deep shit. By the time Rigby was ready to move, Conway was already seated behind the wheel. Goddamn. Gunther was going to be *pissed*.

Rigby looked back at the gas station and then reached into his back pocket and retrieved a satellite phone. It wasn't as fancy looking as the one Conway and the IWAC boys used—Rigby's phone had that long, thick, extendable antenna—but it did have the latest and greatest encryption technology, stuff so advanced that it would take a team of NSA boys weeks to crack it. Charlie dialed the number.

"You got him?" Gunther asked.

"Conway wigged out and hightailed it out of here before I could even get to him."

Gunther didn't say anything. Rigby had known Gunther for three years now—it was Gunther who had rescued him from the streets of L.A. Rigby was seventeen at the time and eating out of trash barrels and forced to do other things to survive, things that a teenage boy should never have to endure. Then like a gift from God came Gunther, his guardian angel; Gunther, who had brought him into the fold and taught him things and showed him a world of unlimited potential and promise.

Rigby, upset that he had disappointed Gunther and nervous that he had blown his opportunity to prove himself, started chattering away: "He made a pay phone call to Bouchard. I got it all on tape. Then Conway called Randy Scott, this guy's inside Praxis right now and he's going to try to shut down access to the suit."

"Dixon's already inside in the lab?"

"As we speak they're downloading the latest version of the software directly into the suit. Now granted, I couldn't hear what this guy Randy was saying on his end because the call was encrypted, but I managed to hear everything Conway was saying and the two of them cooked up a plan—"

"So Conway's going to try to shut these guys down by himself."

"Yeah, him and this guy Randy Scott. They think Angel Eyes is behind this."

"Get everything ready. I'm on the road and will be there in five minutes," Gunther said and hung up.

Inside the mini-mart, Charlie removed the gas station's surveillance tapes and then checked the broom closet. The real gas station attendant was still passed out. Rigby dragged the guy and put him on a chair behind the counter. When the guy woke up a couple of hours from now, he would have the worst hangover of his life.

Rigby put on a pair of latex gloves. As he wiped down the few areas he had touched, he wondered what

Mr. Faust did with all this stolen stuff. Was he collecting it? Selling it? Gunther didn't say anything about it, and Rigby never asked. Then he thought about the suit. To be invisible from everyone, man, you could be God, roaming the earth and carrying out your secret wishes.

Ten minutes from Praxis and relief.

Conway had been barreling down the highway at just above ninety, the ride difficult because of the missing front windshield, the wind gusting past his face with such intensity that his eyes watered. The Palm Pilot was on his lap. He glanced down and noticed that the files were no longer being copied. Randy had knocked Dixon off the server.

But no way to tell if Randy had triggered the lab's alarm system and locked Dixon and Angel Eyes's men inside the building. Conway imagined Angel Eyes and his men as they scrambled to bring the server back online, a process that could take half an hour or more, depending on their skill level. Hopefully, Bouchard's Hazard Team had moved in on Praxis and contained the matter.

Hopefully.

Eight miles away from the company and the traffic on the MoPac expressway came to a grinding halt. Framed against the clear blue sky and sitting perched high on a hill was Praxis, a sprawling, four-floor structure of gray concrete and mirrored blue glass, looking like some sort of futuristic monolith that had descended from the heavens, isolated from other companies and safe from prying eyes, and oddly out of place in the rolling green hills of Spanish-style homes with red-tiled roofs. Conway moved into the breakdown lane and drove the rest of the way. He picked up his phone and called Randy. Far ahead on the right were clusters of people looking no bigger than action figures gathered near the main road and the only entrance to Praxis. *Angel Eyes and his men must still be inside the building.*

Six rings and no answer.

Either Randy had been captured or was hiding somewhere inside Praxis.

Conway hung up and pulled into the small plaza containing a one-hour photo shop and an office supply store. He parked the Pathfinder in one of the shaded spaces, far away from the store and its curious eyes, and shut off the SUV. The hot air throbbed with the traffic from the highway.

Behind the strip mall was a wooded area, its shaded edge holding trash barrels and four redwood picnic tables. All he had to do was walk through the woods, make his way around to the back of Praxis, climb up the embankment, and then he would be able to see the company's main and side entrances. He could watch and report his findings to Bouchard, who should be back at Delburn by now. It beat sitting around and waiting.

He shoved the phone back into its leather case and, Palm Pilot in hand, got out of the Pathfinder and ran behind the strip mall. He tore through the dense growth, ducking under tree limbs, branches snapping back. To his immediate left and rising at what looked like a ninety-degree angle was a steep embankment. He ran up it, struggling, his legs burning, and then five minutes later, his hard work was rewarded.

In the spaces between the trees, Conway could see

the side of the building, the late-morning sun reflecting off the blue-mirrored glass so brightly it made him squint. Dizzy, his face hot and his breath coming in sharp, painful bursts, Conway stumbled around until he found the spot that offered him the best view of the building and then squatted down and surveyed the situation.

The main road from the highway wrapped around the side of the building, past the delivery entrance, and then opened up into the spacious parking lot full of cars. The battered Ford Bronco from the skydiving school was parked at the bottom of the concrete stairs that led to the mailroom, its door held open by a brick. Past the Bronco was a fire truck and another van, this one gray. The vehicles were parked parallel to each other, blocking the main road to prevent anyone from entering or exiting the parking lot. The gray van's driver's-side door was open, waiting for the driver to return.

The front entrance and lobby was made of clear glass. Past the front door was a security guard station. Beyond that were two sets of elevators. No firemen or bomb technicians lingered around, and, he noticed, the security gates had not been deployed. If Randy had triggered the alarm, those gates would have covered each of the company's two exits.

Conway removed the Palm Pilot from his back pocket and checked the screen. The window displaying the download status was still frozen—the software was no longer being downloaded into the suit—but if Angel Eyes had Randy, he would use him to bring the server back online. Once that happened, a few more minutes' worth of work and Angel Eyes and his men would be done and gone.

Conway leaned the Palm upright against the tree so he could see the screen. His phone vibrated against his hip. He removed it from the case and pressed it against his sweaty ear.

"Steve, Keith Harring, Hazard Team leader for Unit Six." The voice was deep and gritty, as if he had sand lodged in his throat. "We were finally able to get through to Delburn. Bouchard filled us in. You get through to Scott?"

"I did."

"Give me your status."

"The lab server is still offline."

"And Scott?"

"I haven't been able to reach him. Where are you?"

"En route to your location. We just left."

Just *left?* Conway felt his body sag. He had hoped Hazard had already moved in.

As if sensing the question, Harring said, "Our communications were being jammed. When we saw what went down at the airport, we knew the gig had gone FUBAR, so we tried another way out—not easy since the place looks like a war zone."

"What about Bouchard?"

"We lost contact. Hold on."

Harring's voice moved away and spoke to someone else, the words inaudible over the sound of car horns blaring and the rapid *click-click-click* of fingers working a keyboard. The airport was max twenty minutes away. Once the lab server came back online, a few more minutes and Angel Eyes would be downloading the software and would be gone well before Hazard arrived.

Harring was back now: "The satellite's locked on your heat signature. The field you're sitting in is clear.

You're the only guy out back. Now listen to me and listen carefully.

"I've got the building's floor and design schematics loaded onto our system. I'm working with a three-dimensional model that allows us to see where they're traveling inside. The satellite will pick up heat signatures and motion. The first floor is clear, and so is the second and third. On the fourth, I'm showing three bodies, all alive, standing outside a door. One is sitting, the other three standing."

"The lab's on the fourth floor," Conway said. "If they're inside the lab, you won't be able to pick up their heat signatures or voices or any transmissions. The entire place is shielded. The others must be in there with Dixon."

"I thought they couldn't get inside the lab without wearing special encoded badges—that the lab's security would go off."

"They could have used Randy to disable the security."

"But not Dixon."

"Dix doesn't have the security clearance."

"Okay, good, that buys us some time. The security room is clear. My guess is that they're saving that for last. Get the suit out first, and then have their guys go inside the security room and remove the surveillance tapes. No way they're going to leave that evidence—wait, we've got action." Harring's voice was tight now, excited. "I'm showing two men standing outside the lab door. They're kicking the guy sitting on the floor, and one of them has a weapon, looks like a submachine gun, he's pointing it at this guy's head."

"Randy," Conway said and felt a heaviness fill his heart. *They've got him.*

"Randy know you're here?"

"He knows I'm alive."

"So these guys are going to try to make him talk."

"Randy won't talk."

"He might if they blow out one of his kneecaps. He's young, Steve. A newbie. He's scared, and if he starts babbling, he'll blow any chance we've got of salvaging this operation."

Below his eyes, Conway saw movement. He looked down at the Palm's screen and saw what was happening.

"The server's back online," he said. "They're downloading the remaining files."

"How long until they're—"

"They're seventy percent done. Ten minutes, maybe five, I don't know, it's too close."

"We won't make it in time."

Two years of hard work, the countless man hours and sleepless nights, the deaths of IWAC team members, Pasha, and now Dixon and Randy were about to be slaughtered.

Harring said, "You have to shut down the server."

"They have Randy. They would have used him to shut off my permissions."

"But they think you're dead, right?"

"They would have shut off my access. It's the smart thing to do."

"But you don't know that. You armed?"

"I've got my Palm Pilot."

"And it has the Air Taser system, right?"

"Yeah."

"I can work with that. Steve, I can watch you on my screen here, watch your back and tell you where to go. The delivery room is clear. You can enter from the side." No urgency in Harring's voice, just a cold, professional precision that reminded Conway of a seasoned coach who was confidently telling the younger player that the bases were loaded, and all he had to do was step up to the plate, hit a line drive, and the game was over.

"You want me to be a running target until you get there," Conway said.

"They won't be able to touch you, I promise."

Time was running down on the Palm Pilot.

It is in the midst of these split-second decisions that character is forged. You don't have time to prepare. You must quickly draw on your inner resources and training, act and hope for the best.

Conway shoved the Palm Pilot into his back pocket and stood up. "I'll make contact with you once I'm inside."

Conway ran up the concrete steps and past the opened door and plunged into the cold semidarkness of the delivery room.

The overhead banks of fluorescent lighting had been shut off. The only source of light came from the opened door and the two computer monitors on each desk, their dark-blue screens glowing against the back wall. The mailroom was long, rectangular and windowless, full of rows of supply cabinets, shelving, and large copying machines. Conway moved behind the counter and walked toward the back of the mailroom, the phone pressed against his ear. Overhead, the air conditioning clicked on, and a rush of cold air blew down from the ceiling.

"I'm inside," Conway whispered, his voice hoarse. "I'll need a minute or so to set up."

"You're clear," Harring said.

Every desktop computer inside the building was hooked into the company's Local Area Network, or LAN. Each employee had a unique user name and password that allowed him access to specific directories and files; other directories and their contents were restricted, permanently out of their reach. As the company's network administrator, Conway had access to all six servers. What he had to do now was reboot one of the mailroom's desktop computers and log on as the administrator, which would allow him to bring the lab's security system back online.

You hope. If they used Randy to shut off your access, you won't be able to do a thing.

Conway moved to the first desk and hit the reboot button on the desktop PC. The computer monitor went black and then came to life again, lines and lines of white text scrolling across the screen as it went through its series of internal tests. Next item: find a headset. Conway searched through drawers, desk tops, and shelving and then found one in the back, lying on top of a copier. He fitted the unit over his head and adjusted the padded microphone so it sat right against the corner of his mouth. All he would have to do was whisper and Harring would hear him. Conway clipped the phone to his belt and then moved back behind the desk and sat down.

On the computer monitor, a window asked him to enter his user ID and password. He typed it in and then paused, his finger hovering above the ENTER key. If Angel Eyes had someone monitoring the network, the second Conway pressed the key, it didn't matter if the password was accepted or denied, they would know someone else was inside the building. If no one was monitoring the network and Conway's passwords were accepted, he could trigger the lab's alarm system. He would be locking himself in here with Angel Eyes.

"They're beating the shit out of Randy," Harring said.

"I'm about to log on. How far away are you?"

"Ten, fifteen minutes."

Conway looked at the ENTER key. *Come on, just let this go through and buy me some time.* He pressed the key and the window disappeared, his information sent into the vast computer matrix for verification.

Shit.

Conway stared at the new window on the monitor. "Denied access," he said. "They've shut me off from the network. I can't do anything from—"

"They're moving," Harring said, his voice loud and tight.

Conway stood up and ran toward the counter, Harring saying, "I'm counting two men, these boys are sprinting and heading straight for the stairs or the elevator, I can't tell which yet. Get to the security room."

Two doors, one leading back outside, the other the stairs. Conway opened the second door to the gray-painted stairwell and ran up the stairs, the squeak and thud of his boots echoing loudly up the stairwell. He opened the door and moved onto the second floor, easing the door back into its frame so it wouldn't make a sound. High above him a door slammed open against a wall, followed by the rush of footsteps, all of it real now, no longer imaginary scenarios.

The door shut, Conway turned and ran down stretches of blue-gray painted hallways ending and beginning, beginning and ending, a maze crafted from a nightmare, until the last hallway disappeared and gave way to an open area of cubicles, private offices, and meeting rooms. The place was strangely empty and quiet. The desktops glowed with the sunlight pouring in from the windows. Conway moved down the final corridor and when it split to the right, he turned and now faced the security-room door. A key-card scanning device was mounted on the wall, located next to the door handle. Conway fished his key card from his front pocket, found it and slid the card through the scanner. The light turned red.

"They've shut off my access to the security room," Conway said. He tried the doorknob; the door shook inside the frame. "I can't get in."

"You got a key?"

"No." The company's office and security manager, Joe Langdon, was the only person who had the keys.

From far down the maze of corridors, Conway heard the second-floor door burst open against the wall and then slam shut.

Harring: "Target two is running in your direction."

The security room was located at the corner of the building in a suite of private offices. The only way out of here was to go back the way he came—the same corridors through which one of Angel Eyes's men was now running.

"I want you to turn the corner and wait," Harring said, his seasoned voice clear and calm. "Target one is in the mailroom looking around, and the one coming in your direction is alone. They probably think you bolted back outside. Get your Palm ready. If you do exactly what I say, we can level the playing field until I get there."

Conway moved past the door, turned the corner, and pressed his back against the wall. To his left and several feet away was an opened door leading into a private office; to his right, the hallway continued for maybe thirty feet, and then the walls disappeared into the wide sea of cubicles he had just passed. Conway looked down at the carpet. Good. The overhead lights didn't throw off his shadow. Palm Pilot in hand, he called up the program that turned the PDA into an Air Taser.

"Our boy just turned the corner and is walking down the final hallway," Harring said. "Stay where you are, regulate your breathing. You don't want him to hear you."

He won't have to see or hear me, all he'll have to do is take a whiff of the air, and he'll know I'm right here. An odor of sweat and grime and dry blood rose from his skin.

Hung on the wall and facing the hallway that contained the security room door was a framed poster of an Americas Cup racing boat diving deep into a towering wave. In the glass's reflection, Conway saw the small, blurred shadow of a man grow larger as he walked up the hallway toward him.

Harring whispered over Conway's earphone: "When I tell you, you're going to turn around and hit him with your Taser. Just remember to stay low."

Conway took slow, deep breaths through his nose and regulated his breathing. He placed his thumb on the Palm's button. The problem with the Palm's Air Taser System was that you only had one shot. Once he pressed the button, he would drain the entire battery. The Palm Pilot became useless until it was recharged. He had only one shot to bring this guy down.

"Twenty feet and closing," Harring whispered, barely audible. "He's moving slowly, looking for you. Stay sharp."

The hum of the fluorescent lighting was maddening. Over the earphone, Conway heard the screech of tires, car horns blaring. His throat was so dry it hurt to swallow.

Harring whispered, "Get ready."

Down to the wire now, Conway could feel it, like an electric current moving through his veins. His fate was about to be decided, everything hinged on him and

(go ahead and say it)

luck. Conway's muscles tensed. Ready.

"Now!" Harring said.

Conway turned the corner, staying low.

The man—dressed in jeans, a black T-shirt, and a baseball cap—had just removed his latex-covered hand away from the doorknob, his right hand fastened around the grip of a submachine gun, when he saw Steve Conway on the floor with one hand on the ground, the other hand holding in the air a Palm Pilot organizer. Startled, the man tried to turn his body and brought the weapon around just as two barbs shot out of the Palm and pierced his leg and chest. The man crumpled to the floor, unconscious.

The Palm was dead. Conway yanked out the barbs, wrapped the wire around the Palm and then shoved the unit into his back pocket. He stood up, grabbed the man's baseball hat and then dragged him into one of the offices. The guy had greasy black hair and pale skin—young, early twenties, too young to be doing this. He knelt down and first removed the weapon, a Heckler and Koch MP-5 submachine gun—the preferred weapon for close quarters combat and used by the FBI's Hostage Rescue Team and terrorist groups. A suppresser was threaded over the barrel and a tactical light was mounted under the forward handguard. The HK, he noticed, had been set to semiautomatic mode.

One shot and this guy would have turned you into hamburger.

"He's down," Conway said. He fastened the machine gun's strap over his shoulder and then started going through the guy's front pockets. Nothing. Conway rolled him over and tried the back pockets. The words "Bomb Squad" were printed on the back of the T-shirt.

Conway checked the guy's waistband and ankles for a hidden weapon and came up empty.

The radio clipped to the man's belt crackled and came to life. The voice spoke in Russian. Conway had studied the language and knew exactly what the Russian man had said: *Demetri, did you find Conway?*

"They know I'm in here," Conway said to Harring. "Where's target one?"

"Still in the mailroom—no, wait, he just ran outside. He's heading toward the van."

They're getting ready to move.

An alarm sounded. Not the fire alarm, no, this one was steady and very distinct: *ding-ding, ding-ding*.

"What's going on?" Harring's voice was barely audible.

"They've activated the lab's security system," Conway said. "They're locking me inside the building."

Right now metal gates similar to the ones city store owners pulled down across their small shops at night to prevent burglaries and vandalism were descending all over the lobby and the delivery entrance. Any window or area on the first floor that could provide an exit would now be gated. Running was useless. Conway was trapped.

Conway thought of the man who had just run outside and wondered, *Why are they deploying the security system now? They're locking themselves inside the building.*

Because they know you're here. They've got you trapped, and now they're coming to take care of you. You walked right into it.

Unless those gates came back up, the Hazard Team would have no way of entering the building—and Conway would have no way of escaping. He stood up and shut the door, quieting the sound of the alarm.

Harring said, "We've got movement."

Conway brought the HK up and pointed it at the door, a new, wired energy surging through his body.

"Six people running out the lab doors and they're all brandishing weapons," Harring said.

"Where's Randy?"

A click over his receiver as Harring swallowed and

then said, "Shit. One of them is dragging Randy back inside the lab."

To kill him, Conway thought. *Angel Eyes is going to kill Randy and Dixon.* Right. The man didn't leave witnesses.

The lab was on the fourth floor, max five minutes away.

You have time, you can still save them.

"I'm going to the lab," Conway said. "What's the best route?"

"The stairwells are clear. Secure the lab, and we'll take the outside perimeter. I'll watch your back. Steve?"

"Yeah."

"Once we arrive, I'll need to redirect my focus to the Hazard Team. I won't be able to watch them and you simultaneously."

"I'll take care of Dixon and Randy."

"Good luck."

Conway opened the door and sprinted through the maze of corridors, the alarm blaring everywhere, the sound like something ripped from a disaster movie, a sinking ship about to go down along with Dixon and Randy, two minutes and counting.

Conway shut the fourth door behind him and crouched against the wall on his right, the alarm drilling inside his head. The hallway continued straight for maybe fifteen feet, broke for the fourth-floor lobby elevators and then continued beyond that to the final corridor that would lead him straight to the lab. Facing him was a railing. Beyond it and far below was the main lobby. A towering wall of mirrored blue glass stretched all the way to the roof.

The alarm stopped. Conway's ears were ringing.

"He's not on the first floor," someone said in a thick Russian accent, the booming voice rising from the lobby. Conway wanted to peek over the railing and see the faces of the men and commit them to memory. He took a step forward and then stopped. No. Too risky.

"You check the security room?" a second voice asked. *Paul, it's the cameraman, Paul.*

"He wasn't in there," the Russian said.

"He's got to be inside the building."

"Find Conway, he's here, hiding."

"The alarm probably scared him off, and he ran back outside," Paul said. "What do you think he's going to do, come charging in here and try to take us down? Relax, Niki, our job is done. Dana's getting the scene set up in the lab. And I got word on Delburn."

"Yeah?"

"Yeah, it's been liquidated."

Conway felt his body sag with defeat. Outside the window and floating in the hard blue sky, he could see the UT watchtower leering at him.

The security gates started to rise, *clank-clank-clank*. Beyond it, Conway heard the faint screech of tires. They were getting ready to run.

Which meant Randy and possibly Dixon had only a few minutes, maybe even a few seconds, to live.

"Harrison should be here," Niki the Russian said.

"He's probably inside the security room pulling the tapes inside as we speak," Paul said. "Our ride's here. Time to boogie."

Over the headset, Harring said, "We're setting up. Secure the lab. Once we've secured the perimeter, I'll call you back."

Conway skulked across the carpet, and when he was in the clear, he stood up and ran down the final hallway of twists and turns, his sweaty finger sliding across the trigger, ready to shoot. A minute later he stood outside the first door that would lead him into the lab's offices and, then, finally, the lab itself. He brought the weapon up, turned the corner, and moved inside the lab's office of cubicles.

Darkness. No windows existed inside these rooms, and the overhead lights were turned off. Where was the switch? He felt the wall. Nothing. He had moved through these rooms hundreds of times, and he knew the layout by heart but couldn't remember seeing light switches. The HK had a tactical light mounted under the stock. Too risky. One of Angel Eyes's men might see the beam of light. Conway stumbled toward the lab, making progress . . . he turned the corner.

The hallway was a tube, long and dark and filled with a steady hum, and at the far end were the pair of steel doors, both open.

The doors should have been shut and locked. It confirmed Conway's suspicion: Angel Eyes had modified the lab's security system.

An inside job, Steve, be careful. Who the fuck knows what else they've done in there.

A dull amber glow from the lab's overhead lighting washed into the corridor. Conway moved down the corridor and saw the ramp of cream-colored tile that led to a staging area. This contained three workstations packed with several desktop computers used for testing various software before it was installed on the company's LAN, Praxis's central nervous system of networked computers. Conway moved past the doors and then placed one foot on the tile ramp, testing his weight. The tiles were removable, the floor underneath hollow to allow the nerd herd easy access to the sprawling nest of wires that hooked up all the servers and telecommunications equipment. Walking across the tiles even in sneakers would echo your footsteps. With his hand on the railing for support, Conway kept low and moved carefully up the ramp. The refrigerated air between the cream-colored walls felt bone-numb, the gray-shadowed world of the lab filled with the mixed beep and hum of the large telecommunications systems. Conway moved past the railing, about to make his way down into the heart of the lab, when he saw the cut and bloodied hand peeking out from behind the chair wheels. Conway moved closer to the hand, the man's face buried in the shadows coming into a sharper focus.

Randy.

Randy's face was cut up and swollen, both eyes completely shut, his lips a wet, torn mess that dripped blood onto the floor. Three of his front teeth were missing.

Conway reached out and touched Randy's neck. The skin was warm, the pulse strong. Conway shook him. No movement, not even a groan.

He must be drugged.

"Please."

Dixon's voice, very soft and choked with tears, drifted up from deep inside the lab, from the staging area where they worked on the combat suit.

"Please," Dixon begged. "Please, don't . . . don't kill me."

"You got one minute to get that software downloaded into the suit or I'm going to paint the walls with your brains."

The male voice belonged to Chris Evans. He was inside the lab with Dixon.

Conway stood up, wondering who else was inside the lab. His head down and his body bent slightly, he crept through the row of bulky telecommunications equipment, the cold air buzzing with a droning mechanical hum and the clicks of machinery. The military suit was stored inside a circular tube made of shatterproof glass, like a rare statue housed inside a museum. Dixon was the only one who could access the suit; the separate biometric security responded only to Dixon's fingerprint and retinal scan, along with a special code, which he changed on a daily basis. A mere touch on the pressure-sensitive glass would signal an alarm and lock up the lab.

Unless Angel Eyes has shut off the security. He's proving to be quite clever.

"I'm done," Dixon said.

"Good. Now get on your knees," Evans said.

"You said—you said you wouldn't." Dixon's babbling voice mounted with terror. "You said all I had to do was help you, and you promised you wouldn't—"

"On your knees or I'll blow your head off."

A body slumped to the floor in a loud, heavy thud. Dixon started to cry.

"I did what you wanted."

The row was about to end, and from around the corner Conway could see the combined blur of two shadows stretched wide across the white tiles.

"Face the wall," Evans said.

"Please, not like . . . not like this—"

"TURN AND FACE THE FUCKING WALL!"

Conway, the skin on his scalp tingling, brought the weapon up and turned the corner.

Dixon and Evans were both dressed in firemen's garb and faced the wall so that only their backs were visible. The helmets they wore shielded their heads so that Conway couldn't see their faces, only their backs. Dix was down on his knees like a man kneeling at church, his body bent slightly forward as one hand grabbed the swivel chair in front of him, his other gloved hand rested by his side, unaware of the handgun already pointed at the back of his head.

Conway aimed at Evans's back and squeezed off two shots, *poof-poof*, each round suppressed by the silencer. Evans fell forward stiffly, as if his entire body was made of wood. Then he tumbled forward and knocked Dixon down against the floor, their helmets scattering across the tile.

The faces of two mannequins stared up at Conway. He looked through the cloud of dust that hung in the cold air and saw the tube that held the suit.

The suit was gone.

"Please," Dixon cried. His recorded voice came from a pair of computer speakers sitting on the table. "I'm begging you, stop, please."

It's a trap.

Conway turned and brought the weapon around and saw a fireman standing in the space between the row of telecommunication equipment. The fireman had already brought the HK submachine gun up and now stared down his sight.

The muzzle flash didn't come from the main chamber at all, but from the long tube mounted beneath the submachine gun's forward handguard, the place where a tactical light should have been mounted. Then Conway's eyes caught it—too large to be a bullet, it was a small cylindrical object, a miniature soda can with fins flying with frightening speed and precision toward him.

Conway tried to turn away and the object slammed into his chest with enough force to knock him off his feet. By the time he fell backward against the floor, the four electrical prongs had already penetrated his skin and were feeding a steady electrical charge through his body. He could feel the thing stuck to his shirt right above his frantic heartbeat.

Heavy footsteps were marching toward him.

Somehow, the HK was still gripped in his hand. He could feel his finger resting on the trigger housing.

Bring the weapon up, Steve.

In his mind he saw himself bringing the weapon up and squeezing off rounds that would shred his advancing adversary. His body ignored the simple task.

Steve, bring the weapon up or it's over.

Conway couldn't move. He was paralyzed. Useless. All he could do was stare up at the dim tubes of fluorescent light with his mouth hanging open while Dixon's voice cried out in the background. "Please . . . I'm begging you . . ."

The footsteps stopped. Conway heard something hard slump against the floor, close to where the mannequins had been standing, but he couldn't turn his head to see. Then the fireman stepped into Conway's line of vision.

The man's mouth and nose were covered by a black neoprene mask, the kind used in skiing. He stood there for a moment and then brought up the Glock, slowly, and pointed it at Conway's face. It was just like that morning with Armand. Only this time, no Hazard Team was going to come rushing in at the last second to save him. Conway stared at the muzzle and knew that his life was over.

"And what do we have here?" Gunther muttered to himself.

Charles Rigby sat in the driver's seat of the 911 Porsche and stared through the tinted windows at the dead-still traffic on the MoPac expressway. He said nothing. After being picked up, he tried to apologize again, and Gunther had given him a look that told him to shut up. Gunther wanted the silence, wanted to use the little time he had to collect his thoughts and see how he could turn this thing around.

What he saw happening on the highway didn't look promising.

Gunther sat low in the passenger's seat of the Porsche, a pair of Viper binoculars mounted on his head and eyes, and zoomed in on the entrance to Praxis. The fire truck with its flashing lights and siren was about to turn onto the highway, the battered Ford Bronco in tow, a revolving red police bubble mounted on the dashboard. Faust wouldn't be able to view this new development. The M.A.R.S. system was back at the skydiving school where Craven was using the equipment to transmit the fingerprints to Faust's condo.

Gunther called Faust. "They're pulling out of Praxis."

"With the suit, I'm sure," Faust said. "They wouldn't come this far and leave without it. Any sign of Stephen?"

Gunther scanned the crowd of faces gathered near the entrance—all clear, no sign of Major Dick either—and then Gunther looked to his left, a strip mall with an office supply store and—

"The Pathfinder Conway hot-wired at the school, it's parked in a lot about a mile away," Gunther said.

"But no sign of Stephen."

"Not that I can see."

"Then he must be inside Praxis. Pull into the lot and make your way inside the building."

"Wait. You want me to go *inside*?"

"Stephen and Mr. Dixon could be trapped or hurt or injured. They may need our assistance."

"If they're inside, then they're already dead." Gunther turned his head and saw the fire truck and Bronco heading up the highway, heading away from him. "These guys are leaving. If we don't pursue the fire truck now, we'll lose them—and the suit."

"We can find the suit later."

"It's here, right in front of us. I can follow these guys and see where they—"

"Remember who we are, Gunther. Remember what we're about."

Gunther tapped Rigby on the shoulder and pointed to the lot.

The fireman had slung back the HK submachine gun and was now kneeling on the floor, his gloved hand holding a Glock handgun that was now pressed against Conway's forehead. The fireman knelt there, waiting.

What the fuck is he waiting for? Conway could feel his heart jackhammering against his chest. All he could do now was lie on the floor and smell the stink rising off his skin.

The fireman clicked back the hammer.

Conway's vision went out of focus. He couldn't breathe. He blinked and then saw

(The gift Pasha had given him last year for his birthday, a photograph of a valley of red tulips bending in the wind, except for one, a yellow tulip, it stands out from the rest of the pack and leans forward into the wind, refusing to bend. "I saw it and the photograph reminded me of you, Stephen.")

the fireman's gloved finger slide up and down the trigger. With his free hand, he waved good-bye, and then Conway saw a pitch-black sky devoid of stars that devoured all of his thoughts and memories.

The fireman pulled the trigger.

The hammer snapped dryly.

The fireman laughed and tossed the gun away. Conway heard it skid across the floor. The fireman stood up and then brought up another weapon and pointed it at Conway's face—no, it wasn't a weapon, it looked like some sort of high-tech spray gun. Two black tubes ran from the bottom of the handgrip and disappeared under the fireman's coat.

The fireman moved the spray nozzle away and pointed it somewhere near Conway's legs and a sound like shaving cream foam shooting out of a canister filled the cold room. Conway could see the spray nozzle being moved across his body, covering both arms, and then the nozzle moved away and was pointed at his face, a viscous, milky liquid dripping off the nozzle and dribbling onto Conway's chin. The fireman stared at his watch for what seemed like a minute, and then got down on one knee and yanked free the stun device that had been stuck to the skin above Conway's heart.

The paralysis vanished. Conway took in a deep rush of air, lifted his head up and saw bands of a thick, whitish gray foam covering his entire body. He tried to move, but the foam had hardened into a stiff, rubber-like substance. He was glued to the floor. The fireman remained kneeling, patient, studying Conway as if he were some sort of exotic, poisonous bug that was now trapped, about to die.

Then the guy reached forward and using the heel of his gloved palm pushed Conway's head to the side, pressing it hard against the floor. Conway saw Randy Scott lying on his side, groaning like a man struggling to emerge from anesthesia. With his other hand the fireman placed his finger inside the HK's trigger housing.

Conway tried to fight it but couldn't move. It was as if dozens of invisible hands had him pinned against the floor.

"WAKE UP, RANDY! MOVE!" Conway's words came

out in a garbled, spittle-filled mess. He tried to yank his hand and head away and—

The shot hit Randy in the stomach; his body arched back as if kicked, the exit wound spraying the back wall and computer equipment a bright red with shattered bone and skin that started to dribble down the computer screen and speakers, where Dixon's voice still cried out for all to stop, that he was sorry, please, let it stop.

The fireman stood up and walked out of the lab.

Randy's chemical haze was gone. His eyes were swollen shut, and his trembling hands felt around the leaking hole in his stomach. He was bleeding out fast.

Conway's left hand was wrapped around his midsection; he wiggled his fingers and felt the phone; it was still clipped against his belt. He pinched it between his two fingers and then slid it toward him. *Don't drop it, you've only got one chance.* Okay, good. Now he could touch all the keys.

"Mittens," Randy said.

"Hold on, Randy."

"Mittens . . . cat food."

"I'll call Delburn and we'll get out of here."

"Cat's name . . . breath . . . smells like cat food."

He's delirious, Conway thought. He wasn't paying attention; he was concentrating on the layout of the phone's keys. *Don't waste time dialing, use the programmed number.* Right, Delburn's number was already programmed in for speed dialing. His finger brushed over the keys and found the program button and hit it. Okay, now the speed-dial number. It was . . . what, one?

No, it's two.

Yes, definitely two. Conway slid his finger over and pressed the number Two key.

An explosion came from down near the lab doors. Conway felt the floor shake beneath him. His finger pressed a key. *Please, God, let it be number two*, he thought. When he looked up and stared down the length of his body, he saw tiles popping up out of the floor as flames shot up toward the ceiling and moved up the walls.

The phone was ringing. The sound was barely audible over the equipment smashing against the floor, but the phone was ringing, he could hear it. Flames fanned up the walls and spread across the ceiling, the fire being fed by the oxygen pouring in from the opened lab doors. In case of a lab fire, the HALON system would deploy a gas that would extinguish the flames without harming the computer equipment.

The system didn't turn on.

Angel Eyes must have disabled it. Fuck.

The fire was moving closer.

You're going to burn to death.

Conway struggled to free himself. Black curls of smoke snaked across the ceiling and slithered down the length of wall. The fire inched closer . . . closer. *Keep trying or you'll burn alive.*

The phone picked up on the other end. "Hello?"

Conway froze. The voice, it didn't sound like anyone at Delburn. It sounded like . . . No. The voice did sound like his friend from Boston, John Riley.

"Hello?"

No, that can't be right.

(You're hallucinating)

(HURRY!)

Conway screamed, *"IT WAS AN INSIDE JOB, WE*

*WERE SET UP. ANGEL EYES KNEW WE WERE
COMING, WE'VE GOT A LEAK."*

"What? Who is this?"

"Mittens!" Randy cried out. "Mittens!"

"Mittens?" the guy—Riley?—asked on the other
end.

The lab had grown hot; Conway could feel the heat
drilling into his skin. Smoke curled around his body. It
was difficult to breathe. "Fire," he said and started
choking. "There's a fire . . . Randy's down. Move the
Hazard inside and help him, I'm trapped—"

Another explosion followed and another, more tiles
popping out of the floor and then raining back down,
the lab bursting with fire. Conway tried to twist away
and couldn't, he was trapped, he didn't see one of the
tiles as it fell down and hit him straight across the forehead.

His body went limp. Conway forgot about the fire,
forgot about the phone and the smoke. He couldn't
hear Randy screaming or see the bright pool of blood
that had formed around Randy's head. Conway was
drifting away.

Wait. He wasn't alone. A woman was kneeling
beside him. Samantha Merrill, his one-time foster
mother. She was dressed in one of her stylish blue suits,
the kind she normally wore for Sunday church. She
stroked his hair and looked down at him with a loving
acceptance, and when she leaned down and kissed him
on the forehead, he could smell the mixture of baby
powder and perfume she wore. Then she looked deep
into his eyes and touched his chin, her voice full of
warmth when she smiled and whispered, *You're finally
going to get what you deserve.*

A WILDERNESS OF MIRRORS

The hospital room's white-painted walls are decorated with cheap, framed watercolors, and the air is stale and uncomfortably warm and as quiet as a tomb. Outside, the day begins its quick winter descent into evening. With his good eye, his right, the one that isn't swollen shut, he stares up at the ceiling and watches the daggers of dying golden sunlight stretch across the white tiles. The stillness makes him feel as if he's inside a confessional. He would like to turn on the TV, to have something to break the silence and distract him from the parade of thoughts inside his head, but he can't find the remote. He suspects the nurse has taken it away. As punishment.

The nurse is a lumpy woman with lacquered gold straw hair tied behind her head with a blue elastic, her face a constant, severe grimace—the look of a woman who believes that life and everyone she has known or met have secretly conspired to keep her down. When she came in here earlier, her eyes were cold and detached as her plump and doughy fingers checked his bandages and changed his IV line. Finished, she shot him a look of such disgust, it made him feel like that piece of waste that stubbornly refuses to be flushed down the toilet.

But he is still gripped by the hope that she will believe him. Steve Conway is young; hope is plentiful. Each foster home brings another possibility, another chance to prove him-

self. This new one, the Merrill home, has lasted longer than the others, and each day when he wakes up in his own room and in his own bed and looks out the back window and sees the backyard with its jungle gym and swimming pool and hears the noise coming from downstairs where Samantha Merrill is getting breakfast ready for him . . . it's like a sunrise in his heart, soft and warm.

The nurse was busy making notes on his chart when he felt the words burning inside his throat. He wet his swollen lips and ran his damaged tongue across the coarse bridge of stitches and took in a deep breath to force out the words.

"I didn't do it."

The nurse ignores him and keeps on writing.

"I didn't do it," he says again. "So stop looking at me like I'm a nobody."

Her eyes move up from the clipboard and sight him, they seem tender now, maybe even concerned for his plight, and for a brief moment he believes that the truth has penetrated her calloused skin. Then her eyes harden, and when she places the chart back down at the end of the bed, he knows that she is just like all the other adults in his world, people who need to label the sick and unfortunate and different, people whose worlds are defined by the boxes into which they place people like himself. The nurse leaves the room without a word. He is alone again, alone with the truth that burns inside his skin and begs for release and understanding, the truth useless because of who he is.

He stares at the ceiling, knowing he can't afford to look out the window. Seeing what's out there . . . he is strong, but the sight of it will destroy him. Instead, he looks at the IV line attached to his hand, the bag and its clear liquid sending pain medication into his system. Three of his ribs are broken, his left eye is swollen shut, his lips are stitched, his nose is broken, and a line of surgical staples runs across *the back of his head where the skin had been ripped open by one of Todd Merrill's many violent kicks. He had heard the word* concussion *tossed around by the doctor. All of it is meaningless. The pain medication has deadened his physical discomfort, but it is useless against his rising anger at the unfairness of what has happened, and it cannot stop the inevitable event that looms on the horizon like a storm cloud.*

The door swings open. He expects to see Nurse Bitch Face or the lardo cop he had spotted earlier outside his room. It's Samantha Merrill, Todd's mother. He is taken aback by the sight of her. Hope rises.

The door shuts. Mrs. Merrill stands in front of the door, her thin body masked in a blanket of soft gray light. Her black hair, threaded with gray, is pulled back into a tight bun—she always wears her hair this way—and the fine, porcelain skin along her face is patted with makeup and stretched tight against the bone of her jawline. She is bundled up in her long cashmere overcoat; her gloved hands hold an expensive purse. Everything about her is expensive and elegant, almost regal, the kind of older woman who can partake of the finer things in life but doesn't brand her good fortune and higher status into your skin with condescending stares or demeaning words. She is above no one and treats everyone she meets as an equal.

"Hello, Stephen." Her voice isn't angry; it's warm and inviting, just like it was on that first day when she brought him to her magnificent Newton home and took him upstairs to show him his bedroom. The memory is overwhelming, so quick and sharp, he feels a sting in his good eye followed by a slight wetness. He blinks it away, knowing he can't afford to indulge in his emotions. Concentrate. Don't give up hope yet. You've still got a chance.

Samantha Merrill walks up next to him and then unbut-

tons her coat. He sees the gold cross pinned to the lapel of her black suit jacket, and when she sits down on the bed and adjusts her scarf, he notices the string of elegant antique pearls draped across the cream-colored fabric of her blouse. The pearls, he knows, were a gift from her great-grandmother. He looks away, his eyes burning, knowing he shouldn't feel ashamed.

"I didn't do it," he blurts out, and his voice breaks. He feels weak and disgusted with himself for a reason he can't pinpoint. This wasn't his fault. But knowing the truth doesn't help purge the feelings.

Mrs. Merrill sits down on the bed and stares down at him, her eyes remote as her attention retreats inside to weigh an important decision. He can smell her perfume, a clean, fruity aroma that reminds him of standing in an apple orchard on a crisp, fall day. He notices that she has not taken off her coat. Her hands remain gloved.

"Stephen, remember last Sunday's sermon when the priest talked about lying."

He nods. He has attended church with the Merrill family every Sunday morning—she had even bought him a nice sport coat to wear; it made him look like one of her sons. Now it hangs in his closet back in his bedroom, and he thinks that he will never wear it again and his eyes well up with tears.

"You know God can see into our hearts, Stephen. He knows when you're lying. You can go to hell for lying. It's a mortal sin."

"I wouldn't lie to you or God." It hurts to talk, but what hurts even more is suffering alone with the truth. "I didn't do it."

"Stephen."

"I said I didn't do it."

"Stephen, I found in your pocket my diamond stud earrings, which were a gift from my mother, and these." She taps

the pearls strung across her neck. "They're not worth anything, but they hold a great deal of sentimental value to me."

He is shaking his head, he is frightened, he is drowning. He grabs the truth and fights against the suffocating tide of feelings. He has been a tough scrapper all his life, and he isn't going to give up now. Not with the truth on his side.

"I don't agree with what Todd did to you—he should never have hit you like that, and he's going to be severely punished for it, believe me," Samantha Merrill says. She takes in a deep breath and then adds, "But I can understand Todd's anger. He thought he was protecting me and the family."

"Todd's a liar and a thief," he says.

Samantha Merrill looks like she has been slapped. Her eyes grow wide in surprise and horror and then she recovers and her eyes narrow with a hard light. He is on dangerous ground. Samantha Merrill is an understanding and patient woman—she has opened up her home to him in a way he could never have dreamed—but the one thing that he has learned during these months with the Merrill family is that Samantha Merrill will not, under any circumstances, tolerate anyone speaking badly of her two sons, Todd and the youngest one, Jarrod.

It doesn't matter. Samantha Merrill needs to hear the truth. Sometimes it hurts, sometimes it frightens us, but she needs to hear it and accept it.

"Todd was inside your bedroom," he says. "I caught him with a handful of money—and your pearls. I told him to put them back, and he told me that he was going to beat me up. When I tried to run outside he caught me and started kicking me and I couldn't move because he's so big."

She looks away from him and stares out the window and he sees that her face has changed. Did she believe him? Had his words forced her to surrender herself to the harsh facts about her son? Don't stop, keep going.

"When Todd heard your car pull up, he didn't expect you home so early, so what he did was he put the stuff from his pockets into mine and made up that story."

Dusk has settled; the room is carved with shadows. Samantha Merrill stares out the window for what seems like a long time. His heart is racing with fear and hope.

"Why would he steal from me?" she asks. Her voice sounds small. Far away.

"To buy dope."

Samantha Merrill's lips crimp together as if to prevent something vile from escaping.

He knows he should stop but doesn't. She needs to hear the truth. It's the only way he can prevent his loss from happening.

"I've seen him do it. Behind the gym after basketball practice. That sickly sweet smell on his clothes—why do you think he washes his clothes the second he gets home? Why he never wants you to pick him up?"

She looks down at the floor and presses a gloved hand against her forehead.

"This isn't the first time you've found stuff missing from inside your house, right? Money's been missing and all this time you thought you misplaced it—"

"I've heard enough," she says and stands up.

"I'm telling you the truth. Todd's not who you think he is. He's a liar and a thief, and he has you and everyone else fooled."

Samantha Merrill slaps him so hard across the face that stars dance across his eyes. She leans into him, her eyes watering and threaded with tiny red veins but at the same time so hard and angry that all he can think about is a crevice suddenly opening up on top of a snow-covered mountain and swallowing him.

"You, Stephen Conway, are the liar and the thief," she

hisses. "The second someone showed you an act of kindness, showed you love and offered you a chance to prove yourself, you took advantage of it. Todd caught you stealing from me—the person who loved and trusted you—and now you have the audacity to lie to me?"

"I didn't steal—"

She strikes him again. It's not the pain that causes him to cry out, it's the fear of what is about to happen next, what he is about to lose.

"You lie and steal because you're an awful person, Stephen Conway—awful—and I will thank the Lord every day for having Todd catch you in the act before we brought you into our home permanently. I'm ashamed to have known you. You're rotten to the core."

His lips quiver as they try to form words. His throat seizes up. Through a watery curtain he watches her blurred shape turn and storm out of the room.

Samantha Merrill and her world, with all its hope and promise, is gone.

Outside the window he sees the homes decorated with hundreds of glowing strings of colored lights, and he realizes that Christmas is only two weeks away. He will be going back to the dreary halls of St. Anthony's Boys Home. Back to the large cafeteria hall with its holiday dinner of rubber turkey and tasteless gravy, back alone with the haunted stares of miserable children who fight and kick and scream themselves to sleep.

He slams his good eye shut and sees himself last Sunday afternoon playing Scrabble with Mr. Merrill in the family room. Outside the windows a light snow was falling, and Samantha Merrill was busy inside the kitchen cooking a roast beef, the aroma wafting through the rooms filled with laughter and talk and mixing with the smell of the burning wood inside a fireplace and the sharp bite of the tall pine

Christmas tree in the corner of the room—it's gone now, it's all gone.

He feels his anger rising and embraces it—embraces its strength. He is a survivor. Fuck you, Samantha Merrill. Fuck you, fuck Todd, I will rise above you. I will rise above you and show you—I will show everyone. Just you wait and see.

Conway's eyes fluttered open. The world was a blur, and his head felt heavy, his mind still clinging to the dream. Why did he dream of Samantha Merrill? He hadn't thought about her in years.

He blinked and slowly the white ceiling tiles came into sharper focus. He lifted up his head—*Jesus Christ*, his temples felt like they had daggers stuck in them—and looked around the room.

A hospital room.

I'm alive.

But possibly disfigured, a voice added.

And then it all came back to him in a frightening rush: the explosions and then the entire lab was on fire, smoke curling up across the ceiling like great black snakes and then . . . he couldn't remember what had happened after that.

Conway closed his eyes. He saw the flames inching closer to him, the heat drilling into his skin . . . a cold sweat broke out all over his body.

I must be in a burn unit.

But there was no pain. *Possibly a morphine drip*, he thought. He turned his head to the right and saw a feeding tube attached to the veins in his hand. The skin was tanned and healthy. With his left hand he reached up and patted down his face. A sizable bandage was strapped across his forehead. Another one was on the back of his head; they had shaved his hair. He didn't know what had happened, but he did know he wasn't facially disfigured.

The door opened and in walked a small, plump nurse with blond hair. Grasped between her chubby hands was a plastic pitcher of water.

"Good, you're awake." Young, maybe mid-twenties, a Texan with a sunny voice, loving her job before the world beat her down. She placed the water pitcher on a tray and then adjusted the controls on the side of his bed. A humming sound of motors working. His head moved up until he was sitting upright. No other patients were in the room. He was alone.

"How you feeling?" she asked as she filled a plastic cup with water.

Conway tried to speak but the words came out in a dry, painful wheeze. He went to moisten his lips. His tongue felt like a piece of wood running over sand-paper.

"Here, get some water in you." She held the straw to his mouth. The water burned at first, then soothed. When she took the water away he swallowed again. His throat throbbed. The soft flesh felt like it had been slashed repeatedly with a razor.

Conway's eyes shifted down to the sheets. His legs were under the white blanket. Wiggling his toes, good, he felt that. Normal looking, no bulky bandages, but that didn't mean they weren't burnt.

"My legs," he croaked.

"Your legs are fine, but you got a nasty gash on your forehead. You cracked your skull open."

He couldn't remember what had caused that. His head felt fogged-in, but he *could* recall pieces. The fire.

Being held against the floor by the sticky foam. The fire-man, probably Angel Eyes himself, grabbing Conway's finger and pulling the trigger. Randy grabbing his stomach. Randy screaming—no, not screaming, he was trying to talk. What was he trying to say? Conway tried to concentrate and couldn't. *Don't force it.*

How did I do that? Conway wondered. All he could remember was the fire and—Randy.

You shot him in the stomach.

Randy had died inside the lab.

"You were under for three days," the nurse said. "We weren't sure you were going to make it."

All Conway heard was *three days.* He had been under for three days. Jesus. What had he missed?

He motioned her closer with his hand. She leaned in, and he could see the perfectly applied makeup on her round face, her eyes lined with heaps of mascara, the tiny stud earrings she wore in each ear.

"Visitors?" he croaked.

"The police have been by."

Conway expected that. "A woman?"

The nurse kept her smile in place. "I haven't seen one, no. Now why don't you just relax and—"

"Anyone else in here?"

"You mean from the Praxis fire?"

"You know about it?"

"Oh yes. It's all over the news. Entire building almost burnt down."

Conway thought about asking her more questions about the fire and decided against it. He needed her to answer a more important question.

"Airport," he croaked. "There was an accident."

"The terrorist attack." The nurse shook her head, a frown on her mouth, and sighed. "What happened to those poor people in those explosions—if they catch this guy Angel Eyes they should hang him from a tree and let people throw rocks at him, stone him to death like they did in the Bible. That's what I think."

"Angel Eyes?"

"That's what the newspapers and TV are calling the guy who did the bombings. He's the leader of some sort of terrorist group."

The nurse's words tumbled inside his head. He stared at her for a moment, not quite sure what to say. Questions lined up like dominoes in his head.

Conway pushed it away. He would deal with that later, but right now, all he cared about was the answer to one question. He formed the words, hope swelling inside him—hoping that Bouchard had been wrong about Pasha.

"Survivors," he said.

"A few. Not many. Some of them came here."

"Her name . . ." Conway had to swallow, start again. "Her name is Pasha Romanov. Is she here?"

No change in expression on the nurse's face. *Please God, let Bouchard be wrong and let her be here.*

"Let me go check. Is there anything else you need?"

Yes. I need you to hit the rewind button and let me go back three days in time. Can you do that?

"Newspapers," he said.

"All three days?"

Conway nodded.

"Let me see what I can do," she said and patted his arm. Then she reached over and grabbed a remote from the nightstand and placed it near his hand. "In case you want to watch some TV. Give me a few minutes, and I'll be back with your papers." The nurse smiled. "You're doing fine, you know. That scar on your forehead will fade in no time. You're lucky to be alive, Mr. Conway."

The helpful and eager smile back in place, she turned and left the room. Conway stared up at the ceiling tiles that glowed red and gold from the evening's sunlight as the word *lucky* tumbled through his head. He tried to focus on the world beyond the door, tried to listen to the scatter of shoes across the floor and the bits of conversation, anything to keep his mind occupied.

It's possible she's alive. Maybe she wasn't inside one of the vans. Maybe she was injured, maybe she was unconscious somewhere in the lot, and they found her and brought her in and she's here and she's fine.

He was looking out the window, watching the sunset, when the door opened.

It wasn't the nurse. The person who stood in the doorway was a small, thin man with chipmunk cheeks shadowed with permanent stubble. He wore a starched white shirt and pale blue jeans, his black cowboy boots pushing his height up to maybe five-five. A large paper cup of coffee was in one hand; the other held several newspapers. Conway's eyes were locked on the badge draped across the man's belt, near the gun holster.

"Detective Lenny Rombardo, Austin police," the man said. "You and I need to talk."

30

Detective Rombardo walked over to the bed with a Marlboro man swagger and tossed the newspapers on Conway's lap. He slid a chair over, sat down, and crossed his legs. His black hair glistened with gel and stuck up on his scalp like porcupine needles.

It wasn't supposed to go down this way. Phase one of the operation was supposed to be completed, the IWAC team moving on to the second and final phase: identifying Angel Eyes and his group. Dixon would be brought into the IWAC fold—not that unusual a move, given his technical skills. Conway should have been lying in his bed back in the condo and thinking about where he was going to go on vacation, maybe do the Caribbean thing with Pasha down in the Cayman Islands.

But it hadn't worked out like that. There would be no phase two of the operation because it had gone FUBAR. Dixon was gone, the IWAC unit had been killed, and Pasha . . . he tried to wipe the thought away and was left with a sharp and throbbing pain like a dagger of ice melting against his heart.

"How's the back of your noodle?" Rombardo asked.

"Fine." The word came out in a dry wheeze.

"You took quite a spill in the lab, cracked the back of your noggin against the floor and then that tile bonked off your forehead and cracked your skull open."

Rombardo blew out a long stream of air as he shook his head. "You're one lucky son of a bitch."

He knows I was inside the lab. Yes, of course he does, that's why he's here. Conway looked back out the window. It was too soon for this. He needed some time to prepare his story, the one that would throw Rombardo and his boys off the scent and away from the IWAC group.

"You remember much?" Rombardo asked.

"I just woke up a few minutes ago and my head's a fog. Can we do this later? Maybe tomorrow morning."

Rombardo grinned. "Relax, I'm on your team," he said.

"My team?"

"I know what went down." Rombardo sipped his coffee and waited for Conway to say something. When he didn't, Rombardo said, "The school. Dixon. What went down in the attic. I know all of it, Steve. Don't worry about the police. I already made the call to your boss. You're protected."

My boss? Does he mean Bouchard? Is he alive? Conway didn't say anything.

"Sorry, my mistake." Rombardo reached inside his shirt pocket and removed a thin black device the size of a pack of playing cards. A green light blinked steadily. "It's amazing to me that the CIA can make a jamming unit this small. Then again, I'm still mystified as to how a copying machine works, so I'm easy to impress." He slid the device back inside his pocket. "Don't worry, we already checked your room and your condo for bugs. It's clean. But after what went down, it doesn't hurt to be extra careful." Rombardo sipped some more of his coffee, his body relaxed, his legs crossed. "We've got you and the perimeter covered. We can talk. It's safe."

Conway remembered Pasha saying something about

having a contact inside the Austin police department in case IWAC ever ran into trouble, but Pasha had never mentioned a specific name. Was Rombardo the real deal? Possible. What was equally possible was that Rombardo was one of Angel Eyes's men sent here on a fact-finding mission. Conway wasn't about to say anything until he talked with Bouchard.

If Bouchard's still alive. Conway wasn't about to ask Rombardo.

"By the look on your face I take it Pasha never mentioned my name to you," Rombardo said.

"No. Where is she?"

Rombardo shifted in his chair, and Conway felt the last lingering threads of hope vanish.

"I'm sorry, Steve."

Conway's eyes jumped up to the ceiling. Lightning quick he slammed the door shut on his thoughts and emotions and would keep them shut until he was alone, away from this guy Rombardo.

"Look. I know this isn't easy for you. I know you just woke up and have no idea about what's gone down and that you're probably feeling a lot of things right now, so let me give you the lowdown on what we know," Rombardo said and then plunged right into it. "The surveillance was blown. That means we have someone working on the inside. That's right, a mole, another real Aldrich Ames special, only this one's got to be close to Bouchard, someone who knows about the group and its activities. Ray told you about this guy McFadden, right?"

Conway didn't say anything.

"Granted, I don't have the inside scoop—the CIA is trying to keep the damage under wraps—but what I can tell you is that this asshole McFadden has, for the past twenty years, been giving up secrets to the Russians," Rombardo said. "This guy forked over all this info on our intelligence systems and sold all this high-tech stuff that was worth millions."

Just like Angel Eyes, Conway thought.

"Worse, the prick fingered Soviet double agents. Fucking blew *major* operations we had going on," Rombardo said. He shook his head and sighed. "This thing's going to be a real pisser to figure out."

Conway looked back at Rombardo.

"Now let me give you the rest of it—the reason why I'm here," Rombardo said. "The fire gutted the entire fourth floor. They were lucky to get you out when they did. Praxis is shut down indefinitely. The press doesn't know you were inside the lab, and they don't know that you were at the skydiving school—they don't know any of it, and they won't because my job is to keep them off the scent. Fortunately, Dixon charged his jump. We wiped the charge off the database, and changed the owner of your Saab to some bogus name out of Dallas. There's no way to connect either you or Dixon back to the school, which, incidentally, burned to the ground. But the press knows about the bomb threat, and they're connecting it back to the bombings at the airport. They're blaming in on Angel Eyes."

"Angel Eyes," Conway said.

"That's right, the press is using that name," Rombardo said. "I don't know how they found out about the name, but the story's gone national. They're calling it a terrorist attack. This story . . . it's taking on a life of its own. You know how it is. The problem is that we're not equipped to deal with this. Technically, we don't even exist."

"Where's Dixon?"

"Disappeared like the rest of them. And before you ask, yes, we checked. His body hasn't turned up. As for the suit . . . well, that's gone too."

If what Rombardo was saying was true, that meant that Harring and his Hazard Team hadn't intercepted Angel Eyes's men. But there was no way to know—not unless Conway called Bouchard.

Rombardo scratched the back of his head. His small fingers were swollen, his eyes puffy from lack of sleep. "Look, Steve, I don't want to overwhelm you. You're tired, you need your rest. I'm here to let you know that you're protected. You're not going to take the fall."

"The fall?"

"If I wasn't on your team, the Austin police would be hauling your ass down to the station for questioning. When they brought you in, your clothes were covered in blood. I confiscated them and had them destroyed— you don't want the DNA tests to come back and say that the blood on your clothes matches the blood of the charred bodies they found at the skydiving school. Same thing with the gun. Your Glock, the one you had hidden in your car, they used it to execute the people at the skydiving school. We found the gun and a bag full of wallets and money belonging to these people in the back seat of the stolen Pathfinder. Don't worry, I took care of it. You're in the clear."

Rombardo's voice and body language seemed so honest and natural that Conway wanted to believe him.

Conway said, "How did I get out of the lab?"

"A fireman picked you up off the floor."

"Picked me up off the floor," Conway repeated, and felt a cold hard truth spring to life inside his chest.

"Several witnesses saw a man with a shaved head carrying you along with a fireman to the ambulance.

Fortunately for you, the lab door was left open—best way to feed the flames. Another minute or so and you would have become a real crispy critter."

Conway had been glued to the floor by the rubber foam; he couldn't have been just picked up.

Rombardo was lying. He wasn't from the IWAC group—and he hadn't been sent here by Bouchard. Conway felt a cold sweat break over his body.

Smiling, Rombardo said, "So, what really went down inside the lab?"

He won't kill you here, Conway thought. *He'll pump you for information first and then report back to Angel Eyes. Just play it cool and make him disappear, and then get on the horn to Bouchard.*

The keypad with the nurse call button was lying just inches from Conway's hand. He didn't take his eyes of Rombardo.

"Steve?"

"What?"

"What happened inside the lab?"

"I don't know," Conway said and then thought, *Too quick, I should have paused.*

"You must remember something."

"I just woke up. My head . . . it feels like a fog."

"Well, take a minute or so and think it through. This is important."

Conway took a few minutes. He thought about Jonathan King's suspicious heart attack in the middle of the night. So many chemicals existed that could mimic a heart attack and then disappear in your blood. The autopsy report would never catch it. *That's what those two dicks were saying in the air, remember? Inject him behind the ear so it looks like a heart attack.*

"I can't remember," Conway said.

"What's the deal?"

"The deal?"

"Yeah, why are you being so evasive?"

"I've never met you before."

"I just told you who I was."

"I don't know what you're talking about."

Rombardo's head tilted to the side, his eyes narrowing, his face quizzical. When he turned to put the coffee cup down on the tray, Conway grabbed the keypad, shoved his hand under the blanket and pressed the call button for the nurse.

Rombardo stood up, his knees cracking, and sat down on the bed next to Conway's waist.

"I think you're failing to grasp the reality of your situation here," Rombardo said, his tone low. "You're supposed to be in our morgue looking like something left on the grill too long. Only you lucked out. You survived. Now what, exactly, do you think is going to happen next? You think, what, you're going to go back to sleep and when you wake up it's all going to be over? That you're going to walk out of here? Angel Eyes doesn't leave loose ends, Steve. He knows you're alive. You need me to help you. I need some answers. Now."

The door opened and the nurse walked in all bright and sunny. "Everything okay, Mr. Conway?"

Conway didn't say anything, didn't take his eyes off Rombardo.

"Everything's fine, nurse," Rombardo said. "Will you excuse us for a moment."

"You can stay right here," Conway said. "Detective Rombardo is on his way out."

Rombardo took in a deep breath through his nose and sighed. Then he ran his tongue over his front teeth, making a sucking sound. He stood up. "Nurse, do me a favor. Call the doctor and ask him to examine Mr. Conway's head. I think he's suffered some serious brain damage."

Rombardo removed a business card from his shirt pocket. He placed it on Conway's chest and then leaned into his ear. Conway could smell the coffee and sour milk on the detective's breath.

"Call me when you find your brain," Rombardo whispered. "But if I were you, I wouldn't take too much time. I have it on good authority that Angel Eyes and his boys are still in town. The next time you close your eyes might be your last."

Rombardo winked, straightened up, and sauntered out of the room.

31

Lunch was a dry tuna salad sandwich on rye bread served on a plate with a bag of chips, the obligatory soggy pickle, and a brownie so dry it crumbled like dust in his mouth. He ate it eagerly and washed the awful taste away with a Dr Pepper. When he was done, he read the past three editions of the local Austin paper.

The airport explosions were being called "a random act of terror" generated by what was believed to be the elusive leader of a global terrorist unit, a man who counterterrorism experts from the CIA and FBI called Angel Eyes. Sources close to the investigation revealed that the random attack was done to "wake America up to their vulnerabilities," and that the FBI and CIA were in the process of exploring a number of different leads.

The papers didn't mention any specific reason for the attack, but compared it to Oklahoma. Without any specifics on Angel Eyes, the papers and media tried to keep interest in the story alive with bold, dramatic color photos and recorded footage of the airport carnage and close-up pictures of the terrified, shocked, and crying faces of the wounded and the lost. Personal profiles of the sixteen people who died from the explosion were written. None of the people mentioned were Delburn employees.

The Praxis fire had also been front-page news, but,

with no mention of the bomb call and the fake firemen and bomb technicians that had scoured through the lab, the story had died. And no mention of Randy Scott's death.

Behind the lines of black text, Conway could see the CIA at work, using its influence and various sources and favors to plant false leads with the hope that the story would die down. And it probably would as long as no one made the connection between the Praxis fire and Angel Eyes.

The story that dominated the news was the discovery of CIA counterterrorism expert John McFadden, who, over a twenty-year period, had launched a one-man spy war that led to the loss of priceless spycraft technology and major assets—a CIA term for valuable double agents. McFadden's victim list, they believed, stretched into well over thirty. Conway read the papers and then followed the story on CNN and found it a perfect match to Rombardo's earlier words.

Conway was exhausted. He had been out cold for three days, and all he wanted to do was sleep. He fought it and kept reading the stories until his eyes started to shut. Conway tossed the newspapers on the chair where Rombardo had sat earlier. *Just close your eyes and get a quick rest.* Right. A quick catnap. That wasn't really sleeping. He would rest and then watch CNN again, see if they had discovered the truth. Conway closed his eyes and within minutes drifted off to a deep sleep.

In the dream he was trapped in the deepest part of the ocean; the water around him was black and as thick as paint and so cold that it chilled him to the bone. Small pairs of green eyes the size of marbles glowed in the murky water and disappeared. From somewhere in front of him he heard someone screaming, muted by the water. It was Pasha's voice. She was screaming for help. *Hang on, Pasha*, he thought as he swam toward her. Pasha's screams grew louder. *Hang on, I'm almost there*. Out of the blackness came the extended jaws of an enormous great white shark, its jagged, arrow-shaped teeth just inches from his face. Conway tried to swim away, but the jaws had already snapped around his body with a terrifying force. He was being ripped apart, about to be eaten alive, chunk by chunk.

Steve Conway did not wake from the dream. The drugs that had been placed in his food guaranteed he would stay under for several hours. He did not stir when the door to his room began to open.

The badge with the photo ID pinned to his white doctor's coat announced him as Dr. Peter Bensen, a visiting neurologist from Houston. Amon Faust wasn't prone to worry or concern the way most people are and, as a result, moved through life with a rare brand of steely confidence. If he was stopped, he could easily answer questions on neurology, and, if someone decided to investigate, a quick call to the Brazosport Memorial Hospital in Houston would verify that Dr. Bensen was indeed a member of the staff.

The door closed with a soft click. Stephen Conway lay still in the bed, his mouth parted open, as if posing a question. The combination of Valium and the sleeping medication Zolpidem that Gunther had mixed into Stephen's lunch and soda would keep Stephen under for several hours. What Faust needed to do would take less than a minute.

The semidark room was lit up with slivers of moonlight. He walked toward the bed, breathing in the air laden with viruses that were now deep inside the soft tissue of his lungs. The thought didn't unnerve him. True, he wished he could be wearing his biohazard mask with its excellent filtering system, but one did not travel outside wearing such things unless one wanted to draw attention.

Next to the bed now and close to the smell of Stephen's body odor and bad breath, packed with dead tuna and disease, too close to the sickening plague of whatever germs lay incubating on the bed sheets. With his latex-covered hand, Faust reached underneath his white coat and removed the thin eight-by-ten-inch envelope wedged between the back waistband of his white pants. He placed it on the nightstand and rested the envelope so that it faced Stephen.

In the sliver of moonlight Stephen's eyes fluttered behind closed lids, moving in all directions, as if trying to sight an invisible enemy that would at any second descend from the sky and destroy him. He swallowed, his brow furrowing. A sweat had broken out on his forehead.

What nightmare has gripped you this time, Stephen?

We never outgrow our childhood pain and fear; we merely catalogue it and, when it becomes visible in our adult life, if we are educated and lucky, we can talk away the anger. Faust did not often reflect on his childhood, but now, staring at Conway, he was aware of the common stigma they both shared: They were both orphans. They had overcome their miserable conditions and had emerged victorious. *We are warriors, you and I. We are gladiators.*

Faust bent forward until his eyes were inches from Stephen's. Gently, he cupped the man's face in his latex-covered hands and using his thumbs pulled back Stephen's eyelids. Stephen Conway stared back at him.

"You don't have to travel this road alone, Stephen. I will be there with you. I will keep you safe. I won't let them hurt you. You have my word."

Faust took notice of the bandage on Stephen's forehead, directly above the eyebrow. He leaned in closer and, on a clean patch of skin, kissed Stephen on the forehead. Faust eased Stephen's head back against the pillow and exited the room.

Gunther was dressed as an orderly and was still regaling the two plump nurses at the nurse's station with an animated story when Faust walked up the hall. He could feel Stephen's sweat—his essence—lingering on his lips.

An orderly stopped emptying the trash to stare at the odd, euphoric look on Dr. Bensen's face. Amon Faust didn't see the man. He was lost deep in the warm beating drums of his heart, enraptured with the thrill of joint exposure, this act of coupling, of becoming one with Stephen, the memory of this shared, intimate moment now forever sealed inside the great expanse of his scarlet kingdom.

John Riley leaned back in his swivel chair and rubbed his eyes. For the past two hours he had been working on an Excel spreadsheet on the computer monitor set up in the Pottery Barn walnut armoire that acted as his desk. Numbers danced in his head. The window on his left was cracked open, and he heard the giggles and laughter of children. He opened his eyes, turned his chair around and leaned forward and pressed his head against the cold glass. It was Halloween night, and kids dressed up in their costumes marched up and down Mount Vernon Street with their parents under the glow of old-fashioned streetlights on Boston's Beacon Hill.

Three years ago, Riley would have been out at a bar getting shit-faced. He'd pick up one of those pretty college girls found in abundance at the local bar, The Hill, and then would invite her back to his old place, drink some more, maybe do a little blow. The next morning he would wake up naked and Jesus, Mary, and Joseph, his mind would be *howling*.

Those days were gone, he reminded himself. A thing of the past. He had shut the door on that world. Forever.

It was all about second chances. That's what his mother had told him. No matter how bad yesterday was, tomorrow was a chance to start over. His mother was full of such sayings. You catch more flies with honey than with vinegar. Don't grow old alone. If you can't love yourself, you can't love anyone else. And his all-time favorite: It's all about choices.

As a kid, even as an adult in his early twenties, John Riley had never paid much attention to her words. They seemed the by-products of another era, some sort of weird *Leave It to Beaver* universe where your dad was an actual physical presence in your life, this warm, caring dude who wore cardigan sweaters and asked you how your school day was while smoking a pipe and petting the happy dog wagging its tail at his feet. Right. Real life was your dad dying in an auto accident just before you were born. Real life was a cramped, two-bedroom apartment with cracked ceilings spotted with brown watermarks, worn tread marks in the dark blue carpet, the windows opened to that awful city smell and neighbors arguing in Spanish and Vietnamese in the armpit of the universe, downtown Lynn, Massachusetts, a place where his mom had to work hard for simple things like food and clothes and school supplies.

And you know the amazing thing? She never complained about it. During those awful early years, she had to work two jobs just to make ends meet. She would drive him to school and then park at Wonderland and then take the Blue Line into downtown Boston to her job as a secretary for an insurance company that gave her flex time and health and dental insurance but couldn't provide the money for the extra things that always popped up, the problems with the Buick station wagon with the big rust pockets—what his friends loved to call the Ass Mobile. Three night-shifts a week and weekend mornings at the local Dunkin Donuts covered the numerous car breakdowns but never enough for a new car. But she never complained. The grind of the second job left her with permanent dark circles under her eyes, but she always came home with a smile and would help him with his homework or just talk. After Sunday morning church, she would take him to Friendly's for cheeseburgers and, if there was money left over at the end of the month, she would take him to a ball game instead of doing something nice for herself.

Not once did she bitch about it. Not *once*. Why should she? Complaining was his full-time job. He had, in fact, carried enough rage for both of them. It came out in odd moments: fights in playgrounds, screaming fits, and later, in college, long bouts of drinking followed by fist fights that left his victims crying and bloodied. He should have seen the warning signs then, but hey, they had been isolated incidents, right? You did that sort of stuff when you were younger. You were supposed to be full of piss and rage, it was okay, this shit happened once in a while. Besides, he had just entered his thirties and was now in full-control, working as a salesman for a hot Internet startup. That part of his life was behind him, right? Oh yeah. Then his mom got breast cancer and everything turned to shit.

His mom, Patricia Riley—good ol' Patty all the girls at Double D called her—had always been a petite woman—the bones of a bird wrapped in skin. The oncologist, Rubenstein, was one of Boston's top cancer specialists, the kind of no-bullshit guy John liked. The doctor laid it on the line: *The cancer's very aggressive, John. It's going to take a toll on her. Your mother's thin to begin with, which concerns me.* John told her to move closer to Boston, where he lived, and insisted on paying her rent. When she didn't argue or put up a fight, he knew right then how scared she was of dying.

The chemotherapy kicked the shit out of her. She couldn't eat, she was nauseous all the time, throwing up. John would go and get her vanilla milkshakes from the same Friendly's in Lynn where they used to go after church, as if this ritual could prevent her from future harm. She drank the vanilla milkshakes, but the chemo left her as weak and emaciated as an AIDS patient.

She'll pull through. She's a good woman. Besides, God owes her one. Church every Sunday, never bitches, and oh God, do you remember the time we found the pocketbook in the woods, the one with the wallet stuffed with over four hundred bucks, and good ol' Patty Riley turned it in? Remember that one, God?

The morning of her final treatment, she didn't buzz him in. He had a spare set of keys, and when he let himself in, he climbed the stairs, thinking she was in the bath. Mom loved to soak in the tub and read her mysteries. When he opened the door and walked through the musty air that seemed too close with the smell of vomit and soap and bleach he knew what had happened to her even before he walked into her bedroom and saw her small body lying deathly still in the tangled mass of white bed sheets glowing with the blades of sunlight from another glorious winter morning.

They hauled her away in an ambulance, and John, true to form, went out and got polluted, did a little coke. Man, did he love to drink. Loved the way the booze put its arm around you like a close friend and wrapped a thick coat of armor around your skin and kept away the hurt, the fear, and all the doubt, the way it kept you from feeling so fucking empty. At night, when the world was spinning and vomit was close, sometimes Riley wondered if his love for the drink came from his father.

Thank God for Booker. True friend, he had stepped right in and helped with the funeral arrangements. Conway had come from Colorado. What the hell was Steve doing in Colorado? The guy traveled all over the place as if he were being chased by bounty hunters. Steve was one of those Microsoft-certified engineers who knew how to troubleshoot servers and LANs, and here he was traveling all the time when he could come back to Boston for some serious coin and be with his friends. Good guy and Riley loved him like a brother, but Steve, man, the guy was locked up tighter than a vault. Stuff goes in but never comes out. Was it because Steve had grown up in and around here in all those shitty foster homes? Riley could relate about wanting to get away from your past. A week after his mother's death, Riley was standing at her grave, the sun so bright it pierced the eyes, and, as he looked out at the field of gravestones, he felt the awful, suffocating weight of the truth come crashing down on him. He was alone. He never knew his grandparents, and his mother was an only child so there weren't any aunts or uncles. I'm alone. I'm totally alone. The truth of his life hit him right there and knocked him flat on his ass. He sat there next to her grave, alone, and cried. And then got shit-faced, of course. Can't break out of character.

Steve could relate. Steve had no family, and now neither did John. Booker, he came from this great family with brothers and sisters—the black version of the *Brady Bunch*, Conway had said jokingly—and what John needed right now was a companion, someone who could understand his pain and fear and not just give him lip service—someone who had fucking *been there*. Book, the guy was living *la vida loca* and had a beautiful wife and twin boys and a booming private investigation business and a sweet, sweet pad in Beacon Hill, this six-foot-nine black guy who dressed in Versace, looking like a cross between a pimp and a gangster as he rubbed elbows with the WASPs and the blue hairs. Now *that* was a funny thought.

The cocaine got way out of control. The days off added up, and Riley lost his job because he wasn't making the numbers. He lost the apartment too, right about the time he got busted for drinking and driving while under the influence big time. He was so fucking polluted he didn't even bother to hide the bag of coke sitting right there on the passenger's seat. Booker had stepped in and pulled some strings and got the sentence commuted to a loss of license for two years and a stay at a drug treatment program—not just some court-mandated shithole either. No, this place was in Tucson, Arizona, a place where celebrities went, and Booker had picked up the entire tab. He even helped Riley pack his bags and bought the plane ticket. Booker hit him with it at the terminal inside Logan: *Clean yourself up and get your life back on track, J.R. If you can't do that, if you're going to be one of these pukes who love their dope more than they love their family, don't bother calling me or coming around my house. My son is not going to have a junkie as his godfather.*

Tough words to hear from a guy you loved and admired, but Riley needed to hear them. They got him through those rough first weeks. Three months inside, doing therapy, and when he was released, he felt cleansed. Born again. All because his friend Booker had stepped in.

And now look at him. A year and a half later, and Riley had cleaned up his life. Book found him a new gig as a salesman for a solid Internet startup with nice stock options and serious pay that allowed him to buy this two-bedroom condo on Mount Vernon street in Beacon Hill, within walking distance to work, and a hop, skip, and a jump to Booker's palace right around the corner. And then there was Renée Kaufmann. Something serious, no more of this bang and scram shit. Riley was thirty-three and tired of running. Time to grow up and be a man. Renée was the director of customer service at the same company where he worked. She was solid and didn't put up with anyone's crap. Beautiful and intelligent and level-headed women like Renée didn't come around that often. Every day may be a new beginning, but a second chance at starting the life you've always dreamed about was as rare as a true friend. You didn't fuck with it.

Riley's kitchen phone rang. He leaned back, reached behind his head and picked the cordless off the dining-room table.

"Hey, babe," Renée Kaufmann said.

"Please tell me you're naked."

"I haven't talked to you in two days and this is the first thing you've got to say to me?" Renée laughed. "You're so classy."

"So are you naked or not?"

"Yes, John. I bumped into a Victoria's Secret model and right now we're dressed up in lingerie and are bouncing up and down on the bed and having a pillow fight."

"And tickling?"

"Lots of tickling. And butterfly kisses too. We're kissing right now."

Riley pushed his chair back to the armoire. He clicked a few keys and on his computer screen a window popped up. Renée Kaufmann, a phone pressed against her ear, sat in front of her laptop computer at a desk inside her hotel room in Amsterdam. She was attending the company's customer service conference.

"You liar," he said.

Renée's wide, toothy smile made her look like Julia Roberts, only Renée had straight blond hair. Riley's flat-screen monitor showed her in crystal-clear clarity. This technical feat was made possible by a digital broadband line, video-conferencing software and the small black orb the size of a golf ball mounted on top of Riley's monitor—the video camera. Renée had a similar one mounted on her laptop. He was testing out this new video-conferencing software for the sales meeting he had in Tahoe next month. Renée's customer-service team would stay in Cambridge and be available to answer customer support questions that might pop up.

"How's the conference going?" he asked.

"Good. You should see this place. There's this church right next door that the hotel bought and fixed up so they could have conferences. It's amazing."

The doorbell rang. Riley ignored it. "So everything's going well," he said.

"Yeah, everything looks fine."

The doorbell rang again.

"Dammit," Riley said.

"What?"

"Someone's at the door."

"Then go answer it and come back. I'll just sit here and relax."

John stood up. He walked past the kitchen and, out of habit, placed the cordless back on its cradle.

Shit. He had just hung up on Renée and—no, wait. The computer microphone headset was already plugged into the computer. He could talk to her on that. Test out how his voice carried over the line. Riley walked through the living room and opened the front door.

A middle-aged man with gray hair parted razor sharp on the side stood in the hallway, wearing a black cashmere coat over a dark-blue suit and black-leather gloves. His face was drawn; serious.

"Mr. Riley?"

This dude better not be a Jehovah's Witness.

"Yes," John said, annoyed. He wanted to get back to Renée, who he hadn't seen or talked to in the past five days.

"My name is Raymond Bouchard." The man extended his hand.

Riley looked at it and said, "I don't mean to be rude, but—"

"I need to talk with you about Steve Conway."

That weird phone call last Friday, that was Steve.

Riley felt something in his stomach lining constrict. He invited the man inside and shut the door.

"Are you alone, Mr. Riley?" The dude looked a lot like a stylish James Brolin—tall, and had that Roman profile going for him, thick gray hair gelled so it looked wet and spiky.

"Yeah. What's going on with Steve? Is he okay?"

"Bear with me. Please shut the windows and shades in your living room."

Riley shot the guy a strange look.

"I know it's an odd request, Mr. Riley, but this is a highly sensitive matter, and I can't risk having someone overhear this."

A highly sensitive matter. Those words kept echoing inside Riley's mind as he walked into the living room and shut the windows and drew the shades. The room fell silent, cut only by the dry snap and pop of the wood burning inside the fireplace. He turned around and saw the serious look on the man's face, and Riley felt a quickening expanse of air move inside his chest and grow tighter, the way he felt that day when the doc delivered the news about his mom's cancer. The news, Riley knew, wasn't going to be good.

Jesus Christ, Steve, what have you gotten yourself into?

"Can I offer you anything to drink? I don't have any booze, but I have just about any kind of soda you want. And coffee."

"No thank you. Let's take a seat."

The guy was taking charge right away. Riley walked him down the hall and into the living room. He took a seat in the corner of the leather couch, leaned forward and placed his elbows on his knees and faced the fire. Bouchard sat across from him in the leather chair. Behind Bouchard was the armoire, the computer screen had gone dark—sleep mode. *Renée*. Shit. Renée was waiting for him; he had forgotten all about her. She'd have to wait a little longer.

"There's been an accident," Bouchard said.

Riley nodded and braced himself.

"A fire. Stephen was caught inside the lab."

Riley's mouth went dry. He took a deep breath and cleared his throat before he spoke. "So Steve is . . . you're telling me Steve is—"

"Alive but unconscious. He almost burned to death."

Riley's mind filled with an image of a burn victim he had seen on those emergency room cable shows. The dude's skin was all red and bloated and peeled back—Mother of God. He looked up from the fire and on the mantel saw the picture of himself and Booker and Steve taken on Booker's boat down at Falmouth, about five years ago? Had it been that long? Riley stared at Steve's face but the picture kept going in and out of focus.

"How bad is it?" Riley asked.

"Miraculously, one of the firemen pulled Stephen out just in time. A few more minutes and he would have been dead. He's still unconscious, and I'm told there may be some brain damage. It's just too early to say, Mr. Riley."

"John. Call me John." *You're old enough to be my pops*, Riley added privately.

Bouchard nodded, reached inside his jacket pocket, and removed a spiral notebook and a Mont Blanc fountain pen. He crossed his legs and got himself settled in the chair. "I need to ask you some questions, John."

"Sure, anything I can do to help Steve out, ask away. I'm sorry, how do you know Steve?"

"He worked for me."

"You're his boss?"

"You could say that." Bouchard paused, tapped his pen against the notebook. *What's with the look?* Riley wondered. If it was as if the guy was deciding just how much to tell him. Then Bouchard broke his gaze, reached inside his jacket again, produced a small black tape recorder, and placed it on the coffee table. A green light was on.

Wait. It wasn't a tape recorder at all. It was . . . Riley didn't know what it was. He leaned forward and studied it.

"It's a jamming unit," Bouchard said.

"A jamming unit," Riley repeated, half-smiling.

Bouchard's face remained serious. "I can't afford to have this conversation picked up. John, what I'm about to tell you is confidential. This conversation has to stay between you and me. If it doesn't, there could be severe legal ramifications for you. Do you understand?"

I understand that you're starting to give me the fucking creeps. Riley was sweating. "Sure," he said. "I understand."

"Don't take this the wrong way, but you have a less than stellar background."

Riley sat upright. "I'm not sure what you're referring to."

"Your drug problems."

Riley's face drained of color. He stared at Bouchard for a long moment, the dude sitting there all confident, maybe even a little smug, and then he thought, *Who the fuck do you think you are? And where the fuck do you get off coming in here and asking questions that are none of your fucking business?*

And then, under his anger, another voice said, *How the hell does he know about your drug problem? This guy a cop?*

"I'm sorry," Bouchard said. "I don't mean to be forward. But my experience with people with drug problems is—"

"That they're all liars," Riley finished for him. "Well, I'm not. Now that we've got that out of the way, how about you tell me what your connection with Steve is."

"Steve worked for me. For the CIA."

Riley started laughing.

Bouchard's face was dead serious. "Steve's been working for me since he got out of college. That's one of the reasons why he moved around so much. I can't get into the specifics, so please, don't ask."

"Wait. Wait a second, back up." This was . . . Riley didn't know what the fuck this was. This conversation was taking on this bizarro aspect that he didn't care for at all. *Let's hit rewind and start over, shall we?*

"I'm sure this seems unbelievable, but you have to trust me when I say I'm telling you the truth. That's why this has to stay confidential. Now tell me, what do you know about Praxis?"

"I know . . ." Riley stopped. He took a moment to regroup and refocus. "Praxis is the company Steve works for. They're based out of Austin."

"That's right. Did he tell you about the company?"

"I know they make fiber-optic cameras. Steve mentioned something about digital . . . replication."

"Digital pixel replication," Bouchard said.

"Right. Steve was their network-security specialist. Microsoft certified and all that stuff."

"That's correct. The technology you just mentioned, Praxis was developing an application for the military called optical camouflage, or cloaking."

"Cloaking. Like the stuff they do on *Star Trek?*"

"Similar, only Praxis was developing the technology for a very high-tech military suit. How it works is that you climb inside the suit, press a few buttons on the wrist-mounted computer and in the blink of an eye you're invisible."

Riley's mother had been a major *Star Trek* addict, so he had seen the show multiple times. He conjured up the image of one of those Klingon Birds of Prey warships vanishing.

Cloaking. Jesus. Could they actually do that? It seemed unbelievable.

"I'm sure you can see the implications if this technology ended up in the wrong hands," Bouchard said. "No one would be safe."

Riley listened, rubbing his palms together. They felt damp and cold.

"Last Friday, a bomb threat was called in to Praxis," Bouchard said. "The company was evacuated, only the firemen and bomb technicians who arrived at the scene weren't who they appeared to be. They were members of a terrorist group. Have you been following the news?"

"Outside of football, no. I've been cooped up in here, working."

"We're certain of two things, John. The military suit

with its optical camouflage technology was stolen, and Stephen went back inside the lab and tried to shut the terrorist group down."

By himself? Riley had an image of Steve rushing inside like James Bond. Steve? The guy who almost passed out the day they went skydiving?

Bouchard said, "We don't know what went down in there, but we do know he tried to call you from inside the lab."

"And you're here because you want to know why Steve called me."

"Stephen's trapped inside the lab, about to burn to death, and instead of calling me or the police or fire department he calls you. You have to admit, it's a little odd." Bouchard added a smile, and his tone had changed, congenial now, like they shared a common interest.

"The truth is that I wasn't sure it was Steve on the phone."

"You didn't recognize your friend's voice?"

"This guy on the phone was screaming about it being an inside job." Riley watched as Bouchard started writing. "The voice . . . it did sound like Steve, but the problem was all this noise in the background."

"Explosions," Bouchard said. "Jellied gasoline in the floor, under the tiles."

Jesus Christ on a Popsicle stick, someone call Tom Clancy. Riley took a deep breath and held it for a moment. Okay. Then he said, "The guy—Steve—he kept screaming. I tried to talk to him, but there was all this stuff going on in the background, like stuff crashing against the floor, and then the line went dead."

"What did you do?"

"I had a hard time believing it was Steve. I didn't

have his work number, so I tried his home number and got an answering machine with a woman's voice on it."

"Did you leave a message?"

"No. I thought I had the wrong number. Is he living with someone?"

"He was." Bouchard stopped writing; he looked upset, as if he knew the woman. "They were quite intimate."

"And Steve doesn't know she's dead."

"Not yet."

John thought of Renée, thought of the times they had shared, memories so vivid and real and a part of his life that if something ever happened to her—

This isn't about her, it's about Steve, so focus, okay?

"You didn't know he was involved with someone?" Bouchard asked.

"No."

"You don't seem surprised."

"Steve's a very private guy, even with his close friends. We used to call him The Vault because stuff would go in and never come out. He was always secretive about who he was dating. Actually, he doesn't date that much. He always had women. He just didn't hang on to them that long."

"Pasha was different." The dude tapped his pen along his pad, preoccupied, as if the dead woman lay at his feet. "John, do you remember anything specific that Stephen said?" he asked and looked up.

"I do remember him saying, 'It was an inside job. We were set up. Angel Eyes knew we were coming, we've got a leak.' "

"He used that name, Angel Eyes?"

"Yes. What does that mean?"

"Angel Eyes is the code name we've given to the

leader of this terrorist unit. Somehow, the press has picked it up."

Riley nodded, his attention turned inward on the specifics of the phone call. His eyes narrowed in thought.

"What is it?" Bouchard asked, pen ready.

"The conversation I had was brief. Maybe fifteen seconds. But I thought I heard the sound of another voice. He was screaming something about . . . I know this is going to sound whacked, but this guy, this other voice, screamed out 'Mittens! Mittens!' That mean anything to you?"

"No. Did you hear anything else?"

"I'm afraid that's all I know."

"Would you be willing to undergo hypnosis?"

"Absolutely. Anything you need."

"John, one last question. You have a girlfriend by the name of Renée Kaufmann."

"What about her?"

"Did you tell her about the phone call?"

"No."

"You're sure."

"Of course I'm sure." Riley saw the look of doubt flash across the man's eyes. "I may have *had* a drug problem, Mr. Bouchard—emphasis on the word *had*—but that doesn't automatically make me a liar."

"When two people are intimate—"

"Renée's been in Amsterdam for the past week running around, and I've been stuck at home working on sales presentations. I haven't told her anything. I haven't told anyone, in fact, not even our other friend, Book. To be honest, I thought the call was a crank or a wrong number and forgot about it."

"Do you have the address and phone number of where your girlfriend is staying in Amsterdam?"

"Why do you need it?"

"John, I want to post some people on you, your girl-friend, Booker and his family."

"Wait. How do you know all these people?"

"It's my job to know," Bouchard said. "The terrorist, Angel Eyes, he's very dangerous."

"Are you trying to tell me we're in—"

"Relax. This is just a precaution. We don't know if Angel Eyes knows about the phone call or not. We want to make sure you're protected. It's standard pro-cedure. Go about your life. We doubt Angel Eyes would try to take you out."

Take me out?

"I need to talk to Renée," Riley said. "Tell her what's going on."

"And you will. Where is she staying?"

"It's the Renaissance Hotel, room number 409."

"John, I cannot stress to you the importance of keep-ing this matter private. This situation is very delicate. Do you understand?"

"Yeah. Yeah, I do." He blew a long stream of air and thought, *What the fuck?*

"Do you mind if I use your phone for a moment?"

"It's in the kitchen. Help yourself," Riley said, dazed.

"I know I've hit you with a lot. Give me a minute, and I'll sit back down and answer any questions you might have." Bouchard stood up and walked behind the couch.

Riley leaned back in his chair, propped his elbow on the armrest and leaned his forehead against his palm. Steve, a CIA guy? Just when you thought you knew someone, boom, you find out that one of your best friends—a guy you thought you knew inside and out—not only worked for the CIA, he pulled some James Bond shit and tried to stop this military suit with this cloaking technology from being stolen. And right now he was lying unconscious in a hospital bed, oblivious to the fact that he was being hunted by a goddamn terrorist with the spooky name of Angel Eyes. The CIA. Jesus. And now the CIA was going to follow him and Renée and Book? This was . . . it was like Riley was living a real life Tom Clancy novel, it all seemed so unreal, so—

Riley felt a sharp sting on his neck. He slapped at it with his left hand and when he moved his hand away he saw a small drop of blood smeared against his palm.

Riley bolted upright, turned around, and saw
Raymond Bouchard standing right behind the couch,
holding the fountain pen in his gloved hand like a dagger. Extended between the pen's gold nib was a two-
inch needle.

He shot me up with something.

Riley's heart hammered inside his chest.
What . . . what the hell is . . . what's going on?

Bouchard capped the pen and fitted it into his coat
pocket and came back with a cell phone. He dialed a
number and pressed it up to his ear.

"Move into position. I'll buzz you in," he said and
walked to the door.

What the fuck? Just a second ago, Riley had been sitting here answering questions, and now this guy—
Steve's fucking boss—had just injected something into
his neck. What the fuck was going on?

Don't panic. If you panic, you can't think, so—

The phone was in the kitchen, mounted on the wall,
just a few steps away.

Hurry up and go for it.

It was like shards of glass had entered his heart. John
Riley clutched his chest, wanting to claw through his
skin and bone. His heart was burning. He reached out
to grab hold of something, lost his balance and fell

backward. The back of his head hit the corner of the glass coffee table, slicing off a flap of skin. But he didn't feel the pain. His heart had already stopped beating. He lay there on his back and stared up at the ceiling. His mind was still alive, it was still screaming at him to stand up, come on, John, you can do it.

He couldn't move.

I'm dying, he thought. *Am I dying?*

His mind had become eerily silent.

Our Father, who art in Heaven, hallowed be Thy name . . .

John Riley said the prayer in his mind while his imagination flashed forward to next week, seeing the look of surprise and joy on Renée Kaufmann's face when he got down on one knee and proposed to her at the Public Garden, how beautiful she would look on their wedding day, here she came walking down the aisle and later that night, they would stay at the Four Seasons. Not bad for a punk from Lynn.

Wait. What was this? It was Renée. She was here with him. She held his hand, and he listened to her voice comfort him: *We'll have beautiful children. You'll be a good father and a good husband. We'll have a great life together, just you wait and see.* She kept talking to him as the violent convulsions racked his body, his mouth opening and closing without sound, his arms and legs flailing like a man trying to reach out and save himself from drowning. Raymond Bouchard looked down at him with his hands in his pockets, his face calm and detached, watching him die with the patient energy of a man waiting for his train to come in and take him home.

The front door swung open and in walked a thin, wiry man wearing a blue North Face down parka, designer glasses with thick black frames. A blue Red Sox baseball cap covered his recently dyed hair. The twenty-eight-year-old Owen Lee no longer looked the part of Chris Evans, the Texan skydiver.

Twenty-eight and he looks like a boy, Raymond Bouchard thought. At that age, you *were* a boy, but computers were a young man's game, and these boys not only ruled the computer world, they could keep up with the overwhelming expanse of technology and all of its mind-numbing minutiae.

Lee shut the door behind him, moved into the living room and stopped dead in his tracks. "Jesus," he said. "I didn't know you were going to kill him."

Bouchard leaned over John Riley's body, picked up the jamming unit from the floor and turned it off. "Does the word *mittens* mean anything to you?"

"No. Why?"

"According to John Riley, another person was screaming this word inside the lab."

"Randy Scott."

Bouchard nodded. "He was the only person in the lab. As for Stephen calling Mr. Riley, it looks like it was an accident."

"This word *mittens*. You think it's decryption code?"

"Possible. Only Randy Scott would know, and he's dead."

"If Misha had stuck to the script, we wouldn't be in this mess," Lee said. "He's the one who decided to fuck with the tapes at Delburn."

Bouchard didn't say anything. He didn't want to get into it with Owen. "Any word on Stephen's condition?"

"The word came down when you were in here. Conway's awake." Lee took off his cap and rubbed back his hair. "The security on that suit is locked tighter than a flea's ass. I can't hack my way past it. I tried. I might have a fighting chance if you gave me access to the NSA computers—"

"Out of the question," Bouchard said. He could keep them off the radar screen, but some things were simply out of the question.

"Then I hope the word *mittens* is the decryption code, because Dixon sure doesn't know it." Lee chewed his gum, his eyes reflective. "Our Russian partners are getting worked up. Misha, he's a fucking loon."

"Put him out of your mind."

"Easy for you to say. You weren't there when he did his . . . thing with Dixon."

"Can't stomach this?" Bouchard said.

"This isn't a normal gig and you know it. Look, I explained to Misha that we didn't encrypt the software they downloaded into the suit. That Randy did it at the last second and changed the code without our knowledge. The dude stood there and looked at me as if I was something stuck to his shoes. Those eyes . . . It was like I was throwing rocks down into a well that had no bottom. The guy's not a good listener. And he's not big on patience either."

"You have the drugs?"

"Right here," Lee said, tapping his jacket pocket with his gloved hand.

Raymond had investigated John Riley's background and knew of the man's battle with cocaine and alcohol, the stint at the celebrity dry-out clinic in Arizona. When John Riley's body was discovered, the autopsy would reveal the cause of death as a simple drug overdose. Case closed.

"Stage the scene," Raymond said. "After that, I want a standard surveillance rig, just in case. Might as well cover all the bases. The girlfriend, Kaufmann, she's staying at the Renaissance Hotel in Amsterdam."

Lee's eyes brightened. "You're shitting me. That's where Cole is staying. He's heading up the Fletcher gig."

Malcolm Fletcher was the name of a renegade FBI profiler responsible for the death of one of Jonathan Cole's men, Victor Dragos. Cole was leading the hunt.

"I'll call Mr. Cole and tell him to pay Ms. Kaufmann a visit and see what she knows," Bouchard said. "You have the woman's apartment bugged?"

"Her place and this place. She called him just a few minutes before you got here, then Riley hung up on her. I heard the whole thing. We've got it on tape. Now we've got to talk about the Russians."

"We'll talk about it later."

"No, we've got to talk about it *now*. We've got to find a way to get out from under them. These guys are fucking animals. They're not like the Italians. *La Cosa Nostra*, those guys are dangerous motherfuckers, but they operate by a strict code and have a certain sense of honor, but Misha and his gang . . . Misha's talking about how he and his buddies took turns beating the shit out of this fifteen-year-old prostitute. She lost one of her eyes and is in a wheelchair for the rest of her life and Misha's standing there in front of me laughing it up."

"Maybe it's time we introduce Cole to Misha."

"He won't do it." Lee considered a private thought, and then added, "Cole is unstable. You do realize this."

"I realize he's a major liability. You tired of playing his house boy?"

"You know I am."

"Then we'll work something out."

"Like what?"

"It's time to take Cole out of the picture."

"Sure, why not. It's not like our plate's full."

"I'm serious," Raymond said. "I'll bring him here and wipe him out."

"Right now, I'm more concerned about the Russians."

"I'm working on it," Bouchard said, and felt the anger he had been nursing for the past four years rise to the surface. He looked at the clock mounted on the wall above the mantel. It was late. He realized he hadn't eaten. "I'm going out for a while," he said. "I'm going to turn my phone off. I don't want to be disturbed."

"You've got a transmitter in your phone. If there's a problem, I know how to find you," Lee said and got to work.

A celebration: Dinner at the excellent Aujourd-hui at Boston's Four Seasons Hotel. The maître d' sat Raymond at a private corner table that overlooked the restaurant's long, wide room of matronly diners and offered a second floor window view of the spectacular Public Garden. He ordered quickly, taking the wine steward's suggestion for a bottle of red that would complement the main course of beef. When the wine came, Raymond declined the obligatory first taste, telling the steward abruptly that it was fine, knowing his tone was rude. Raymond didn't care. He wanted to be left alone.

Wine in hand, he settled back into the soft comfort of his high-back chair, his eyes wandering the room, taking in the people. A lot of the patrons were twentysomething men—all of them multimillionaires from hot Internet startups, what he called New Money. But the other selection, the Old Money crowd, the crowd Raymond had grown up with, dominated the room. Distinguished older cocksuckers dressed in their stale Brooks Brothers suits, dining with their wives, who had silver hair and saggy tits and faces stretched tight from plastic surgery.

Some of the women were noticeably younger, their beauty a sharp contrast in the sea of weathered, lined faces.

Cunts, all of them.

Raymond loved the way the word sounded inside his head. *Cunts. Tits.* The rhythmic language of cretins and the uneducated. Growing up, he had never been allowed to use such words in his daily speech; he still didn't. But his interior life was vastly different than the one he projected to others. He often bridled when he heard such words spoken out loud.

Well, that wasn't exactly true.

He said *cunt* several times when thinking about Toni, now his ex-wife. That was coming up on three years now. Toni-the-Cunt was the reason why he was in this mess with the Russians. The memory was there, always there—mental herpes that refused to go away.

Toni had come from serious family money. She never had to hold a full-time job—not unless you considered attending society and political functions and ass-kissing an occupation. Her only dream, the same swan song of all women, was to have kids. She had been married once, and when they tried to have kids, they found out she had fertility problems. The guy up and left. The problem was Toni liked to eat and her figure reflected it.

When she turned thirty-six, her biological clock already on its downward spiral, the unmarried hag had secretly started exploring artificial insemination and adoption. Her father, a man who had been raised in a world of privilege in New Orleans and had gone on to become one of those blue-blood lawyers who had invested wisely in real estate and the stock market, had discovered his daughter's plans. *Artificial insemination? Have you lost your goddamn mind, woman? Children need a father in their lives. You can't find a man on your own, then that's the Lord's way of telling you it ain't meant to be.*

Toni threatened to go ahead and do it anyway. Pops

threw his trump card: If she went ahead and had a baby without being married, the allowance would be cut off, and she would not see one penny of the family fortune. The only thing Toni loved more than her dream of having a family was her daddy's money and the lifestyle it provided her.

She was just pushing thirty-nine when they met at a society function, and Raymond was already into his mid-forties, established and doing well, but not well enough to live the sort of lifestyle he felt a man of his intellectual stature deserved. He had been born into it, had sampled the life to the age where he was old enough to appreciate it, and it could still have been his if his pathetic excuse for a father had learned to manage his business.

Or maybe it would have turned out differently if you hadn't married Janet. Another one from the Cunt Express. Married when they were both twenty-three, they had relatively nothing in common except not wanting children and demanding the finer things in life. Time marched on, and when Raymond's CIA salary didn't provide the life Janet wanted, the rift between them grew. After eight years of marriage with a missing husband who worked nights and weekends and had secret affairs, she left, taking with her the house and car and a good chunk of his salary. The judge, of course, was a woman. Cunts always stuck together so naturally, Janet got everything, and he got stuck with the massive credit-card debt and worked to pay for her fucking tennis lessons and facials.

And now here came the plump and needy and ridiculously rich Toni looking for the same love she sought from her overbearing father. When it came to spotting a good opportunity, Raymond was like a shark sensing blood in the water. Toni, he knew, could be molded and managed. Raymond had molded operatives for a living; he knew how to play the part, how to press down on a nerve and when to ease up. She liked the fact that he was a founding partner for an e-business consulting company called Bradfield (she would never know he was CIA); she responded to his good looks and charm. Her eyes lit up like a pinball machine when he started in on how much he loved kids.

The vasectomy was a simple procedure performed right in the doctor's office. Snip-snip, and a few weeks later—no sperm.

Toni didn't know about it. Sure, there was that period of four weeks when he couldn't have sex because of a pulled groin, but after Raymond got the doctor's go-ahead, he jumped back into the part, doing it to her every night, even coming home early from work to service her (and that's exactly what it was, with those wide hips and lumpy white skin, he had to close his eyes every time and think of that woman he was seeing, that pretty thing with the long blond hair and an ass and tits that made your hands ache with want). Then he did the doctor thing, even going inside the bathroom to produce sperm for testing. Raymond had the sample in his coat pocket, given to him by one of his men. The test results were fine. He didn't have a problem. He was fertile. They kept trying.

Toni turned forty. . . .

They explored fertility options. Toni's age made it next to impossible to get pregnant, but to be sure, Raymond paid off the doctor to make sure it never happened. Raymond collected skeletons for a living. Turning a man into a puppet was easy when you had the right nerve to press.

Toni turned forty-one . . . forty-two. . . .

Good-bye baby, hello good life.

At least that was the way it was supposed to work.

Toni was supposed to grieve and get on with her life. And Raymond didn't have to worry about Toni wanting to adopt. Her father, Harrison Winthrop, was not going to be the grandfather to another man's child. Toni would grieve, do the therapy thing, pig out, pop pills, and be overly dramatic in the way she always was, help me, someone help me, the sky is falling. Meanwhile, Raymond would play the part of the sympathetic husband, listening to her constant griping, comforting her when she cried. All he had to do was look around the house he lived in, its sprawling grounds, the lifestyle that once was promised to him now a reality, and he knew he could put up with anything.

But the world has a funny away of biting you back.

Raymond came home one night, late, opened the front door and stepped into the dark foyer. He was about to go upstairs when he saw a flame jump from a lighter in the darkness of the living room, an orange and yellow halo of light spreading across the face of Harrison Winthrop.

"Sit down, boy. You and me need to have a chat," Winthrop said.

Raymond turned on a light. Winthrop wore a black suit and sat on the couch with his legs crossed, his left arm propped up on the armrest, a Churchill-size cigar clasped in the tiny fingers of his small hands. His white hair was immaculately combed, his powder blue eyes serene behind the wisps of smoke drifting up across his face.

A cold pain shot up through Raymond's stomach and

ran all the way up into his head. For a moment he couldn't breathe; it was as if all the air had been sucked out of the room. He opened his mouth to speak.

"Now the affairs, I can see that," Winthrop said. His voice was neutral, as if this discussion was simply a business meeting. "Nothing wrong with a man wanting to get his pencil sharpened every now and then as long as it's done in good taste. Toni ain't never been a pretty girl, and the Lord didn't give her that many marbles either, but he did give her a heart of gold and what you did to my baby girl was downright cruel."

Winthrop took a puff on his cigar. "I know all about the vasectomy," he said in a long trail of smoke.

"I saw your medical file. You got the vasectomy not two months after your marriage, right in Dr. Brocade's office. And don't bother asking me how I found out, because I'm not going to tell you. What I will tell you is that you're out of the picture."

Raymond sat in his living room with its antique furniture and went into shock. It was like that day when he came home from school, just two weeks after burying his father, and found repossession men moving his world into two moving vans. That day he had stood paralyzed with fear. Now, older and wiser, his brain desperately sought some neutral ground where it could formulate some explanation that would extricate him from this situation.

"Where's Toni?" Raymond asked.

"At home with her momma. Ever since she learned that her opportunity to have kids is gone, she hasn't been right in the head."

"Does she know about—"

"Of course she doesn't. You think I'm going to tell

my baby that the man she loves is a monster? You know what that will do to her?"

A thought came into Raymond's mind. He almost smiled.

Winthrop leaned forward, placing his elbows on his small knees. "Now you listen up and listen good, because I'm only going to say this once. You're going to leave, tonight. The divorce will be rushed through, nice and quick, and you're not going to be in our lives anymore. You understand me, boy?"

Raymond didn't like the word *boy*, and he didn't care for Winthrop's self-righteous Southern tone.

"I've put four years into this marriage," Raymond said.

"And for that you will be duly compensated."

"How much?"

"Half a million. Cash."

"That's insulting."

"That's the deal. If you don't like it, go pound sand."

"What do you think the knowledge of the vasectomy will do to her fragile mental condition? I hope she isn't suicidal."

"Boy, this isn't a negotiation. You either take the money and run, or tomorrow morning you wake up and your private life will be national front-page news and you won't get a cent. Bradfield, that company you work for, you think I don't know it's a CIA front? You think I don't know what you do for a living?"

Raymond had his poker face on. "I think there are drugs in your cigar."

"And I think you're one stupid son of a bitch. You're not the only one who can make bodies disappear."

"That sounds like a threat."

"It's a fact, sir." Winthrop smiled, and then tapped

the end of his cigar against the edge of the coffee table, watching as the ashes drifted to the hardwood floor.

Raymond stared at the man's green eyes that crinkled at the corners. *He's got you by the balls and you know it.*

"What about the house?"

"I'm going to hang on to it until the real-estate market shoots back up," Winthrop said. "Don't think I'm not aware of your connections, how you collect people in your pocket. Don't make the foolish mistake of believing that you're the only one who has connections. If anything happens to me or my family, I'll release everything I've got on you along with a few other tidbits to your superiors—and the media, of course. The media hounds will lap this story right up. I'll let you suffer for a while, the CIA will boot your worthless ass out, and then at some point you'll disappear." Winthrop smiled again, and Raymond wanted to reach over and punch it right off the old goat's face. "I'm giving you the easy way out. Don't be blinded by greed."

Roll the dice and fight or take the half million?

Half a million in cash wasn't a bad severance package.

"You got the money here?" Raymond asked.

"No, a financial planner's got it."

"Yours?" Winthrop's planner was a magician with money.

"Someone else. Conflict of interest. Now, you do what this man says, he'll invest the money for you and make you a rich man in a year. This guy's that good. I figured that little extra touch will keep you happy and away from me and my family. Of course, if you decide to piss it away, that's your problem."

Raymond used the financial planner, and by the end of the year, with the stock market soaring into the stratosphere, had tripled his money. Winthrop and his family were distant memories. Raymond had his money, and with some patience and planning would have his old life back. Then Raymond walked into the two-bedroom condo he was renting and found the stinking, massive figure of Misha Ronkil, the Russian mob's most notorious hit man, hunched over the architectural plans for Raymond's new home.

"Pull up a chair, Big Ray," Misha wheezed. "I've got one hell of a story to tell you."

The financial planner worked for the Russian mob. All of the money Raymond made was through stock scams. Nobody knew about it yet, and no one would know about it as long as he played along. If he didn't, well, Misha said his boss had ways of making the evidence look more damaging. *Maybe no jail time, Ray, but no permanent CIA gig either.* If the CIA cut him loose, Raymond would have to protect himself against the Russians. Not a realistic option.

"You and I have this common problem with this rat fuck Angel Eyes," Misha said. "He's been in Russia stealing some of our stuff, and we found out he's doing it here in the States. You got the inside line on the stuff we want. So unless you want to spend the rest of your days bagging groceries and looking over your shoulder for me, you better give us access to all those goodies. Like this military suit you're developing that allows you to become invisible."

Four years now and Misha and his boss still had Raymond by the balls. Imagine, a section chief for CIA special ops, a puppet for the Russian mob. Funny how the world has a way of biting you back. Twice.

You've got to get out from under them.

Jonathan Cole could do it. The problem was that the

son of a bitch didn't accept assignments. He *chose* them. In fact, all this time he had been wandering the planet, doing his own thing until the Malcolm Fletcher operation came along and suddenly Jonathan Cole was on the phone, wanting in.

Raymond Bouchard broke out of his reverie and was back in the restaurant with its warm air filled with hushed conversations and the *clink* of antique silver brushing against fine china. He had to find a way out of this fucking mess—and quick. As he drank his wine, his eyes happened to wander over to the restaurant entrance where Misha was tossing his overcoat to the maître d', the Russian's hungry eyes scanning the room like a panther in search of wounded prey.

38

Raymond felt his back stiffen.

Get out of here, a voice said.

Too late. Misha's eyes settled on his.

The densely packed three-hundred-pound animal, draped in an awful black double-breasted suit with a gray undershirt, lumbered his way through the dining room, flexing his fists as if preparing for a brawl. Sometimes he moved closer to one of the tables to inspect the food, his face curious but mostly disgusted, his queerly set dark eyes giving him the strained expression of an intellectually challenged man trying to solve a complicated puzzle.

But the look of mild retardation was deceptive, for while Misha's younger associates tended to view him as some sort of middle-aged professional wrestler whose body had turned to hard fat from years of steroid abuse, the fact was that Misha was one of the Red Mafiya's most feared enforcers. His cruelty was legendary. Raymond recalled one story of how Misha made a woman eat a bowl of what he called homemade Grapenuts: small rocks and sand mixed with milk. When Misha finished force-feeding the nineteen-year-old prostitute, he threw her into an ice-cold bathtub, tossed in a plugged-in radio and took pictures while the electricity thrashed her body. He later sent copies of the pictures to the young girl's family.

Misha walked up to Raymond's table. The waiter, his throat working nervously, slid out a chair next to the window. "What's with you and the foo-foo food?" Misha asked as he sat down, his voice a dry wheeze. He sounded like an emphysema patient. He folded his hands on the table and grinned, while chewing a thick wad of gum. He snapped the gum and said, "You ain't going faggot on us, are you?"

His English was excellent, his speech patterns and colloquialisms molded from hanging out with members of the Italian mob and from watching *The Sopranos*, which he thought was the funniest comedy show on TV.

Raymond looked around him to make sure no one was within hearing and then leaned in closer to Misha. The warm, pleasant air, once rich with the fragrance of wine and gourmet food, was now fouled by Misha's cheap cologne and the combined stench of cigar and booze.

"Misha, we talked about this."

Misha said nothing, just smiled. His brown teeth were small and pointed, carnivorous, useful for when he bit women during sex. It was his way of branding them, he said. His black hair and goatee were trimmed close to the skin, and his dark eyes had the vacuous look of a tunnel.

"Relax, Ray, the feddies don't know I'm here."

Typical mob mentality; neither Misha nor his cohorts knew the meaning of discretion. They imagined themselves as gods who could walk on water, above the laws of man, and as a result, came and went without thought or consideration for the aftermath their actions always produced. Raymond remembered a story about Misha from his Brighton Beach days when, in a parking lot in broad daylight, he grabbed a fellow Russian gangster by the throat, picked him up with one hand while the other pumped nine shots from a Beretta into the man's stomach in front of seven eyewitnesses, all of whom later stated that they hadn't seen the shooter.

That sort of intimidation may have worked with the locals, but it wouldn't fly with the FBI's Russian mob unit, whose members were working around the clock investigating Misha's boss, the seemingly untouchable Alexi Zvereva, on several stock scams on Wall Street. The thought of what they would find made Raymond cringe.

"What's wrong, Ray? You look like you're going to have an accident in your pants." Misha snapped his gum and without moving his eyes from Bouchard said to the waiter, "The fuck you staring at?"

"I didn't want to interrupt your conversation, sir. I was waiting for you—"

"Give me a menu."

"We're leaving," Bouchard said.

"No, we're *not*," Misha replied and snapped the menu out of the waiter's hands. Raymond shooed the waiter away, and then leaned in closer to Misha.

"You know how dangerous this is," Raymond hissed, his face flushed.

"You talking about the John McFadden spy case that's all over the news?"

"That and the fact that the FBI has you and your boss locked in its crosshairs. This—this is *insane*. I'm leaving."

"Keep your ass parked in that chair."

Misha said it in such a way that Raymond didn't move. He moved back a little but kept his hands folded on the table. Misha smiled.

"Seriously, what's with this place? Everyone acts like

they got something plugging up their butthole—look at those two faggots in the corner staring at me. I got a bad case of BO or something?"

Bouchard, sensing that the attention in the room had turned to them, said, "Misha, *please*. You're creating a scene. At least watch your language and keep your voice down."

"Yeah, yeah, yeah," Misha said, waving his hand dismissively. He looked over the menu, blew out a long pink bubble and then snapped it. He handed the menu back to the waiter and said, "I'll have the caviar for starters, the good stuff, not the cheap shit, followed by the chef's tasting menu. And bring another bottle of this foofy wine. Then I want you and your buddy over there leaning against the wall to scram. Be fucking polite and give us some privacy."

Raymond shifted in his chair. The wine was over three hundred dollars a bottle.

"Excellent choice, sir," the waiter said and turned, thankful to be gone.

Misha watched the waiter leave and then surveyed the room, watching with amusement as everyone turned back to their plates and conversations. "What were you doing in that apartment?" he asked.

Fuck. He's been following me.

Misha looked back at Bouchard for an answer.

"Interviewing a source," Raymond replied and felt a sinking feeling inside his chest. He glanced out the window and looked at the people bundled up in their coats walking along the sidewalks under the streetlights and the bald trees, a knot twisting inside his stomach. *If he finds out what happened, he'll hand it over to his boss, and Alexi will have another fucking thing to hold over my head.*

Not unless you kill them off, a voice countered.

"Why are you following me, Misha?"

"Alexi wants to make sure nothing happens to you. You're our most prized asset." Misha grinned and blinked an eye at him. "By the way, I appreciate you letting my boys take a look around Delburn. The place was a gold mine of info on this cocksucker Angel Eyes."

"I didn't sanction your men to destroy my communications systems."

"I wanted it to look authentic. The boys at Delburn didn't mind."

Raymond had authorized the hit. It didn't bother him. He felt no guilt because this was business. His men understood that when they signed on.

"Because of what you did at Delburn, I have no way of knowing what Conway talked about inside the lab," Bouchard said.

"I was there. He didn't say anything interesting." Misha grinned and blew out another bubble.

Raymond looked at Misha, at his big shit-eating grin, and thought, *Go ahead and keep smiling, you stupid fucking pig. Your days are numbered.*

"Relax, it was a clean hit," Misha said. "Looks like Angel Eyes raided the place and then went apeshit. Now all you need to do is press a few buttons on a keyboard and these guys will disappear."

"It doesn't work that way."

"Pin it all on Angel Eyes."

Raymond *had* pinned it on Angel Eyes. In fact, he had planted electronic trails suggesting that John McFadden, the CIA operative turned Russian spy, had access to certain restricted computer folders on the IWAC group. McFadden was viewed as the source of the leak. But that didn't mean Raymond could be careless.

"Look, my boys took care of Delburn," Misha said. "But you're not living up to your part of the bargain."

"What are you talking about?"

"Conway. He comes charging inside Praxis like fucking Rambo and tries to take us down. You were supposed to take care of him."

"I led him right to you."

"And the fucker survived. I would have killed him except you wanted to make it look like an accident. Like him and that guy Randy Scott got into it and Conway shot him. Next thing I hear a fireman rescued him."

"It wasn't us."

"Then who the fuck was it?"

"Maybe it was an actual fireman."

The waiter came by with a crystal bowl of caviar surrounded by crackers on a china plate and set it on the table in front of Misha. The Russian's eyes didn't move off Raymond's face. He kept staring and chewed his gum as the waiter opened the second bottle of wine and exited.

"One of my guys, he stuck around and guess what he sees?" Misha said. "He sees this guy with a shaved head, he's not a fireman or policeman, this guy goes running inside Praxis and comes out carrying Conway. You know how I know Egghead isn't legit? The real firemen and police arrive, and Cueball bolts."

"Misha, I don't know what you're—"

"Hey, don't interrupt, it's bad fucking manners. So we're inside the lab, downloading the new software into the suit, just like you told us to do, and then out of nowhere this skinny fuck Randy Scott, a member of *your* team, tries to shut us down. And here's the fucking kicker. We leave with the suit and take it to the safe house just like you said and now we can't get the fucking thing to work because the software your guy downloaded into the suit is fucking encrypted."

"I didn't have anything to do with that."

"Someone told Randy to do it, and the guy only reported to one guy."

"You have Dixon. Ask him."

"He don't know the code."

"Then he's lying to you."

"See, here's the thing, Ray. I *know* when a guy's lying to me, and this guy Dixon, he ain't lying. He don't know shit." Misha swiped his index finger through the crystal bowl and then sucked the caviar off his finger and pointed it at Bouchard. "You're a smart guy, Ray. You've been playing this game for a long time. You know what it takes to work a good scheme. You know what I think? I think maybe one of your CIA pals rescued Conway. I think maybe you called the firemen and police yourself. I think you're trying to figure out a way to fuck us. If I was in your shoes, I'd be working day and night trying to figure out a way to not only get myself off the fish hook but to find a way to take Alexi off the board. And me."

"The deal was for me to deliver the suit. I held up my end of the bargain. As for this temporary wrinkle—"

"It ain't a wrinkle, it's a major fucking problem. Without the decryption code, the suit is useless. Dixon don't know it. I'm thinking Conway does. He may have heard things while he was inside the lab, and he worked with that guy Randy, right?"

"You want my permission to go pick him up? Fine. You've got it."

"He won't give the code to me."

"He will if you apply the right pressure."

"I can chop off Conway's fingers and toes one at a

time, and he'll never hand the code. He'd rather die. He's actually one of these moral motherfuckers who's got a conscience and is all patriotic and shit." Misha blew out a bubble; it was spotted with bits of caviar.

"I think you're being a tad melodramatic."

"The problem is that you pencil-pushing types can't spot real talent when you see it." Misha reached inside his suit jacket and came back with a matchbook. He tossed it on the table. "That's my cell phone number. I'm going to leave a present for Conway. Once he opens it, he's going to be calling you every five minutes. Call me when he gives you the code."

"And if he doesn't deliver it?"

"Then kiss your balls good-bye, 'cause I've got my orders to turn you into a fucking limp dick. And that's just the appetizer. I'll send you some pictures, give you some choices for the main course."

Misha stood up and wiped his mouth with the linen napkin, then wadded it up into a ball and stuffed it inside the bowl of caviar, his eyes smiling. Without a word, he turned and sauntered out of the room just as the waiter came by with the first course.

His meal and evening ruined, Raymond asked for the bill. He paid in cash, the one remaining commodity that didn't leave an electronic trail, and left the restaurant.

Halloween night and the evening air had a sharp chill. Raymond Bouchard bundled up his coat, about to take a brisk walk to clear his head when he saw a white Fox 25 news van pull up to the side of the road. Owen Lee was behind the wheel, his bloodless face as white as parchment as he motioned for Raymond to get inside the van.

39

The crude Russian gone, the restaurant settled back into its warm luxury.

"This has certainly been a night of surprises," Faust said.

Gunther nodded. He rubbed the back of his neck, working it like he had a muscle spasm that wouldn't go away.

"Misha always manages to leave an impression," Faust said.

"And quite the odor." A few minutes had passed since Misha had left, and the air still lingered with the stench of dried sweat and testosterone mixed with wet cigars and cheap cologne. Gunther stared at the now-empty table where Bouchard and Misha had sat and wondered what it would be like to kill such an animal.

As if reading his mind, Faust said, "Misha is very dangerous, Gunther."

"You've told me that before."

"Icarus was warned not to fly too close to the sun. The boy didn't heed his father's advice and, as a result, the wax that affixed his wings to his back melted. He plummeted into the sea. Promise me you'll stay away from him."

"That might be difficult now that he's involved with this case."

"Leave Misha to me."

"What do you think is his connection to Bouchard?"

"I'm sure that will become known soon. Imagine, Raymond Bouchard connected with Misha Ronkil. The gyre is widening, Gunther. The falcon can no longer hear the falconer."

"You're speaking in riddles again."

"Raymond's world is beginning to unravel. Didn't you get a good look at his face? It's not surprising. The arrogant can never see how they set the stage for their own demise."

Gunther nodded. Using his fork, he pushed his meat around his plate and then said, "What do you think Bouchard was doing inside that apartment?"

Faust smiled pleasantly. "Trying to keep his world from unraveling."

Gunther looked up from his plate and put his fork down. "You don't seem concerned about any of this," he said and settled back in his chair.

"Concerned? No. Raymond lacks creativity; his thought process is dreadfully linear. True, he took us by surprise in Austin, but the men working for him collectively suffer from *folie à deux*. It makes their thinking and their actions for this next stage *highly* predictable."

Gunther nodded, not really understanding.

"You haven't touched your meal," Faust said. He, of course, was not eating. He did not eat out at restaurants, even ones as splendid as Aujourd-hui. All those diseased hands touching his food, plates, and silverware—the thought was nauseating. But he did partake of the wine, knowing of its well-documented medicinal value, and asked the wine steward to leave the bottle on the table without opening it. First Faust had wiped down the bottle using the sterilized swabs he kept in a kit on his breast pocket, and then he had wiped down the glass.

"You saw the front page of the *New York Times?*" Gunther asked.

"The article about the CIA mole, Peter McFadden." Gunther knew that McFadden was Faust's CIA contact. "Yes. It's all over the news."

"Aren't you worried McFadden might blab on us?"

"No."

"I envy your confidence."

"There's no reason to worry. McFadden doesn't know about us." *And he'll be dead by the end of tomorrow,* Faust added privately. He had several other contacts besides McFadden, contacts well placed with the CIA and FBI. "Mr. McFadden is not what's really on your mind, is it?"

"It's the suit."

"I thought so. You feel you let me down."

"If I had arrived there just a few minutes earlier—"

"I asked you to stay and help Mr. Craven get set up to retrieve the fingerprints. We fed the fingerprints to our FBI contact and now know that the CIA is involved. I asked you to go inside the lab to rescue Stephen and you did. You were the one who discovered the phone call on Stephen's cellular phone." The name John Riley and the phone number had been displayed on the phone's LCD screen. "Come, Gunther. We have much to celebrate."

"They're questioning McFadden around the clock. He's all over the news and so are you. They're blaming you for what happened in Austin. We're out in the public eye. It's only going to get worse."

"We know that a high ranking CIA field officer is not only involved with a prominent figure from the

Russian Mafiya, he's somehow connected to the stolen military suit from Praxis. We know this because the men who entered that Beacon Hill condo were the same men we saw at the skydiving school in Texas."

"We should have bugged the place first. That way we could have heard what went on inside Riley's condo. But we sat back and let those CIA dudes—"

"We'll find the answers soon enough, Gunther. That's why I had you place the call to the Boston police. Let them do the work for us."

"Another contact?"

Faust smiled. "This evening was intended to be a celebration, not a business meeting. Please. Relax and enjoy yourself."

"Everything's unfolding around us, and you're acting like it's no big deal."

"You should really try painting, Gunther. It helps soothe the mind."

"One last question."

"For you, anything."

"All these years I've worked with you to steal this technology—"

"We're not stealing, Gunther. We're keeping these weapons out of the hands of animals like Raymond Bouchard and Misha."

"I know. I understand."

"Then what is your question?"

"What are you doing with all this stuff?"

Faust's eyes were lit with a private thought. "All good things, Gunther, come to those who wait."

Inside the back of the Fox 25 News van was a mobile operations center used for surveillance. The interior was warm, the darkness cut by the light glowing from the four flat-screen color monitors with interior shots of John Riley's condo. The space between the wall-mounted surveillance and computer equipment was narrow but roomy enough to allow Raymond Bouchard to cross his legs. He leaned back in his chair, drumming the fingers of his left hand across the console as he watched the monitor on his left: two Boston detectives, their hands covered in latex, stood above John Riley's body while a crime-scene photographer took pictures.

"Who called the police?" Bouchard asked, and yanked his attention to Owen Lee, who sat in the chair next to him.

"You know what this is?" Lee slid an object down the console. It was roughly the size of a golf ball, black, and mounted on a small stand that had a wire running from it. What held Raymond's attention was the small lens inside the ball's center.

"A Web cam," Raymond said, the gears of his mind already in motion.

"We found it after you left. It was inside the armoire, mounted on top of the computer monitor. It wasn't there the other day when we searched the condo." Lee's voice was tight. "Riley must have brought it home from work today."

Raymond cleared his throat. "What are you trying to tell me, Owen?"

"We ran a trace on the line. It led back to Amsterdam. To the Renaissance Hotel."

"Where Riley's girlfriend is staying."

"She saw the entire thing, Ray."

Raymond's head filled with a white noise. He sat motionless, his eyes locked on the monitor showing John Riley's dead body.

"I used a jamming unit," he said.

"But after you killed Riley, you picked it up and shut it off—I saw you. What you and I talked about, she heard it. She heard it and saw everything, Ray. *Everything.*"

"And then she called the police."

"We were lucky enough to plant the surveillance equipment and the drugs," Lee said. "We had to escape by the fire exit."

"She's only one person. We can discredit her."

"What if she has evidence?"

"Like what?"

"Ray, that video-conferencing software Riley was using, all you need to do is press a button and it will start recording. Riley also had a microphone plugged into his computer." Owen Lee's eyes danced with a nervous energy.

Raymond felt the veins tighten in his head. He placed his forehead on the fingers of his left hand and massaged the skin. His eyes cut sideways, out the van's front windshield, where people bundled in their winter coats marched up and down the streets and jogged through the slow traffic. They were near the Boston

Common. The traffic was heavy, the night air peppered with red brake lights, the storefronts dark.

"She doesn't know who we are," Raymond said and looked back at the monitors.

"It won't take her long to figure it out. Goddammit, Ray, I told you not to go in there. I told you to let me handle it."

On monitor one, detectives dusted for prints inside the living room. On another monitor, a shot of the bedroom, the gram bags of cocaine Lee had planted were now lined up on the bedspread. It was supposed to be a simple drug overdose. Case closed. But now, because of an oversight on his part, the simple plan was about to escalate into a disaster. The Boston cops were treating it as a possible homicide, and if what Lee was saying was true about the girlfriend recording—*fuck*. Raymond took a deep breath.

"I'll have a copy of the 911 call she placed within an hour," Lee said. A pause, then he added, "On the bright side, I don't think she'll go to the police right away. Right now, she's in shock. She knows she's dealing with pros. She's going to want to flesh out a plan, think this through. That buys us some time."

"You talk with Cole?"

"He's not picking up."

"Just find her," Raymond said. When he closed his eyes, he saw himself at sixteen, alone in his dark bedroom and wrapped up in a blanket on the mattress on the floor. The house had been stripped bare of all of its valuables, his mother down the hall and crying into the night, refusing to accept her new fate.

41

Six o'clock on a Friday evening in Austin. The air had finally cooled, and the pleasant breeze was full with the smell of barbecued steaks and hamburgers wafting up from a nearby grill and charged with the sounds of neighbors out in the backyard talking to one another and kids giggling and laughing as they splashed around in the condo's community pool. Conway, still dressed in his sweat-soaked gray sweatshirt and Red Sox baseball cap, sat on his shaded brick patio next to a black wrought-iron table where he and Pasha had shared many weekend breakfasts. Only now Conway was alone.

Twenty minutes ago, he had come home from the gym and instead of grabbing his pre-made Myoplex protein shake from the refrigerator, he grabbed a Blue Moon beer and headed out to the patio along with his backpack that held a musty-smelling towel and his spare Glock. As he looked around the pool, all he could see were the photos.

They were waiting for him in the hospital room. The day of Rombardo's visit, Conway had woken up sometime during the night, the room dark and quiet and lit up only by moonlight, and on the nightstand, leaning against the phone, he saw an 8-by-10 envelope with his name. Inside he had found a stack of color photographs: Dixon lying unconscious on top of the battered

Ford Bronco; a picture of the skydiving instructor Chris Evans removing Dixon's watch and clothes; shoving everything inside a blue pillowcase; a close-up of Chris Evans standing outside the registration office door with a Glock in his hand; and here was a close-up of Pasha in sunglasses as she walked between rows of cars at the airport. A red X had been drawn through her face. And the last picture: Conway walking out of Delburn Systems that morning after his briefing, on his way to pick up Dixon. Bold red lettering was written across the bottom: YOU'RE NEXT.

Conway stared at the picture and knew that his mind had punched a nonrefundable one-way ticket to insomnia.

But no red X had been drawn over Dixon. Did that mean he was still alive?

Possible. Dixon knew how to operate all the various aspects of the military suit. That was worth something. But not for long. Once Dixon had transferred his knowledge to Angel Eyes, he would be killed.

And you. You already know too much.

Using pay phones, Conway placed several calls to Delburn Systems at various times. Each call went unanswered. He did a couple of quick drive-bys, one in the morning and one in the late afternoon, and each time the parking lot was deserted.

In case of an emergency, Conway was to call Bouchard's private number. He did that and also sent him a coded e-mail. Conway had been out of the hospital for five days and still no word from Bouchard. Conway had no way of knowing if the man was alive. If he was, he would have responded by now.

And no word from Rombardo either. A few minutes' worth of investigative work had revealed that Leonard

Rombardo was, in fact, a detective with the Austin police. The man hadn't stopped by or called. Neither had anyone else from the Austin force. Very odd. Had someone from the CIA stepped in and told the police to back off?

Conway finished off his beer, grabbed his backpack, and then stood up and walked through the opened screen door. The condo felt as cold and as desolate as a tomb. He put the empty beer bottle on the table, opened the refrigerator door, and grabbed another bottle of Blue Moon beer. Opening the bottle, he drank half of it as he thought about the master bedroom, the only part of the condo he hadn't visited since returning home. He finished off the beer, grabbed the rest of the six pack, and headed back outside. An hour later, with four beers in him, he felt bloated and numb and had a good buzz going.

He had every intention of going upstairs and taking a shower, maybe going out and grabbing something to eat. Everything he needed was in the second floor bathroom next to the guest bedroom, where he had been sleeping. Conway turned on the water and stripped down to his boxers. In the mirror he saw the round scar the size of a half dollar on his left collarbone, peering at him like the eye of a Cyclops, and the new scar, the healing, stitched gash on his forehead. He remembered a line from Cormac McCarthy's *All the Pretty Horses*, something about how scars have the power to remind us that our past is real and cannot be forgotten. Conway stared at the old, fading scar on his collarbone and the new one to add to his collection, two different stories that showed how close to death he had come. He had been lucky

(again)

but not Pasha. Her body had not turned up at the hospital. She was dead. Gone.

An urge came to him. Drunk, Conway left the water running and walked down the hall and for the first time since he arrived home opened the door and stepped inside the master bedroom.

The king-size bed was still unmade, exactly the way it looked on the morning they had last made love. That's right, made love. He could say it now. It wasn't just sex, it wasn't fucking, ladies and gentleman—they had made love. He *loved* her. Funny how loss and being shitfaced gave you the courage to say the words you had been so afraid to speak.

Pasha's tank top and panties were on the floor near the nightstand. He pushed away the white comforter, lay down on her side of the bed and pressed his face against the sheets. He could still smell a hint of her almond soap and the coconut butter cream she used on her skin. He turned his head to the left and saw the whirlpool bath in the master bathroom, and his mind replayed one of those simple moments each of us took for granted.

A Sunday a few months back, they had both gone for a long run together early in the morning before the sun came up, a solid five miles through dense air already dripping with heat and humidity. The final stretch, he had to push to keep up with her—Jesus, she was fast—and she knew this and wouldn't cut him any slack. Everything with her was competition. When he was a rookie and still wet behind the ears, she pushed him harder than the others, her voice hard and cold at times but never mean-spirited, the way a good teacher recognizes your potential and with a few carefully placed words can make you shatter your own constructed barriers and show you a reserve of strength and ambition that you weren't aware existed within yourself.

When they got back inside the condo, their bodies dripping with sweat, he went for her first, tearing off her clothes and then she removed his, both of them naked and wrestling each other for control, playful yet competitive. He managed to get her down against the kitchen floor, their wet bodies sliding against each other and the tile, Pasha fighting him, her strength amazing. She got some footing and flipped him around and like a panther springing into action got on top of him and pinned his wrists to the floor, bending them until he stopped fighting her. When he lay still, his heart hammering against his chest, she moved both hands behind his head and mounted him. The sex was incredible.

Pasha loved to pamper herself by taking long baths. Every Sunday after their run, she would spend a good hour or more in the Jacuzzi, either reading a book on Zen meditation or listening to music on her CD Walkman (she loved old jazz). He sat in their small office with his feet up on the desk and read the Sunday paper, and as he listened to the combined whir of the whirlpool jets and smelled the clean scent of the almond soap drifting through the air, he felt a sense of home, of belonging, that the two of them had formed an unspoken union and would move through the world together as one. He put the paper down and walked inside the bathroom. Pasha had her headphones on; she watched him as he removed his clothes and got inside the tub with her. She removed her headphones and looked at him, knowing him well enough to know he was about to say something important.

The words were there. He had been with a good number of women before her, and while some of them had spoken these words to him, he had never said them or felt them. Or maybe he hadn't wanted to say them until now.

Pasha looked at him. The words were there, assembled and ready, he could feel them about to come out.

"I know, Stephen," she said. "I know."

She straddled him, wrapping her arms and legs around his back, and they sat in the warm water whirling with the hum of jets, her blond hair extended over his eyes as he looked outside the window and saw the deep gold color of the rising Austin sun.

The phone was ringing.

Conway opened his eyes. The bedroom was dark. The bright neon number on the clock read 1:30 A.M. He had fallen asleep. He propped himself up on one elbow, reached over to the nightstand, and grabbed the cordless phone. The caller had already hung up.

His head felt groggy, his mouth pasty with a cottony film. He sucked the stale, bad taste out of his mouth and swallowed. He heard the sound of running water. The shower. Right, he had left the shower running in the guest bathroom. He swung his feet over the side of the bed. Drain his kidneys, get some water and some aspirin, and then head back to bed.

Downstairs, a glass shattered against the floor.

Someone was inside the condo.

And then he remembered: *You left the screen door open. Move, it's going down.*

The Glock was in the guest bathroom. Wide awake and wearing only his boxers, Conway moved down the hall in his bare feet. Inside the bathroom now, he reached inside the backpack, removed the Glock and headed toward the stairs. He stopped when he reached the landing. Soft candlelight glowed across the foyer tiles. The front door, he noticed, was shut.

Conway moved down the stairs as alert as the lingering alcohol would allow. He stepped onto the cold tile, turned the corner, and looked down the gunsight into the kitchen.

The beer bottle that he had left on the corner of the

counter near the opened patio door was now shattered on the floor. Someone had knocked it over. That same person had also gone inside one of the kitchen cabinets, removed the small red and gold candles and had arranged them in a circle around the table. The wicks were lit, the walls dancing with flames. Lying in the center of the table was a small box wrapped in red gift paper printed with the words "Get Well Soon."

Walking around the broken glass, Conway shut the sliding door, locked it, and then began the tedious process of checking all the rooms. The intruder was gone. Conway walked back into the kitchen and picked up the package. It felt light, almost weightless.

A bomb? No. Too light. Besides, the intruder wouldn't go through all this elaborate preparation to hand deliver a bomb. Still holding the gun, he tore the paper off and then lifted up the box top.

A shiny compact disc lay on top of white tissue paper. Then he noticed what looked like dried flecks of blood on the tissue paper. A closer inspection revealed another item hidden behind the CD.

A cold sweat broke along his hairline.

The phone rang again.

The package still in his hands, he reached for the cordless phone mounted against the wall. The receiver felt loose and wet in his palm when he brought it up against his ear.

"Hello, Stephen."

It was like staring at a cemetery plot and hearing the voice of the dead screaming out to you. It took a moment to get the word out.

"Pasha."

"Come to Delburn," Pasha Romanov said. "And make sure you're alone. You're being watched."

42

The elevator door opened and Conway stepped into the quiet, dim lobby. The glass door was open, held in place by a rubber wedge. The world beyond the glass door was dark, lit only by the dim sources of light bleeding from downtown Austin.

Delburn Systems was one long rectangular cube of open space crowded with desks stacked with phones and computer equipment. Large, empty shipping boxes littered the floor; days old empty Starbucks coffee cups, doughnut and pizza boxes and fast-food containers were piled inside overflowing trash cans. The floor-to-ceiling windows that ran the perimeter of the building looked out at the black night sky without stars. The downtown nightlife of the campus was about to come to a close at the ungodly hour of 2:00 A.M.

Conway walked across the carpet with the box held firmly in his right hand and searched for Pasha. The big room buzzed with the kind of uneasy silence he associated with funeral homes. The cool air was stale and filled with disuse, as if the place had been closed for days. And then a familiar odor behind it: wet copper. Blood. He stopped walking.

Nobody answered the phone because nobody was here, Conway thought, and his mind tumbled back to his gruesome discovery inside the skydiving school's attic.

He didn't like stumbling through the darkness. The Glock was wedged in his back waistband. He stopped walking and reached across the desk, about to turn on one of the banker's lamps.

"Leave the lights off," Pasha said.

Conway turned and saw Pasha emerge from the conference room. She stepped into the soft, translucent light coming from the outside window. The skin above her left eyebrow was stitched in several places, and her forehead was marred with crusted scrape marks. A bandage covered most of her left cheek, and her eyes were puffy, the skin bruised yellow and purple. The dark blue suit she wore was sleek and angular.

For a brief moment, he forgot what was in the box, what had happened inside the lab and whatever went down here. All he could do was stare, breathless. Seeing her like this, in the flesh—*alive*—it felt like a dream. Like a gift from God.

"Stephen." Her voice was dry and hoarse. Weak.

Conway placed the box on top of the desk, walked over to her, and gently placed his hands on her shoulders, about to bring her close to him when he saw her wince. It was then that he noticed that her blond hair was tied behind her head, exposing the disfigured ear— something she went to great lengths to hide, even from him.

Pasha caught him looking. "It happened when I was fifteen. When I was living with my father," she said. "My mother died giving birth to me."

Sharing was very unlike Pasha. Conway moved away from her, sat on the edge of the desk and waited.

"We were living in Donetsk," Pasha said. She placed her hands behind her back and then leaned her back against the wall, only a couple of feet away from him.

"My father owned a very successful jewelry store. We lived well—not by American standards, mind you. I'm saying we always had fresh fruit and fresh meat. I didn't know my father was dealing in black-market items. It was the only way to survive. I didn't know that then. Now, in Russia, everyone deals with the black market. But you already know such things, having studied the language and country while you were in college."

Conway found himself listening intently, not sure where she was going with this, not wanting to interrupt the flow of this rare, private moment.

"A very powerful head of the Mafiya, a *vor z zakonye*, came to my father's shop and told him to sell the business for some cheap sum of money. My father refused. The *vor* sent two of his henchmen to the house. A fat, smelly animal named Misha raped me on the kitchen table while my father sat in a chair with a gun pointed at his head. My father never once tried to move, never cried out for it to stop." Her voice was devoid of any feeling, as if this story was about some fictional character. "I didn't blame him for it, or when he looked at me, disgusted. I actually forgave him. That may sound bizarre to you, but this man was my world. I depended on him for my survival."

Pasha's eyes were impossible to read.

"My father still refused to sell the business. Pride," she said, shaking her head. "The next time Misha came, not only did he fuck me again in front of my father, when he was done, he placed my head on the wood stove and burnt my ear off." The final words came out dry, matter-of-factly. "That's when I saw it in my father's eyes, that sense of relief," Pasha said. "He was secretly hoping that they would kill me. I always sensed he blamed me for my mother's death, that he was angry that he had to support me. When I told him I was pregnant, he threw me out of the house. Standing out in the cold, I realized that I was totally alone, that I would have to take care of myself. It is what you would call a defining moment."

What do you say to something like this? Conway asked himself. Sorry? He decided to say nothing.

"Aren't you going to ask me what happened to the baby?" she asked.

"What matters to me is that you're alive."

"I aborted it. The doctor didn't use sterilized equipment. I had a massive infection and almost died. I can never have kids." Conway heard what sounded like, what, a hint of regret?

"Why are you telling me this?" he asked.

Pasha looked out the window, her face dim in the light as her eyes searched downtown Austin.

"Misha's here in Austin," she said and looked back at him. "Misha's the one who left you that package."

"How do you—"

"I saw him."

"*Saw* him? How?"

"All the rooms inside our condo have well-concealed surveillance cameras. Only two people have access to them. Myself and Raymond. I've been watching you from here, in my office. I've had you under surveillance since you left the hospital. And to answer your next question, yes, I'm sure it was Misha. You don't forget someone like him. I know it sounds odd, him involved in this case after all these years, but it *was* him. Did you talk to Detective Rombardo?"

"He came to the hospital."

"I need to know what you told him."

"I've never met the guy before. I thought he might

be connected with Angel Eyes. What do you think I told him?"

"But he told you he was with our group."

"Rombardo was missing some key facts."

"Like what?"

"For one, he thinks Bouchard is alive."

"He is."

"How do you—"

"I'll get to that later. Tell me more about your meeting with Rombardo."

"Rombardo said a fireman came inside the lab and picked me up off the floor. That was impossible. I was glued to the floor by this thick, rubbery foam—the stuff Jonathan King developed. There's no way anyone could have come in and picked me up."

Pasha shook her head and sighed. "The gray powder."

"What are you talking about?"

"When you were brought in, Rombardo confiscated your clothes and found a gray, powdery substance. He told me about it. I didn't know what it was. But from what you just told me, it must be the residue from the sticky foam. The heat from the fire must have broken the foam down. Rombardo wasn't lying to you. He didn't know."

"Rombardo hasn't stopped by or called since that day at the hospital."

"That's because he's missing."

Conway felt a cold, hollow knocking inside his chest.

"Rombardo was supposed to report back to me after he saw you at the hospital. He never did," Pasha said. "The Austin police are looking into his disappearance. Didn't you read today's paper?"

"No."

"Stephen, I need you to tell me what happened that day. All of it."

Conway pinched his temples between his thumb and middle finger and stared at the carpet for a moment. He was bone-tired, his eyes so exhausted they wanted to shut. What he needed was some time to process all of this, some time to sleep.

For the next hour, he explained to Pasha in detail everything that had happened that day. When he was done, she moved next to him and opened up the box top. Her hands moved over the tissue paper and then stopped.

"My guess is that it belongs to Dixon," Conway said.

Her Palm Pilot was clipped to her belt. Pasha removed it with one hand, the other reaching inside the box and coming back with the severed pinkie finger. She pressed the fingertip against the Palm's screen, holding it there for a moment, and then moved it away.

"It's Dixon's finger," Pasha said. She dropped the finger back inside the box. "Have you viewed the CD?"

"Not yet."

Pasha grabbed the CD and limped her way inside the conference room. Conway followed. The shades were drawn, the area almost completely black, but Pasha knew her way around. She fed the CD into the computer and then grabbed a remote control and turned on the wall-mounted TV. A light hiss of static on the small speakers as the CD started to play and then, bright and vivid on the flat-screen TV, came the recorded image of Major Dixon screaming.

Dixon is nude, leaning back in the kind of surgical chair found in a dentist's office. His legs are bound to the stirrups by leather straps; his arms are fastened to the chair's pale blue armrests and his hands dangle off the end, his fingers wriggling as if searching for the key that will unlock him from this nightmare. His boyish, haggard body is bathed in a spotlight so intense it makes his skin glow white.

From somewhere in the dungeon of gray walls comes the sound of heels clicking across the floor. Dixon wants to lift his head but can't; two leather straps—one fastened across his forehead, the other around his neck—have his head pinned against the headrest.

A small metal cart with a stainless steel tray moves into the frame and is placed near Dixon's left hand. He tries to turn his head and can't, and then he struggles to free himself and can't because he is trapped. His wild, frightened eyes are only able to see the shadows of the predators moving across the ceiling.

The camera lens pulls back, stops. Standing slightly behind Dixon's chair is a man dressed in black pants and a white tank top undershirt that swells with a hard, wide belly. The man's hands are thick and meaty with fingers like sausages, his brown forearms popping with veins and covered with coarse black hair. His face is out of view. He reaches out of the camera's lens and then starts plunking down surgical instruments on top of the cart's stainless-steel table.

Clink, a scalpel.

Clink, a vial of clear fluid.

Clink, a meat cleaver.

Dixon can't see the tray or the instruments, but he can hear the clink-clink sound, and his imagination goes into overdrive. He has an idea what is coming. His eyes clamp shut and he starts sobbing, his thin, boyish body convulsing.

The man finishes plunking down the instruments and turns his body toward Dixon, his face still out of view. His left arm looks like a telephone pole; a panther and a dragon have been tattooed on the meat of his upper biceps.

"Dixon." The torturer's voice is Russian, deep, with a wheeze.

"That," Pasha said, "is Misha. I'd recognize that voice anywhere. And the tattoo. He's a veteran of the Gulag."

"Open your eyes and look at me," Misha says. His English is remarkable.

Dixon's eyes shoot wide open, as if God Himself has spoken.

"I told you what would happen if you lied to me, yes?"

"I haven't lied to you." Dixon's voice sounds like the rattle of china about to break. "I've answered every question you had about the suit, about the cloaking technology, about Steve Conway—"

"Yes, I know you were being honest about Mr. Conway. How do I know this? I saw the hurt in your eyes. Don't blame yourself, Dix. Conway is a professional liar by trade. He uses people and throws them away like toilet paper."

Dixon closes his eyes again and clenches his teeth and mumbles something under his breath.

"Please," Misha says. "Share."

"I hope he rots in hell." The words came out seething.

"He will. But to get there, he'll have to pass through me first," Misha says. "Back to business: I have questions that need answers. You're tired, I'll give you a practice one to get you in the mood. What hand do you write with?"

"My right."

"Good. See, that was easy. Now for the second question. As you know, the wrist-mounted computer on the suit engages the cloaking technology. The computer is asking for a key or a password. Without the password, the suit won't work."

"I already gave it to you."

"It doesn't work. The new version of the software you told us to download into the combat suit, it was encrypted."

Dixon's mouth opens, shuts, and opens again, as if swallowing words. "But I didn't encrypt it. It must have been Randy. He booted us off the servers and when you brought him into the lab he must have encrypted the software. Find Randy and ask him. He'll know the code."

A long pause follows. Then Misha leans forward and grabs Dixon's left hand and pins it against the steel tray. Dixon tries to move his hand away and can't. It's pinned against the tray, wiggling, like a fish impaled on a spear.

"I swear to God I didn't encrypt the software, I don't know anything about it!" Dixon screams. "If I had it I would give it to you, please oh dear Jesus, please, you've got to believe me!"

Misha's other hand, his right, grabs the meat cleaver. Dixon is staring at the ceiling, eyes wide in terror. His mouth is working but no sound comes out.

The Russian's fingers tighten around the cleaver's handle, the muscles in his forearms flexing, he is raising the cleaver slowly, up past Dixon's eyes, Dixon is shaking his head, no, please no.

"Last time, Dix: What is the decryption key?"

"Please. Please. I'm begging you. Please listen to—NO!"

The cleaver comes down, whomp! *and chops off Dixon's pinkie finger. Blood sprays against Misha's white tank top. Dixon's eyes bulge and then roll back up to the ceiling, his body convulsing against the straps, spittle flying out of his mouth as he roars with pain.*

"What is the decryption key?" Misha screams, raising the cleaver again.

"MOTHER OF GOD I DON'T KNOW, I SWEAR TO GOD I DON'T—"

The cleaver came down again and Conway jerked his head away from the screen. Behind him came the sound of the cleaver striking against the metal, *whomp!*, followed by a fresh roar of pain.

"Don't worry, Dix, I won't let you bleed to death. Now just hold still while I seal those stumps for you with my blow-torch," Misha says.

Pasha shut the monitor off. The screen went dark and with the shades drawn the conference room plunged back into darkness. She stared at the screen, her face as remote and cold as a stone soldier overlooking a field of graves. In the silence Conway could still hear Dixon's screaming, could still see the terror in his eyes.

Conway couldn't stand still; it was like his whole body was vibrating. He started pacing.

Pasha said, "How did you manage to encrypt the software?"

"I didn't. It had to have been Randy."

"So you don't know the decryption code."

"I know the one Dixon does."

"Which appears to be incorrect."

"My guess is that when they had Randy bring the

server back online, they made him finish the software download. That must have been when he changed the decryption key."

"You said Randy told you something inside the lab."

"I remember Randy saying the word *mittens.*"

"Maybe that's the decryption code."

"Or maybe Randy was delirious." Conway thought back to that moment. It was still hazy. The more he tried to concentrate, the hazier it got. The events of that day were hiding, being stubborn, refusing to come out and show themselves.

"They won't kill him," Pasha said. "They need him to show them how to operate the suit. That buys us some time."

"Wait. The suit has a transponder locked inside the wrist computer. In case a man is down, the army could locate him using a satellite." Conway picked up the phone, hit the button for an outside line and started dialing.

"Who are you calling?"

"Bouchard."

Pasha reached down and planted her thumb on the button to kill the call.

Conway stared at her. "What are you doing?"

"We can't call Raymond," she said.

"Why the hell not?"

"Because he's the reason why this operation failed," Pasha said. "Raymond Bouchard sold us out."

Conway was about to ask the obvious question and then stopped. Pasha was not given to flights of fancy. If what she was saying was true

(it can't be)

then she would have some evidence to back it up. Conway placed the phone back down on its cradle and waited.

"I want to show you something," Pasha said.

Conway followed Pasha out of the conference room and back into the main area of the company. She walked in the semidarkness, moved behind the desk, and made her way to the second conference room. The door was already open. She moved her hand inside and turned on the lights.

Blood screamed from the carpet and white walls where it was splattered in odd angles. Conway looked at the spray patterns and knew exactly what had happened even before Pasha said the words.

"The six remaining members of our team were led in here and shot," Pasha said.

"You find the bodies?"

"Someone removed them."

"Someone being Angel Eyes and his Russian friends."

"This bloodshed—Angel Eyes wouldn't do this. It's not his style."

"Killing everyone would be the only way to overtake this place. Besides, we don't know *what* his style is. Christ, we don't even know his real name."

"So you think he did this."

"I think he would have done anything to get that suit. And he did. Mission accomplished."

Pasha clicked off the lights. Back to darkness. She moved away from the door, staying away from the window, then folded her hands behind her back and leaned against the wall, her broken face covered by the shadows.

"At the airport, I saw a small, furry man seated at the terminal where Dixon was to make the exchange with Angel Eyes," she said. "I didn't know who this man was, but he looked familiar. I went outside for a walk. Then our two trucks started blowing up, and the next thing I knew my head was split open on the back bumper of a car." Pasha gimped over to the desk and then leaned against the window. "I finally remembered the man's name. Mark Alves. Short guy with lots of hair, Raymond called him the Elf. He's a black-op specialist."

"So?"

"So why was this person sitting at the airport?"

"Maybe this guy Alves was part of the Hazard Team Bouchard brought in," Conway said. "He told me you knew about it."

"Yes, he told me."

"And you know about McFadden."

"Yes."

"So what happened to Bouchard's Hazard Team?"

Pasha paused, then said, "I don't know."

"What did Bouchard say?"

She didn't answer.

"Pasha?"

"I haven't talked with him."

"So he doesn't know you're alive."

"Correct."

That surprised him. No, more like shocked him. Pasha held the man in high regard.

Pasha said, "When you drove to the gas station, you called Delburn and they patched you through to Raymond."

"That's right."

"I checked the call logs. Bouchard wasn't at Delburn when he talked to you."

"He was talking from a phone inside his car," Conway said and filled her in on his conversation with Bouchard at the gas station.

"You don't find that awfully convenient?"

"I find it lucky."

"This man from Raymond's Hazard Team who called you, Keith Harring. He instructed you to go inside Praxis. Guided you through the company, told you to make your way inside the lab."

"That's right."

"Don't you see it, Stephen? They were waiting for you inside the lab. They knew you were coming. They staged the scene and used Harring to lure you inside. You were supposed to have *died* in there, and I was supposed to have died at the airport. It was only by a stroke of luck that we both survived."

"Angel Eyes used his men to impersonate the people at the skydiving school. He—"

"The idea to go skydiving was Dixon's idea. Nobody

put him up to it. Angel Eyes didn't know—*we* did. *We* had advance notice. In that time, Raymond could have easily handpicked a team to impersonate the skydiving instructors and doctored the files so they looked legit— which they did."

"Jesus Christ."

"And Raymond knew all the specifics of the lab's security—knew how to turn it off. Raymond had the inside line all this time, Stephen."

"Don't say it." Conway could feel his anger reaching the boiling level. He was tired and didn't feel like pulling it back.

"Why are you being so stubborn, Stephen?"

"Because you're standing there and telling me with a straight face that our boss sold us out. This is Raymond Bouchard we're talking about, Pasha. He took a bullet for you once, remember? We were setting up the command post and you were inside the truck, about to hand him a box when he heard gunfire and shoved you back inside the truck. Took one right in the arm."

"I'm familiar with the incident."

Familiar with the incident. Jesus Christ. Conway said, "The problem is that we have a leak. Someone who had access to classified information on us and our team and sold us out. That much I *do* know."

Pasha crossed her arms over her chest and stared at the floor.

"Have you read the front page of the *New York Times?*" Conway asked.

"You're referring to John McFadden," she said.

"Raymond said he talked with you about this on the morning of the operation. My guess is that you both decided not to tell me. Didn't want to fuel my paranoia."

"Correct."

"So in the week you decided not to call me, did you spend any time investigating McFadden?"

"I did."

"And?"

"And he had the security clearances. Or so the computer says."

"So now you think the computer's lying to you."

"You of all people know how easy it is to doctor those things."

"You search the computer systems here?"

"Our communications system that tracks and records all the IWAC conversations was destroyed. The backup tapes were also removed, so I don't know where Raymond was when he called you." Her voice was so calm, so level when she spoke, it was as if her words contained an inoperable truth. "And before you ask, the answer is yes, someone raided the databases for information on Angel Eyes."

"What about the tape backups and blueprints on the suit?" They were stored at a private company called Wentz Enterprises.

"They're missing," Pasha said.

"Sounds like Angel Eyes to me."

"Stephen, you cannot ignore the possibility that Raymond—"

"I deal with facts. Fact: We know that John McFadden has sold out us and some of our top agents to the Russians. We also know that Misha, a member of the Russian Mafiya, is involved in this case. Fact: Delburn Systems was raided for information on Angel Eyes."

"It could have very well been staged."

"And how do you explain the pictures left for me

inside the hospital room? Why would Bouchard go to all that trouble?"

"I'm looking into it."

"And why would he be connected to Misha?"

"Again, I'm looking into it."

"Come to me with hard facts and then we'll talk," Conway said.

"I think the larger issue is that you're afraid I may be right."

"I think the explosion seriously fucked up your head."

Pasha turned and limped her way to the window. She stared outside, her face as remote and cold as a storm soldier overlooking a field of graves.

Nice job, ace. Why don't you just go over there and kick her in the head to drive your point home.

The wall clock read ten minutes before four. He didn't want to think anymore. All he wanted was to go home with Pasha and get some serious sleep, talk about it in the morning when he was rested. He rubbed his eyes to get some wetness in them, then stood up and joined Pasha at the window.

"I'm sorry," he said.

Pasha leaned against the wall, quiet. He stared at her, this intelligent and resourceful woman who possessed such unnatural strength and character, her body haggard and bruised and mending. Her eyes remained still and did not move when she spoke.

"I realize what I am suggesting. I know who Raymond is. What he means to you." Pasha turned her broken face to him. "I was the one who rushed into that basement and saved you from Armand. You were on the floor, your heart had stopped beating. I kept you alive until the paramedics arrived."

"I know."

"And when you left without me for Colorado and wanted to be alone, I watched you, made sure you were safe, had people in place when Armand's team made another rush at you. You've trusted me all this time. I've never lied to you. Why won't you trust me now?"

Conway didn't have an answer for her. She was right, of course. She had never lied to him. She had been his protector, his teacher and mentor and lover, and with the exception of his two friends back east, Pasha Romanov was the one person in this life he knew he could trust.

"All I'm asking is for some time to look into things," Pasha said. "If I'm wrong about Raymond, then I'm wrong, but the only way I can do my job is to make sure he doesn't know I'm alive. I think I'm being fair. In fact, I know I am."

"What do you want me to do?"

"I want you to meet with Raymond tomorrow. He's coming to Austin."

"How do you know that?"

"After you left the condo, an encrypted e-mail was sent to our home computer. I already read it. He wants to meet you at Mount Bonnell tomorrow evening. Tell him about Rombardo but don't tell him about me. This meeting never took place."

Pasha reached inside her suit-jacket pocket and came back with a Palm Pilot wrapped with an elastic band. She handed it to him. Conway flipped the Palm Pilot over and saw a credit card and the torn piece of a matchbook that had a phone number written on it.

"I have a phone listed under Sally Johnson," Pasha said. "That's the number on the matchbook. Call me only in an emergency. You're probably being watched and traced."

"What's the credit card for?"

"It contains a transmitter. Carry it with you at all times. That way I can track you."

"To do it, you'll have to stay close. This doesn't have a great range."

"I have the equipment."

Conway looked into her eyes and in that moment felt some deep part of himself become whole.

Pasha leaned forward, carefully, kissed him on the mouth, and then slid her cheek against his. He could feel her breath whispering against his ear.

"I'll find out who did this to us," Pasha said.

"We both will. If you find out anything, drop it in my locker at the gym. You know the combination."

Gently, Pasha moved away from him. He was about to walk out the conference room door when she called out for him.

"Stephen?"

Conway turned back to her.

"You can trust me, Stephen. Always. I'll never lie to you."

"I know."

Satisfied, Conway turned and left her alone in the darkness.

Raymond Bouchard, an only child, was sixteen years old when his father had the bright idea of committing suicide at home. His father sat in his favorite leather chair, the one by the bedroom window where he would read his history books and smoke his cigars, and wrapped his lips around the double barrels of a shotgun. Using his bare toe (suicide rule number one: always use the bare toe because with socks you might slip and fuck up the job), he blew his problems out onto the back wall of family portraits. The maid was off that day, and his mother was, of course, at the club.

Raymond discovered his father's body. For a reason to this day he couldn't explain, he went outside and waited on the porch for his mother to return, and when she did, around five, sunbaked and shit-faced as always, he told her that Dad was upstairs and had something important to show her.

The child psychologist, a chubby man with a beard and glasses who fancied himself an intellectual, had wanted to know why Raymond didn't call the police or cry. The shrink was especially fascinated by the manner in which Raymond chose to tell his mother. The reason Raymond gave was that he didn't know the man. His father, a businessman who owned and operated several shoe stores, was an invisible presence in the family's life. Raymond knew the man only as The Provider, the one who had provided the lavish mansion in Dover, Massachusetts; the country club memberships; the twice-yearly flights to Paris so his mother could go shopping. What was the point of grieving for someone you didn't know or love? Then the shrink started in with questions about Raymond's mother, Fiona.

Fiona had refused to discuss the incident. How could she? The textbook narcissist was too immersed in her rage about the position she had been left in, the one who now had to take control and sort out this financial mess and for once play the dual role of mother and adult. She, like her husband, like Raymond himself, was an only child; no aunts or uncles came by the house, no neighbors or friends, not even his father's business associates. It was as if everyone viewed the suicide as some sort of lethal airborne virus.

For hours she would scream at her husband as if he was still a living presence in the house. You filthy son of a bitch. You fucking coward. You selfish, no good prick. She would keep up with it, even at night, and Raymond would lie still in his bed and listen to her ranting, wondering more about the fear that was fueling her voice. He knew about the will—had heard her talking it over with the lawyer. His father had drained all the accounts to pay off bad debts and had left her with nothing. Less than a week after the funeral (a miserable turnout; Raymond had seen more people waiting inside a dentist's office) the moving trucks came and packed his world into boxes and took it all away. They moved to a cramped home in Arlington, Virginia, where seven years later, his mother married an investment banker. The man stayed a year and left with his secretary.

To escape, Raymond would seek refuge in the shower. He still did. Now, alone in steam and the hot water that pounded around him with the cleansing intensity of a thunderstorm stripping the city of its grime, Raymond Bouchard could relax and think. Three days had passed since the Boston incident and no word from Jonathan Cole. Bouchard had no idea if Cole had found John Riley's girlfriend, Renée Kaufmann, or if Cole was, in fact, even looking for her.

Cole was good but had for reasons unknown become unpredictable and unstable. Somewhere in his mid-forties, Cole had begun to see himself as some sort of mythological underworld deity who possessed special powers that the world needed in order to survive. He took on side projects, mercy or vigilante killings that had nothing to do with company business. Assignments were taken and rejected based on the unknown internal design of his dyslexic moral framework. It was time to deactivate him—but first, sic Cole on Misha.

The water started to cool. He shut the water off and opened up the glass door. The entire bathroom was filled with a cloud of steam so thick he couldn't see the blue-and-gray tile, the two sinks, or in the corner, the three-person whirlpool bath with the windows that overlooked the backyard stretch of woods. Then he remembered: He had forgotten to turn on the fan.

Raymond reached out into the mist and reached for the towel on the hook only to discover it wasn't there. Odd. He remembered placing it there. Raymond was a strict creature of habit; the barometer of his mood was based on the order he injected into his life. This past year, he had started to notice his forgetfulness, little things like misplacing his keys and wallet, or worse, forgetting who he was calling after dialing a number. A fresh towel was in the linen closet; that much he remembered.

Dripping wet, he stepped onto cold tiled floor and almost tripped. *Careful.* At fifty-three, he was in great shape—he could still see most of his abdominal muscles, how many fifty-year-old men could brag about such an accomplishment—but if he slipped and fell, he wouldn't heal as fast. Taking slow, measured steps, he watched his feet as he made his way through the fog to the linen closet, regretful that he was unable to take a moment to view his body in the mirror.

"Hello, Raymond."

Startled by the familiar voice, Raymond turned, slipped and fell backward. His hands reached out to absorb the impact, but his body was slippery, and when he landed flat on his ass, he fell sideways and slammed his head against the door. He grimaced and clutched the back of his head, the pain bursting behind his eyes like dozens of exploding fireworks.

"Careful. If you split your head open and pass out, you wouldn't be able to call an ambulance. You could die right here on the floor. Alone."

Raymond slid to his right side and winced—fuck, the pain was brutal. He looked up and through the steam saw the pair of black work boots on the tile, stone-colored pants against the edge of the whirlpool bath, a white shirt and the tanned, familiar face of Jonathan Cole. Dizzy, Raymond pushed himself up to his knees. Cole threw a towel at him.

Raymond found anger in any form distasteful and ugly; he had seen it transform grown men into petulant little boys. When he felt the heat rise into his throat, he swallowed it back. He needed Cole's skills. *Let Cole be the alpha dog.*

"Do you have Renée Kaufmann?" Raymond asked. He rested his back against the linen-closet door and propped his arms on his knees.

"No."

"Where is she?"

"My guess is she's back here."

"Didn't you check the flights?"

"I did. She didn't fly under her own name. This woman is no dummy, Raymond."

"If you don't have her, then why are you here?"

"You called and I came."

"I didn't ask for you to meet me here, in my house."

"And I didn't ask to be pulled from the Fletcher case. I finally managed to track him down, and you've denied me access to my men."

"They don't work for you, Jonathan. They work for me."

"I'm taking them with me. Today."

"You work for the Agency, Jonathan. You have a problem remembering that I'm your boss."

"You don't own me. I'm not your dog that you can call."

"I have a project that requires your specialized cleaning services."

"Housekeeping matters bore me. Send one of your stable boys."

"I need you."

That made Cole pause. A moment later, he asked, "What do I get out of it?"

"Freedom."

Cole leaned forward, his elbows sliding across his thighs and then stopping to rest on his knees. Cole's fine blond hair was parted on the side and neatly combed, his face tanned, the skin stretched tight. With his all-American boyish good looks and his casual dress, he looked like the kind of dedicated father seen in the stands at his son's hockey game.

"I'm listening," Cole said.

"You know Misha Ronkil?"

"I'm familiar with his sloppy work."

"I want you to kill him."

"Misha's a hot zone. The feds are keeping a close eye on him and Alexi."

Raymond knew that the best way to get Cole to come over to the other side of the fence was to feed into the man's savior complex. For once, Raymond told the truth.

"So you sold out your own men to save your hide," Cole said when Raymond was done.

"Misha is out of control. He won't listen to reason."

"Because he wants the decryption code for this military suit. Why is this suit so important? You didn't say."

Again, Raymond fed into the man's God complex. "The suit offers total invisibility using a technology called optical camouflage."

"Cloaking."

"Yes. You climb inside the suit, punch in the code, and you're invisible."

Some of the steam had cleared; Raymond could see the possibilities working behind Cole's blue eyes. *That's it, take the bait, you arrogant fuck.* Raymond kept his face neutral and hid his pleasure.

"Who has the code?" Cole asked.

"I believe Steve Conway."

"The only survivor of your IWAC group."

"That's right. I'm meeting him later today. I'm going to send him to Boston."

"To attend his friend's funeral. The man you killed."

"Conway believes Angel Eyes is behind all of this. You'll be Conway's handler. Once he hands over the code, you'll kill him. I want every loose end tied up."

"I haven't accepted the job yet."

"I'm offering you your freedom."

"I don't believe you'd let me go so easily, Raymond."

"I'm going to retire soon. I want to be left alone. Name your terms."

"I want the military suit."

Cole would never get it, of course. Raymond pretended to think about it. Then he said, "You get the Russians out of my life, you can have it."

Cole smiled. "Then we have ourselves a deal."

"You need to find the Kaufmann woman. She might have recorded evidence of what happened inside the condo."

"She'll pop up at the funeral."

"Or she won't. She could go to the police or worse, the feds."

"Did Owen post people?"

"We've got the Boston PD and the federal building at Government Center covered. If she goes in, we'll catch her. We know what she looks like."

"I'll be in Boston tonight. Send Conway to me." Cole stood up and walked over to the door. His hand on the knob, he looked down at the naked Raymond Bouchard. "I heard you injected this man Riley with cocaine and rat poison." Cole grinned. "I never thought you were capable of such things."

"I'll contact you after I talk to Conway."

"Just one last item. If you try to fuck me, Raymond, I'll eat you alive, piece by piece."

Reaching the top of Mount Bonnell required a steep climb of one-hundred-plus stone steps that left even the athletic winded. Those willing to undertake it were rewarded with sweeping, panoramic views of Austin and Hill counties.

It was a quarter to six, and Conway stood in a round clearing that held a circular stone table with benches. The sun was setting, and right now the place was dead. But that would change later tonight, when teenagers and UT college kids looking for privacy or a romantic place to drink or talk or to get high or get laid would sneak inside sometime after 10:00 P.M., the time the park closed. Such an undertaking was dangerous. With only the light from the stars and moon as your guide, and with steep cliffs surrounding you, a slip or a false move could result in death. Not long ago, three pledges plummeted to their deaths when a UT fraternity had the bright idea of staging a hazing ritual here.

"Stephen."

Conway turned around. Framed against the darkening sky was Raymond Bouchard, dressed in a commanding black suit and jacket, his tie blowing in the breeze. A thin film of dust covered his black shoes. A pair of blue mirrored Revo sunglasses hid his eyes.

"Let's take a walk," Bouchard said and without waiting, turned and started down a path. Conway jogged over to catch up.

Bouchard did not appear to be in a rush; he ambled his way through the bumpy, winding path with his hands deep in his pockets, his head bowed forward as he watched his feet moving across the dirt. Conway didn't talk, just followed. He looked into the infinite expanse of stars and wondered if a satellite were locked on them right now, watching, ready to record his voice and analyze it later. Computers now had the ability to tell whether or not someone was lying.

Pasha's words from just last night: *You can trust me, Stephen. Always. I'll never lie to you.*

All day Conway had thought of this moment, rehearsing what he would say, how he would answer Bouchard's questions. Lying to the man would jeopardize the one thing he cared for besides Pasha: his career. But Pasha . . . Conway's need to protect her was so intense he was willing to take on any risk, including lying to his boss. She had saved his life—twice now—and he loved her, so naturally, he felt protective and loyal.

But even if those two conditions weren't involved, he still would have granted Pasha's request for secrecy. His time served in foster homes and the orphanage had taught him how to ferret out liars and people's hidden agendas. Conway was sure of one thing on this earth: Pasha Romanov was not a liar. Private, maybe even secretive, but trustworthy.

A few minutes later, Bouchard stopped walking. They stood near the edge of a cliff that overlooked the sweeping flat earth of Austin, the bridge, and below it, the river littered with powerboats and sailboats whose canvas sails swelled in the wind.

"I'm sorry it took me so long to get back to you,"

Bouchard said, his voice scratchy. He coughed to clear his throat. "My hands have been full. I take it you've seen the news about Angel Eyes."

"And McFadden."

Bouchard gritted his teeth, the muscles along his jawline flexing. "His treason is taking on epidemic proportions. It's a goddamn mess," he said. Over his shoulder, the sky had grown darker. He took off his sunglasses and tucked them inside his jacket pocket. Even in the twilight his eyes looked worn. "I'm sorry about Pasha, Stephen. I know how important she was to you."

Conway played the role of the grieving lover. "Her body," he started, and cleared his throat.

"We haven't ID'd any of the bodies yet. It's . . ." Bouchard started to say and then his voice trailed off. He shoved his hands into his pockets, shook his head, and sighed, and as he looked out at the water below, he jiggled his change and keys. "It's going to be a long and painful process. What happened here . . . I've never lost men like that. I'm still having a hard time accepting what happened."

Conway studied the man for a moment. His grief seemed genuine. Conway removed the 8-by-10-inch envelope wedged in his back waistband and handed it to Bouchard.

"Angel Eyes left these for me in my hospital room," Conway said. "While I was sleeping."

As Bouchard went through the pictures, studying each with great care, Conway watched his boss's face, checking for surprise, shock—something that would validate Pasha's theory. The man's face was as readable as stone. If anything, he looked shell-shocked.

"Why would Angel Eyes leave those pictures?" Conway asked.

"To keep you on the edge. To let you know he was coming."

"Dixon's alive."

Bouchard looked up from the pictures, the meaning in his eyes veiled. From his back pocket Conway removed the jewel case that contained a burned copy of Dixon's torture session and held it up in the air. He kept the original for himself.

"Last night someone left this compact disc inside the condo. I was afraid the CD might be infected with a virus, and since my home PC doesn't have the latest virus updates, I drove over to Delburn and used one of our secured computers."

"How did you get in?" Bouchard asked. Conway didn't work there and didn't have a key. But Pasha did.

"Pasha's keys. She left a spare set at the condo," Conway lied. "Nobody's answering the phone. Where's the rest of the team?"

"They're all dead."

"Including your Hazard Team?"

Bouchard nodded. Conway watched him carefully now.

"Steve, when you called Delburn, the switchboard patched your call to my car. I was on my way to the safe house I keep here in Austin. The DO of Operations called and wanted to talk to me about McFadden—the shit had hit the fan big time back at headquarters. I had classified files on a compromised operation that McFadden worked on. We had hours to go before the exchange at the airport, so I decided to drive out. I was about twenty minutes away from Delburn when you called. When we got off the phone, I turned around and headed back to Delburn." Bouchard looked disgusted. "They were all dead."

"What happened to all the bodies?"

"A special team came in and removed them."

Right. Can't have the local police investigating the matter, Conway thought.

"Same with the Hazard Team and surveillance team that was supposed to be guarding you. They were killed with nerve gas. Someone rigged the vans," Bouchard said. "Someone sold us out."

"McFadden?"

"Yes. It was John."

"You know him?"

"John used to work for me. We used to be good friends." Bouchard's tone was flat, almost detached. "He and I were at the funeral for one of my men. We were both pallbearers. I found out this week that McFadden sold him out for five grand, and there was the son of a bitch on the opposite side of me that day, choking back tears." Bouchard slid the pictures back into the envelope, rolled it up and tapped it against his leg. "All those years we were searching for the mole and that *fuck* was right under my nose, selling us all out."

"So you knew we had a mole."

"What we knew was that for the past ten years, a man we called Hijack was selling out some of our top agents. The problem is McFadden didn't have any abnormalities in his background. McFadden's a die-hard Catholic. Has four kids, went to church every Sunday, didn't have any marital problems, didn't drink or gamble or have any additional source of income. He passed all the five-year background checks. He knew how to play the game. When it came to tradecraft, McFadden was a pro."

"Then why did he sell us out?"

"We'll never know."

"Not talking?"

"He's dead."

Conway felt his heartbeat surge.

"He went to sleep last night and never woke up," Bouchard said. "Poisoned, probably. We're looking into it. As for why he sold us out, it's going to be one of the great mysteries of life."

If Bouchard was lying, he was a great actor. Still, Conway heeded Pasha's words and studied the man.

"Why would Angel Eyes take over Delburn?" Conway asked. "It doesn't fit his MO."

"Simple. It's our base of operations. Once inside, he would be able to locate all of our surveillance and Hazard Teams, would be able to overhear any conversation. He took what he needed and then started wiping us out." Bouchard looked at the CD gripped in Conway's hand and said, "What's on it?"

"Dixon's torture session. Angel Eyes thinks Dixon knows the decryption code."

"He does."

"It doesn't work. The code's been changed. Without the decryption code, the suit is worthless."

"Unless Angel Eyes can hack his way past it."

"Unlikely."

"Nice work, Stephen. Because of you, the suit is safe."

"I didn't encrypt the software. It was Randy."

"So you don't know the decryption code?"

"I don't remember much from the lab. A tile fell on my forehead and cracked my skull open. After that, it's all one big blur."

"Do you remember what happened that day?"

"Most of it."

"Tell me."

Conway did, in great detail, including his conversation with Rombardo—Conway told the man everything except his early-morning meeting with Pasha. Thirty minutes later, when he had finished talking, Bouchard was quiet. The wind had picked up and moved around them, and the air was noticeably cooler.

"Keith Harring and his men never made it out of the airport," Bouchard said. "The person who called you was an imposter. Angel Eyes used Harring's name to lure you inside the lab. Steve, do you think Dix was in on it?"

"No. Up in the plane, he was scared to death. It wasn't an act."

"Angel Eyes must have been monitoring us all this time. That's the only way he could know about Harring—the only way he could stay ahead of us. Jesus Christ. I can't believe how smoothly he pulled this off."

"Why didn't you contact me once you got to Delburn?"

"I tried calling you from the car and couldn't get through. When I got back to Delburn, the majority of the communications equipment had been destroyed. I couldn't call you. Angel Eyes also took the tape backups. He raided the place, Steve, and destroyed everyone and everything there. I drove to Praxis but by the time I got there Angel Eyes was long gone."

Conway said, "I take it Rombardo didn't relay my message."

"No, he didn't."

"So he's one of us."

"He's our liaison inside the Austin police." Bouchard stared out at some point below the cliff. He seemed focused on a thought. "I can't lock onto the suit's emergency transponder."

"Why?"

"To activate the transponder, the suit needs to be on, and you can't turn it on unless you access the computer system on the wrist unit. But if you had the decryption code, you would be able to turn on the computer and activate the transponder."

"I don't know the code," Conway said.

"Randy must have told you something in the lab."

"He was dying. He wasn't making any sense."

"Tell me."

"Randy said the words *mittens* and *cat food*."

"Randy owned a cat, right?"

"The girl he met down here, she sometimes kept it at his apartment. This evil black thing called Lissy. Scratched the hell out of everyone and everything." Conway handed Bouchard the CD. "They've already chopped off two of Dixon's fingers. If we don't find him soon, they're won't be much left."

"When Angel Eyes figures out that Dixon doesn't know the decryption code, he'll target the person who does."

"Randy's dead."

"Which means you're next in line."

Bouchard considered a private question. He studied the ground for a moment, and when he looked up, his eyes seemed clouded.

"Stephen, when I got back to Delburn, the communications system was destroyed. Fortunately, the system mails an encrypted copy of each call to an offsite office. When you were at the lab, you said you made a final call to Delburn."

"That's right. I told you what I said."

"Yes, you did. My question is, do you know who answered the phone?"

"It was loud. There were explosions, I couldn't hear, but it was a man's voice. I thought I was . . . I thought I was going to die so I told the team member what I knew."

"But did you recognize the voice on the other end?"

Conway thought about it. "No. For a brief second, I thought I had called a friend of mine, John Riley."

"You did."

For a moment Conway was too stunned to speak.

Then he saw the tightening in Bouchard's eyes, felt the way the air seemed to grow colder. Conway felt his stomach tighten as Bouchard took in a deep breath and formed his next choice of words.

"John Riley," Bouchard said.

"What's wrong?"

"He's dead, Stephen. Angel Eyes killed him."

Shock mushroomed from deep in Conway's stomach and then spread across his skin, making it tingle. *It's a mistake*, a voice reassured him. *John Riley has nothing to do with the CIA or Angel Eyes, Bouchard's got it wrong.*

Conway met Bouchard's sad gaze and an icy vapor filled his heart.

"I'm sorry, Stephen. It's true."

Bouchard went to put his hand on Conway's shoulder but he had pulled away and turned into the wind. He wasn't going to let his emotions get him, not here in front of his boss. *Pull it together, man.*

"How did he die?" Conway asked, his mind filling with the images from Dixon's torture video.

"That's not important."

"Tell me."

Conway could hear Bouchard shift his weight, the man's shoes crunching under the rocks as he moved closer and then stopped.

"Cocaine laced with rat poison," Bouchard said. "I'm not going to lie to you, Stephen. It was an awful way to go."

Conway placed his hands on his hips and looked down at the brightly lit boats the size of bath toys moving across the water. Then he closed his eyes and saw a pitch-black sky. How he wanted to be swallowed inside that void, to feel nothing. Old memories of Riley, events he hadn't thought about in years, all of them came to him in a rush. He couldn't shut them off. Odd how the mind loved to betray you at your most vulnerable moments.

"I remember an interesting story from your personal file," Bouchard said, his voice closer now, directly behind him. "That foster family that took you in, the Merrills, their eldest son, Todd, almost beat you to death that day he supposedly caught you helping yourself to the mother's jewelry. The mother came home just in time and had you rushed to the hospital. The police found the pearl necklace inside your jeans pocket and sent you back to St. Anthony's. You were thirteen."

Conway opened his eyes and stared at the water.

"Three years, and during that time you picked up weight lifting and trained in kenpo karate, focusing on it with such intensity that it frightened your teachers and counselors back at the boy's home. You told them you were channeling your anger, but what you were really doing was compartmentalizing it, using it to prepare yourself for your showdown with Todd Merrill. You thought about him day and night. Then, one summer night when you knew he was alone, you went up to his house. When he opened the door and saw you, he didn't have a chance, did he?"

Conway turned around and faced Bouchard.

"The extensive plastic surgery never removed all the scars," Bouchard continued. "Every time he looked in the mirror, all he would see would be that day you kept smashing his face against the bathroom mirror, kept kicking him while he was on the ground, the way he curled up on the bathroom floor, crying and shaking, begging for you to stop. That earned you a one-year stint in a juvenile correction center. The parents would have pressed for a stiffer sentence if they hadn't just discovered that their son was busted at school for being a dealer. It's not the sort of thing one likes to advertise. Not in Newton, anyway."

"That was a long time ago," Conway said, his voice steady. "I'm not proud of that moment."

"But you don't regret doing it, do you?"

"I'm not sure what you're asking me."

"If you can package your grief and rage on John Riley's death, if you can keep your head clear and focused, then I can use you in Boston."

"Boston?"

"Two days ago Echelon picked up a transmission from a cell phone. The message said, 'The suit is useless to us without the decryption code. Dixon doesn't know it. Pick Conway up.' He believes you know the decryption code."

"But why would Angel Eyes want Riley—" Conway's throat seized up at the thought of the word *dead*. "His men were inside the lab, at Delburn—they know Riley doesn't know the decryption code."

"It's payback for what happened inside the lab. More importantly, your friend's death keeps you out in the open, keeps you visible."

"What you need is for me to act as a lightning rod," Conway said. "The bait to bring Angel Eyes in."

"He knows you'll be coming home for the funeral."

"And then he'll try to pick me up."

"If you don't want in, I understand. I can hide you so Angel Eyes will never be able to find you. But that won't stop him from striking again at what's closest to your heart."

"Book," Conway said. Jackson Booker, or Book, was now the only remaining member of Conway's self-labeled family. Booker and Pasha, the only two people left. If they were taken from him—

Don't think about it.

"I've got to call and warn Book," Conway said.

"This operation is classified, Stephen."

"I'm not going to leave him hanging in the wind."

"I've already put people on Booker and his family. They're being watched around the clock."

"So was Dixon."

"Stephen, I'm personally overseeing this operation. There will be *no* mistakes." The world had turned dark. The full moon's silver light sparkled on the slick black waters below like slivers of mirrored glass. "You're the best shot to draw Angel Eyes out— and to save Dixon. He's alive. They'll keep him alive until the suit is operational."

Bouchard reached inside his suit-jacket pocket and handed Conway a small cell phone and a bulky white envelope bound with elastic. Conway opened the envelope and in the moonlight saw the cash, all one-hundred-dollar bills, and a plane ticket for Boston. The flight left early tomorrow morning.

"I can use your help, Stephen, but the decision is yours. You've already put your life on the line. God knows I'll understand if you say no."

Cowardice ranked right up there with stealing and lying. Conway had never run away or turned his back on anything in his life. He wasn't about to start now.

"I'm in."

"Jonathan Cole will be your handler," Bouchard said. "He's already in Boston heading up the operation. His number is written on the back of your plane ticket.

After the funeral is over, and once you feel settled, call him. You are to report to no one but him or me, understand?"

Conway nodded.

"On your belt, is that your Palm Pilot?"

"The detective, Rombardo, gave it back to me," Conway lied.

"Let me have it. Mr. Cole will provide you with a new one that's retrofitted with new transmitters and new features. He'll also provide you with new gear when you meet up with him in Boston."

Conway handed the Palm Pilot to Bouchard, who took it and then turned it over with both hands, staring at it like it was some weird, foreign contraption.

"I'm sorry about what happened to your friend," Bouchard said. "I'm sure he meant the world to you."

Conway felt a heavy hand wrap around his neck, squeeze it in a fatherly fashion, and then drop away. He stood motionless, listening to the sound of Bouchard's shoes crunching across the gravel grow distant. A moment later there was only the wind. Confident he was alone, Conway surrendered himself to the cold truth, grateful for the darkness that hid him.

An hour until the flight back to Virginia, Raymond Bouchard parked the rental, a roomy Ford Explorer, in the most remote location at the airport, backing the SUV up against the wall so he could look out the front window and see anyone who might approach him. What he wanted was privacy. He removed the laptop from his briefcase and got to work.

Raymond had watched the video all the way through and had just started going through the pictures when his satellite phone rang. He placed the pictures on the passenger's seat, on top of his laptop and Stephen's Palm Pilot, and then picked up the phone and dialed the number. Next came the familiar deep, dry wheeze of Misha's voice.

"Brighten up my day," Misha said.

"Go secure," Bouchard said. *Beep*, and the encryption technology engaged.

"Give me the code, Ray."

On the drive to the airport, Raymond had felt it, the opportunity to trap Misha and his boss, Alexi, and take them out of the way. What Raymond needed now was some time to think over the possibilities and flesh them out with Cole. He would have to stall Misha.

"The decryption code is Lucky Charms," Bouchard said.

"Lucky Charms? What the fuck is that?"

"The name of a breakfast cereal."

"Hold on," Misha said.

Over the phone came the sound of footsteps clicking across a hard floor, and Misha talking in Russian, his voice audible but far away. Raymond looked through the front windshield and watched the sprinkling of people wander through the parking lot and thought about the woman, Renée Kaufmann, who had so far proved to be elusive. How long would she stay hidden? John Riley's wake was tomorrow. Would she dare show up? Grief could be overpowering. *Make it easy for me*.

Misha was back on the line: "The code don't work."

"Try Count Chocula."

"Count *what*?"

"Count Chocula. C-H-O-C-U-L-A. Apparently Randy Scott was a big fan of breakfast cereals," Raymond said, his smile widening.

Another pause, and then Misha's voice burst back on the line, agitated as he said, "The suit's still locked up."

"My suggestion is to go through all the breakfast cereals."

"Alexi wants the code. Tonight."

"I gave you what Conway told me."

"Conway saw the video?"

"He saw it all," Bouchard said, his eyes cutting sideways to the surveillance pictures that had been left next to Conway's bed. "It rattled him, and he gave me the decryption code."

Misha's throat clicked when he swallowed. "This is starting to feel like a bad hand job," he said.

"I can't conjure Randy Scott up from the dead. You killed him, remember?"

"Let me tell you a story, Big Ray. Last night I'm at

Alexi's place, he's entertaining some very important people, he's got these fucking high-class broads all over the place, they're dressed to the nines and got their tits hanging out, they're taking guys upstairs two at a time, doing girl-on-girl, two-on-two, tag teams, orgies. They're on their knees and blowing these guys under the table while we're eating, it's like something out of that flick *Caligula*."

"Misha—"

"Now Alexi, he wants to know the status on the suit, so I tell him. You know what this guy does? He gets up and overturns the fucking table, I'm talking one of these solid oak jobs that seats like twenty-four people. Food's going everywhere, Alexi's screaming at me, he's picking up this rare china off the floor, this stuff that costs half a grand for a single plate, and this crazy son of a bitch starts throwing it against the wall. Broads are fleeing the place in terror. You getting the full picture?"

"Yeah, Alexi threw a temper tantrum."

"He ordered me to remove one of your testicles as a down payment for your cooperation."

Raymond felt a drop of sweat run down his armpit.

"And that's just for starters," Misha said. "You know that story about the guy who meets the hot-looking broad at the bar, takes her home, and then wakes up in a bath full of ice with a kidney missing? Alexi's big into the organ donation program."

"And how's that going to solve our problem?"

"Our problem? No, *your* problem. You think because you got some fancy fucking degree you can try to fist us by holding onto the decryption key? You know who you're fucking with here?"

"You should try living up to your end of the bargain."

"The fuck you talking about?"

"Lenny Rombardo."

"Who?"

"The detective from the Austin police. Our liaison. He went into the hospital to question Conway and now he's missing."

"So why you telling me this shit?"

"Where is he, Misha?"

"How the fuck do I know? Ray, if I was you, I'd get to a doctor quick and get your brain pan checked out because you're starting to have some serious fucking delusions. I don't know this guy Rombardo, I don't want to know him, I don't care if he's banging my mother's corpse. You know what you need? A little incentive to get your priorities in order."

"Goddammit, Misha, will you listen—"

Screams exploded over the line.

Startled, Raymond nearly dropped the phone. The screaming continued, then came a man crying for it to stop. It was the voice of Major Dixon.

Misha was back on the line, his breath gasping against the receiver.

"I just clipped off Major Dick's pinkie toe with a pair of garden shears. Imagine how you're going to sound when I remove *both* your kidneys," Misha said and hung up.

In the parking lot below, Pasha Romanov removed her headphones and held them in her hands for a moment. She sat in the back of the surveillance van, the only one left from Delburn Systems. The inside of the van was dark and warm, and her ears were ringing with a high-pitched whine. A wired energy, the fight-or-flight adrenaline high she experienced when sparring, filled her legs.

Raymond's not that far away, a voice said. *His flight doesn't leave for another half hour. You can book it over to his rental. Imagine the look of surprise on his face when he sees you.*

Or the look on his face when she had Raymond on his knees, his hand clasped in one of hers. She would bend it forward, threatening to snap his wrist, the pain causing him to confess all of it. He would beg for it to stop, keep begging.

One swift kick and she could kill him without breaking a sweat.

She practically had a confession; the bug she had planted in Stephen's Palm Pilot had picked up Raymond talking to Misha. Pasha only wished she could have heard what Misha had said in return. Raymond's phone wasn't bugged, and they were talking over an encrypted line. She had only heard Raymond, but what she had heard was enough.

Killing Raymond. The thought wrapped around her like a warm blanket.

Do it.

Pasha did not get up. She remained seated and watched her thumbs trace the rubbery edges of the headphones.

Raymond had the suit. And he had Dixon, who was, at the moment, still alive and hidden somewhere in Boston along with the nightmare from her childhood, Misha.

She thought about Raymond again and wondered how long he would beg for his life.

If you kill Raymond, you'll sentence Dixon to death.

Yes. If Raymond was killed, Misha would have free rein and what then? Dixon would be dismembered piece by piece. The fact that Dix was still alive was amazing. Misha did not do well when things did not go his way. Somehow, Raymond had managed to control the animal. How long would that last?

Not long. Misha was a headcase. He once had a meltdown at a mob-owned restaurant when the cook failed to cook his steak tips the right way. The cook ended up needing facial reconstructive surgery.

Time was running out. She had to go to Boston and find Dixon. Quick.

And she had to be there to protect Stephen.

The sharp bite of betrayal still stinging her skin, she started working the computer keys to take the recorded conversation and burn it onto a blank compact disc. While she waited for the copy, she checked out her appearance in the rearview mirror.

Her hair was still the same length but dyed black; the contacts gave her eyes a chemical green color. A prosthetic ear now covered the ear stump. CIA prosthetics were amazing; they weren't like the peel-away faces from those amusing *Mission Impossible* movies, but they came close.

The computer beeped. The CD tray slid open and offered up the shiny silver disk. Pasha grabbed it, got behind the wheel, and started the van. The Levi's jeans and the plain gray sweatshirt and hiking boots she wore were comfortable but lacked the refined elegance of Armani. Boston would be cold; that meant the opportunity to wear additional layers, combining different outfits and looks. More chances to disguise herself.

Pasha pulled out of the parking space. The van had been recently painted black to cover the Delburn logo. The Texas license plate matched the driver's license she had created. In the event she was pulled over for speeding, everything would match and check out. She had several different IDs at her disposal.

Pasha had maintained a separate safe house apartment here in Austin in the event an operation had been compromised. Inside the house was a cache of untraceable weapons and some rather interesting gadgets, along with encrypted laptop computers, a fax machine, and computers with secured lines into the CIA computers. The printing equipment could manufacture licenses, passports, anything one needed for a new life. The money she had stockpiled could allow her to stay hidden for months and, if necessary, a couple of years as long as she lived frugally. She couldn't use the credit cards—that would alert Raymond—but she had more than enough cash to set up a base in Boston and live well.

As she drove out of the airport, Pasha wondered if Raymond would discover that the only van left at Delburn was now in fact missing. Probably not.

Raymond had his hands full at the moment. He was in deep with Misha, that much Pasha knew, but for what? What did the Russian have on him? That thought kept her mind busy until she was well on the highway, heading north on the road to discovery. Pasha slid the disc into the CD player, fast forwarding to the part where Raymond talked to Misha. She thought of Misha, imagining how the animal's face would transform itself when she made him feed his own prick into a meat grinder.

It's the second Saturday in December, sunny and surprisingly warm. Conway sits alone in a chair on the rooftop of the Delta Chi fraternity house. It's a little after eleven in the morning. He drinks coffee that's spiked with Jack Daniel's.

Cars are parked in the front of the house, along the side, and in the parking lot behind him. Finals are officially over. Last night, everyone celebrated the eve of their release. This morning, everyone is going home for Christmas break. Downstairs, he watches Pete Bartlow carrying a duffel bag full of clothes to his parent's sleek black Mercedes. He tosses the bag into the trunk, looks up and happens to see Conway and waves good-bye. Conway waves back. For the next three hours he watches everyone else leave for break. By the time two o'clock rolls around the fraternity house is dead. He is no longer drinking coffee but Jack straight on ice.

Conway opens the door to his room and turns on his stereo, a cheap plastic model by Sound Design that he bought at Goodwill for fifteen bucks. The radio works but the tape deck eats tapes. Some song by Aerosmith is on. He plops down on the couch and leans back, propping his head on a pillow. He balances the drink on his stomach and looks around the room.

The walls are decorated with the free video posters he takes home after his shift. He doesn't own any pictures. The couch he sits on was rescued from the trash, and the mattress *was free, the sheets and pillow and extra set were given to him by one of the fraternity brothers. On the floor by the cheap metal desk is a stack of nine library books. A lot of Stephen King. If you wanted to forget your current surroundings and be transported into a world where you would be entertained and scared shitless, then Stephen King was your man. As Conway sips his drink, he thinks about which book he should read on Christmas day. This has become an annual tradition for him. He buys a bottle of Crown Royal, picks a book and spends the day drinking and reading. Last year it was the remarkable novel* Sophie's Choice, *and the year before that, John Fowles's excellent novel* The Magus. *This year it's going to be John Irving's* The World According to Garp. *Then there's King to get him through the rest of winter break.*

Conway stares at the Irving book. How would The World According to Steve Conway *read? Lots of blank pages. No pictures.*

His room door slams open and in walks John Riley. "I've been looking all over for you. Where the fuck you been hiding?" He has the kind of expansive smile and deep, steady voice that makes you believe in the power of his words—a natural salesman in the making.

"I've been here all day," Conway said.

"You still haven't told me what you're doing for break."

"Working."

"No shit." Like Conway, John Riley is putting himself through college. School breaks and holidays are not vacations; they are opportunities to earn money. "What I'm asking is what are you doing for work?"

"Bartending at The Cliffs."

"Are you fucking serious?"

"I'm serious."

"That bar draws on a good night two people. And that's

including the bartender who, I may add, is a dick. That ain't going to cover the bills."

"I'm looking for something to do during the day."

"You find anything yet?"

"I'm looking into a few things."

"You like painting?"

"I'm more into doodling."

"I mean can you paint walls, shithead."

"I like money."

"I'm painting full-time, about ten hours a day, more if I want it. I'm talking some really good coin, time-and-a-half, too. If it goes well, the guy will hire us for the summer."

"Us?"

"That's what I'm saying. We leave tonight."

"What?"

"You can stay with us. I already cleared it with my mom. The apartment's small, you'll have to sleep on the couch, but she's cool with that."

"I appreciate the offer but—"

"Don't start in with this shit. What are you going to do, stay here and what, spend all your free time thinking? You think more than Einstein and you're not half as smart."

Conway shook his head, laughing.

"Seriously, you need the money, and the guy I'm working for needs a body. I already told him you'd do it."

"John—"

"Look, this will be a good time. My buddy from home works over in Marblehead at this bar. He'll hook us up with drinks, and these girls I know, they'll be home on break from Emerson. Emerson broads are so notoriously horny, my brother. They're known to fuck guys as ugly and as desperate as you."

"Wow. How can I pass that up?"

"That's what I'm saying. You in or what?"

Conway looks at the stack of books and thinks about the four weeks stretched in front of him. He's eighteen and this will be his first Christmas spent with a real family. Real food too, not that canned crap they served each year at St. Anthony's.

"Okay. I'm in."

"Good," Riley said. "Just one rule. Don't be spanking your meat puppet in the bathroom. You don't want my mom to catch you. She'll make you say the rosary and like forty Hail Marys or something."

"Doesn't the door lock?"

"That's what I thought until two years ago. Brother, she hasn't looked the same at me since. Come on, I'll help you pack."

Conway woke up with a start. The new James Lee Burke hardcover was opened across his lap. He was on the plane, on a direct flight to Boston. He must have dozed off.

The stewardess was suddenly right next to him. "Can I get you something, sir?" she asked in a bubbly voice.

"Coffee would be great."

Conway sat in the corner seat, next to the window, far away from the other handful of first-class passengers. He had never flown first class before. The leather seats were more comfortable than coach, wider, the leg room generous. He wondered if this was Bouchard's gift to him, an act of kindness to show that Bouchard understood that losing John Riley equaled the loss of a brother.

The stewardess came by with a china cup of coffee and placed it on the tray with two creamers and a small container of sugar. Conway opened one of the creamers and poured it into the cup, watching it swirl inside the black liquid, and in his mind saw a black cloud as thick as ink twisting its way through John Riley's veins, the combination of rat poison and cocaine swallowing blood and tissue, tearing into his heart like a rabid animal.

Did Riley try to fight it? Did he cry out for help? Or was it too late? Had he already crossed that threshold, his body growing still, unable to function, his mind surrendering to the fact that it was too late? What had John Riley's last moments been like?

Bouchard's words from yesterday: *I'm not going to lie to you, Steve. It was an awful way to go.*

Conway saw John Riley convulsing on the floor. Saw John Riley crying out in pain, crying out for help. John Riley, his friend, was dying.

Dead.

Because of me.

And now Dixon was held captive, surrounded by jackals feeding off his pain, alone with the knowledge that no one was coming to rescue him.

I won't let you down, Dix. I promise.

Then a voice added, *If Angel Eyes thinks you know the code, he'll kill Dixon. Do you know the code, Steve?*

Since that night he had met Pasha at Delburn, Conway had thought about Randy's last words: *mittens* and *cat food*. What did it mean? Conway had tried to recreate those final moments inside the lab; but the memory was hazy, full of black holes. He kept turning the words over and over in his mind, racking his brain for a solution.

Twenty minutes later and he still had no idea what the words meant.

Don't force it, Steve. It will come.

It had better come soon. Dixon's life was on the line.

If Conway could figure out the decryption code, then maybe he could use it as a bargaining chip to save Dixon.

The plane touched down at Logan airport. Outside the window and framed against the hard blue sky of a clear November morning were the skyscrapers of downtown Boston. Conway had come home, and Angel Eyes was somewhere out there, waiting.

Booker was late. Conway sat down in a bank of seats located in front of floor-to-ceiling windows that overlooked the runway. He draped his arms across the tops of the chairs and waited, back in Boston for the first time in over five years.

The thing about Boston was that nobody seemed to smile. In fact, they all looked pissed. Well-dressed people bustled about the crowded airport, everyone in a rush as they talked on their cell phones, others walking with their heads down, frowning or locked in deep thought, every face having that particular hard, serious gaze, what Conway called "The fuck do you want?" look. Boston was the opposite of Vail or even Austin, where life moved at a much slower pace. People you didn't know would stop to say hi, maybe even ask you how your day was and engage in idle conversation while you were waiting for a bus, all of it done with a smile. Maybe it wasn't sincere, but at least it was cordial.

But he still loved Boston, missed its unpredictable weather and the people and the air that always seemed to be crackling with an energy and life he had never experienced anywhere else.

Boston was home.

If you missed it so much, then why were you so anxious to leave? a voice asked.

A large black man turned the corner. He glided up the corridor with a cool, easy rhythm, the solidity of his three-hundred-pound presence, his six-foot-eight frame and the slow, methodical deliberation of his movements giving him the aura of Darth Vader. People moved out of the way and turned their heads and gawked, their eyes guarded and nervous. Jackson Booker lumbered on and chewed his gum, oblivious or not caring, Conway never knew which.

Conway remained seated. Book was dressed completely in black: the stylish overcoat, trendy suit and shoes, even the hip sunglasses—all of it by Versace. His shaved head gleamed in the overhead fluorescent light, the muscles along his jaw flexing as he methodically worked the gum. He had been a football star at the University of New Hampshire, but two bum knees had prevented him from being drafted to the NFL.

"You with Puff Daddy?" Conway said, grinning.

"It's P-Diddy. Can't you honkies get anything right?" His words, like his movements, glided on their own rhythm, his voice deep and sleepy: an edgy Barry White. "Sorry I'm late," Booker said. "Cracker held me up at the security gate."

"Guy probably thought you were a master criminal."

Book blew a pink bubble, popped it. "You think?"

"You definitely give off that vibe."

"And here I was thinking I was the CEO of a highly successful global security agency." Book shifted the wad of bubble gum to the other side of his mouth. "The wake's not until four. It's just after noon. Let's go grab lunch."

"I'm not real hungry."

"Then you can come with me and watch what I eat. You and I need to talk."

The Oak Room, located inside the prestigious Fairmont Copley Hotel, was a dimly lit bar that reminded Conway of the kind of enormous library found inside a Newport mansion. The high mahogany walls were decorated with various paintings, the maroon carpet stamped with what appeared to be family crests. In the center of the room was a piano, played at night while you dined on the upper level that offered window views of the beautifully lit city.

The bar was at half capacity when the maître d' seated Booker and Conway in the corner, near the tall pane window overlooking St. James Street and the red carpet that led up to the hotel entrance. Booker ordered a Poland Springs with a lime; Conway went straight for the gin and tonic. He sat with his back to the window, the November sun warm on his back. He had already polished off one drink and had asked for another. He declined lunch.

"Going liquid this early is a bad idea, bro," Booker said after the waiter had left.

"I had something to eat on the plane."

Booker leaned back in his chair, crossed his legs, and popped cashews one at a time into his mouth. The car ride had been quiet, the death of their friend lay between them. Conway didn't want to talk. What he really wanted was to be left alone and get drunk.

"How's Austin?" Booker asked after a moment. His coat was off but his sunglasses were still on.

"Hot and humid. During the summer, it gets so bad you have to stay inside. Everyone has air conditioning."

"You hate the heat."

"You get used to it."

"Praxis must be laying down some serious benjamins."

"I do okay," Conway said, knowing where the discussion was headed.

"These alpha-geeks I got working for me, they don't like to collaborate, they don't like to ask questions, they all want to be the top dog but lack social skills. You got all the skills and can speak their language."

"Why do I have a feeling you're about to offer me a job again?"

"You know all of the tech-talk, you come in and wrangle the nerd herd, do some security work, and put that kenpo training of yours into action. A lot of the boys I got are big but they're not second-degree black belts."

"Playing bodyguard to overpriced movie stars when they come into town?"

"You rather stay in Texas and sweat your balls off?"

"Austin's nice. I enjoy it."

"You think you can enjoy making one fifty large?"

"You don't work with or for close friends. It's a rule."

"You've used that one on me before. You going say no again, be creative, come up with some new material."

"Why you want me so bad? There are dozens of guys out there who have more technical experience than I do."

"Besides my wife, I trust two people on this planet,"

Booker said. "I'm about to bury one, and the other is sitting across from me."

Conway didn't know what to say; intimate, touchy-feely conversations like this made him nervous. He polished off his gin and tonic. A good buzz was coming; he could feel it building, warm and comforting.

Drink all you want, Steve. Nothing's going to change the fact that John Riley's dead.

He wanted to shut the voice up. Drown it with alcohol. Conway signaled the waiter and ordered another. Booker turned his head to the side, as if he had had enough of this particular conversation, and for several minutes watched the two elderly women a few tables over share a pot of tea and a club sandwich. A couple of older men were here dressed in suits. Conway wondered if Angel Eyes was in the room or somewhere close, watching them.

The waiter came by with a fresh drink. Conway waited until the man disappeared and then said, "What did you want to talk to me about?"

"J.R.'s girlfriend," Book said.

"I didn't think Miranda was still in the picture."

"Not Miranda, Renée Kaufmann. She worked with him at that Internet startup in Cambridge."

"The name doesn't ring a bell." Which didn't surprise him. Since his arrival in Austin, he had been consumed with working on Dixon and creating the trap to catch Angel Eyes. Conway's efforts at keeping in touch were lackluster at best. Lots of e-mails and some phone calls with just some quick hellos, but nothing of substance.

"J.R. said he was thinking of getting married. I think he may have picked out a ring," Booker said. "At least that's what he told me."

"How's she taking it?"

"Don't know. She's disappeared."

Conway stared at the chunks of ice floating in the tall glass.

"She was supposed to return from Amsterdam two days ago," Book said. "Renée hasn't been back to work, and she hasn't been back to her apartment."

Conway felt a spasm in his stomach. *Angel Eyes has her. He's going to use her as a bargaining chip. Now her life is on the chopping block.*

(because of you)

"The autopsy report confirmed that it was OD."

"You told me that over the phone," Conway said, his voice hoarse. When he returned from his meeting with Bouchard on Mount Bonnell, he had come back to the condo and seen the single blink of the red light on the answering machine and in the darkness listened to Booker's message to call immediately. Book said it was an OD, then explained how J.R. got a little too heavily into alcohol and coke after the death of his mother, the driving accident that could have resulted in his death, Booker's intervention, and Riley's treatment at the celebrity detox unit in Tucson. All of it shocked Conway. He had no idea.

"What I didn't tell you was that it was cocaine and rat poison," Booker said.

Conway nodded and kept his eyes blank.

"And I didn't tell where J.R. shot up," Booker said. "The needle mark was on his neck. That's a last resort for a junkie. You got no veins left, you try the neck. J.R. didn't have any tracks on his arms, never did. He wasn't a junkie."

Conway was quiet, the truth about how Riley really

died burning across his skin. He wanted to unburden himself of it and couldn't.

"J.R. liked to snort it, always rubbing his nose, telling me he's got allergies in the winter. Mirror and the dollar bill, that's how he liked to get high," Booker said. "Not this needle in the neck shit."

"So what are you saying?"

"J.R. was murdered."

Conway finished off his drink and then rubbed out a tingling sensation on the back of his neck.

"Friend of mine on the force, he told me about a 911 call someone placed," Booker said. "Caller said a homicide was about to take place, left the address, and described the condo but didn't use J.R.'s name."

"Renée?"

"No. A guy. Dude didn't leave his name."

"So there's a witness."

"Maybe. The 911 caller, he didn't sound upset. Sounded like he was reading off his laundry list."

"Can you get a copy of this call?"

"Why?"

"I'd like to hear it."

"You all right?"

"J.R. never told me about any of his problems."

"He tried to keep them hidden. Badly, I might add."

"But he confided in you, right?"

"Probably didn't want to look like a failure in your eyes."

"What?"

"He admired you. You had a shitty life from day one. You never complained about it. You started out with nothing and made something of yourself. You were always in control. He admired that."

"Why couldn't he talk to me about his problems?"

"He said that you were never around."

Book didn't mean it as a dig, but it was the truth. Conway was never around. He bounced all over the country and was hard to get in touch with; he was home late every night. His world—his surrogate family—had been the IWAC team.

And now they're all dead.

Conway stared at his friend and a voice said, *He could be dead tomorrow.* Conway finished his drink.

"Booze is only going to make it worse," Booker said. "Keeping it bottled up's not helping either."

"I'll keep that in mind, thanks."

Booker shook his head, a smirk on the corner of his mouth.

"I've known you for eleven years now, and every time I talk with you, it's like I'm trying to crack a safe," he said. "What the hell you hiding, anyway?"

At first Conway was grateful for the alcohol. It silenced the collective din of voices inside his head, numbed his frayed nerves, and made him feel impervious to the low throb of the funeral-home organ music and the muted sobs of the mourners.

Don't look at the casket, don't think about the music, and you'll get through this. Conway repeated the words over and over. For two hours he kept it together, shaking hands and engaging in idle chitchat with John Riley's Boston friends and coworkers, Booker next to him, ominously quiet. Then the time had passed, and the people had left, and it was only Conway and Booker who stood inside the room. Camille, a fellow UNH graduate and a friend of Conway's since college, had left to go home to relieve Book's mother, who had been baby-sitting the twin boys, four-year-olds Trey and Troy.

Conway stood with his hands in his pockets, his eyes fastened on the floor. The alcohol had abandoned him. Now he felt fatigued and drained, and the voices of regret and guilt he thought he had bottled were set free, rising from the depths with a renewed energy and life.

"Renée never showed up," Booker said, his voice booming inside the small room. A deep sigh, and then he added, "Maybe she'll be at the funeral tomorrow."

Or maybe Angel Eyes already has her. Maybe she's already dead. Conway's head felt light. The room was warm and close with the smell of air freshener and chemicals.

"I've got to wrap up a few things," Booker said. "I've got a room made up for you at the condo."

"The hotel's fine."

Booker stood there for a moment, about to say something, Conway could feel it. Instead, Book turned and sauntered out of the room in that slow, drowsy way of his and opened up the front door. Conway heard it shut, leaving him alone. He stood there, motionless, like a man who couldn't decide if he wanted to cross a bridge or turn around and just go home.

John Riley was a close friend—the guy was like a brother to you and now you just want to turn and walk away because you can't deal with it? That's the cheap way out and you know it.

Conway was aware of his breath, the dryness in his throat and the tightness inside his chest as he took measured steps toward the casket. His heart tripping, he knelt down and made the sign of the cross, folding his hands across the railing, his fingers hovering just inches away from John Riley's sleeping, waxlike face.

He died of a combination of rat poison and cocaine. It was an awful way to go, Stephen.

Riley on the day they went skydiving, when they were both safe on the ground: *God protects people like you and me, Stevie.*

John Riley lay in the white-silk bedding of the coffin, dressed in a dark-blue suit and tie, looking like a man who had fallen asleep on the commuter train after a long, hard day.

Only he's never waking up.

Stop it.

You can't run away from it, Stephen. He's dead because of you. Get used to it. No matter where you go, no matter how much time has passed, you will never be able to change that fact.

Conway took a deep breath and pushed back the tide of feelings, not wanting to give in to them, but they were there, refusing to be ignored, building like the pressure behind a dam. The harder he tried to push it away the more intense the feelings became.

Conway reached out and grabbed Riley's wrist and squeezed it, the skin cold and stiff against his warm palm, and in that instant, Conway felt the finality of his friend's short journey.

"I'm sorry, John. Wherever you are, I hope you can find it in your heart to forgive me."

Conway looked away at the flowers, saw the small cards hooked on green spears poking up from the bright sea of color petals. *Our deepest sympathy. We're sorry for your loss. Our prayers are with you and your family in your time of need.* His eyes stopped on the card belonging to the basket directly above the casket, the one signed Winston Smith: *You live in a wilderness of mirrors, Stephen. Be careful. Jackals surround you.*

Conway stood up so quickly he almost tripped. He tore the card away. His entire body was shaking. Out of the corner of his eye, he saw someone enter the room. Conway wheeled around. It was the funeral director, a pudgy man with carefully combed brown hair and a deep red rose pinned to the lapel of his black suit.

"Mr. Conway?" The man's tone was low, respectful. "Daniel Murray, funeral director. You have a phone call," he said and handed Conway a cordless phone.

"Who is it?"

"A man named Jonathan Cole."

His handler. Right.

"Hello," Conway said, wondering why Cole hadn't called the cell phone. He noticed that the funeral director had not moved away.

"Stephen, this is Jonathan Cole. Meet me tomorrow at the Holocaust Memorial, on Congress Street, at eleven o'clock."

Cole hung up. Conway handed the funeral director the phone.

"I was instructed to give this to you." Murray held up a small, cream-colored envelope wedged between two small fingers.

Conway took it. No name or postmark on the front, but it was sealed.

Conway opened the envelope. Inside was a handwritten note from Renée Kaufmann.

Steve,

I can't talk to you on the phone because I think it's tapped and they could trace me. I'm in Boston, but I don't think they know I'm here. Meet me tomorrow at the New England Aquarium at noon, top floor, near the shark tank. I know who killed John and I have evidence to prove it. Come alone and be careful. I think you're being followed.

But is this really her? Conway wondered. *You've never met her before. It could be a trap.*

It was possible that Booker would recognize the handwriting. But that meant involving Booker in this, and the less he knew, the better.

Conway stared at the note. *What if it isn't a trap?*
Only one way to find out.

Conway said, "Who gave this to you?"

"A young gentlemen here at the wake," Murray said. "He asked specifically to give this to you when you were alone. I'm sorry for your loss," he said and left the room.

The New England Holocaust Memorial runs parallel to Boston's ever-busy Congress Street. At the far end is Curley Memorial Plaza, an area of benches that holds the sitting bronze of the Boston Mayor James Curley. Another bronze statue of the controversial mayor stands in the center of red brick, his hands folded behind his back, his eyes permanently cast over the architectural splendor of Faneuil Hall and beyond it, the towering, monolithic skyscrapers that comprise the heart of downtown Boston.

Outside in the cold November air, Amon Faust walked down the blue-gray granite path, his gloved hands clasped behind his back. Six rectangular towers of glass stretched beyond the trees and reached up into the hard blue sky as if they were conduits to heaven. It was a quarter to eleven on a Friday morning, the air crisp and cold but still lacking the bite of winter. No one was inside the memorial, and Stephen Conway wouldn't be here until eleven.

Faust entered the tower for the concentration camp Auschwitz-Birkenau and stood on the venting grate that hissed white clouds of steam. Etched in the glass were thousands and thousands of prison numbers—the enormity of a human life and its soul compressed into a cold, random number. Faust wondered if these numbers held any meaning anymore. Fifty years had passed since the great beast Hitler unleashed his evil, and people were no longer afraid. What if Hitler had technology on his side? What if he had armed his troops with blinding laser weapons and military suits that rendered them invisible to the enemy? Could Hitler then have carried out his world vision?

Look at these people, bundled in their coats as they rushed to meetings and important lunches. This new generation didn't mourn history; they were no longer haunted by it. Time had wiped the slate clean and filled fresh new minds with MTV and empty TV talk shows and programs like *Survivor*—laughable, given where he stood right now—and the talk of money, it was always money, they were consumed by their spreadsheets and financial projections.

The time was ripe for their downfall.

Faust's skin tingled. The glass towers seemed to give off a charge, as if the screams of the dead had been sealed inside the glass. He reached out and ran his gloved hand against the glass. To feel it all, to actually connect to the beauty of Hitler's vision of a sanitized world, Faust would have to touch the glass with his bare hand. The thought made him dizzy with anticipation.

Two specialized sterilized wipes were inside his jacket pocket—one to clean, one to wipe. He could use one to clean the glass and touch it with his bare hand, and then use the other wipe to disinfect. The small bottle of hand sanitizer he carried with him at all times would destroy any lingering germs.

Faust unwrapped the wipe from its foil container and cleaned off a good section of glass, committing the area to memory, and then carried the infected wipe to the barrel and threw it away. He would burn the gloves later.

He walked back to the same spot and then removed his glove, the cold air washing across his warm, damp skin. Alone inside the memorial, Faust pressed his palm against the glass, closed his eyes and in his mind saw this street in the vivid, singular vision of his brave new world.

The winter sky is the color of blood. The sun has started to set; a light snow is falling over the bodies of the dead, hundreds of them, their twisted, mangled corpses line the streets and steps leading up to Government Center. Some have collapsed against the hoods of their cars or against the steering wheels, others are hunched over restaurant tables, sprawled on the street. Some clutch the cell phones they used to call 911 for help. Their faces are the color of eggplant; blood dribbles from their mouths and noses. They have drowned in their own fluid.

The virus is called Chloe Six, a genetically engineered strain of influenza created in Russia that had, at one point, been designed as a bioweapon against the U.S. It was intended to re-create the 1918 influenza epidemic which, in only a few months, killed more than twenty million people worldwide. Only a few knew of Chloe Six's existence, or its antidote, both of which are stored in the sacred vaults of the Centers for Disease Control.

Faust knows the CDC's layout quite well. For years, he has been preparing for this moment. He knows the security measures and how to bypass them. When he slips outside the CDC and walks through the darkness, he is invisible to the world. He is wearing the military suit. Stored inside a special pack are the Chloe Six specimens and the world's only antidote.

Faust walks down the bloody street, smiling as he

breathes in the wonderfully cold air, the snow a pleasant tingle on his scalp. He has nothing to fear. Like Gunther, like all the ones Faust has chosen for his brave new world, he is inoculated, safe from the deadly virus. The dead look up at him, their mouths frozen open in horror; some look away, their hollowed-out eyes pointed toward the heavens. The cell phones and pagers clipped to their belts and clutched in their hands and strewn about the street are still alive, glowing with power and waiting for a command. Nothing will come. The old world now lay dead. A new god has emerged, about to rule a new world.

"JUST SELL THE FUCKING THING!" a man shouted.

Faust's eyes flew open. His hand still pressed against the glass, he turned around and saw a tall man with slicked-back black hair, pacing around the bronze statue in Curley Memorial Plaza with a cell phone pressed against his ear.

"Yeah, Alex, I read the fucking P/E report," the man said into his cell phone. The man's other gloved hand held a Starbucks coffee cup; he took a long draw from it and then yanked it away from his mouth, nearly spitting out his coffee. "Forget the long-term growth, I'm talking about the here and now, Alex, and I'm telling you I'm not going to take a bath on that stock, so sell the fucking dog before it fucking tanks."

"Do you *mind*, sir," Faust said.

The young man stopped pacing and stared from behind his designer sunglasses, his mouth parted open, insulted and shocked that someone had interrupted him.

"Show some respect," Faust said. "You're in the presence of the dead."

"Mind your own business," the man snapped and

then turned around and went back to his noisy conversation.

Oh so oblivious. They couldn't see that the center of their world was already falling apart, that the great rough beast had already slouched its way toward Bethlehem to be born and was now lurking in their midst, the darkness about to drop again and unleash the blood-dimmed tide. Quote them Yeats and could they claim the beauty of the poem and grasp its meaning? Not unless it was rapped by an illiterate black street gangsta with a mouth full of gold teeth on MTV.

Time to flush and begin again. Time for a new world. A world without end. Amen.

"Mr. Cole?"

Faust turned around and saw Stephen Conway standing on the venting grid in the second tower of glass, his face mournful.

Faust smiled. Time for the lesson to begin.

"Good morning, Stephen," Amon Faust said.

"Am I interrupting?" The man's tone was low, his sad eyes moving toward the glass where Faust's hand was still pressed.

"Of course not. But thank you for asking," Faust said and his hand slid away. The hand wipe was already gripped in his other gloved hand. He started scrubbing his bare skin. Stephen watched. "One cannot be too careful with viruses. Especially this time of year."

Stephen nodded. His eyes moved around the prison numbers etched into the glass, his head tilting up into the sky.

"Staggering, isn't it?" Faust said.

"It seems almost unbelievable."

"That's because you're young. The young like to forget. It reminds me of an article I read in *Newsweek*. A twenty-three-year-old Polish man opened up a nightclub in Oswiecim, one mile down the road from the infamous Auschwitz-Birkenau death camp. The nightclub that hosts topless women wrestling in a pit of Jell-O sits on the same site of an SS-run tannery in which hundreds of Jews lost their lives." Faust's eyes roved across the numbers. "All those people trapped in those camps, on their way to the gas chambers, praying for help . . . God could have stopped it all but didn't. Do you think God wept, Stephen?"

"I'm not religious."

Faust smiled. "All that time at St. Anthony's didn't instill the fear of eternal wrath into you?"

Conway shoved his hands into his pockets. "I see you've read my file."

"And I see you're avoiding my question."

"I don't have much use for religion."

"Why?"

"It has no practical value here. Especially today. We've become tolerant to corruption."

"Yes. Society as a whole has moved away from God. Evil lives among us and we're blind to it. The great beast has slouched home and secretly, we're relieved."

Conway nodded, his eyes shifting over Faust's shoulder, to the Curley Memorial Park where a guy paced back and forth and blabbered on his cell phone.

"Forgive my diatribe, Stephen. I don't mean to lecture. I'm old, and I don't like the path the world has taken. I find it unsettling. I often wonder what it would be like if the whole planet started over again. Do you ever have those dreams where you're surrounded by people like yourself, people who appreciate you and who you are?"

"Everyone does."

"I think it could happen, you know. If the right person came into power, we could have a world whose foundation isn't built on lies and deceit. One without all this needless pain and suffering and death."

"It's a thought." Stephen was still distracted. "Jesus, I wish that guy would shut up."

Faust put a hand on Stephen's shoulder and ushered him to the last tower, out of hearing distance from the rude gentleman. Steam hissed and rose between them. Faust could smell Stephen's youth, his need for the world to exist in black-and-white, right-and-wrong—all of it was still there, it hadn't formed that thick, impenetrable callous across his skin. In time, Stephen could be molded and shaped.

But first, find a way to get inside.

"Last night when I called you at the wake, I was rather rude. I didn't want to intrude on your mourning," Faust said. "I'm so sorry for your loss, Stephen. To lose someone so close to you—someone you considered a family member, it must be devastating."

"Bouchard said Angel Eyes is in town."

"Yes. He's very close."

"What's the latest intel?"

"We're investigating some leads. First, I'd like to know your thoughts on this man Angel Eyes."

"I'm sure Bouchard filled you in."

"He did. And now I'd like to hear your thoughts."

Conway looked out at the traffic for a moment and gathered his thoughts. "What's to say?" he said and looked back. "He's managed to stay off our radar screen. He's achieved this by using, we think, a number of people he has planted on the inside."

"Like John McFadden."

"Who's now dead."

"Yes. Very suspicious."

"We can never get a lock on the guy. The psychological profile defines him as a psychopath."

"I'm not interested in what computers think. Tell me your thoughts."

"He steals the technology, and then he kills people. That would place him within the definition of having a psychopathic personality."

"How do you know he kills all his victims?"

"They wind up dead or missing."

"Missing doesn't mean they're dead."

"Their bodies haven't turned up yet. We know he killed two people: Jonathan King and Alex Matthews."

"Jonathan King," Faust said, frowning. "Refresh my memory."

"Invented a new type of sticky foam—the same stuff used on me in the lab. Angel Eyes or one of his henchmen beat him unconscious and poured Drano down his throat. He woke up in the hospital and suffered brain damage and couldn't talk but wrote down the name Angel Eyes. I'm sure Bouchard told you this."

"Yes. He did. But my question to you, Stephen, is how can you be sure it was Angel Eyes?"

"He killed Randy Scott. I was inside the lab when it happened. And then there's Alan Matthews."

"And now your friend John Riley. The one you buried today."

Conway cleared his throat. "You sound like you sympathize with this guy."

"Man is not one-dimensional. His thinking, his motivations, and his needs, the expanse of his inner world—his soul, if you believe in such things—cannot be compressed into neat, linear words that you feed into a computer. Man is not a piece of code."

"You make it sound like you have the inside line on this guy."

Faust smiled. "You might say that."

"I'm listening."

"Don't limit the scope of your thinking. If you do, your target becomes elusive. You'll be hunting an apparition that exists only in your head. For example, what if I told you that Alan Matthews was consumed by greed. That if he didn't sell the technology to Angel Eyes, he would have sold it to someone else. Like your friend Armand."

"That doesn't mean Matthews deserved to die."

"Did Armand deserve to die?"

"He rolled the dice."

"But did you *mourn* over his death?"

"Of course not."

"Your moral landscape is very black-and-white, isn't it?" Faust said. "By your definition, is Angel Eyes evil?"

"Anyone who kills someone purely for personal gain is, in my book, evil."

"What if I showed you that all of his efforts were designed for a higher purpose?"

"That doesn't give him the right to kill people for gain."

"Isn't that what you and your IWAC team do? Take down people who are threats?"

"I'll be sure and ask him these questions when we meet."

"And then you'll kill him."

"I didn't say that."

"It's all right to admit it, Stephen. Frankly, I'd want to kill someone who betrayed me."

Stephen nodded, but his expression didn't change. Faust was pleased. The foundation was laid. He would shape the next course of events to reveal Raymond Bouchard's betrayal and Stephen's inner world, the one he had so carefully constructed, would be leveled. He would be ripe for transformation. Faust would take him into the fold and would, over time, mold him. *I have so many things to teach you, Stephen.*

Faust said, "The technology that Angel Eyes steals, what do you think he's doing with it?"

"We know he's not selling the devices. They haven't turned up on the black market. I think he's collecting."

"Interesting theory. What would he be collecting these items for?"

"When we catch him, then we'll know what he's up to."

"Yes. I'm sure some revelation is at hand."

Conway reached into his pocket and came back with a small card. He handed it to Faust. "I found that in a bouquet at the funeral home last night," Conway said.

"It's signed Winston Smith."

"It's one of Angel Eyes's aliases. We know that because Matthews left a detailed verbal diary on his dealings with the man. That's how we found out about his next targets: Praxis and Dixon."

"How does Angel Eyes find out about these targets? Any thoughts?"

"Given what happened at Praxis and the recent revelations in the papers, I'd say the leak is this guy McFadden."

Faust stared at the card. "Does the name Winston hold any significance?"

"Winston Smith is the name of the main character from Orwell's *1984*."

"Yes. The man converted by Big Brother. The one who waits for the bullet to enter his brain."

"Besides King, Alan Matthews was the only witness who has seen Angel Eyes. Now we might have another." Again Conway reached inside his pocket and came back with a card, only this one was slightly bigger. He handed it over and said, "This is from Renée Kaufmann, John Riley's girlfriend. She had it waiting for me at the funeral home last night. She was in Amsterdam when Riley was killed."

"And now she's waiting for you at the Aquarium."

Conway nodded. "We have a witness who's seen Angel Eyes's real face."

"The note says she has evidence to back it up. What do you think that means?"

"I don't know. Maybe she recorded something."

"This is quite a breakthrough."

"I want to bring her in. I want her protected."

"I agree. Stephen, do you think Angel Eyes knows about the woman?"

"I don't know. Right now, I think he's focused on me. He thinks I know the decryption code."

"Do you?"

Conway mentioned the last words Randy had spoken to him. "They mean something, I'm sure," he said. "But what happened inside the lab is still hazy. Any leads on Dixon?"

"I'm sure he's close to the suit. Stephen, before our visit, you talked with Raymond?"

"In Austin. He wanted to be updated about what happened in the lab."

"Walk me through your conversation. I want to make sure Raymond hasn't missed anything."

Conway did. When he was done, Faust held up the card from Renée Kaufmann and said, "Have you told Raymond about this most recent development?"

"He told me to go directly through you. He also said you'd give me a new Palm Pilot, a watch, and a phone."

"Those items aren't ready yet. You're staying at the Fairmont Copley, correct?"

"Room 602."

"I'll drop them by later. The next time you talk to Raymond, tell him he should read *Spiritus Mundi*."

"What's that?"

"A medieval text for Christians. It lays out what Christians need to do in order to die in the grace of God."

"I don't understand."

"Don't worry. He will." Faust glanced down at his watch. Ten minutes before noon. The Aquarium was a good fifteen-minute walk. "You better get going. When you find Ms. Kaufmann, bring her outside. I'll be there with a van, waiting. I'll keep her safe, Stephen. And you. Remember that. There are not many people you can trust in this world, but you can trust me. I'm a man of my word."

Conway nodded, turned around, and started a light jog down the path carved through the glass towers. He had reached the end of the last tower when Faust called for him. Conway turned around, his pale face almost white in the sunlight.

"'The best lack all conviction, while the worst are full of passionate intensity,'" Faust said. "It's a line from Yeats's poem 'The Second Coming.' Don't underestimate the depths of human cruelty."

Faust removed his cell phone and hit the speed dial for the programmed number, his eyes tracking Stephen until he disappeared into the mob loitering around Faneuil Hall.

"It seems that software they downloaded into the suit was encrypted," Faust said. His eyes had settled on the disrespectful young man who was still screaming into his cell phone. "They need a decryption code in order to operate it. Otherwise, the suit is useless."

"And they're keeping Conway alive because they think he knows the code," Gunther said.

"Yes. Raymond believed that John Riley knew it. Stephen accidentally called him from inside the lab. And it gets better. They're pinning the death of a man named Jonathan King on us."

"Who's that?"

"The chemist of some sticky foam. Apparently, he's the one who originated the name Angel Eyes."

"So Bouchard's been stealing items for a while now."

"Yes. Where are you?"

"I'm sitting on a bench, looking directly at the front entrance of the Copley Fairmont."

"And how is Mr. Cole?"

"Still under. He won't be coming up for a while. I

planted the bugs and transmitters but I didn't find anything useful to get us closer to the suit."

"And the rest of Mr. Cole's brood?"

"The guy shadowing Conway and the surveillance team they had covering him have all been taken down. When Cole wakes up and finds out what happened to his men, he'll talk to Bouchard. It won't take them long to figure out we're involved. We're not living in the shadows anymore."

"I have a witness who not only saw Raymond kill Mr. Riley but claims to have evidence to back it up. She's at the Aquarium, waiting for Stephen. I want to bring them both in."

"You think Bouchard will hand over the suit for the woman?"

"Raymond's soul operates on currency. If we have the woman and evidence and threaten him with exposure, Raymond will hand over the suit." Faust would not put the woman in danger. She would be brought into the fold, safe from harm. *But I will use her to bring you trembling to your knees, Raymond*, he said to himself.

Gunther said, "A van just pulled up in front of the hotel."

"The Russians?"

"CIA. One of them I recognize from Austin. Five new players, they're moving inside the hotel."

"Probably on their way to see Mr. Cole. Any sign of Misha?"

"No. It's weird. It's like he's disappeared."

"Misha isn't one to hide, and he's predictably impatient. I'm sure he's restless by now. My guess is that he's sick of playing by Raymond's rules. Move your team to the Aquarium and call me so we can coordinate our efforts. We cannot leave any room for failure. If Raymond's men get Ms. Kaufmann first, her fate will be sealed."

"Understood."

"Be careful, Gunther. The vultures are circling," Faust said and hung up. He put his phone away and walked out of the memorial toward Curley Park, his arms by his sides and stretched wide to allow his gloved hands a final run across glass.

Outside of the towers, Faust removed his sunglasses from his inside jacket pocket and walked toward the young man still engrossed in his conversation. A few feet behind him, a black limousine had pulled up against the curb.

Faust held the sunglasses in one hand and let them dangle by his side. Mounted on the belly of his forearm and hidden underneath the coat was a unit with a retractable blade. He scratched his forearm and with the press of a button the blade sprang from the unit. His gloved hand, the one holding the sunglasses, hid the blade from view. Smiling, Faust approached the man.

"Richie, hold on," the man said, and then pulled the phone away from his ear, his attention locked on the advancing Faust. "What's the problem now?"

To the casual observer, Faust looked like he was about to walk past the man. Faust lifted his hand to put his sunglasses on, moving his wrist up to give the blade room to cut. In a swift, practiced motion the blade sliced the man's throat so quickly that he didn't realize what had just happened.

Three steps and Faust reached out and opened the

door to the limo. He climbed inside the car and shut the door, and through the tinted window watched the gentleman on his knees, gasping, his pale, trembling hands clutching at the gash in his throat, desperately trying to stop the bloody tide.

The inside of the New England Aquarium was deceptively small. In the center was a mammoth circular glass fish tank with a concrete ramp that spiraled all the way to the top. The glass was segregated into sections, allowing different, boxed-in views of the tank. Arranged outside the tank were several rock formations in water that held dozens of Little Blue Penguins. An Aquarium employee dressed in a wet suit stood in water that glowed aquamarine from the underwater lights. He fed the penguins from a bucket of fish. A group of kids leaned spellbound against the handrail, as the man talked over his headset microphone about the feeding habits of penguins.

It was just after noon, and the Aquarium was scattered with mothers pushing infants in carriers or holding the hands of toddlers who kept pointing with wide-eyed fascination at the exotic, colorful fish gliding through the dusty-colored water and dodging their way in and out of the spaces between rock and coral formations.

Last night, before going to the hotel, Conway had stopped by Booker's condo in Beacon Hill to see the kids. He scanned the photographs hung on the various walls and asked if Renée Kaufmann was in any of them. Booker had pointed to a woman with straight, long blond hair and a magnetic Julia Roberts kind of smile.

Conway didn't see her on the first floor, so he moved past a surly Boston cop who was watching a group of teenagers inside the gift shop. Conway walked up the ramp, the panels glowing with color pictures and facts about the various fish inside the tank, the air dark and warm and packed with the close, humid smell of salt and dead seaweed. When the ramp ended at a stairwell with a sign that said Caribbean Coral Reef, he walked up the last set of steps. At the top, he saw a mother holding a boy of about five in her arms, so he could look down into the tank. An enormous turtle broke against the surface and submerged in a cone of bubbles. Against the far wall was a blue neon strip molded into several waves or shark fins, Conway couldn't tell which.

"Mommy, where are the sharks?" the boy asked, excited.

"They're swimming with the other fishes, see?" The woman held the boy slightly over the tank. "The man will be upstairs in twenty minutes and he'll tell you all about them. Then maybe we can watch the diver feed them."

"Stephen?" a woman whispered.

Conway turned around. Renée Kaufmann stood on the steps that led up to an employee's-only area. With her arms wrapped around her body as if chilled, she walked over to him. She was petite, about five-five, and thin, one of those girls who probably had a naturally high metabolism and never had to diet. She wore a long tan-colored winter coat and blue knit hat that covered her ears and hair.

"I recognized you from John's pictures." Renée licked her cracked lips, her throat working as she swallowed. The skin beneath her round blue eyes was puffed and bruised from lack of sleep. She leaned in closer, and Conway could smell an unwashed odor rise up from her clothes. "Did you come here alone?" she whispered.

"I did. No one followed me. How did you get in here?"

"A friend who works here. You didn't tell anyone about me, did you? I mean, I know Booker has a background in this sort of thing, but I figured—I don't know what I figured. Maybe I should have called him first. I don't know."

"Relax. It's okay."

Renée crimped her lips. She took a deep breath and then said, "Did you go to the funeral?"

"Yes. Yes, I did. Booker handled everything."

"He always does." She looked exhausted and angry and terrified all at once.

"I wanted to call Book—he's the best one to handle this sort of thing, he's in the business and he knows people, he helped John when he got busted on that DWI, but after what I saw, what they did to John . . ." Renée's voice broke, her eyes growing wet as she covered her mouth with her gloved hand to stifle her cries. "I didn't want to put Book in danger. He has a wife and kids, and if something happened to them I couldn't live with that. But you're involved. They're after you."

"Let's go over here and talk." Conway touched her arm and ushered her over to the corner, away from the mother who was watching them. "Who's after me?"

Renée looked over her shoulder, her eyes scanning the area for the enemies who could at any moment now descend on her, and then looked back at him. "One of them was called Owen," she said.

"Owen what?"

"Just Owen. I was in Amsterdam on business, at a conference, and John wanted to test out this video conferencing software he just bought. He thought it would be a good way to keep in touch." Renée dabbed at her eyes. "I was in my hotel room, on my laptop, talking to him when the doorbell rang. John went to answer it and when he came back, the video went fuzzy. I couldn't see or hear anything."

"Tell me what you saw."

"After John . . ." The words came out in a sputter, wet, clogged by her grief. "After he collapsed, the man reached down and picked something up off the floor. After that I could see and hear everything."

A jamming unit.

"They wanted to talk to John about some phone call you made to him from inside some lab," Renée said. "Is that true?"

Conway nodded and felt the sadness and guilt he had experienced at the grave site earlier this morning return, blossoming again inside his heart. "What did this man look like?" he asked.

"Tall, with gray hair and blue eyes. Nice clothes."

"Was his name Raymond Bouchard?"

"They never said."

Could be Raymond, could be Angel Eyes. Conway placed his elbows against the guardrail and leaned forward so he could watch the front entrance. Out of the corner of his eye he could see the tears running down Renée's cheeks.

"What did John tell him?" Conway asked.

"Something about a friend of yours saying the words *mittens* and *cat food*."

If that was true—if Angel Eyes was the one inside the condo—then he already knew the decryption code.

Unless those words didn't work. Conway turned his head back to Renée. "You're sure about all of this?"

"I've watched the video over and over again, those were the words John said you used."

"Wait. What do you mean you watched the video?"

"I recorded it."

"That's the evidence you were talking about?"

Renée nodded. Conway couldn't believe what he was hearing.

"It was an accident," she said. "I didn't know how to use the software. It was defaulted to record."

"You're telling me you have the whole thing taped?"

"I packed up my laptop and luckily grabbed a flight leaving Amsterdam an hour later. A friend drove me to the airport. I had her buy me the ticket. I flew under her name."

"You have the tape on you now?"

"I burned it onto a CD. John has a safety deposit box at the Eastern Bank, on Broadway in Lynn. Last year, when my apartment got broken into, he put me on the list so I could use it. I have all my mother's jewelry stored inside there."

Renée Kaufmann had recorded *everything* and now it was waiting inside a safety deposit box in Lynn.

"I feel like I'm living inside a nightmare," she said, her voice quiet, racked with sobs. "Every person who looks at me, I think they're going to grab me right there and I feel like screaming. I can't go to my apartment. That's the first place they think I'll go, and I don't want to stay with friends, I'm sure they're being watched. I've been living on the street for days, using what cash I have left to check in and out of cheap motels. I can't sleep and I'm running out of money and I don't know who to turn to."

"You don't have to run anymore. I can protect you."

"How? How are you going to protect me?"

"I have people waiting for you outside."

"Boston cops? The FBI? I won't be safe with any of them, Stephen, and neither will you."

"These people are from the CIA."

She looked at him, dumbfounded.

"You can trust them," Conway said.

Renée's puffy eyes narrowed, her mouth hanging open. "You're with the CIA?"

"I'll explain this to you later, but right now we need to get you out of here," Conway said. He reached out and grabbed her arm.

She looked over his shoulder and her eyes grew wide. She stumbled backward and fell against the floor. Conway turned around and stood face to face with the man from Dixon's torture video, the animal who had raped Pasha Romanov as a young girl: the massive, intimidating figure of Misha Ronkil.

"Don't try and be a fucking hero," Misha said, and raised a nine-millimeter Beretta with an attached silencer and pointed it at Conway's face. "Keep your mouth shut and your voice down and everyone's going to come out of this golden."

Behind Misha, on the steps leading up to the tank, Conway saw two hulking figures dressed as Boston cops. Only they weren't cops; one of them came toward Misha while the other remained on the steps, telling people who wanted to come up to the tank that it was closed for the moment. The advancing cop was bloated with steroids and had a crewcut. He grabbed Renée by the arm.

Renée screamed out for help. The cop punched her across the mouth and Renée buckled to her knees. Conway made a move and Misha was there in front of him with the gun.

He'll shoot you right here, a voice said. *These guys have no boundaries. Let the cop take Renée outside where Cole and his men are waiting. He'll move people on her so just let her go and you can take care of Misha.*

Which wouldn't be easy. The man was *massive;* his entire bulk seemed to occupy the small space, his barrel-size chest looking like it was about to burst from underneath the blue shirt.

Renée was on the floor, bleeding and dazed. The cop handcuffed her and then yanked her up and led her away. The other cop remained on the stairs, keeping people from coming up. Conway was alone with Misha now. The cool, semidark air smelled of water and a foul combination of dried sweat mixed with cologne, and another odor, one that made Conway think of sour milk and musty towels.

Pasha's words came back to him: *A fat, smelly animal named Misha raped me on the kitchen table while my father sat in a chair with a gun pointed at his head . . . Misha came back again. Not only did he fuck me again in front of my father, but when Misha was done, he placed my head on the wood stove, burning my ear off.*

"Now it's your turn to go," Misha said.

The light from the water tank cast white water rings that glowed across the ceiling and walls. Below, a crying Renée was hauled out of the Aquarium.

You've got to stall him. Cole's going to have his hands full when he makes a run to get Renée Kaufmann.

"I want to make a deal," Conway said.

"You don't make deals. You do what you're told."

"I know how to operate the suit."

"So does Major Dick."

"I can hack my way past the security and get you inside the suit, show you how it works."

Misha was quiet, listening or thinking, Conway couldn't tell.

"You take me to where the suit is, I'll unlock all of it," Conway said. "All you have to do is let Dixon and the girl go and take me as your prisoner instead. You take me in, I unlock the suit, and everyone walks away clean, win-win."

Misha fired a shot. The silenced round hit the floor.

"The next time it's your fucking kneecap," Misha said. "Now move it."

"You know about the transponder, right?"

"The what?"

"The suit is equipped with a transponder," Conway said. "The second the decryption code is entered, the transponder is automatically activated. We'll be able to track the location of that suit with the satellite."

"Can you shut it off?"

"Only if you bring Dixon and the girl to me."

With his other hand Misha reached inside his jacket and came out with a knife that looked like a miniature machete. Knife in hand, he put the gun away. His face was a dark red, his trembling body energized with adrenaline and anger, his muscles flexing, ready.

"I'm sick of dealing with you CIA fucks," Misha said. Spittle flew out of his mouth as he talked. "Now you're going to give me exactly what I fucking want, right here, right fucking now or I'm going to take it out of you in chunks."

Conway had to draw him in. It was the only way to get the knife from Misha.

You hope. The guy is massive. And don't forget about the other cop on the stairs.

Cole's men should have been in here by now. What was taking them so long?

Misha lunged forward; Conway jumped back and hit the wall. The knife was less than a foot away from his face. Then Misha shifted the blade in his hand so the tip was pointed down toward the floor. Then he raised the knife and brought the blade down in a frightening arc.

That was his mistake. Conway's instinct and martial arts training took over. His rear foot slid out to the side, and as Misha's hand came down with the knife, Conway used the animal's momentum and brought the blade down so it missed him and instead sunk deep into Misha's knee.

Misha roared in pain, all of his attention focused on the blade that had pierced through to the back of his leg. Quickly, Conway gripped the knife hard and twisted it and then yanked it up so it the blade sliced up through his leg, blood pouring all over his hands. Then he released his grip, raked his elbow up the length of Misha's arm and using all of his strength snapped the animal's head back.

Conway thought Misha would fall back. He didn't. His pumpkin-size head simply bounced back, his tolerance for pain amazing. Misha grabbed Conway with both of his meaty hands and lifted him into the air. Conway's arms came up from his sides, about to execute a move that would release him from the man's grip, when he felt the back of his calves hit the edge of the water tank. *Jesus Christ, he's going to throw me into the tank.* He was already over the edge, his back inside the cold water, it was too late, he was going to go under. Conway clutched Misha's meaty arm and yanked him along with him into the tank, they were underwater now, the world a blur of shadows and colorful shapes as they both sank toward the bottom of the aquarium.

Pasha Romanov had been shadowing Stephen since his arrival in Boston. Two men, no doubt belonging to Misha, had been following him. Last night, at the wake, after Stephen had left, Pasha had watched one of these men walk inside the funeral home. When he came back out, she had tailed him until they reached the highway, when he must have sensed that he was being followed and shook her. She drove the van back to Stephen's hotel and had followed him this morning to the Aquarium. She didn't like the idea of Stephen going inside alone, so she went in after him.

The Aquarium was small, with not much room to hide. She walked around in the cool air searching for him, the brim of the blue Red Sox baseball cap pulled down low to cover her eyes. She wasn't worried about being spotted. She wore jeans and sneakers and a bulky winter coat packed with down; a polar fleece headband covered her ears, her eyes hidden behind sunglasses.

Where was he? He wasn't on the first floor. He couldn't have left; that much she knew. A moment later she saw a small, bloodied woman being hauled out the front door by a Boston cop. She was about to make her way up the winding ramp when she heard a woman scream.

Pasha turned and saw the horrified expression of a

young mother scooping up her toddler into her arms, the boy still pointing at the glass aquarium tank where Stephen was trapped at the bottom, on his back, Misha straddling him but trying to break free of Stephen's grip. A knife was stuck in Misha's knee; blood rose up through the water like clouds of red ink, rising past his clenched teeth and drifting up and past the group of sand sharks circling overhead.

The sharks had sensed the blood in the water and were swimming fast toward Misha and Stephen.

Pasha unzipped her coat and ran toward the tank. The young mother ran past her. The cool air became charged with adrenaline as other people screamed and ran for the exits. A handful of others remained frozen in place, too afraid or mesmerized to move. They stood around the large section of glass, their feet planted as they watched in wonder and mounting terror at the unbelievable spectacle that was about to unfold right in front of them.

"Holy *shit*, look!" a man yelled, backing up as he pointed at the glass.

The first shark sunk its teeth deep into Misha's arm and started twisting its powerful head side to side, its razor-sharp teeth ripping off a chunk of meat. A burst of blood formed a watery red cloud around Misha's face as he turned and tried to fend off the attack with his free hand, the second shark having already moved in for the kill and sunk its teeth into Misha's shoulder. Stephen lay on his back, sand swirling around him, his body wedged against the rocks and tank, trapped, the sharks feeding just a few feet above him.

Stephen will never make it to the surface. You've got to get him out now. Do it before security gets here.

"Get out of the way," Pasha said, knocking people

down to get to the glass. She knelt down, just inches from Stephen. From behind the glass she saw Misha's muted, agonizing screams of pain and saw Stephen's wide, frightened eyes in the water.

Pasha pulled out her gun, holding up her Glock so everyone could see it. Pandemonium broke out, everyone was fleeing toward the exits in a stampede, adults screaming, children crying. The glass was too thick; she couldn't shoot through it. Pasha holstered her Glock and came back with Primacord and a charge. She had been carrying it with her for days in case she had to take down some of Misha's men in a hurry.

Moving quick, Pasha knelt down and worked the strip of Primacord in a straight line along the bottom of the glass, making an X. Stephen's face was pressed against the glass. He turned and with wide, frightened eyes looked at her. Did he recognize her? Pasha moved her face close to the glass, hoping he could make out her blurred face.

"You, back away, now!" a man yelled behind her. She looked over her shoulder and saw a Boston policeman. The accent was Russian. *One of Misha's.* She turned her attention back to the tank.

Footsteps rushed toward her.

Hurry up and get it done. Pasha finished shaping the explosives. She placed the charge against the glass, entered 10 seconds into the timer. The other two sharks had descended on Misha's body and were tearing him apart in bursts of bright pink clouds. A sickening crunch of bone as one shark snapped its powerful jaw on Misha's head. Conway's face was turning red from lack of oxygen. The sharks were feeding less than a foot away from him.

Angry, powerful hands descended on her, lifting her

up. Pasha didn't fight it; she let the two guards pick her up, wanting them to think they could handle a woman. She surrendered herself, letting her body go lax, and when she felt their grip loosen, she raked her elbow against the nose of one of the guards, shattering it. When the man let go of his grip, Pasha planted her feet, turned and used a side-kick to blow out the second man's knee. His body crumbled forward, and Pasha finished him off with a kick to the groin and then a roundhouse to the stomach, sending him flying backward across the floor.

Pasha ran back to the charge and hit the button for the timer.

10.

9.

You can't stay. You've got to get out now, before the real police come.

Pasha ran past the groaning, bleeding men and headed for the door. A tall guy with a shaved head seemed to be coming for her. She tucked in her body, threw her shoulder into him and sent the guy flying against the wall. Pasha ran out the door and sprinted through the cold, November sunshine, the piercing wail of police sirens close. A Boston police cruiser, its lights flashing and its siren wailing, came to a screeching halt along with a van near the Aquarium entrance. Pasha ran in the opposite direction.

Stephen will survive this. He'll be fine. Jail will keep him safe. She kept telling herself this as she fled through the traffic-packed streets of Boston, her mind forming a plan to strike deep into Raymond Bouchard's poisoned heart.

Conway needed air. He looked up and in a blurred mess of red saw what remained of Misha's carcass being torn apart by the sharks only a few feet above. He had to make a break for the surface, but there was no way to get to the top of the tank without being attacked. Deep in the water and needing oxygen, his frightened mind pieced together words from one of those Discovery Channel shows on shark attacks: *They're afraid of humans. Don't start thrashing about in the water, they'll think you're a wounded harp seal and descend on you. If a shark attacks, hit it in the nose.*

He pushed himself off the floor and had started to swim up when he saw a bright flash followed by a rumble of thunder rock against the pebbled bottom of the Aquarium tank. Conway turned his head, looked down and saw what looked like . . . it looked like a *hole* had been blown through the glass.

Conway was being pulled. Then, it was like being caught in an undertow, and the next sensation he had was of being spit through the hole in the glass in a rush of water.

He hit the Aquarium's hard floor, tumbled and rolled, and then his body stopped moving. He lay on his stomach, gasping for air. He pushed himself up onto his knees and looked up.

The explosion had cut a large hole inside the glass; sharks and fish and Misha's body parts poured out onto the floor in a rush of water, the tank draining fast. Fish flopped about on the floor. People were screaming.

Gunshots.

Conway turned and saw a young, bald muscle-head holding a gun; the man had just shot two Boston cops who had their guns drawn. Two cops lay against the floor, covered in water and blood. The one near Conway had a shattered kneecap and a broken nose. It was the Russian Conway had seen earlier, the one who had been with Misha at the top of the stairs.

The bald guy ran to Conway. "They're not real cops. They're from Misha's gang," he said.

All Conway could do was gasp for air. He took the man's hand when he heard another gunshot. The bald guy crumpled to his knees and fell against Conway, and they were both knocked to the ground. The bald man lay on top of Conway. Blue-uniformed Boston patrolmen, their guns drawn, were running this way.

"Bouchard's dirty," the bald guy said. Blood was rushing from the gunshot in his stomach. "He's setting you up. Stay away from him and his partner, Cole. You can't trust them."

And then pairs of rough hands descended on Conway like lobster claws.

Angel Eyes's men, they're about to grab you.

Fight it.

Conway tried and couldn't. His strength was gone.

"Stephen, we're on your team," one of the cops said against Conway's ear. A towel was thrown over his face. "Keep that towel draped over your head," someone said. "Hold it in place. We don't want the security cameras to see you."

"Get him outside," another man said. "I'll see if I can grab the security tapes and meet up with you at the rendezvous point."

"Hurry up, the Boston police are on their way."

Conway was pulled up to his feet. The towel held over his face and his body hunched forward, he was escorted out of the Aquarium, the men holding him shouting, "Boston police, out of the way, get out of the way!" Through the gap in the towel he saw the back door of a black van open. Conway was tossed inside. Two men stepped inside with him and slammed the back door shut. The van lurched forward in a screech of tires, Conway lying on his stomach against the cold floor, sucking in air, his eyes closed and thinking of Pasha. It was her face he had seen against the glass, he was sure of it. Pasha had placed the explosives and had saved his life. Again.

The towel still draped around his head, Conway pushed himself up onto his hands and knees and tried to gulp in air between coughs. His face was hot and his lungs burned, his temples pounding so hard that it felt as if the veins were going to burst inside his head. The memory of what had happened inside the shark tank just moments ago still trembled inside his skin. He could still feel that choking sensation of the cold water rushing down his throat, Misha above him, his screams garbled as he was torn apart.

The van hit a bump. Conway lost his balance and slammed against the floor. He lay there against the cold, vibrating steel floor, not wanting to get up. The air was warm and humming with the sounds of the van's racing engine and the tires moving across the pavement. A cellular phone rang.

"You might want to sit up, Steve, and get comfortable. The ride's going to be a little shaky until we hit the highway."

Conway didn't recognize the bright, confident voice.

"Who we got in pursuit?" the same voice asked.

"Surveillance says we're in the clear," another voice responded, this one behind Conway, in the back of the van.

"And the Aquarium tapes?"

"In our possession and on their way to the rendezvous point. The Aquarium's a hot zone. Boston cops are on the scene. We're going to have to do some major spin control to keep the focus away from us."

"Stephen, looks like you're going to make it out of this nice and clean. But to be safe, I suggest you cut your hair, grow a beard or a goatee. Go with the goatee. It will give you an edge."

Conway pushed himself up so he was sitting down. Breathing was painful, and he still felt dazed, unable to hold on to one particular thought. He ran the towel over his damp head and face, still coughing, then slung it around his shoulders. He pressed his back against the van's side wall.

The middle-aged man sitting on a cooler near the van's sliding door looked like a construction worker for the Big Dig. He wore mud-streaked jeans and Timberland work boots and a burnt orange Dickeys winter coat draped over a gray sweatshirt. His baby-fine blond hair was parted to the side, his skin tanned.

Two other people were in here besides the blond man: the driver, dressed in the blue uniform of a Boston patrolman, and in the back, sitting against the opposite wall, his elbows propped up on his knees and tapping a cell phone against his calf, a tall man who was also dressed like a Boston cop. Conway didn't recognize any of them.

The blond-haired man picked up a tightly wrapped white towel from the floor and pressed it against the back of his head. He saw the question in Conway's eyes and answered it for him.

"Happened in my hotel room, can you believe it? Here I am, getting out the shower, I only got a towel wrapped around me, and when I stepped into the bedroom someone smacked the back of my head. There I am, lying on the floor buck naked and unconscious while some dude goes through my things." The guy shook his head with a wry grin, like he couldn't believe he stepped right into it. "Then the surveillance van, all the gear we had inside, it suddenly craps out, just went up in smoke, everything fried. Lucky we had alternate equipment to track you. That transmitter in your phone has a two-mile radius. We locked onto the frequency just before you decided to go for a swim." The man smiled, his eyes crinkling at the corners. "Looks like Angel Eyes tried to take a run at you."

Conway took in a deep breath, winced. He closed his eyes and saw the mess of events playing inside his head. What he wanted was some time alone to sift through all of this shit.

"The guy I had follow you to the funeral, Tony, the Lynn police just found his body sitting inside his car. Someone used his brains to redecorate the upholstery and back window. Look, I underestimated the guy's potential, and we got caught with our pants down. It won't happen again. We haven't been formally introduced. Ray told me to leave you alone until after the funeral. I'm Jonathan Cole."

Conway opened his eyes. He wasn't in the van. Right now, he was back inside the still-fresh memory from this morning, back in the cold air smelling of dead leaves and packed with the foreboding chill of a long winter, approaching the middle-aged man who stood with his eyes closed and his bare hand pressed against the glass. *He introduced himself as Jonathan Cole, knew all the specifics about the Austin fiasco.*

But if this blond guy was really Cole, then who the fuck was the guy from this morning?

I think you know the answer to that question.

He thought back to the man he had met this morning. The man seemed so polished, so sure of himself. Then came the words from the funeral home card: *You live in a wilderness of mirrors, Stephen. Be careful. Jackals surround you.* A warning? Then Conway thought back to the pictures left for him in the hospital room. *You're next.*

Had Angel Eyes been trying to warn him about Bouchard?

Angel Eyes had the opportunity to take you at the Holocaust Memorial. You thought he was your handler. So the big question is, if Angel Eyes has the suit and needs the decryption code, then why didn't he take you in?

Conway felt himself turn away from the answer.

You can't ignore the possibility anymore.

"You okay, Steve?" Cole asked.

"Kaufmann," Conway wheezed, his voice barely audible.

"What about her?"

"You got her?"

"Got her? What are you talking about?"

"They took her away. Outside," Conway said. "Didn't you intercept her?"

"I had no idea she was there."

It was a setup.

Renée Kaufmann was gone.

Next came the voice from just moments ago, the young bald guy from the Aquarium: *Bouchard's dirty. He's setting you up. Stay away from him and his partner, Cole. You can't trust them.*

Another person telling Conway not to trust Bouchard.

Why would Bouchard sell us out?

The answer's waiting for you on a CD at the bank in Lynn.

Was the bald muscle-head connected to Pasha? What the *fuck* was going on?

If what the dude from the Aquarium said is true, then it confirms Pasha's theory, so tread carefully.

But first, he had to figure a way out of this mess.

"What went down in there?" Cole asked. "Who blew you out of the tank?"

Conway kept his eyes veiled. He had to protect Pasha, the only person he could trust. He ran the towel over the back of his neck and said, "It wasn't one of your guys?"

"If it was, I wouldn't be asking the question." Cole was grinning, his tone polite. "I was hoping you could tell me."

"I was underwater, everything was blurry, happening fast. I had no idea who it was. Next thing I know, I'm being spit out of the tank and tossed onto the floor."

"And the guy you were talking to?"

"He shot two cops," Conway said. "Misha's men."

"Who?"

"Misha Ronkil, one of the Russian mob's top hit men. He came with two of his crew dressed as Boston cops."

"This bald guy, you know him?"

"Never saw him before. You?"

Cole shook his head. "He say anything?"

"He said to come out with him. That he was there to help me."

Cole let his gaze linger. Conway held it for a moment and then casually looked away and out the front window at the highway. The van was heading north on Route 95. It moved into the right lane and took an exit for Somerville.

The two men stared at Conway, waiting. It was possible, very possible, that these men were hiding Dixon. Conway felt confined.

An idea came to him. He reached inside his back pocket and removed his wallet. He opened it up and saw the note from the funeral home wedged in the slot right in front of the credit card Pasha had given him, the one with the transmitter. Was she tailing him right now? Conway hoped so.

The card was wet, but the writing was in ballpoint, so it hadn't been blurred by the water. He carefully removed the card and handed it to Cole.

"What do you think it means?"

Cole read it and then said, "Who knows? He's probably trying to get inside your head."

The van stopped. Conway craned his head and saw that they had pulled into a Mobil gas station. The man in the back, the one dressed as a cop, opened the back doors, got out and jogged over to the mini-mart. The driver remained behind the wheel, the engine running.

"Take a ride with me," Cole said. He opened the van's sliding door and stepped out into the cold November day.

"Where are we going?"

"For a ride. Come on, I promise I won't bite."

With his thumb, Conway slid Pasha's credit card out of his wallet. He wedged it into the space under the driver's seat, got out and slid the door shut.

It was a gamble, sure, but maybe this van was going back to wherever Dixon was being kept. Conway hoped that Pasha was nearby, that she would follow this van, thinking he was inside. He had memorized the number she had given him back in Austin. He would call her later tonight. Hopefully, she would have answers. Or better yet, she would have Dix and Renée Kaufmann.

Inside the Jaguar with its black leather seats, Cole put in a Miles Davis CD, the volume turned low. They drove through the streets of Somerville, Cole tapping his fingers against the steering wheel and staring out the front window as he ran through a private store of options. Several minutes later, they were on the high-way heading south, back to Boston.

"That was one hell of a ride back there," Cole said.

Conway nodded.

"It's okay to be a little shook up," Cole said. "God knows I would be. Nothing worse than drowning. Except maybe being burnt alive."

Conway kept looking out the front window, watching the traffic. A minute or so passed before Cole spoke again.

"What did Renée Kaufmann want to talk to you about?"

"Why didn't you ask me inside the van?" Conway said.

"I wanted to ask you in private."

Conway couldn't see a way around it. "She left a note for me with the director of the funeral home, asking me to meet her at the Aquarium," he said. "I went up to the top floor and found her, and that's when

Misha came in. He took her away before I got a chance to talk with her."

"And now Misha's shark food."

"You sound crushed."

Cole laughed. "Actually, I couldn't think of a better ending for Misha. This note from the funeral home, you got it with you?"

Conway had the note in his back pocket. It was wet, dissolved probably. "I shredded it," he said.

Cole pulled over into the breakdown lane, parked the car, left it running. He twisted sideways, his left hand still draped over the steering wheel.

"You mind if I search you?" he asked, smiling.

"Go for it."

Cole looked like he was considering it. Then his eyes cut sideways, out the front window. He licked his lips and then rubbed them together for a moment.

"The guy sitting in the back of the van with us, Parker, he look familiar to you?"

"No," Conway said.

"He should. He was at the funeral home, the night of your friend's wake."

Conway thought back to it but couldn't remember seeing his face.

"After you left, he talked to the funeral director and then went to a pay phone and placed a phone call. I traced the number. It belongs to a man named Chris Wiley. He's a counterterrroism expert with the FBI. He's also a friend of John McFadden."

"The dead mole."

Cole looked back at Conway. "You're starting to see the big picture? We got a goddamn spy network within the CIA. Can you imagine what would happen if this sort of news got out?"

"You're sure about this?"

"I'm sure about Parker. He bought a Rolex in downtown Boston a few days ago. I replaced it with an identical watch, only this one had a bug in it. I heard him talking with the funeral director and heard the whole conversation with McFadden's friend, Wiley. Raymond thinks—and I happen to agree with him—that these two boneheads are part of a spy ring that is feeding information to Angel Eyes."

It made perfect sense, of course. But how did Conway know this guy was telling the truth?

You live in a wilderness of mirrors. Be careful, Stephen. Jackals surround you.

"This guy Parker, he's been with Bouchard since the beginning. Parker's run all sorts of black ops," Cole said. "When you finally figure out the decryption code and hand it over to Bouchard, Parker's going to blow a bullet through the back of Ray's head. So when you do figure out the code, you are to tell no one but me. Understand?"

"Sure."

"Why do I get the feeling you and I are not on the level here?"

"You calling me a liar?"

"I think you just survived one hell of an underwater ride and right now you're confused and scared and to top it off, you have this psycho playing head games with you. I don't think you know who to believe."

Conway stared out the window at the passing traffic and thought, *Why didn't Angel Eyes take me in when he had the chance?*

"Has he made contact with you?"

"No," Conway lied.

"Don't let him get inside your head and make you start thinking you can't trust the good guys."

Conway looked back at him. "I know who to trust," he said.

Cole reached inside his jacket pocket and came back with three items: a Palm Pilot, a phone, and a bulky Citizen's diver's watch. He handed them to Conway.

"The watch is a little different," Cole said. "Release this button here and you have a garroting wire so sharp you can cut off a person's head. You get in an emergency situation, you press down on the glass and it turns on the emergency transponder and throws me into action. If for some reason you can't activate it, don't worry. There's a transmitter inside the watch. I can track you down anywhere."

Conway fastened the watch to his wrist. It felt heavy. Bulky.

"The Palm's different too," Cole said. "It's based on the IIIc model and has the same color screen and functionality as the one you're used to, only this one's a tad bit wider. That's because there's a sheet of Semtex inside. You hold down these two buttons and then the program comes up on the screen, see?" Cole showed him. On the color screen came a box asking him to place in a time. "Enter the time, hit the button here, and you got yourself an improvised explosive device that can take down a car. The Palm acts as the charge. Just make sure you're far away when this puppy goes off."

Conway thought, *I'm going to have a bomb attached to my hip.*

"The phone Raymond gave you," Cole said.

Conway reached into his pocket and brought out the phone. It was wet, worthless. He handed it over.

"Here, take mine," Cole said. "Before you take the car back to the city, stop somewhere and buy some new clothes and get a haircut. And I want you to stay with your buddy, Booker. Stick with him. That way I can watch both of you."

"Where you want me to drop you off?"

"I'm going to get off here."

Cole opened the door, the inside of the car filled with the rush of traffic whizzing by. Conway climbed behind the wheel, but Cole didn't shut the door. He leaned one arm on the opened door, the other on the roof, and looked down into the car.

"Steve, I know you're dealing with a lot right now. I can appreciate what you're feeling. But remember this: Angel Eyes was the one who killed your friend."

Only one way to find out.

"We're on the same team, Steve. You understand?"

"Absolutely."

"My numbers are programmed into your phone. Call me if you find out anything."

Conway looked up and smiled. "You can take that to the bank."

The neighborhood in this section of Lynn was made up of the lower-middle-class homes that had seen better days, the kind of place that acted like a black hole where you could disappear off the face of the earth. No one paid attention to you, they didn't want to stop and talk. No one cared. It was the perfect place to conduct personal matters without raising suspicion.

Cole pulled his car, a rented Nissan Maxima, into the driveway of a house on the end of the street, near the Commons. The ramshackle, two-floor unit had a fresh coat of yellow paint and a chain-linked, fenced-in backyard that was full of rotting leaves, decaying dog turds, and a rusted swing set that leaned to the side, as if it were sinking into the ground. It was after five, the world dark now, the front and back porch lights turned off, the shades drawn.

Cole got out of the car and walked up the rickety back steps. He opened the back door and moved into the kitchen with the peeling blue-and-white diamond-patterned linoleum floor and oak cabinets hung crookedly on nicotine stained rose wallpaper. The air was stale, heavy with the noxious fumes of takeout Chinese food.

Inside the living room, the TV was on, turned to the top news story of the day: the Aquarium bombing. Cole moved through the living room and walked down the small length of hallway. The basement door was cracked open. Far below, waiting in the sound-proofed, gray-concrete belly of the house, he heard the whimpered cries behind the prayers coming from a TV gospel show.

Through the bedroom door on the right, the light inside dimmed, Cole saw Raymond Bouchard leaning against the wall. Ray rubbed his forehead with one hand as he stared with wide, still eyes at a silent video screen that played recorded footage of the person who set up the strip of explosives against the Aquarium tank. Steve Conway was inside the water, trapped below the bulk of Misha, who was being ripped apart by the three sand sharks.

"Who do you think it is?" It was the voice of the techno-weenie, Owen Lee, the man-boy wearing his baseball cap backward and sucking a lollipop as he sat in a swivel chair in front of a grouping of desks that held surveillance and digital editing equipment.

"Pasha," Bouchard said, and then ground his teeth together.

"I thought she was dead."

"Her body hasn't turned up."

"You sure it's her? These Aquarium tapes don't have sound, so I can't hear her voice. And the way those two Russian dudes went down? I don't think a chick could do that."

"You've never seen Pasha in action. *I* have."

"Let me play around with the tape, find the best angle for the face. Then I can enhance the image and we'll know for sure."

"How long will that take?"

"Give me an hour."

Ray's head slumped forward. Cole smiled to himself. *Time is running out for you, Ray. The small holes in the dam are leaking, threatening to burst at any moment now, and once the tidal wave breaks free, nothing will be able to stop the force that will topple your personal empire.* How fun it was going to be to watch Ray drown, slowly, inch by inch.

On the screen the explosion followed, water and fish and what was left of Misha pouring onto the floor in a gushing waterfall. Cole stood in the hallway, in the shadows, invisible as he watched. Slaughter them all now? Tempting.

The stolen military suit and its cloaking abilities hung downstairs, waiting for him. All Cole needed was the decryption code. Then he could slip inside and become invisible to the world. Forever.

On the video monitor one of Misha's men, a Russian dressed up as a Boston cop, was up on his feet, his gun drawn and pointed at the back of Conway's head. Conway was oblivious as he crouched on all fours hacking up water. Gunshots and the Russian went down and here came a new player, a white man with a shaved head. Look behind you. Too late. The other Russian with the busted leg fired off a shot and Egghead was on the floor, clutching his stomach, already bleeding out.

"The guy's mouth is moving," Lee said. "He's trying to say something to Conway."

"Can you isolate it?"

"Like I said, this video doesn't have sound, but I can zoom on the guy's face, have the computer try to read his lips."

"I want to know what he said, and I want to know who the hell this person is."

Cole could hear the strain in Raymond's voice, trying to hold up the foundation to his empire. Time to remove another brick from the wall.

"Don't bother," Cole said. "The bald man belongs to Angel Eyes."

Bouchard and Lee jumped at the sound of Cole's voice. Then Raymond moved off the wall, coming closer, his eyes bloodshot. Owen Lee went back to working on the computer, the muscles in his back tense.

"How do you know this?" Bouchard demanded.

"Angel Eyes is in Boston."

Bouchard was speechless. His throat swallowed at a feverish pitch.

"He ambushed me and my men at the hotel today," Cole said.

"Wait—when did this happen?"

"This morning."

"Why the *fuck* didn't you call me? Why didn't your men—"

"They work for me. At least, some of them do," Cole said, and focused his eyes on Lee, who wouldn't turn around.

"Impossible," Bouchard said. "There is no way Angel Eyes could know we're here."

"Apparently you have a leak."

"McFadden? He didn't know about us. That part I made up."

"Say what you want, but Angel Eyes is not only in the game, he's become a major player."

"Did Conway give you the decryption code?"

"He claims he doesn't know it."

"That's bullshit."

"Maybe. He's been fed a lot of different stories. I can tell you this much: our boy is spooked."

"You saying he's holding out?"

"I'm saying he doesn't know who to trust." Cole reached into his shirt pocket, retrieved the small card Conway found stuck in the flowers at the funeral home, and handed it to Raymond.

"You had someone follow Conway to the funeral home," Raymond said, his eyes glued to the card.

"Yes. Tony Romano."

"What did he say? Did Conway talk to anyone?"

"Someone blew Tony's brains out this morning. I didn't get a chance to talk to him."

Raymond started pacing. He pressed his hand against his forehead, his eyes wide with disbelief. The rare sight of the emperor becoming unglued. Marvelous.

"We also have a problem with Misha's boss, Alexi," Cole said. "Misha's shark bait, and two of his prized goons are lying dead in the morgue dressed as Boston cops. The FBI is going to put the heat on Alexi."

"We can pin Misha's death on Angel Eyes."

"Alexi doesn't listen to reason."

"Then I'll bring him here and you'll kill him."

"The body count's getting high, Ray."

"If Angel Eyes took you and your men down, he could have taken Conway in. Why would he let him go?"

"My guess is that Angel Eyes wanted to use Conway to bring the girl out. That way, he would not only have the person with the decryption code, he would have the witness to her boyfriend's murder. Those are powerful bargaining chips for the suit. Personally, I don't think he's after the suit. I think he wants something far more valuable."

"What could be more valuable than the suit?"

"Your head hanging above his mantel."

Raymond stared at the floor as the idea sank in.

"You used his name to stage a phony raid and he found out. The whole world knows about him now. You have the suit he was after and to top it off, today one of his men got killed trying to save Conway," Cole said. "I don't know the guy personally, but if I had to guess, I'd say he's rather pissed off."

"What did the girl want?"

"You mean Renée Kaufmann."

"Who the fuck do you think I'm talking about?"

"I don't know. They didn't get a chance to talk."

"That's what Conway told you."

"Yes."

"Then he's fucking lying."

Raymond was coming unglued. Wonderful. Cole said, "Have you talked to her?"

Raymond took a breath and unconsciously looked down at his hand and flexed his fingers. They were cut and looked swollen.

"Couldn't make her talk, Ray?"

"She's downstairs, waiting for you. I want answers and I want them tonight. Understand?"

"So Miss Kaufmann's alive?"

"Of course she's alive. You think I killed her?"

"I thought you might have stuck a syringe full of rat poison in her neck. For fun."

Owen Lee said, "The person who blew Conway out of the tank was Pasha Romanov."

Cole and Raymond turned to Lee, who swiveled around in his chair and moved to the side. On the color screen was a blown-up picture of a woman wearing a baseball cap. It was clearly Pasha.

"One other thing," Lee said and took the grape lollipop out of his mouth. His tongue and part of his lips were stained purple. "I managed to isolate what the bald dude was saying to Conway."

"I thought the video didn't have sound," Bouchard said.

"It doesn't, but our computer has software that can read lips."

"What did he say?"

"He said, 'Bouchard's dirty. He's setting you up. Stay away from him and his partner, Cole. You can't trust them.'"

Cole saw the anger and fear spark in Raymond's eyes. He drank it in and smiled. Enough. Time to get to work.

"We'll deal with Stephen tomorrow. Right now, I'm going to have a talk with Renée, see what she told Stephen," Cole said. "In the interim, Raymond, please try to keep yourself together. The ride is going to get *very* bumpy."

When she was eleven, Renée Kaufmann learned that her grandfather had terminal lung cancer. She didn't believe it. This man had survived the worst hell on earth, the Holocaust, and although she didn't know the specifics of his ordeal (Zayde *never* talked about it), he did say, once, that he knew he would survive that never-ending stretch of nightmare because he had prayed to God every day. God, he had told Renée, never let good people down.

So when Zayde got sick, Renée knew God wouldn't let her down. She went to Temple, she prayed, she believed in God, she could feel Him deep in her heart, the kind of warm comfort that reminded her of the way bed sheets smelled after coming out of the dryer. Deep in her heart she knew God wouldn't take away such a brave man from her, this old man with thick glasses who loved to do magic tricks with cards and make coins materialize into dollar bills, his clothes always smelling of smoke and Vicks Vapor Rub. Besides, Grandpa looked fine. But here was her mother crying in the bedroom, her father next to her, trying to comfort her but not knowing how, Renée standing in the hallway and watching, not knowing that the second man she loved would collapse from a heart attack a year later in the basement while working on a cabinet for her mother.

Zayde sat upright in the hospital bed, his smile bright (he was always smiling) when she came in, alone, Mom waiting out in the hallway.

"Well, hi there, Button!" He loved to call her Button because, even at eleven, she was so small.

"Mom says you have cancer."

"You were always blunt, Renée." Then he laughed and coughed and hacked, the deep, wheezing sounds of a man struggling to breathe. "Don't ever lose that. It will help you weed out the bad ones later in life."

"You didn't answer my question."

No change of expression in his face. He reached over and grabbed the paper cup of water and drank it out of a straw, his eyes dropping to the bed, glancing at the skin of his wrist painted with the blue numbers. In the harsh sunlight pouring in from the window, he suddenly looked so old and frail.

"Come sit with me," he said, patting the bed with a shaking hand.

Renée sat next to him, close to his sour breath and the smell of medicine and alcohol, her eyes staring at the hanging bottle of clear fluid attached to a tube that ran into Zayde's wrist.

"You don't look sick," she said.

"I am, Button."

"Are you in pain?" she asked, her voice low, afraid of the answer, but more afraid if he said yes, she knew, even at that age, there would be nothing she could do to take his pain away.

"I'm never in pain."

"Never?"

"No. I want to share something with you. A secret." He leaned in closer, conspiratorial. When he whispered, she could smell the smoke on his breath. "When

I was stuck in the camp, I would close my eyes and think of a special place that no one could touch. It's beautiful. It's full of gardens and open fields, the sky is always blue and the air is cool and sweet and smells like apples. But what makes it so special is that your great-grandmother and grandfather are there, my friends, my dog Piper, all of the people and things I've ever loved are always there, waiting for me."

"What are you saying?" She was trembling and didn't know why.

"Build a special place inside yourself and don't let anyone touch it. When you get older, you'll discover that the world has a nasty habit of kicking good people. Sometimes they get hurt. It's not God's fault, it's just the way the world works, Button. When that happens, escape to that place and remember all the good things you have in your life."

Renée was there now. Her eyes were clamped shut and in her mind she saw the old farmhouse she had always envisioned buying someday, the bedroom window overlooking a valley of trees, the leaves those burning colors of red and orange and yellow and gold. She was there right now, far away from the basement with its musty air lingering with piss and waste and sweat, far away from the sensation of her full bladder and the pounding cuts and bumps on her face from the man who had hit her—the same man who had killed John—and far away from a more frightening sight: the terrified expression of the skinny man bound to the same dentist-type chair next to her, the man with two missing fingers.

John is here, he's lying on his back in the bed they had first made love in, his naked body white even in the dimming sunlight. She sits on top of him, riding him, he is so gentle as he touches her, then he slaps her rump and starts wiggling his body while he yells out, "Who's your daddy? Who's your daddy?"

She laughs—you have to laugh when you're around John, you can't help yourself—and she swats him on the arm. Then he sits up in bed and brings her close to him, his face serious, and buries his face against her chest as if he is trying to find a way to burrow past her skin and take her with him to a place that doesn't exist in the real world, a place where two hearts are safe to whisper promises and share secrets and laugh and live forever.

"Renée."

The voice was bright and warm. Renée opened her eyes, not wanting to leave the place in her mind, and looked down the length of her bound body. She saw a man with blond hair standing at the foot of the chair. He looked like a construction worker who had come home to his family. His eyes were a deep blue, kind.

Smiling, the man with the blond hair walked around to the side of her head and knelt down. Renée heard something scrape against the floor, something that sounded like metal. She could feel the man's breath washing over her ear. She couldn't look at him—her head was bound against the chair's headrest.

"Are you okay?" the man whispered. "Talk, but keep your voice down."

She didn't respond, didn't move. She wanted to lose herself back inside the vividness of a magic fall day where John waited for her. *Concentrate.* She tried to rebuild the image in her mind but it wouldn't form.

"Relax, Renée. I'm a friend of Stephen's."

Stephen Conway. The name brought back all of her rage. This was his fault. He was mixed up in some sort of CIA bullshit and had mixed John up in it and now

John—her life—was dead because of Steve Conway.

"I'm here to help you and the guy next to you, Dixon. I can't remove the straps yet. I have to wait until some of them leave and then I can bust both of you out of here, okay?"

Was what this man saying true? Could he be here to help? Really? Before John, she had dated enough men to know that, by nature, they were full of secrets, often greedy, being kind and polite and charming so they could talk you out of your pants, only needing you if you had something of value to them. Still, she wanted to believe him.

"Steve told you he was CIA, right?"

The man's voice sounded so kind, so gentle and confident. Risk answering the question?

She nodded.

"So you did talk with him," the man said.

"A little." Her lip was split and swollen, but her voice was strong. Hearing it renewed her hope.

"Why did you want to meet him alone?"

She swallowed and said, "You said you talked with him."

"Briefly. We got split up." The man swallowed and then sighed. "They got him, Renée. He's in danger. That's why I need to know what you talked about. I know you saw what happened in the condo."

A voice cried out, telling her to stop talking. But she didn't want to stop. She wanted to purge this dark and terrible knowledge from her heart once and for all.

"A man with gray hair came down here and hit me," she said. She closed her eyes and felt the welts throbbing across her face and head.

"His name is Raymond Bouchard."

Renée took in a deep breath. Tears welled up along

the rims. "It was the same man who killed John. He came down here and started hitting me."

The blond man stroked her head. "Shhh, it's okay. Raymond Bouchard will get what's coming to him, believe me. Now just take your time and tell me what happened."

"They killed John, and then they said they were going to kill Steve."

"They?"

"Bouchard and another guy, the one who planted the drugs."

"Do you know his name?"

"Owen Lee."

"Go on."

"They planted the drugs around the condo to make it look like an OD. Then they talked about Steve, what they were going to do to him and this other guy named Jonathan Cole."

She felt the man's hand stop moving and heard his breath catch in his throat. Then he breathed again, only now it sounded like the labored breath of a man recovering from an unexpected blow.

Something's wrong. She tried to squirm away from his touch. Her bladder was swollen like a water-filled balloon threatening to burst.

"You have quite a memory, Renée. Not too many people could remember this level of detail." The cheer and warmth was gone from the man's voice, as if the words she had spoken had caused him injury. She didn't know why, but his tone reminded her of the character Ralph Fiennes played in *Schindler's List*, the SS commander. Every time he spoke, it was like death wrapping itself around your skin.

"I have to pee," she said.

"How were they going to kill Cole?"

"Please. I can't hold it anymore," she said again, hating herself for sounding so weak.

"Then piss in your seat."

In that moment she knew she had mistakenly walked down a corridor from which there was no return.

"What's the decryption code?"

"I don't know," she said.

"One last time. What's the code?"

The man next to her—Dixon—was screaming from behind his strip of duct tape.

The blond man sank his teeth into her ear and then shook his head wildly like a dog trying to tear away the last remaining strip of meat from a bone. Renée screamed, writhing against the restraints that dug into her skin, and kept screaming when the blond man stood up and spit her ear onto her lap. Blood was smeared across his mouth and chin, dripping. He smiled and brought up the circular saw, its ragged teeth shining under the light, and turned it on, the whining screech of the blade drowning out the sound of the screams.

Renée Kaufmann shut her eyes. This time John was there, waiting for her on one of the paths carved out in the magnificent stretch of woods behind the farmhouse. John took her close to him and wrapped his big arms around her back and hugged her tight.

"Just hold on, Renée, it will be over in a moment and you'll be here with me, with all of us." John whispered the words against her ear over and over again. The whining screech of the blade moved closer.

The black van was perfect for this neighborhood. It was scratched, dented and dinged, but not as bad as the others, decade-old junkers plagued with rust and missing fenders and blown-out rear windows that were now covered with garbage bags and fastened to the car with duct tape. A strong wind blew, shaking the branches of the bald maple trees, and kicked the empty beer cans across the sidewalk and lawns, the air cold and sharp enough to keep everyone indoors.

Pasha Romanov sat on a chair in the back of the van, her body tucked behind the front seats, a pair of night-vision goggles strapped across her head. Her breath fogged around her as she looked through the misty green prism of light and stared at the yellow house at the end of the street. She had been parked here since late this afternoon. It was now after nine.

Just under an hour ago, she had watched a blue Nissan Maxima pull into the driveway. When the car door opened, a man with neatly combed blond hair and a burnt-orange jacket stepped out and walked up the back porch steps. It was the same man she had seen earlier at the Mobil station. There, he had slid behind the wheel of a shiny black Jaguar, not a Nissan, his passenger a bedraggled Stephen Conway.

Pasha knew Stephen was alive before seeing him at

the gas station. After leaving the Aquarium, she had booked it straight to the van and used the surveillance gear to lock onto the transmitter in Stephen's credit card. She caught up to the white van on the highway, shadowing it, far enough away not to attract any attention. She saw the van take the exit and followed. The white van had pulled off the road and was now parked near the pay phone of a Mobil station, and there was Stephen, alive. Pasha didn't pause; she drove past them for about half a mile, pulled into a strip mall, turned around and waited for the Jaguar to move.

When she reached the highway, she expected to be following the Jaguar. Instead, she was following the white van. And she had no idea where Stephen was, since the only means of tracking him, the credit card, was inside the van. Stephen was gone.

Or had he purposely left the credit card in the van? Had Stephen discovered something?

Pasha followed the van to this house, parked where she was now sitting and for the past three hours watched as various men came and went. In the daylight, she had used a set of binoculars hooked up to a laptop computer that allowed her to zoom in on the faces and take high-resolution pictures. By the time four o'clock rolled around, the world fading into darkness, seven men had entered the house, including the blond man.

The real surprise came just after five. A silver Honda pulled into the pitch-black driveway and out climbed the familiar figure of Raymond Bouchard, wearing a hat, his Roman profile and squarely-set jaw unmistakable even in the misty world of the night-vision.

It was clear that the house was serving as a base of

operations. What wasn't clear was whether or not Major Dixon or the suit was inside.

In her mind Pasha saw the naked and bound figure of Major Dixon from the torture video, twisting beneath his restraints, screaming for it to stop. In her hands was a Glock, the barrel threaded with the silencer, and on the floor next to her were two Heckler and Koch MP-6 submachine guns with attached suppressors and laser sights. More than enough firepower.

She ran her finger over the trigger, staring at the house, thinking.

She was only one person. And right now she did not know the layout of the house, and she didn't know the best entry point. Later, in the early morning hours, she would leave the van and take a walk, and from a safe location survey the house. That meant more waiting. She thought of Raymond and wanted to burst in there now. Kept thinking about it.

She wanted to call Stephen now and find out what had happened inside the Aquarium. The problem was that his hotel room was probably bugged. And he would have people following him, listening. If she called, if she tried to approach him when the heat was on, Raymond would discover that she was alive and would put his men on alert. They would secure the house, might even kill Dixon. Best to wait.

Raymond would leave at some point tonight, taking some of his men with him, and thereby reducing the number inside the house. She would case the house tomorrow, watching and planning. Later, when the sky had grown dark and the world had settled into sleep, Pasha would strike. The combat gear she needed was stored here in the van.

Pasha kept watching the house, rubbing the trigger

of her pistol for comfort. But the feeling wasn't as soothing as the image playing inside her head: that of the treacherous fuck Raymond Bouchard curled into a fetal position, crippled and crying as she introduced him to new levels of pain.

The man known only as *Angel Eyes* stands on a grate hissing with steam. He is covered in a thick white fog, but Conway can see the back of the man's pale head and his hand pressed against the cold glass of the Holocaust Memorial as if locked in prayer.

Conway takes a step closer and feels the air drop dramatically, bone-chilling now, and laced with an electrical charge that makes his muscles tremble with anticipation. He can feel the power radiating off the man's skin. A well-contained storm, violence that, once unleashed, knew no match. Conway had felt this power only twice in his life. The first time was while watching his kenpo karate instructor break through five wood boards with a single kick; the second time was in college, at a keg party after a football game where three steroid-induced douche bags who loved to fight decided to take on Booker. Conway watched Book toss them aside as if they were made of paper, watched his meaty fists shaped like blocks of concrete send his opponents crumbling to their knees in painful tremors.

Only this power is different. It is stronger, darker, and more terrifying, the kind of breathing entity that once forced adults and children to march into the sealed chambers with showers that filled with gas and screams and cries to God for mercy and forgiveness.

"It's not what you think, Stephen. I'm trying to stop it

from happening again," Angel Eyes says, his back covered in steam and shadows. Overhead, the once blue sky is now roiling with dark clouds the color of ink. The streets turn dark; it starts to snow. Then a shot rings out.

Car doors fly open and the drivers and occupants flee in terror, everyone running up stairs and bolting down streets to the building doors that offer safety. Conway doesn't see the shooter but he sees something more disturbing. Dozens of white wolves have appeared on the streets and steps leading up to Government Center. They emerge from the grass and bushes that surround the memorial, their jaws are open, their breaths steaming in the air, their blue eyes locked in a predatory stare on a man who lies twisting with pain on his back in the middle of the road.

It's Randy Scott.

He turns his head and his frightened eyes lock on Conway. Randy reaches out for help, his fingers trembling and dripping red. The wolves sniff the air, their eyes growing wide as they lock on the scent of the blood.

Conway steps off the grate and makes a move up the slope when Angel Eyes calls out to him.

"It's a trap, Stephen."

"If I don't help Randy, he'll die."

"He's dead already."

"I don't believe you."

"You have no reason not to believe me. Why do you willingly trust Raymond?"

Conway doesn't have an answer ready.

"What frightens you more, Stephen? Discovering the truth about Raymond, or shattering your inner world?"

Angel Eyes speaks with a cunning superiority, the words burrowing past Conway's skin and scaling his protective walls and barriers and then settling deep in those vulnerable, private places he kept hidden from the rest of the world.

"*You're so eager to impress, so eager to be accepted and valued in this slick den of thieves, that you're blind to the jackals that surround you. Like Dixon and Randy, you're a means to an end. You're disposable. I bet that thought keeps the engine running long into the night.*"

Randy cries out for help. Conway moves up the slope. The wolves start to advance. Angel Eyes speaks to him one last time.

"*You live in a wilderness of mirrors, Stephen. Jackals surround you. The choice is yours. I'm not going to warn you again.*"

Conway runs out into the street. Dozens of glowing, predatory blue eyes bear down on him. Randy is on his back; his trembling hands are working to try to keep the blood from leaving the gunshot wound in his stomach.

"*Hang on, Randy. I'll call for help.*"

But Randy isn't listening. His gaze is still, focused, what people call the thousand-yard stare. The wolves are approaching them.

"*Mittens,*" Randy says. "*Cat food.*"

"*You're not making any sense.*"

Randy twists his head to Conway. "*My cat's breath smells like cat food,*" he says. "*My cat's name is Mittens. My cat's breath smells like cat food. My cat's name is Mittens. Who said that, Steve?*"

"*You're delirious.*"

"*You know me, Steve. You know what I like to watch?*"

"*TV. Sports.*"

"*And cartoons.*"

It's like watching a hidden object rise from the depths of the ocean and break the surface. It's all clear now. It makes sense.

"The Simpsons," *Conway says.*

"*Right. Ralph Wiggim, remember him? The little retard*

*who runs around saying those stupid things that make me
laugh so hard I come close to pissing myself? I tried to tell you
the code inside the lab in a way so they wouldn't figure it out.
Only you're not a good listener, Steve. You never were. You
can't even see what's happening around you."*

*Randy's hand comes up with a Glock. He presses it against
Conway's head, and when Randy smiles, his teeth are yellow
and crooked, his breath packed with the overpowering stench
of nicotine.*

*"Nobody's going to save your ass this time," Randy says,
but it's Armand's voice, and he fires a round into Conway's
head.*

Conway woke up in a tangle of sheets. His chest and
head were drenched with sweat, and his heart was
pounding so hard and fast that he felt dizzy. He wiped
his face, slid his feet over the bed and placed them on
the cold hardwood floor. He was inside one of the spare
bedrooms in Booker's penthouse condo in Beacon Hill.
Conway had gone back to the hotel, packed his stuff,
and come directly here, wanting to stick close to his
friend.

*The dream is a warning. They took Renée and they'll try
to take Booker.*

Or worse, try to hurt someone from Book's family.

A floor-to-ceiling window faced him. Outside, the
first snowstorm of the season was in full force. Boston's
downtown cluster of buildings glowed with squares of
white and yellow light. Behind the bedroom door,
Booker and his family were fast asleep.

You have to tell him.

It was against protocol. A serious breach of—

Fuck protocol. You want another dead friend?

Conway thought about the 911 call. Book had provided him with a copy of the tape. The voice on the 911 call was an identical match to the bald guy at the Aquarium. The man reported a murder in progress but didn't give a description of the killer.

Another piece of the puzzle. But what did it mean?

A ringing sound made Conway jump.

It wasn't his cell phone. When Conway had returned from the hotel, a package was waiting for him at the front desk in the lobby of Booker's condo building. Inside the box was a cell phone and a note telling Conway to leave the phone turned on. He rushed over to the nightstand, grabbed the phone and pressed it up against his ear.

"Hello?"

"Having trouble sleeping, Stephen?" Angel Eyes asked.

"I hope you don't mind me calling at such a late hour," he said. "After the day's events, I thought you would be up, ruminating. How are you coping?"

The man's tone was distant; a dry click separated the words. Gone was the confidence Conway had witnessed earlier today. It was almost as if the man was . . . what, grieving?

"I'm fine," Conway said, dazed and yet somewhat curious. "Why did you leave me this phone at the front desk?"

"So we could talk privately, on a secured line. Or have you invited your friends to listen?"

"It's just you and me." His IWAC cell phone, the Palm Pilot, and watch given to him just hours ago by Cole, all of those items had been placed inside a freezer bag and stuffed into his gym bag. That and his suitcase full of clothes were now sitting on the floor in Booker's living room. Conway didn't want Cole overhearing any conversation.

"I've been thinking about you a lot today, Stephen. I never met my parents. Like you, I had to fend for myself. I spent most of my life as a runaway in Europe. I was homeless for good periods of my life. Like you, I was so full of rage. I read that you carved up Todd Merrill's face with glass."

"What do you mean you read?"

"Welcome to the electronic age. There are no more secrets." Angel Eyes took in a deep draw of air and then sighed. "Did you ever try to track down your birth mother?"

Conway didn't say anything. The problem was, the image of the man he had carried for so long inside his head—this faceless entity that stole high-tech weapons and killed people or made them disappear, this intelligent *uber*-villain the CIA knew only as Angel Eyes—didn't match the polished gentleman from earlier today. Conway was still trying to figure the guy out, to discover the true agenda locked behind the surface smile and cunning words that, once formed and sharpened, had the ability to flay the soul.

"Am I getting too personal?" Angel Eyes asked.

"The past is the past. I don't think about it."

"It's okay to be vulnerable with me, Stephen. It doesn't make you less of a man. I certainly don't think any less of you. You are, in fact, one of the bravest people I've ever met."

Conway's heart was tripping inside his chest with an anxiety he couldn't name. *Must be the dream, what it meant.* Yes. The dream was still fresh in his mind. He stared out the window at the snow that was coating the city in a fine white blanket.

"I was roughly your age when I decided to undertake one of the most terrifying journeys of my life," Angel Eyes said. "It didn't take much to unshroud the mystery. Two weeks' worth of work and I tracked her down to this disgusting flat in London. There she was, this small, petite creature with chemically treated blond hair and bad eyesight, her spine twisted with osteoporosis, clearly in pain as she tended to the flowers in her garden. The poor thing had to use a walker to get around. For days I watched her from my car. No visitors or friends ever came by. It was heartbreaking."

"What was her name?"

"What's important, Stephen, was what I did. I rang her doorbell and had my first panic attack. There I was, standing on her porch, and I thought I was going to faint. I looked through the door's paneled window and saw her arthritic claw fumbling at the lock, and I ran away. Can you imagine that? Me, a grown man, very successful, and I ran away and buried my hands in my face and cried like a child. I was terrified at what I would discover. It took a couple of days, but I came to my senses and went back just in time to see her body being wheeled into the back of an ambulance. She had died in her sleep." Angel Eyes sighed against the receiver. A wet click in his throat and then he said, "All those questions . . . they went unanswered. Failing to gather the courage to talk to her was one of the worst mistakes I ever made. I regret it to this day, Stephen. Don't make the same mistake."

"This is why you called me? Because of your mother?"

"No. I needed someone to talk to. A companion who would understand the depth and severity of my loss."

"*Your* loss," Conway said, his voice rising before he could stop it, the anger leaking out from behind the locked door. In his mind he saw it all in a rush: the bodies of the dead IWAC members; Pasha bruised and walking as if she were crippled; and John Riley as he twisted on the floor, his shaking hand gripping his chest, wanting to claw through the skin and break apart the bone and stop the spasms in his heart, his final breaths becoming shorter, more painful.

"Today, at the Aquarium, the man who came in to help you, his name was Gunther." Angel Eyes's voice caught. "I've known him since he was a boy."

Conway started pacing the floor, his palms ringing, wanting to hit something.

This guy can deliver you Dixon and the suit

(Can he? Or is it Raymond—)

but you've got to play his game. You're the only person who's seen this guy up close and lived and now you got him on the phone, Jesus Christ, Steve, don't blow it because you're pissed off. You might not have this opportunity again.

"I've lost men before, people I've liked and respected, but this . . .   This is the first time I've lost someone close to me. Someone I cared for and loved. Deeply." Angel Eyes swallowed audibly. When he cleared his throat and spoke, his voice almost trembled. "This boy was my life and now he's gone."

Conway could feel the words burning on his tongue. He leaned forward and placed one hand against the window.

"Why are you being so quiet, Stephen?"

"What do you want me to say?"

"How about thank you?"

"For what?"

"Gunther saved your life, Stephen. Twice."

Conway turned his head away from the window. He hadn't expected that.

"When you were spit out of the tank, you had a gun pointed to the back of your head. One of Misha's men was dressed as a police officer," Angel Eyes said. Darker. "Gunther shot him before he had a chance to blow your head off."

Conway felt drops of sweat slide down his armpits.

"The second time was at Praxis, just as the suit was

leaving," Angel Eyes said. "I had a chance to save you or to go after the suit. Gunther went in and found you unconscious. He carried you out of the lab and dropped you outside, where the EMTs rescued you."

"So what's your interest in all of this?"

"Like you, I'm trying to make the world a safer place. Only you're working for the wrong team."

"So you admit to wanting the suit."

"Of course."

"Why?"

"To keep it out of the hands of the people you work for."

"And why should I believe you?"

"Why the recalcitrance, Stephen? Didn't you talk with Renée Kaufmann?"

"Why don't you ask her yourself?"

"She's not with me, Stephen."

"Then where is she?" Conway asked. Deep in his heart, he already knew the answer.

"Why don't you ask Raymond or his partner, Mr. Cole. You have their numbers."

Conway didn't say anything.

"Misha didn't work for me, Stephen. I make it a habit of not associating with liars and thieves. I was delighted to hear of Misha's denouement inside the tank. My only complaint is that it should have been slower."

"I didn't talk with her," Conway said again.

"I haven't lied to you, Stephen, and I never will. I despise it. I expect you to honor me with the same courtesy."

"*Honor* you?"

"What terrifies you more, Stephen? The truth or the fact that you've placed your loyalties, your trust and your life—the very *essence* of who you are—with jackals, men who view you as nothing more than a means to an end. You've been used."

Conway thought of the CD waiting for him at the bank. Then he thought of the bald man at the Aquarium—the man Angel Eyes had called Gunther—on his knees and clutching his stomach as he whispered his final words: *Bouchard's dirty. He's setting you up. Stay away from him and his partner, Cole. You can't trust them.* This was the same man who had called 911 and reported John Riley's murder.

"I don't know what you're talking about," Conway said.

"Burying your head in the sand will not make the truth go away."

"Dixon has nothing to do with this."

"You're right. He's an innocent victim."

So casual in the way he said it, it took Conway aback. "Release Dixon and I'll give you the decryption code," he said.

"So you do know the code."

Conway saw Randy speaking the decryption code in the dream and knew it was true. "Once I know Dixon is safe, I'll deliver you the code," he said.

"Poor, poor, Stephen. The vultures are circling, and all you want to do is cover your eyes."

Conway had a feeling of sinking in quicksand, of losing ground in the conversation. "Don't play innocent. You killed Alan Matthews."

"Yes."

That took Conway aback.

"Alan Matthews was a budding pedophile. It was only much later, after I had already gone into business with him, that we found pictures of nude little boys in a lock box inside his condo. That's why he couldn't get it up for the girls—or for the guys. Alan's true desires rested in smooth, hairless skin. Money can buy almost anything, Stephen. Especially secrecy."

"So you admit to killing him."

"I wasn't going to finance his prepubescent cravings. And Matthews was greedy. But his greed didn't hold a candle to the people who own your soul."

"That didn't give you the right to kill him."

"And what gave you the right to permanently disfigure Todd Merrill's face?"

"What about Jonathan King? What you did to him was—"

"I didn't do anything to him, Stephen. I've never even met the man. If you want to know the truth, turn your attention to the animals lurking in your backyard."

"And the others? What happened to them?"

"They're all safe."

"I don't believe you."

"Would you like to talk with them?"

"You know where they are?"

"Of course. They work for me now."

Conway's head echoed with competing voices.

"Let me tell you something about yourself, Stephen. What keeps you awake at night is your desperate need to have the world exist in black and white. Right and wrong, good and bad, all if it neatly labeled and stored away in your safe mental storage jars. Such thinking is admirable given your background. But this sanitized version of the world doesn't exist, Stephen. Life breathes in shades of gray. Holding on to such secular belief structures in your current profession is not only foolish, it's dangerous."

Conway's throat felt dry, his heart tripping inside his chest with anticipation of a possible knowledge he didn't want to accept. For a moment, he couldn't speak.

"I can give you the life you crave, Stephen. I can help fill those missing pockets because once they were missing in me too, Stephen." A pause, then his voice was lower, as if whispering a secret. "I can show you worlds you couldn't possibly imagine."

"Your friend, Gunther, I know he called 911," Conway said. "I've listened to the tape and I recognized his voice. Tell me what you saw."

"Prometheus confined all of man's evils inside a box. Pandora opened the box and unleashed all the evils back into the world. So it will be with you. Revelations are at hand, Stephen. Be prepared to have your foundation shaken to its core."

Conway could feel a cold sweat break across his skin.

"One last thing, Stephen. Your mother's among the living. Her first name is Claire," Angel Eyes said and hung up.

Conway tossed the phone onto the bed. Sleep was gone. His mind was too charged up, too busy searching for answers inside an endless loop that he could never seem to shut off. He leaned one arm against the cool window and looked at the city, his old home, swirling with snow and memories, the raw wind outside howling against the building.

Bouchard's dirty. He's setting you up. Stay away from him and his partner, Cole. You can't trust them.

I haven't lied to you, Stephen, and I never will. I despise it.

Revelations are at hand, Stephen. Be prepared to have your foundation shaken to its core.

What if Angel Eyes was telling the truth?

Conway wanted to talk with Pasha. He would have to figure out a way to do it without tipping off . . .

Go ahead and say it, Stephen. Figure out a way to do it without tipping off Raymond or Cole.

Conway's throat ached. He wanted something cold to drink. He opened the bedroom door, about to step out and navigate his way through the semidarkness to the kitchen, when he heard Booker's wife, Camille.

"Dammit, Book, I want to talk about this. Now."

Camille was talking in a hushed but urgent tone. Conway turned and looked down the long hallway. Their bedroom door was cracked open, but the lights were off, the bedroom dark. Booker said something that Conway couldn't hear.

"How the hell do you expect me to sleep?" Camille said, angry. "Every time I shut my eyes all I can see are my babies—*our* babies—being blown apart and you want me to sleep? What's wrong with you?"

"I told you, it's hype," Booker said, louder now.

"*Hype?* When someone says they're going to shoot your kids, it's not hype, it's a goddamn *threat.*" Camille's voice broke. She choked back tears.

"You're letting these people get to you," Booker said. "I'll talk with Steve tomorrow."

Conway, a sick feeling in his stomach, stepped out into the hallway so he could better hear the conversation.

Camille said, "And what are we supposed to do? Stay inside the house all day and wait?"

"You can't do that for one day?"

"I want Steve out of here."

"And leave him hanging in the wind? That's what you're asking."

"Baby, I love Steve, but this, this is just too dangerous. Whatever he's mixed up in, we've got nothing to do with it. I'm not going to put our kids' lives on the line—I already did that once with John Riley and I'm not—"

"Camille—"

"Don't. You weren't there. I came home and there he was passed out on the couch from drugs while Trey and Troy are sitting on the floor screaming because they're hungry and wet." Camille was crying now. "Why do you do this? Why do you have to put everything you love on the line? And for what? All those times we caught John Riley getting high, we opened our doors and our hearts for him and what does he do? Keeps getting high on coke, keeps getting shit-faced until he almost gets himself killed and who comes in and cleans up the mess? Who picks up the tab for his detox center and pays for the funeral?"

Booker was quiet.

"This is *my* family. *Our* family, Book. I'm not putting them in danger. This isn't just about you. I have a vote in this too."

Another period of silence followed. All Conway could hear was the beating of his heart.

"You got anything to say?" Camille asked.

"Your brother Michael."

"Don't go there," she replied, defensive.

"I gave him a job with a good salary. I educated him about the business, I even helped pay for his college education." Booker's deep voice was so calm you couldn't tell if he was mad or upset or excited. He just kept on talking in that cool tone. "And how did your brother repay me? By skimming money from my company for months and racking up credit card debts in my name to the tune of thirty gees because he's in big with gambling, he's got a major league problem no one knew about."

"Baby—"

"And when it all hit the fan and your parents were here crying 'cause they didn't want him to go to jail or to get his legs broken by the dudes coming to collect the vig, guys who threatened to shut off his light permanently, who bailed him out, Camille?"

"That's different. Michael's family. You stick together with family."

"Right. So why you asking me to throw Steve to the wolves?"

Booker's condo was on the corner of Anderson Street in Beacon Hill, the penthouse suite, a sprawling maze of two floors made of hardwood, three fireplaces, a state-of-the-art alarm and surround-sound speaker system, and floor-to-ceiling windows that offered sweeping, panoramic views of downtown Boston. Booker's wife, Camille, was busy cooking egg-white omelets in a contemporary kitchen of black granite the size of a small apartment. Booker sat at the head of the breakfast table, drinking coffee as he stared down at the front page of the *Boston Globe*. It was just after 6:00 A.M. and the air inside the condo was warm and pleasant with the scents of coffee and toast and eggs, the window behind Booker full of the bright hard blue sky of a picture-perfect November morning.

Conway drank his coffee, his eyes shifting over to the front page of the *Globe*. AQUARIUM NIGHTMARE was splashed across the front page in bold letters and underneath the title, three fuzzy color photos of an "unknown" man being spit out of the tank. Conway stared at the pictures of himself, his face averted from the camera, and rubbed his palm and fingers over the spiked ends of his freshly cut hair.

"What do you make of that?" Booker asked, his expression and tone, as always, unreadable.

"Pretty wild. What are they saying on the news?"

"You didn't catch it?"

"I was out most of the day."

"Yeah, that beauty parlor stuff takes up a lot of time." Booker grinned, his eyes moving away from the paper to Conway's new haircut and his unshaven face. "You starting to get that city look. Going out and hitting the clubs. You planning on sticking around?"

"I figured I'd go with you to work today, see if I can figure out where you landed the gelt for such a place like this."

"Only way a brother can do it: hard work."

Camille walked out from behind the island counter and moved into the kitchen carrying two plates stacked with omelets and wheat toast. She was tall for a woman, almost five-ten, her body long and slender under the jeans and red cardigan sweater. Her hair was tied up in a bun, her face free of makeup and still radiating that tough but youthful look of the nineteen-year-old business major from UNH who had fought her way through college and life with a blend of natural intelligence and street smarts. Camille was gentle and loved to laugh, but she also was outspoken and rarely held her feelings back; you always knew where you stood with her at any given moment. Conway had known her since college and knew that right now she was biting down hard on subject matter that had, for the time being, divided the air between her and her husband.

Conway hated the uneasy silence; it reminded him of foster homes. The eternal stranger with the unknown history, the one always stared at and studied like a zoo specimen. When Camille placed the plate of food in front of him, he said, "Thanks again for letting me stay with you, Camille."

"You're welcome, Steve." But the words were forced and so was the smile. She placed a steaming plate of food down in front of Booker, her body rigid, and walked back into the kitchen where she picked up the orange halves and started making freshly squeezed juice.

"This is quite the pad," Conway said, wanting to take off the edge. "When am I going to see this place on *Cribs*?"

"On what?" Booker said.

"*MTV Cribs*." Conway looked at the massive living room with its big-screen TV. Color security cameras were mounted above the screen. "That where you and the soldiers kick back and watch *Scarface*?"

"I get it. Us black folks get our homes featured on *MTV Cribs* while the old and crusted cracker types get *Architectural Digest*."

"You tell Steve about the phone call?" Camille asked.

Book didn't look at her. "I was getting to it," he said. "A woman called for you yesterday. She asked if you were staying here, Camille said yes, and then the woman said she would call back and hung up."

"She didn't leave a phone number?"

"She said you would how to get in contact with her. Said she had some good news for you."

Conway nodded and ate a piece of toast. *Had to be Pasha.* He glanced at his gym bag in the living room. The mikes in his watch, Palm, and cell phone were stuffed deep in his bag, so Cole and Raymond couldn't listen to this conversation.

"Who's the girl?" Booker asked, his eyes even.

"Must be someone from work checking in on me. I left this number."

"And here I was, hoping you had a steady. How long you out here for?"

"A couple of weeks. More if I need it. You got time to show me around the company this morning?"

"Only if you're serious about keeping your ass here."

"It's a possibility," Conway said.

"Book's been asking you for years to come work for him," Camille said. She had stopped squeezing the oranges. The red-colored fingernails of her right hand danced across the lever of the juicer. "Why the sudden interest now?" she asked.

"Life is short," Conway said. "I'd like to explore my options."

"You're right, Steve. Life is very short. It's a very precious thing that should never be taken for granted," Camille said, her eyes locked on her husband the entire time.

Booker's company was located on the twenty-first floor of 100 Summer Street in Downtown Crossing— less than a fifteen-minute walk from his Beacon Hill condo. Conway followed Book through the narrow maze of one-way streets shaded by the tall, red brick-faced apartments, condos, and townhouses. The first snowstorm of the season had left a little over two inches of snow. Thirtysomethings were out walking their dogs or strolling their kids bundled in coats and hats and mittens; others were brushing off their cars or on their way to work, well-dressed city professionals in a race to get downtown, everyone's face red, their breaths puffing in the cold, sharp morning air.

Book lumbered with his hands in his pockets and chewed his gum with methodical care. He said nothing, his eyes covered behind his black-lens sunglasses. They crossed the street and walked down the steps, and entered Boston Common. The wind picked up again and rattled the branches of the balding trees.

"Late yesterday afternoon, Camille took Troy and Trey to the Public Garden and her cell phone rang," Booker said. They were walking through the park now, heading toward Tremont. "Some dude gets on and says, 'I've got Troy locked in my crosshairs right now. You tell Conway to deliver the decryption code by tomorrow or I'll blow one through the head of your little boy.'"

"Those were the exact words?" Conway asked. He felt pins and needles dance across his scalp and race down his spine. He looked around. No people close by.

"I asked Camille for the exact words. That's what she told me."

Angel Eyes wouldn't speak like that. The words didn't match the polished man Conway had talked with on the phone last night.

It's got to be Cole.

A moment later, they crossed the always busy Tremont Street and walked down Winter Street, a small, red-brick-lined alley that led straight into the heart of Downtown Crossing. Set up on the corner of Filene's department store was a grocer with a green apron selling fresh fruits and vegetables and fresh-cut flowers out of pots. Crowds of people poured out of the T's orange line stop and marched down Summer Street's cobblestone walk toward work.

Any one of these people could be part of Angel Eyes's group—or Cole's. Conway had left his stuff in Booker's condo, but that didn't mean someone close by couldn't pick up on his conversation.

Booker's in danger. You've got to tell him the truth.

But not here. Cole's men could be lurking close by with surveillance gear. It was easy to do.

A Starbucks was on his right. Conway had an idea.

"Let's grab some coffee," Conway said.

"I got coffee at the office."

"But not those fancy croissants you love." Conway opened the door and with a jerk of his head motioned for Booker to join him.

The walls of the Starbucks coffeehouse were painted in shades of yellow and gold; the place buzzed with activity and energized jazz music, the warm, rich air packed with the soothing aroma of fresh coffee and perfume from the well-dressed, good-looking women who crowded the counters as they waited for their venti-size lattes and cappuccinos. A few minutes passed, and a tired kid with blond hair and a pierced nose yelled out, "Next."

Conway ordered a large coffee and two croissants and handed the kid his Visa card. When the kid handed Conway the receipt to sign, Conway signed one copy and on the back of the other wrote a note: *We're being followed and watched. Will explain everything but need a room where we can talk without fear of electromagnetic eavesdropping.*

Conway held out the receipt so Booker could read the writing and said, "Hold this for me, will you? I've got my hands full."

Conway grabbed the plastic bag and his coffee and headed out the door.

Booker's office was long and wide and had the mark of a professional interior decorator. A mahogany bookcase lined the far east wall, the shelves filled with framed pictures of Booker with his family and friends and various A-list actors and several high-profile Boston politicians. No overhead lights, just desk lamps that, along with Miles Davis playing low over the ceiling-mounted speakers, gave the room a warm, inviting feel.

His secretary, a bubbly, beautiful redhead named Robin Tigges, came inside the office holding a silver tray with milk, sugar, and plates for the croissants. She was dressed in a gray power suit and wore a gold watch and tasteful gold loop earrings. She placed the tray on the small table next to Conway's chair and then left the office, shutting the door behind her.

Booker sat behind a mahogany desk that was the size of a moat. A small, white circular device the size of a fire alarm was on his desk. He pressed a button and the light on the device turned green.

"It's safe to talk, even if you're wired," Booker said, his tone all business. "You wired now?"

"Not anymore."

"Where is it?"

"The items are stored inside a freezer bag inside my gym bag at your condo."

Conway sat in one of the two oversize leather chairs backed up against the wall. Behind Booker were windows partially overwhelmed by the view of a drab, gray-concrete skyscraper. As Conway stared at the world outside, he replayed the events from Austin, John Riley's death, and meeting Angel Eyes—all of it so overwhelming, avalanches threatening to topple. *Where to begin?*

"Why you wired?" Booker said.

Conway looked back at Booker, who chewed his gum, waiting for an answer. *The man sitting across from you is the last remaining member of your family,* a voice said. *His wife and his kids have been targeted. No more secrets, Steve. You owe it to Booker, and you owe it to Riley. Fuck protocol and get it all out in the open. Now.*

"I can't help you unless you talk," Booker said.

"I work for the CIA."

Booker stopped chewing his gum. The skin stretched tight across his face. His eyes were motionless. It was the first time Conway had seen his friend surprised. Booker leaned forward in his chair and spread his arms across his desk.

"You telling me you're a spook?"

"It's a unit called IWAC," Conway said. "Information Warfare Analysis Center. We deal with technology proliferation. We're after a guy known only as Angel Eyes. He's been stealing high-tech, cutting-edge military weapons—stuff that could destroy a nation if it got in the wrong hands."

"I got ex-CIA guys here. Never heard of IWAC."

"That's because it doesn't exist."

"Black op?"

"Something like that. We're not on the radar screen."

"Explains why you moved around so much, why you

couldn't stick around here. Got to keep the secrecy thing going."

"In part."

"Yeah, the other part is you enjoy playing the emotional nomad. Don't like to let anyone in. CIA loves guys like you. No family, no kids or connections, you get wiped off the planet nobody going to start asking the wrong questions."

"I met Renée Kaufmann yesterday."

Booker leaned back in his chair. "Goddamn, you're full of surprises this morning. And it's only nine."

"She left a note for me at the funeral home. She asked me to meet her yesterday. Alone. At the Aquarium."

"Let me guess. That picture of the guy in the tank on the newspaper and on the news, that was you."

Conway nodded.

"Who blew the hole in the tank?" Booker asked.

"Pasha Romanov, an IWAC member who is supposed to be dead."

"And the shark food?"

"A Russian mobster named Misha. He was looking for the decryption code for a high-tech military suit that uses a technology called optical camouflage. The company in Austin—Praxis—they were developing this technology along with the army. The operation went south. I was inside the lab when it went down."

The guilt that had been festering inside his chest rose again, swelling, like a tidal wave about to come crashing down, overwhelming in its intensity. He tried to push it back and a voice said, *Get it all out in the open.* He looked back up at Booker. "I thought I hit the speed dial to call for our backup team. I accidentally called John Riley."

Booker stared back for a moment, unblinking, and then slowly turned and faced the window. Outside, a plane climbed high into the blue sky. On the opposite building, the sun reflected like balls of white fire in the dozens of windows. Several minutes passed. The Miles Davis song ended and the CD player shifted to another compact disc, some classical thing.

"Renée didn't want to put you or your family in danger, that's why she wanted to meet alone with me," Conway said. "The people who killed Riley, Renée saw the entire thing. My name was mentioned. I was the next target. That's why she wanted to meet me. They think I know the code."

"Do you?"

"I think so."

"So now they see you hanging around me and my family, and they're going to come after us. Use us as a bargaining tool to get the code from you."

"That's the way it looks."

"Where's Renée now?"

"I have no idea," Conway said, and felt suffused with guilt again, as if he had willingly led her into the slaughter. It wasn't supposed to go down like this.

She could be alive. She'd make a powerful bargaining chip.

Conway took in a deep breath and then said, "She saw the entire thing, Book. And she recorded it."

Booker turned around.

"Video-conferencing software," Conway said. "She burned it onto a CD. It's stored in a safety deposit box. At the Eastern Bank on Broadway in Lynn."

"So why didn't you drive there and get it? You got CIA backing you up, why you here telling me all this?"

"The people who killed Riley . . ." Conway's face clouded. He leaned forward and propped his elbows on his knees and stared at the floor. "I think these people are on my side of the fence."

"You know this for a fact?"

"Yesterday, at the Aquarium, one of Angel Eyes's men saved my life and then warned me about my boss."

"Angel Eyes," Book said. "That's the dude from Texas who blew up the airport parking lot."

Conway nodded, rubbed his palms together. He told Book the rest of what had happened in Austin. When he was done, Conway said, "All this time, I've been told that Angel Eyes killed Riley out of revenge, to bring me here to Boston."

"Because Angel Eyes wants the decryption code."

Conway nodded. "Before I met with Renée, I was supposed to meet with my handler. Only it was Angel Eyes. Right there he had the opportunity to create some clever lie and take me in. But he didn't. He let me go so I could rescue Renée."

"And you believe, what, he's on your side?"

"I don't know what to believe anymore."

"One thing I do know. A contact I got in the department, I bumped into him last night. The cops who were shot at the Aquarium weren't real cops. They're Russian gangsters."

"I want to get inside that safety deposit box. Can you get me an ID with Riley's name on it?"

"I can have that made within an hour. Now we need to make arrangements."

"*We* don't need to do anything. This is my mess. I'll clean it up."

"With what? You just said your boys are dirty."

"I don't know that for sure."

"But you will when you see the CD. You expect me to sit here and leave you to fend for yourself? Not my style, hoss."

"These guys are pros. They wipe people off the

board without getting their hands dirty. Go home and be with Camille and—"

"Camille and the boys are going to stay home. They're covered, and they're safe." Booker picked up the phone and hit an extension. "Bobby? Gather up the boys and meet me in my office." Then Book hung up the phone and looked at Conway from across the desk, his eyes veiled.

"All this time, you've been a spook." Book grinned, flashed his white teeth. "Never would have guessed that one."

I have a feeling my employment days are numbered, Conway said to himself. "I need a phone, preferably one with one-twenty-eight-bit encryption," he said.

"I got access to stuff the NSA boys can't crack. Who you need to call?"

"Pasha."

"That your spook girlfriend? The one who called the house?"

"Yeah."

Booker stared at him, preparing a question.

"I trust her," Conway said.

"How much?"

"As much as I trust you."

Booker nodded, blew out a bubble and then popped it. "You CIA guys love to give code names to operations, right?"

"Yeah."

"We'll call this one Operation Oreo. Soft white center protected by hard black shells. Don't worry, Steve, the guys after you, they ain't going to be pissing in the playground much longer."

71

Jonathan Cole sat in a swivel chair in the back of a bulky Channel 5 Action News van that was parked near the State House. He drank a cup of green tea with skim milk—serenity tea, the woman at Starbucks had called it—and over the steam watched as Owen Lee sat hunched over the controls of the surveillance equipment. Owen had the ear pad of a headphone set against the side of his head. Lee's partner, Mark Alves, also known as the Elf, sat behind the wheel.

Lee tossed the headphones onto the console and pivoted around in his swivel chair. He wore jeans, Timberland boots, and a red bandana. When he removed the Blow-Pop from his mouth, his lips made a wet, smacking sound. A gold loop dangled from each ear.

"I still can't hear a goddamn thing," Lee said.

"Then move your men closer," Cole said. They had men with surveillance equipment shadowing Conway.

"I can't without spooking Conway. The dude's a pro. Why the fuck would he remove all of his gear? I can't hear anything off the bugs."

Because I called and threatened to kill his friend's kids— that's why. Cole placed the call late yesterday afternoon. He wanted to throw Conway's balance off, overload his brain with concern for the safety of his friend's family.

By the end of this evening, Cole would have Conway *and* the cloaking suit.

"I say we bring him in now," Lee said. "Make him spill what he knows."

"He won't talk."

"What did you manage to get out of the girl? You were down there for a long time."

"Renée told me she witnessed everything and burned it onto a CD."

Lee swallowed and licked his lips. He looked pale. The Elf turned around in the driver's seat. Cole drank his tea, waited, enjoying this.

"A CD," Lee said.

"Yes."

"Where is it?" Lee asked.

"She wouldn't say." Which was true. The woman's heart gave out from terror or blood loss, Cole wasn't sure, but she stopped talking and faded away before giving up the location of the CD.

But he *was* sure that Steve Conway knew about the CD and its location, and that Conway was going to use his friend to help him retrieve it. If Cole could get his hands on the CD, he would trade it for the cloaking suit. That morning inside the bathroom, he knew that Raymond had no intention of handing it over. Cole always suspected Raymond wanted him out of the way. The woman's story now confirmed it.

"She say anything else?" Lee asked.

She also tipped me off on what you and Raymond have planned for me. I'm going to love watching you scream, Owen.

Cole said, "Did you bug Mr. Booker's office?"

"No."

"Why not?"

"Can't get inside there without tripping the alarms. I tried, believe me. Look, I think Conway's onto us. We should bring him in, right now."

"Stephen doesn't trust anyone and doesn't want to talk. Everyone around him is lying and scheming. Frankly, I can't blame him for being secretive."

"That what he told you during your private ride yesterday?"

"Something like that."

"Yesterday at the Aquarium, the broad must have told Conway something. He's got to know about the CD."

"We'll follow Stephen and see what the day brings us. Are you feeling okay, Owen? You're sweating."

"I don't like having this psycho Angel Eyes in the picture."

"I thought it might have had something to do with hosing down the basement."

Lee wiped his brow against the sleeve of his sweatshirt. "I just want to put this gig behind me. Take some time off."

"Patience, Owen. Everyone's going to get exactly what they deserve."

72

Booker pulled his black Lincoln Navigator against the curb, right in front of the Eastern Bank on Broadway in Lynn, a half-hour ride north of Boston. It was just after three-thirty in the afternoon, and as always during this time of the year in New England, the light in the sky was performing its quick fade. In less than an hour, the world would turn pitch black. Conway watched the people, tough lower-middle-class types, walk in and out of the bank.

"Lynn, Lynn, the city of sin," Booker said. "You ever spend any time here?"

Conway thought about his Palm Pilot and watch. He told Booker about how each item worked, and after much discussion, Conway went back to the condo to retrieve the gear from his gym bag. He hoped Cole and his men were tracking him right now. It was the only way the plan would work. So he kept talking.

"I had a short stay in a foster home right across the street, up on that hill. Boynton Street," Conway said. Through the bank's glass doors he could see the small line of people huddled between the red ropes as they waited for the next teller. Inside the bank, he spotted two of Booker's men, black guys dressed in identical sharp blue suits, black overcoats, and black shoes, both of them carrying burgundy-colored leather briefcases.

Conway was dressed in the same suit and carried an identical briefcase. Booker's men stood against the wall near the chairs where people were seated as they waited to talk to a bank representative. Beyond the desks was the entrance to the safety-deposit boxes.

Conway shifted his attention and looked back out the front window. One van, black, was parked across the street in front of the small, modest, ramshackle homes. Was Cole in there? Or Angel Eyes.

I won't let them hurt you, Stephen, Angel Eyes had said. *I'll protect you. I give you my word.*

The world was darkening and Angel Eyes was somewhere out there, hiding. Planning.

"You nervous?" Booker asked. He knew this conversation was being monitored.

"Angel Eyes is here. The second I step back out of the bank I'm a target."

"We went over this."

"I know."

Conway turned to Booker, who leaned against the driver's-side window and chewed his gum, his eyes serene, as if he had kicked back in a beach chair and was now looking out at the calm water lapping under a magnificent sunset. The SUV's windows contained a transparent layer of armor made up of resilient polycarbonate, similar to that used in military jet canopies.

The Lincoln Navigator was an armored vehicle with a level-five rating, its shell strong enough to withstand a shot from a high-powered military rifle. The entire SUV, in fact, came with an exhaustive list of features: concealed gunports that allowed a passenger to safely return fire from within the vehicle; an encrypted satellite-communications system; hands-free night-vision goggles to allow the driver to turn off the headlights and drive in the dark; a kidnap recovery system; and a host of countersurveillance measures to protect the occupants. Booker had used the armored SUV for the company's bodyguard work, mainly high-profile celebrities and government officials who needed to feel reassured by the extra protection in a vehicle that by all rights belonged in a James Bond movie. The same company who had provided the armored SUVs to Booker's company had worked on vehicles for the president and a number of prominent senators and businessmen.

"Want to run through the game plan one more time?" Booker asked.

Conway shook his head. He reached down and picked up his briefcase.

"I'll call you when I'm ready," he said, and opened the door and stepped out into the raw November air that whipped around him.

Cole was on the encrypted phone, speaking to the van across the street: "Stephen is to be picked up when he steps out of the bank," Cole said. "He isn't to be harmed. When you have him, bring him to me."

Cole hung up. He sat in his swivel chair in the warm, growing darkness inside the back of the van, which was parked in a diner lot at the end of the block, less than 100 feet away from the bank.

The driver's door opened and in came the Elf holding two white paper bags—take-out food from the diner. He handed one to Lee and then turned around and settled behind the wheel. Lee sat the bag up on the console and took out the cup of coffee. On the color monitor, the black Lincoln Navigator slid away from the curb. Outside the front window, Lee could see the other van parked across the street, the one with the sniper.

Lee flipped back the lid on the coffee and listened over his headphones. If Conway played the CD in the bank, Lee would be able to hear the recorded conversation between him and Raymond over the bug in Conway's watch. It was all there—including Raymond's order to take Cole off the playing board.

Lee moved one of the headphone's pads off his ear and said, "We should pick Conway up. Now."

"We will. When he leaves the bank," Cole said.

"Why not get him in the room?"

"The bank is monitored by security cameras. Plus, it's a confined space. We have no way of controlling what might go down in there, but when Conway steps outside, he's ours."

Lee shook his head.

"Problem, Owen?"

"This reminds me of the Mosier gig. I told you the guy was suicidal. I told you to pick him up before he met our operative and what happened? Mosier shoots the guy in the back of the head and then decides to dine on a bullet himself. A year's worth of work got flushed."

"Your voice is off, Owen. This isn't like you."

"We couldn't hear what Conway and his crew were planning at the office, and now suddenly we can hear everything? Plus, we got this psycho Angel Eyes to deal with. What if he's inside the bank right now and makes a run on Conway while we're sitting out here waiting?"

Cole didn't respond.

Lee gulped about a quarter of his coffee, set it down on the console, and then grabbed his black North Face jacket from the floor and put it on over his sweatshirt. He said, "Last night you carved that broad into dozens of pieces. She wasn't a threat at all, but this guy Angel Eyes, he's a major threat to the success of this operation and you won't take it seriously. He knows we're here. That's why we should go inside the bank—*now*."

"Don't you wish you could be inside there with Stephen," Cole said. "To watch his face when he discovers his boss injecting rat poison into his friend's neck. Talk about a Kodak moment. The bug in Stephen's watch—I want to listen. Play it over the speakers. I want to hear *everything*."

Lee turned around, faced the monitor, and grabbed his coffee from the console. As he drank it, his left hand slid inside his jacket. He could feel the .38 in the hidden pocket. No way was Cole going to hear what happened in Riley's condo. Lee undid the snap and got himself ready.

An attractive young woman with blond hair pulled back into a bun ushered Conway into a private room so he could view the contents of the safety deposit box. Typical bank décor: silk potted plant in the corner, a cheap framed watercolor painting of flowers hanging on the drab cream-colored wall, and a table made of pressed wood complete with one of those plastic, hard-back chairs.

Conway placed the steel-gray safety-deposit box on the table and smiled at the woman as she shut the door. Then he locked it and got to work.

Booker's laptop was in the briefcase. Conway parked the briefcase on top of the table and then removed the small Sony laptop and a pair of Sony Walkman headphones. He didn't want Cole or his men overhearing this just yet. Conway placed the laptop on the desk, flipped opened the screen and powered it on. While the laptop booted up, he flipped open the safety deposit box lid and inside saw the CD locked in a clear jewel case.

John Riley's final conversation with Renée Kaufmann, his final moment of life—his murderer— every question Conway needed answered was stored on this shiny silver platter, waiting to be unlocked.

Pandora opened the box and unleashed all the evils back

into the world, Angel Eyes had said. *So it will be with you. Revelations are at hand, Stephen. Be prepared to have your foundation shaken to its core.*

His chest felt tight. Different images and imaginary scenarios swirled around in his head.

The laptop was ready now. Waiting.

Are you sure you're ready to confront this?

A press of the button and the laptop's CD tray slid open. Conway removed the CD from the jewel case, placed it on the tray, and then slid the tray shut. A whirl as the computer came to life, the laser reading contents stored on the CD. Conway sat down in the chair and moved his body close to the desk. His face hovered just inches from the laptop's small screen.

The Windows Media Player program opened up and there, alive on the tiny window, was Riley's crooked Irish nose and smile as he looked directly at a Web camera mounted on top of his monitor. The picture quality was so real, so lifelike on the active matrix screen, it was as if his friend were merely standing behind a window.

Conway slipped the headphones over his ears. Riley talked about video conferencing software and Renée gave an update on Amsterdam—a doorbell rang. Riley stood up and walked to the door, oblivious to the fact that he was about to invite his killer inside. Out of the camera's frame, a door opened. Muted conversation, too far away to be heard.

Here it comes.

Lines of static flashed across the screen.

Had to be a jamming unit.

The white lines grew and the picture started to blur, the words garbled. Conway couldn't make out Riley's face or the face of the man he had let inside.

Shit. Slowly, Conway fast-forwarded through the static.

The man in the chair stood up. Conway hit the PLAY button. The static was still there, the words inaudible, but through the static he could make out the blurred figure of John Riley sitting on the couch.

The screen was swimming with static now. Conway couldn't see a thing.

Revelations are at hand, Stephen.

Then the static was gone. Conway looked at the man standing over John Riley's body and felt a sharp, cold chill explode at the base of his spine and burst across his face so fast that his skin tingled.

On the screen Raymond Bouchard held a jamming unit in his hand. Inside the condo with him was the man who had posed as skydiving instructor Chris Evans. Conway listened as Bouchard instructed the man called Owen Lee to plant the drugs around the condo. Listened as Bouchard and Owen Lee talked about Misha.

The Austin operation was a lie. Staged.

Angel Eyes's involvement: a lie.

Everything over the past three years, all that work—all of it was one big fucking lie. Raymond Bouchard had staged an operation and massacred his own people so he could own the military suit and its cloaking technology.

Pasha, what she said . . . she had been right all along.

For a moment Conway felt numb and useless as his heart struggled to fight off an awful and now undeniable truth.

The phone in his briefcase rang.

His hands shaking, Conway took off his headphones and then reached inside the briefcase and removed the new phone that Jonathan Cole had given him. Conway pressed the phone against his ear, knowing that Cole would be listening.

"You ready?" Booker asked.

"Yeah." Conway's voice was dry and tight.

"Exit by the back door like we talked about. See you in ten," Booker said, sticking to the script. A click and he was gone.

Conway placed the phone on the desk. On the screen Bouchard explained how they would use Jonathan Cole to get Renée Kaufmann.

Lies. All of it *lies*.

Bouchard calmly walked out of the condo, back out into the clean air—back out into his life.

You lying son of a bitch.

If Conway brought this evidence to the CIA, they would try to sweep it under the rug, keep it nice and quiet. Had to protect the Agency. Conway wanted Raymond Bouchard to go down in flames—in front of the world. He wasn't about to give him an opportunity to hide.

You're right, of course. But you know being right and having the truth on your side doesn't change political agendas. You carry out your plan, your CIA career will be over.

On screen Conway saw Owen Lee and a short, dark man Lee called the Elf plant the drugs around Riley's apartment and talk about where to place the surveillance gear. He slammed the laptop shut, ripped off his earphones, and shoved it inside the briefcase. He had to leave his watch on. He wanted Cole and his men to be able to track him.

Inside the briefcase was a rubber Halloween mask. Conway removed it and looked at the stark white face and red hair—the mask of serial killer Michael Myers from the *Halloween* horror movies. Conway fitted the mask over his head and then put on his black leather gloves to hide the skin color of his hands. He knew Cole had men waiting outside, maybe even inside the bank, ready to pick him up. Hopefully, the mask and the elaborate setup to follow would confuse Cole just enough to allow Conway to pass off the briefcase with the evidence.

Conway's phone rang again. He hit the button and pressed the phone against his rubber ear.

"Don't be afraid, Stephen," Angel Eyes said. "I'll protect you. I give you my word. We'll travel this road together."

Conway hung up and shoved the phone inside his pocket. Then he locked the briefcase and moved behind the door, his hand on the doorknob, ready. His equilibrium seemed off. He felt like a man who had staggered away from a terrible accident. He sucked in air. He could smell his stale, sour breath along with the rubbery stench of the mask.

The fire alarm sounded. Conway opened the door and ran, navigating his way through the short maze, and then headed into the lobby. Four of Booker's men were dressed identically, all of them wearing the same masks and holding the same briefcases, people already on the floor, cowering, thinking it was a robbery. Booker's men fell into line with Conway. He exchanged briefcases with one of them and then they all raced for the front door.

Owen Lee couldn't believe his fucking luck. Man. He expected to hear the CD play over the speakers inside the van—Cole had leaned forward in his chair, waiting, and Lee's hand gripped the revolver inside his jacket.

But no sound ever came. Conway must have plugged headphones into the laptop. They could hear the dude breathing heavy, then heard the phone ring twice and listened as he talked to Booker and then to that spooky motherfucker Angel Eyes.

Cole was only a couple of feet away. Lee thought, *Kill him now.*

And he would have if it weren't for the fire alarm. He could hear the goddamn drilling sound here in the van, a block away.

Cole, calm and in control—cocky was what it was— on the headset to the men: "Stephen's going to exit the back. Be ready."

Lee's attention shifted to the monitor showing the back door—wait, what the fuck was this: on monitor four, here came Conway bursting through the *front* entrance, the area lit up by the bank's outside door lights. The glass door burst wide open and oh shit, here came four—no *five*, guys, all of them running. They were all dressed in long black jackets and held brief-cases and—what the *fuck*, all of their faces were covered by masks with creepy orange hair that stuck straight up.

"What the hell is this shit?" Owen said.

"He's trying to confuse us. Lock onto his transmitters."

Lee worked the console, his heart beating against his ribs. It didn't feel right. And why was he sweating so much? He had done this shit hundreds of times and never had he sweated like this.

Cole had moved directly behind him. *Shoot him now.* No. Got to deal with Conway first.

New action on monitor two, a live shot from the van across the street: five black Lincoln Navigators had pulled up against the curb. The people about to enter the bank had thrown themselves against the snow-covered ground and lawn, their shaking hands covering their heads. Conway and his boys were at the SUVs.

"I've got all of Conway's transmitters locked: He's the middle guy, right here," Lee said and tapped a finger against at the screen. "What do you want to do?"

Cole spoke into the headset to the sniper: "Take them down."

Conway was inside. The SUV, its engine throbbing beneath him, hadn't moved away yet. The first vehicle pulled away. Through the eye slits in the mask Conway saw Booker, his face calm as he gripped the steering wheel, ready to move.

Something slammed into the back window. A spider web of cracks bled off from the center hole, the round deflected by the SUV's bulletproof glass. More rounds deflected off the glass of the surrounding SUVs.

The Navigator peeled away from the curb in a screech of rubber. Another shot hit Booker's window, right where his head was. Book ignored it; he was locked in some other place, concentrating, the same look Pasha had that night in Colorado when a sniper hit the van window, her expression never breaking once as the van fishtailed over a snow-whipped street glowing under a blanket of silver moonlight that rained bullets.

"The Navigators are bulletproof," Owen Lee said. *Steve, you clever motherfucker.*

On the color screen, Owen watched as the pack of SUVs pulled away from the curb. "I still got Conway's vehicle locked," Lee said. He looked up through the van's front window and saw the SUVs race past them. In fact, *everything* was racing. His heart, his vision—man, he was *soaring.* It was like that time down in Tijuana when he was banging this seventeen-year-old whore, snorting coke off of her back, higher than a kite, *sweeeet* Jesus, and just as he was about to come he thought he was going to black out. But this . . . he felt like he was swimming away. It didn't feel right.

"Guys are calling in," Lee said. Now he felt short of breath. "How . . . how you want to play it?"

Cole spoke his orders into the headset. Each unit was to break off and follow one of the Lincoln Navigators. While he spoke, Lee made a clumsy attempt to grab the gun. Cole grabbed him by the throat, pushed him back out of his chair, and pinned Lee against the floor. Cole's free hand pried the .38 away from the jacket.

"You were going to use *this?*" Cole said. "This wouldn't have even put a *dent* in me."

Owen Lee tried to move and couldn't. His eyes were open; he could see but he couldn't blink. Cole moved in closer.

"You're going to be paralyzed for several hours," Cole said. "Your friend the Elf drugged your food and coffee. For me."

What's the first rule in this business, Owen? Trust no one.

Lee wanted to talk, to try to barter for his life with the information he had on Bouchard, but his mouth wouldn't work. Nothing was working, but he could feel *everything:* the grip around his throat and the weight of Cole's body. And to top it off, it was becoming a struggle to breathe. Like he only had half of one lung working. But his mind was fine, nothing hazy there, and the voices screaming inside his head were clear and so loud.

Cole turned Lee onto his side. Out the front window the black sky was peppered with bright stars. It reminded Lee of a time long ago when he was a kid. Cole used flex-cuffs and bound Lee's hands and feet, and then moved his mouth closer to Lee's ear.

"When I'm done with Conway, you and I are going to take a ride up north to a cabin," Cole whispered, his voice breathy. Excited. "The only way you'll be able to scream is in your head. Why don't you start practicing now." Cole sunk his teeth into Lee's ear.

Nothing in his life so far matched the pain he felt as his ear was ripped away from his head. In his mind he screamed for it to stop—could hear himself screaming—and what came next was a memory from his childhood: the time he had stolen the highly prized boombox from his neighbor's back porch. Ten years old and the prize tucked under his arm and he ran like lightning across the dirt backyard in the dead of night with the neighbor's snarling bulldog mutt chasing after him. Lee had climbed the chain link fence and jumped, his right hand stretched out to the side, confident he was in the clear when he ran forward and was jerked back, the spike of pain in his wrist unbearable. He looked back and in the moonlight saw that the fence's barb-shaped tip had penetrated his wrist and had popped through to the other side, ripping through his flesh and muscle when he had tried to run. Blood squirting everywhere, Lee dropped the boom box and screamed and screamed, squares of yellow lights popping up in the windows of the neighborhood, the black sky filled with stars just like tonight, thousands of eyes that stared down on him, not caring.

Mark Alves, the Elf, sat behind the wheel, his eyes riveted on the rearview mirror. He felt his stomach flip and then flip again and then felt the bile shoot up his throat. What was happening in the back . . . he had heard stories about Cole but what Alves was seeing made him want to run out from the van. He had his hand on the door. He squeezed it, about to open it, when the nagging voice called out:

You check the account to see if Cole made the deposit?

Shit, no, he hadn't checked the Cayman Islands account. Four hundred G's . . . that's a lot of cash to give up.

You leave now, you leave without the money. You want to give it up?

No. And the strange thing was, he couldn't take his eyes away from the rearview mirror. Owen Lee lay on the floor, absolutely still, his eyes wide and staring straight at him as if to say *Look what you've done. You've fucked me and good.* Not my problem, dude. I needed the money—you knew that—and you decided to play your cards and I played mine. Shit happens.

Cole, on his knees and hunched forward over Lee's body, suddenly straightened as if startled by a sound.

He turned his head around slowly, the ear still in his mouth. Then the ear dropped.

"Want a taste, Mr. Alves?"

"No," the Elf wheezed. *That could be you*, he thought and almost pissed himself.

"Then *drive*."

Alves peeled out of the parking lot. Stay on Conway and then let the cannibal psycho go after him, get Cole the fuck out of here. Alves would use the computer here in the back, check his account, and if the money was there, transfer it to another account. And after that? Fake his death, run away, do something. Mark Alves never wanted to see Cole again.

Booker headed down Route One South toward Boston. Traffic was light; Booker and the other SUVs cruised up the highway at a steady eight-five. The world outside the windows was full of bright signs for stores and strip malls and gas stations. The SUV was warm, lit up by the dials on the control panel. Miles Davis played over the speakers.

Conway had taken off his mask, but he could still smell the aroma of the sweaty rubber. The fleet of SUVs had split up. When he left the room, he exchanged briefcases with one of Booker's men. Conway kept the watch, Palm, and the phone, knowing that Cole would lock on the transmitters and follow this vehicle. The CD was on its way to Booker's contact at the Channel Five news station in Needham, and with any luck, Cole and his men would be following him.

"My boss, Raymond Bouchard, he killed Riley. I got it all on this CD," Conway said. He stared at the depth sensor in his watch and thought, *I hope you're listening, Raymond*. "You got your FBI contact all lined up?"

"It's all set," Booker said. "He'll meet us with his team. All we have to do is hand him the CD and he'll take it from there."

There was no way Cole would let that happen. He would try to intercept this vehicle and put a stop to it. That's what Conway wanted. Now all they had to do was to get to Roxbury.

The penthouse suite inside the nine-unit condo on Devonshire is less than a two-minute walk from the heart of downtown Boston even under the worst weather conditions. The suite comes with its own private parking garage and a separate elevator which is accessible only by key—a remnant from the previous owner, a basketball player from the glory days of the Boston Celtics who demanded privacy and discretion. The other owners must pass through the front doors and enter the lobby where a security man who doubles as a concierge sits behind a wonderfully crafted desk bathed in soft light.

None of the owners or the security personnel have ever met Simon LeCruix personally—in fact, no one who lives in the building can claim they've met the man. But they *do* know the story of how Mr. LeCruix paid a staggering seven-figure sum to gut the entire suite and rebuild it from scratch, a three-year project that included a changing chamber behind the door, complete with two special HEPA-filtered devices, scrubbing stations and lockers that held boxes of latex gloves, surgical masks and Tyvek sterile garb. No one knew why Mr. LeCruix needed such an area, or why the same group of well-groomed men would periodically visit him.

Inside the suite now, the rooms dark and cold, always cold to keep whatever lingering germs and viruses that might have survived the scrubbing with the Vesphene/Spor-Klenz cleaning solution from incubating. The suite's layout was almost a mirror image of the one in Austin, right down to the choice of furniture and its arrangement.

This strict order was also imposed on the owner's thoughts. For years, the rooms of his mind have been clean and ordered, a majestic, sweeping museum of stored emotions and experiences and adventures that have been neatly labeled and could be, at a moment's notice, examined with total clarity.

Gunther's death had changed that. The once-splendid rooms in Amon Faust's mind, these crafted private sanctuaries that had held glorious memories and tastes and secrets, have been ransacked, their contents destroyed, the glass containers and picture frames and vivid filmstrips of a perfect life now shattered against the floor, burned and defaced.

Faust had spent the better part of the day inside his office, sitting with his back against the wall, his eyes closed, focusing his mental energy on the task of cleaning. Deep, slow breaths kept the volatile mix of rage and regret and loss and grief from consuming him. It was critical to keep his mind clear. It was the only way he could help Stephen through this next maze. Faust couldn't afford another mistake. Another loss.

The phone rang.

He opened his eyes. Outside the pair of sliding glass doors that led out to the patio was a black sky alive with the full moon, its silver light washing over the hardwood floor decorated with dozens of pictures of Gunther taken at various stages of his life. The photographs were arranged in ascending order, a series of molts that charted Gunther's inspiring transformation from a troubled, violent boy to a handsome, intelligent Renaissance man capable of so many wonders. The pictures captured the boy's essence in various phases, and as Faust viewed them, a part of him believed that Gunther was still alive, still a viable presence in his life, and not a carved up piece of meat waiting to be dissected on an autopsy table.

The headset was already in place. Faust hit the TALK button.

"Conway has left the bank."

The voice belonged to Charles Rigby, the chubby, apt pupil who had worked closely with Gunther in Austin. Gunther had believed the man possessed the necessary skills to be not only a leader, but an effective member of Faust's family. Privately, Faust wondered if Gunther's vision was clouded by the fact that up until five years ago Rigby was living on the streets of Los Angeles, forced out of his house because his parents had discovered the true nature of their son's sexual proclivities.

Time to test the young man's abilities.

"Cole and his men took shots at Booker and his crew," Rigby said.

Faust straightened up. "Stephen?"

"Unharmed. Didn't you watch it on your computer screen? I had one of the men transmit the images to your—"

"Where is Stephen now, Mr. Rigby?"

"Traveling down Route One South, headed toward Boston."

"And who do we have following?"

"Two vans, one of them containing Jonathan Cole.

The bugs we planted inside the vans are working. We can hear everything. One new development: our man inside the bank saw Conway exchange briefcases. Conway's still wearing the gear with the transmitters."

Of course he wants Cole and his brood to follow. Stephen's acting as the decoy while the CD moves in another direction. Interesting.

Faust looked down at his hands. Grasped between his long, slender fingers was a head shot of Stephen as he ran across the field. Such determination and raw energy, such intelligence in those eyes. All that potential waiting to be tapped and shaped. *What new secrets will you share with me tonight, Stephen?*

"Conway's setting the stage for something," Rigby said. "What it is we don't know, since Booker's place is sealed tight. It's got all the latest goodies to prevent eavesdropping. I know Gunther wanted to get inside there, but even he said—"

"Stephen is to be protected at all costs."

"I won't let you down."

"See that you don't."

The plan didn't allow for traffic jams. They had made it over the Tobin Bridge without a problem, but when they came out of the tunnel, the traffic was backed up on the expressway, bumper to bumper, because of what looked like a two-car accident up ahead. Conway could see a pulsing storm of blue and white cruiser lights and a parked ambulance grouped near the exit for Storrow Drive. The Lincoln came to a complete stop. Conway shifted in his seat and looked out the windows, scanning the area.

"Relax," Booker said. He blew out a long pink bubble and snapped it. "These guys aren't going to make a move with the cops right up there, not in front of all these witnesses."

"They're desperate. They can't afford to let the CD get out in the open."

"Desperate don't mean foolish. They're smart. They're going to sit back and watch where we're going, then they'll access the situation and make their move when they think no one is looking."

Earlier, using the encrypted phone in Booker's office, Conway had tried to call Pasha. She didn't pick up but he was surprised to hear a prerecorded operator's voice come on and ask to leave a message. Conway did; he left the number to Booker's office and cell phone. Time to try her again.

Booker's phone rang. He removed it from his belt. He listened and stared out the window, his face remote, the SUV inching forward toward the Storrow Drive exit.

"It's for you," Booker said and handed over the phone.

Conway pressed the phone against his ear. Rows of cars lined the Southeast Expressway; hundreds of red brake lights glowed like pairs of eyes under the black sky.

"How are you coping, Stephen?" Angel Eyes asked.

"How did you get this number?"

"I have many friends."

"I'm still having trouble processing your interest in all of this."

"What did Raymond say?"

"I didn't ask him."

"Why not? You seem to take everything the man says at face value."

"I want to hear it from you."

"Like you, my moral fabric is woven in terms of black and white. Right and wrong. What I want, Stephen, is the very same thing you've pledged your life, up until this point, to fight: to keep the world safe from those want to cause it harm—people like your boss, your mentor, and father figure, Raymond Bouchard."

"That still doesn't explain your interest in the suit."

"Right now the suit is a one-of-a-kind item. It hasn't become a mass-produced weapon of destruction—yet."

"Let's discuss your secret agenda."

"Only if you discuss yours."

"Mine?"

"Yes. You, the emotional orphan who must perform heroic acts of bravery to prove your worth in a company of men who don't deserve to share the air you breathe. It's been your life-long mission to prove to yourself that you are not the picture of the worthless orphan you carry in your head. The liars and thieves and white-trash teachers that provided the moral framework of your childhood—you have risen above them, Stephen. Yet you live in constant fear that you don't possess the secret treasures and gifts that make you desirable to others. That's why you can't get close to people."

"Psychoanalysis bores me."

"No, it *terrifies* you. You'd have to map out all those undiscovered countries within yourself—places that will always be unfamiliar terrain. After the Armand shooting, I bet you flirted with post-traumatic stress disorder, and your peers suggested therapy, didn't they? But you didn't go because you don't have the answers to the questions about your origins. You have no idea what makes you tick. Each day is a mystery. You're the puzzle that when put together never forms a complete picture."

Conway felt alarms going off, but behind the noise and the commotion and the driving need to get to the next destination, a well-buried part of himself had opened up to Angel Eyes's words, knowing what the man had just said was true.

He's sucking you in. Don't let someone else use you, Steve.

"When faced with the choice between saving your life and retrieving the military suit, I chose *you*, Stephen. I saved *your* life. When you went in to find Ms. Kaufmann, I sent in the person I loved the most to protect you. You, Stephen Conway, are alive because of me."

"Why me?"

"Despite your complicated rearing, the worlds you've been forced to inhabit—despite all the ugliness you've seen, you still want to believe in good. In the purity of what you're doing. I find that remarkable."

Car horns blared. Booker was trying to move the SUV into the next lane, but nobody was letting him in.

"I can help you erase your doubts, Stephen. I can provide you with the answers to your origins, the names of your mother and father—all those questions you have about yourself, I can answer. The life you so desperately want can be yours."

"Tell me where Dixon and Kaufmann are."

"Turn around in your seat and ask that question to the people who are coming for you."

The phone pressed against his ear, Conway turned around and saw dozens of headlights pointed at him. He tried to look beyond them and didn't see anything, just a lot of fancy sports cars, a few trucks and—

Five men, Conway counted five, peeked out of the darkness and dodged their way through the narrow spaces between the cars, the strong wind trying to blow them back. They were all dressed in bulky down parkas with hoods and wore gloves and were coming this way, closing fast.

To see them, Angel Eyes must be close.

"We need to get out of here, Book. Now."

"I see them. They can't get in here. They can plant a bomb on this car and they won't be able to get in."

On the phone Angel Eyes said, "I'm a man of my word, Stephen. I said I will protect you, and I will. Just remember to keep an open mind later. For now, keep your eyes shut."

Shut my eyes? What the hell is he talking about?

The back window deflected three shots.

"Hold on," Booker said and planted his foot hard on the gas pedal.

The SUV had dual-ram bumpers that could ram through blockcades. Book smashed into the right side of a Saab with enough force to knock the driver into the passenger's seat. Conway fell forward, bracing himself by reaching out for the dashboard, and dropped the phone. Car horns blared in all directions. Booker kept pushing his way through. The startled and angry faces of the drivers in the surrounding cars tried to move their vehicles out of the way, seeing that the owner of the Lincoln Navigator wasn't about to stop.

Booker yelled over the car horns. "All I need to do is get through this opening— The *fuck* is this shit?"

Seven cars up, the back of a white van had opened; three men dressed head-to-toe in the kind of black, close-quarter combat gear worn by the FBI's Hostage Rescue Team exploded onto the bridge and came charging toward them, night-vision goggles strapped across their faces.

But it was the bulky, square-shaped backpacks and the rifles that looked like props from a science fiction movie that held Conway's attention.

The blinding laser rifle.

How did Angel Eyes get a hold of—

Gunshots rang out. One of Angel Eyes's black-dressed combat men stopped running. Now standing only a few feet away from the front hood of the Lincoln Navigator, the man brought the weapon up, his eyes covered by protective gear, and stared down the scope of the rifle that was pointed in their direction.

"Get down and keep your eyes shut!" Conway screamed, and then grabbed Booker by the back of the shirt and pulled his friend's massive bulk down into the seat.

More shots pinged off the SUV. Booker and Conway lay twisted against the seat, Conway's face pressed against the soft leather, his eyes shut. Outside, beyond the SUV's protective armor, Conway could hear car doors slamming shut. People screamed. Then he heard something heavy thump against the front hood of the Lincoln Navigator and behind the commotion, a voice screamed out in pain and horror.

"My eyes! Oh my God my eyes I can't fucking see!"

Another voice, trembling, sobbing, right outside the window: *"I'm blind! I'm blind!"*

Pinned against the soft leather, Conway close enough to smell the bubble gum in his friend's mouth, he recalled the video-test footage of the blinding laser weapon that, on its highest setting, ruptured the cells in the eye and caused permanent and irreversible blindness.

Angel Eyes's voice came from the phone resting on the floor: "It's safe to open your eyes now, Stephen."

Conway grabbed the phone and straightened up. Blinking, he looked outside the window. Car doors hung open while people fled down the expressway, tripping over each other and falling, everyone running away from the three black-dressed combat men who were now climbing back inside the van.

One of Cole's men was sprawled across the front of the hood, both of his shaking hands gripping his face. Conway could see blood dripping between the man's fingers. Another was wandering up the street, blinded, his hands reaching out and touching cars as he screamed for someone to help him.

"You better get moving, Stephen," Angel Eyes said, his voice so calm it sounded mechanical. "I just received word that two more vans are closing in on your location, and have orders to kill you and your friend."

Booker had already straightened up. Settled back behind the wheel, he punched his foot on the gas, the engine racing, and like a bullet determined to sink deep into bone, the SUV's massive frame and weight plowed ahead and smashed the two small cars out of the way in shrieks of crunching metal. The last image Conway had before they broke free and took the Storrow Exit was that of the startled expression of a uniformed cop on the horn, calling for reinforcements.

The Elf did what he was told: he stayed close to the Lincoln Navigator.

The SUV skidded down deserted and dark streets. They were now deep in the heart of the projects, the Elf closing on the SUV. In the back, Cole leaned down on the floor and looked out the front window, one hand on the back of the Elf's headrest for support, the creepy motherfucker's mouth so close to his ear that he could hear the guy making these wet, smacking sounds.

"Stay close and don't lose him," Cole said, and the Elf got a strong whiff of Owen Lee's blood coming from the man's mouth. Then he thought about last night, Cole down in the basement doing his thing with the girl and the screaming, Jesus Mary Mother of God, he hadn't signed on for this. It was supposed to be a simple gig. All of this torture, it was totally unnecessary. There were other avenues to explore, things like truth serum, and Bouchard knew that. Last night, Alves had come back to the house and saw Cole march up from the basement, the dude splattered in blood. When Cole walked into the back room, Bouchard's face didn't even change expression.

"You get the code?" Bouchard asked.

"No. She was too busy screaming." Cole smiled. His teeth were red, his eyes shining and bright, the look of a man who had just stepped off the most thrilling roller coaster ride of his life, and right then everyone knew Cole had done the biting thing again. "Want a taste, Raymond?"

The Elf had caught the peculiar look in Bouchard's eyes. The dude was jealous that Cole got to enjoy the release, got to enjoy the taste. That was why Bouchard had insisted on going inside the Boston condo alone, why he stuck the needle full of cocaine and rat poison into the guy's neck even though there was a more humane way to pull the guy's plug. No, Bouchard had *wanted* to watch John Riley suffer. Just like Cole, Bouchard got off on it. Bouchard like to play in the same sandbox but didn't like getting his hands dirty. At that moment, the Elf didn't know what was worse: the devil you didn't know or the devil you did.

The thing of it was Cole *knew* he was being set up. The broad must have spilled something because after Bouchard left, Cole looked at Owen Lee and said, "You have something you want to tell me, Owen?" And Owen, the fucking idiot that he was, just shook his head no. The Elf thought about what had just happened to the girl, and when Owen left the house to get some smokes, he called Cole and struck up a deal.

The Elf looked out the window. They were in the projects now. As he chased the SUV, he suddenly didn't care about the money. All he cared about was getting the fuck OUT. Go down to the Caribbean and spend some time popping college broads out looking for dick, then fake his own death and start over somewhere in the Midwest, maybe give the nine-to-five thing a try. Other guys had done it.

"When I tell you, pull up alongside of them and run them off the road," Cole said.

The SUV took a sharp right. The huge Lincoln Navigator looked like it was about to tip over but instead, it shot up a narrow one way street. The Elf was on him.

He saw them first, shining in the van's headlights, metal strips with the spiked ends dropping from the unit underneath the Navigator—road spikes used to stop high-speed pursuits. The spikes were bouncing all over the street.

The Elf hit the breaks but the van had already run over them. The front tires deflated. *Oh shit*. He turned the wheel but had already lost control of the van. He slammed dead-on into a row of parked cars.

The seat belt threw him back against the seat—kept him from flying out the window. Cole hit the back of his chair and bounced backward, back toward the drugged Owen Lee. Cole wasn't moving, but the Elf could. He was dazed and probably had suffered massive whiplash, but he could move.

Now's your chance. Get the fuck out of here.

His head throbbing, the Elf unlocked his seat belt and checked his door. It opened, and he had room to get out. Dazed, he stepped outside.

A tall and mean-looking brother stood against the side of the van, the dude's skin as dark as the night sky, his hair braided so close to his scalp it looked like a hedge maze.

"You fucked up my ride, bro," the man said, and then cocked his head to the side and smiled, flashing a mouthful of gold teeth. Out of the darkness came two more homies, the pair dressed in Tommy Hilfiger, loud and bright colors. The three punks grinned ear to ear, amused.

The Elf swallowed. *Just play it cool.*

"Let's be cool, okay? I've got my wallet right here," the Elf said. He reached inside his jacket for the Glock hanging in the shoulder holster.

"Fucking midget's packing," one of the brothers said, and the next thing the Elf felt was a hail of fists that plunged him screaming into darkness.

The apartment made a jail cell look like a resort get-away. Past the front door was a narrow foyer where you barely had enough room to hang your coat; take three steps and you were standing in the common room, with low ceilings and battle-scarred walls with chipped white paint and graffiti. A hallway led down to a bedroom where a mattress lay on the floor, covered by a crumpled white sheet; dirty clothes were balled in a corner.

The place should have been condemned—and probably would have been, too, if a building inspector could have entered this neighborhood without fear of his losing his life. It was said that even the police avoided this section of Roxbury.

All the lights inside the dilapidated apartment were turned off. The semidark room was lit up by slivers of a urine-colored streetlight, one of the few that hadn't been shot out. The warm air was packed with the thick, overpowering stench of mold and cigarettes and marijuana smoke mixed with days-old Burger King food and beer cans that were piled high in the uncovered wastebasket from the attached kitchen. Gang-bangers in their late teens to early twenties, all of them schooled on the street and dressed in expensive street threads and wearing mint baseball caps worn at odd angles, lumbered about the living room, their hard faces boiling with testosterone and rage and itching for the chance to get it on with either of the two white motherfuckers tied down to the cheap kitchen chairs that sat facing a large screen, brand new HDTV.

Conway leaned his back against the kitchen wall, his attention riveted to the center of the common room. The short guy with the black hair and the furry neck Conway recognized from the video. The Elf looked nervous; he kept swallowing and wouldn't look up.

But not Cole. Despite the fact he was bound and immobile, his face cut up and bruised and bleeding from the beating he had endured outside, the man seemed completely relaxed. His blue eyes tracked each of the gang-bangers who loitered inside the room, their anxious fingers sliding up and down the triggers of their MAC 10s and handguns, and viewed them as if they were nothing more than harmless characters playing in a movie.

A kid no older than sixteen punched Cole across the mouth with a right hook that would have made Mike Tyson proud. Cole, bound to the chair, tumbled against the floor. The kid reached over and pulled Cole back up. His nose was broken; a red river poured out of his nostrils and dribbled onto his chin and chest.

"That's what you get for eye-fucking me, motherfucker," the kid spat.

Cole examined his lap where his blood dripped from his chin and splashed like the steady drops of a summer rain shower, his eyes still, reflective.

"Dude knows how to take a hit," Booker said to Conway. They were alone in the kitchen. "These two boys from your backyard?"

"The guy who just got clocked is my CIA handler,

Jonathan Cole. The other guy is the Elf. He planted the drugs around John Riley's apartment."

"What about the vegetable with the missing ear we found lying in the van?"

"Owen Lee, the Elf's partner. Lee played the part of the skydiving instructor back in Texas. He and the Elf placed the surveillance gear inside Riley's apartment. All three of them work for Bouchard."

"Black ops guys?"

"Something like that. Don't these windows have blinds?"

"Place ain't the Four Seasons, hoss."

"Cole's friends are going to be here soon."

"So let them come. People are out front, watching. We're safe. These boys are the real deal. They don't fuck around."

"You mean these gang-bangers."

"They prefer the more politically correct term of urban relocation specialists." Booker grinned. "You lucky I got such high connections."

Outside the window and across the street was another tenement building full of dark and mostly broken windows. Conway didn't know what was more frightening: the truth he had discovered on the CD or Angel Eyes's unpredictability. The guy and his men had a knack of materializing out of thin air at exactly the right moment.

Conway checked his watch. 5:40 P.M. In another twenty minutes, the six o'clock news would come on. His eyes shifted over to the common room. He could feel the comfortable weight of the Glock stuck in the back of his waistband.

"I want to be alone with them."

"What you scheming inside your head?"

"Cole knows where Dixon and Kaufmann are hidden," Conway said. "Knows where Bouchard is staying."

"And you think he's going to give them up?"

Conway looked down at the kitchen floor that had missing squares of linoleum. Someone had brought up one of those Rubbermaid gas cans. Booker followed Conway's gaze.

"Ain't your style, hoss."

Conway didn't say anything.

"You've always had trouble playing in that zone. You like things nice and clean, black and white. Me, I'm used to the gray areas."

"Move your boys out."

"Once you step over that line, you're a lifetime member."

"You better move your boys outside."

Booker didn't say anything for a moment.

"Going to leave a couple of boys posted outside the door though, to make sure you're protected. Wear this," Booker said and handed over his headset and a new cell phone to Conway. "Keep this on, I'll call you if anything pops up."

Conway took the gear and put it on. He had already dumped the watch and the phone but hung on to the Palm Pilot. With its Air Taser system and explosives, the device was just too handy to dump.

Booker made a motion to one of the boys and then a moment later everyone left the room. The apartment door shut.

Silence.

Conway stood in the warm semidarkness, not really in the room but inside his head. He saw Major Dixon strapped to a chair, the meat cleaver coming down and severing the finger because he had failed to deliver the decryption code needed for the military suit. And next came the fresh image of John Riley on the floor in his condo, dead from the rat poison injected into his neck. And what about Renée Kaufmann? What fate awaited her?

All these people dead, tortured. All because of Raymond Bouchard's orders—orders that these men carried out.

Conway glanced over at the TV and thought about what was going to happen next. It wasn't good enough. Bouchard should be tied to a car bumper and dragged around from city to city.

Booker's right. This ain't your style.

And what is *my style?* Conway wondered. The last six years of his life had been based on the lies and deception manufactured by a man who had pledged ideals and honesty and morals. Conway gazed inward at that untouched private sanctuary deep within himself, the place where he sought refuge and where few people had been allowed entrance. What he pictured was a church ransacked of its sacred items, the space that was once a haven for reflection and retreat now defiled, filled with a cold air charged with the kind of rage that demanded an outlet, a release. And there, standing in the middle of it all, his satisfaction well hidden as he led the secret pillaging, was Raymond Bouchard.

Conway picked up the box of matches from the kitchen counter. He saw the cut and bloodied faces waiting for him in the next room and took a step forward, knowing he was about to step over a line and take a journey that would forever alter the way he had come to view himself.

Conway stuffed the box of matches into his back pocket and then turned on the TV, making sure it was tuned to Channel Five. A commercial for Tide detergent played inside the common room, the volume at a good level but not so loud that he would have to yell over the TV. Then he turned around and faced the two men.

The furry one, the Elf, was nothing more than a gofer, doing what he was told. Conway was more interested in Jonathan Cole, the black op specialist and assassin. Conway walked over to Cole and ripped the piece of duct tape off his mouth. The guy didn't even wince.

"I know Raymond Bouchard's behind this. Behind everything," Conway said. His voice sounded deep, steady, foreign to him. "I saw the video from beginning to end. They were going to use you and kill you."

No surprise in Cole's face. He moved his tongue around the inside of his mouth and teeth, inspecting the damage.

"The guy in the corner behind you, the Elf, I saw him on the video," Conway said. "He helped Owen Lee, the vegetable we found lying in the van, plant the drugs and surveillance gear inside my friend's apartment."

Cole spit out a bloody clump on the floor, right next

to Conway's black shoe. "Where is Mr. Lee now?" he asked.

"On his way to the hospital. Looks like someone chewed his ear off. Any idea what happened?"

Cole made a wet, smacking sound with his lips. "None," he said.

Why the fuck is he acting so calm?

The only answer Conway came up with was that Cole was trying to stall to gain some time. Cole wasn't stupid. He had to know his men couldn't sneak into this part of town. The streets were covered.

Don't underestimate him, a voice warned.

"Do you have the video with you?" Cole asked. "I'd like to watch it."

"Where are you hiding Dixon and Renée Kaufmann?"

"If I tell you, what do I get?"

"You get to live."

"So if I don't tell you, you'll do what, torture me? Kill me?" Cole coughed, grinned. "You don't send in a Boy Scout to a, how shall I say, an information gathering session."

Conway stepped back into the kitchen. He picked up the jug of gasoline, unscrewed the black cap, and came back into the living room and started dumping gasoline over Cole's head. The guy clamped his eyes shut and winced as the gas burned the gashes on his face. When the tank was half empty, Conway placed it back on the floor and then reached into his pocket and came back with a box of wooden cigar matches.

"You give up Dixon and Kaufmann and I promise not to turn you into a human candlestick," Conway said. "That's the deal."

"What about the suit?"

"I don't give a flying fuck about the suit."

"And what about Raymond? Do you give a flying fuck about him?"

"Bouchard will get what's coming to him."

"He'll snake his way out of it. I've seen him do it dozens of times."

"Not this time."

"Raymond Bouchard's a powerful man," Cole said. "He has a powerful agency at his disposal. As long as he's alive, you'll never be safe."

"Last time: Where are you hiding Dixon and Kaufmann?"

"You're not the only one in this room who's been betrayed. I know what Raymond had planned for me. I think I have a right to justice. Instead, you've got me tied up here, threatening me with torture. You kill me, you'll be killing an innocent man."

"Stop pretending you're a cherry. I know what you do for a living."

"I've got nothing to do with what happened to you in Austin, or what happened to your friend. If you watched the video, then you know that."

"Renée Kaufman. Where is she?"

"She's dead."

Conway felt something hot and sharp pierce his stomach.

"Raymond Bouchard tortured Renée Kaufmann for information on you and the location of the CD, and she wouldn't speak," Cole said. "Then he cut her into bits."

Over Cole's shoulder, Conway saw the Elf's eyes pop up in surprise before they dropped back down to the floor.

Cole's lying.

"Bouchard's moved Dixon," Cole said. "Now that

you know the code, Dixon's going to get turned into fer-
tilizer. I can help you, Steve. I can help you save Dixon.
I know where Raymond is staying. You let me out of
here, I'll take you to him. You can bring your friends
along too, if you don't trust me. You want to save
Dixon, then you have to release me. That's the deal. It's
not up for negotiation."

Conway picked up the gas tank, stormed over to the
Elf and started dumping gas on him, the stocky, furry
animal twisting against his restraints, screaming behind
the tape. The gas fumes were overpowering. If Conway
lit a match now, the whole room would blow.

The can empty, Conway tossed it aside, hearing it
bounce against the floor, and opened the window behind
the Elf. The cold winter air rushed inside, clearing the
the room of fumes, making it easier to breathe. Conway
removed the box of matches, took out a match, and then
ripped off the piece of tape from the Elf's mouth. He
held the unlit match in front of the Elf's face.

"The flames will eat away at the tape and rope, but
by the time you're free, you'll be permanently disfigured," Conway said, his anger separating each word.
"You want to spend the rest of your life in a burn unit?
Or you want to walk out of here in one piece?"

"Torturing is the business of cowards, Stephen,"
Cole said.

Conway's eyes and attention remained focused on the
Elf. He said, "You don't answer my question, I'll turn
you into a human candle."

The Elf's eyes kept bouncing from the match to
Cole.

"Your choice," Conway said and then lit the match.

The Elf jumped as if shocked, his mouth open in
horror. His beaten, bloody face glowed in the flame's

soft yellow and orange light. Conway moved the match closer.

"*Jesus Christ, okay, don't fucking do it!*" the Elf screamed.

Conway recognized the voice and froze. "Keith Harring," he said.

"That's correct," Cole said. "Mr. Alves played the part of Keith Harring to lure you inside Praxis to have you killed. The man you met inside the lab was Misha. You were supposed to die in the fire, Stephen. They were supposed to blame the whole episode on you and your colleague, Randy Scott. That's why Misha had you shoot him. Raymond Bouchard wanted everyone wiped out, only you survived."

"*Fucking listen to me!*" the Elf screamed. "*Cole is the one who tortured the girl and chopped her up and bit off Owen Lee's ear. I fucking saw it!*"

"You wouldn't be lying to me, would you?" Conway asked and moved the flame closer.

"*Jesus Fucking Christ, get that away!*" The Elf stopped and then sucked in air. He looked like was on the verge of tears. "Dude, I'm begging you, man, please."

"My Palm Pilot is equipped with a transmitter, right?"

"And a bug, yeah, we can listen in on you." The Elf's eyes were locked on the flame slowly burning its way through the long wooden matchstick.

"Where's the surveillance van now?"

"Downstairs, all fucked up. Nobody else can track you, I swear."

"Where's Dixon?"

"If I give you the address you've got to let me go."

"This match is starting to get hot. I don't know how long I can hold it."

"Cole's men are coming for you, right now," the Elf stammered. He swallowed and stammered again. "They'll come in here, they'll kill me, you, all of us, don't you fucking get it?"

This guy tried to kill you. You almost burned to death inside the lab. Throw the match and let him burn.

"Where's Dixon?" Conway said and moved the flame closer to the Elf's gasoline-soaked lap, ready to turn him into a candle. *Let them all burn.*

"*Lynn, 27 Park Street, yellow house on the corner!*" the Elf screamed.

Cole, very calm, said, "I wouldn't believe a word the man says. He's a professional liar, one of Bouchard's herd."

Conway said, "How many men guarding the house."

"Last count, five," the Elf said.

"Alarm system?"

"Code's nineteen thirteen. Keypad's inside the front door. Dixon's in the basement. The broad's clothes are still there. You'll see what happened. Mary, Mother of God, I'm telling you the truth. Take me there, leave me bound up, I don't care, just don't fucking burn me and don't leave me here! He's bit Lee's ear and tore it off— *blow the match out! BLOW IT OUT!!!*"

Conway blew out the flame. Coming from outside, he heard a slightly muted sound, *thump-thump-thump.*

Booker's voice, loud and urgent, burst over on Conway's ear piece: "I can't believe what I'm seeing. A goddamn Blackhawk helicopter just materialized out of thin air, two buildings down. It's hovering right above the roof."

The stolen Blackhawk helicopter with the optical camouflage.

Angel Eyes was here.

"I'm watching men rappelling onto the roof—three, I'm counting three men, and they're dressed in close-quarter combat gear," Booker said. "Same dudes from earlier, armed with the laser rifles. The chopper's moving to another roof. You got what you need?"

"Most of it."

"My chopper's already on its way. They'll be there in five. Get your ass to the roof."

Outside, car engines raced. Men shouted orders. Car doors slammed.

Automatic gunfire erupted on the dark street.

The guy Booker had posted outside the apartment door opened it, poked his bandanna-covered head inside and with a mouthful of gold teeth said, "Let's move."

Conway blew out the match. He stood up and refastened the strip of tape across the Elf's mouth. Conway checked his watch. A few minutes before six.

"You'll never make it out of here alive," Cole said.

"Tell that to Angel Eyes. He's on his way to see you," Conway said, and turned toward the door. Before he ran out of the room, he dropped the small box of matches on the floor, fully aware of what he was doing. Conway headed up the dank stairwell, smiling in the darkness at the sick pleasure that had lined his heart.

Raymond Bouchard was back in the shower, back to thinking in his favorite place, tucked alone in this womb of steam and hot water. He didn't know why, but he was thinking about his father.

No, that wasn't exactly true. In times of stress, when all the walls seemed to be closing in and hope about to run out, Raymond often thought about his father, wondering what new direction the man's life would have taken if he had just made the simple decision to hang on, to just press forward through the temporary stretch of blackness and emerge on the other side, stronger.

Inside the shower, as he worked the white soap into a lather, he saw himself that day as he walked up the steps, on his way to his room. His parents' door was open just a crack, but it was enough for him to see the bright, angry splatter of blood that fanned up the white wall and marred the group of wedding and family pictures with a series of angry, wet lashes, like razor cuts. Raymond remembered his vision locking on one picture, his parents grouped around him after a Little League game, his smiling face the only one spared by the blood, an omen as if to say, *You will be the only one to survive this.*

Which was true. His mother didn't last much longer. Ten years later, she got cancer and decided to cash in her chips and forgo the chemotherapy. Raymond paid for the funeral but didn't attend it.

He was never one to indulge in the *why* of life. He preferred to deal in reality. He could shape it, control it, change its history to suit his needs. People and problems could be sold and purchased, molded or destroyed or made to disappear, depending on what was needed.

What was needed here was confidence. He had been in numerous precarious situations and had survived them. This time would be no different. This wasn't a mess, it was a situation—nothing more than a series of minor setbacks. Break them down into small, digestible units, and the larger problem could be contained and managed like radioactive spills.

First, use Stephen to draw out Pasha. She had to be close, watching him. Bring them both in, find out what they know, then remove them both from the equation, permanently. Same with Conway's friend, Booker. Plant the evidence and stories and erase any trail that led back to himself. Problem solved.

And what about Misha's boss, Alexi?

Blame the whole situation on Angel Eyes. Tell Alexi that Angel Eyes killed Misha and stole the military suit.

Angel Eyes was trickier. The man had stepped out of the shadows and had, for reasons that still perplexed Raymond, taken an active interest in Conway. Hopefully he would draw Angel Eyes out and then Cole, forever thrilled with the hunt, would take the mysterious figure out of the game.

Sounds great, Raymond, but the only problem is that Angel Eyes is proving himself to be a powerful adversary.

But the man wasn't made of vapor. He was human, and he was here in Boston. And, like Pasha, the man would protect Stephen.

Angel Eyes is proving to be elusive.

So far. The point was, he was a man and all men bleed. One good shot and he'd be out of the picture. Cole, Owen Lee—someone would kill him.

Satisfied that this situation, which would have overwhelmed his mental weakling of a father, was now clearly labeled and defined, Raymond Bouchard shut the water off, pulled the curtain back, and then stepped into the bathroom of sand-colored tile. The door was cracked open; most of the steam had cleared. He toweled himself off in front of the mirror, studying himself at different angles, all of which left him feeling satisfied. He tossed the towel onto the floor and put on the white terrycloth Four Seasons robe, and walked out into the grand bedroom decorated with French walnut furniture.

The window offered a view of the park. It was dark now and the city had come to life. From the sixth floor he watched the people milling about Charles and Boylston streets. He spied a young couple making out right below him. The man's hand was under her coat and grabbing her tits—Raymond smiled at the word, and smiled even more when the man's hands cupped the woman's ass displayed so finely in a pair of black leather pants. Raymond continued to stare, invisible, like God.

If you had the suit, you could be invisible.

Raymond looked up, startled, and saw his reflection in the mirror.

The suit's your size; you could fit into it without a problem. If you had the decryption code, you could use the suit whenever you wanted. You've studied the design, you know how it works.

"I could kill Alexi," Raymond mumbled to himself. "Get him out of the way."

And Angel Eyes.

That's right. He could follow Stephen himself, and when Angel Eyes stepped into the picture, the son of a bitch wouldn't even see the shot coming.

The truth is, if you had that suit, you could get rid of anyone. And if this suddenly turned sour—I'm not saying it will, but if it did—you could climb inside that suit and nobody would be able to find you.

The thing was, he *did* have the suit. It was, what, half an hour's drive from here? Kill the men he had guarding the suit and then steal it—blame it all on the mysterious Angel Eyes. Then bring in Conway and have him fork over the decryption code.

Raymond took off his robe and dressed quickly. He was hovering over his suitcase, packing, when his cell phone rang. *Probably Cole calling to tell me he's got Conway.* Raymond picked up the phone from his briefcase, anxious to hear the good news.

"Give it to me."

"I don't like you using my name, Raymond."

The calm voice had a cold, mechanical quality to it, and sounded slightly British—as if a robotic Patrick Stewart were on the phone.

"Who is this?" Raymond demanded.

"The man you're pinning all your sins on."

Raymond Bouchard straightened up.

"The whole world is watching your star performance on television," Angel Eyes said.

Star performance? What the hell is he talking about?

The TV was housed in the walnut armoire and turned off, but the cable box was on, already turned on to Channel Five.

"Go ahead and take a look, Raymond. I have forever."

Raymond stepped forward, reached out and turned

on the TV. A hum as the screen came to life and then Raymond saw himself standing over John Riley's dead body.

In his mind's eye Raymond saw Owen Lee sitting in the back of the surveillance van the night Riley was killed, Owen holding up the black, golf-balled–sized device with the camera lens. *It's a Web cam. . . . We found it inside the armoire, mounted on top of the computer monitor . . . Riley's girlfriend . . . she saw the entire thing . . . it's possible she recorded us.*

Angel Eyes said, "How does it feel to be the center of national attention?"

Raymond pressed the UP button on the cable box. Next channel, there he was, talking to Owen Lee about planting the drugs in the apartment to make it look like an OD. Next channel, Owen talked about killing Misha. About killing Cole.

"I thought about calling the police, and then I remembered the skills of your friend Mr. Cole, the one you set up to get killed," Angel Eyes said. "Mr. Cole's on his way to see you. *Bon appétit*, Raymond."

Raymond Bouchard didn't see the floor or the wonderful room, all he could see behind his eyes, branded, was the picture that everyone all over the country, maybe even the world, had just seen: the image of himself standing over John Riley's dead body. It was like . . . it was like he had stepped sideways into another dimension, back in time to that day from his childhood when he had come home and discovered the two moving vans parked in the driveway. Right now, he felt the way his mother must have that day, useless, powerless against the men who were removing their lives.

Just a few minutes ago, everything had been under control. And now . . . and now . . .

That inner voice came on, it was very cool, very collected, and Raymond listened to it: *You've got your gun. Grab your suitcase, drive to Lynn, and get the suit before Cole gets here.*

Inside the elevator, Raymond put on his sunglasses and pushed his damp hair down across his scalp, giving him a George Clooney kind of hairdo. The elevator doors chimed open. *Take it easy. Act normal. Remember who you are.*

The suitcase strap slung over his shoulder, Raymond moved into the lobby and then walked toward the front entrance, taking his time and staring straight ahead as people whisked past him. Casually, he moved out the doors and stepped into the cold night air. A young black man dressed in the cap and white gloves of proper valet attire stared at him for a moment.

It's the sunglasses. You're wearing them at night, guy probably thinks you're a celebrity. Just relax and smile, act casual.

"Good evening, sir."

"I just need my car," Raymond said. His voice sounded confident, firm. "It's a black Dodge Durango." He gave the man the license plate number and watched as the valet nodded and then disappeared.

From behind his black lenses, Raymond watched the faces of the people who walked in and out of the hotel. He didn't see Cole. But Cole was an expert at disguising himself. It would be hard to find him if he was—

Sirens. Raymond heard sirens.

The noise grew louder. Police? Ambulance? Fire? His muscles tensed, ready to run. But where? Where was he going to run to? His car pulled up to the front. Raymond tipped the man and got in. Three police cruisers whizzed by the hotel in a wail of sirens and then disappeared, taking his panic with them.

It wasn't until he was out of the city, traveling on Route One North, passing through the city of Saugus, that he felt himself start to relax. He was inside the car, alone; nobody knew where he was. He was safe; protected. Once he had the suit, he would be invisible.

Inside his pocket, his cell phone rang. He ignored it and drove faster.

Both sides of the highway were filled with brightly lit strip malls, gas stations, and retail stores. He had turned the radio to the twenty-four-hour news station, the AM channel, WBZ, and listened for a breaking news report. Fifteen minutes and no news about what he had just witnessed on TV.

Wait. Was it a trick?

Get the suit.

Raymond turned off the highway and onto 144 East, the route that would take him straight into Lynn. He heard a hissing sound.

He turned off the radio. The noise was faint but was definitely coming from inside the car. *What the hell is that?* He shut off the heat. The hissing was still there. He couldn't smell anything.

A press of the button and the interior light turned on. Raymond looked around as he drove. Nothing on the floor, and it sounded like it was coming from under his seat. He reached under and instantly felt something hard, something made of metal, and pulled it out and examined it in the small strip of light.

A canister hooked up to what appeared to be a remote-control device, the nozzle hissing air.

Get out of the car.

Raymond rolled down one window, tossed the canister outside, and using the automatic controls, rolled down the other windows. He drove faster.

His eyes started to burn.

Don't scratch them. Keep driving.

Minutes later, his chest felt tight. He tried to suck in the cold air but it was becoming too difficult to breathe. Tear gas, was that what was inside the canister? Or was it something worse? He kept trying to breathe. It was getting worse. He pulled the Durango to a side street. He couldn't call the police or go to the hospital, but if he could just lie somewhere and wait for the effects to wear off, he would be fine. Raymond collapsed against the steering wheel, against the horn, struggling to breathe.

A moment later, the car door opened.

Raymond Bouchard saw a pair of latex-covered hands grab him and push him back against the seat. He couldn't see the person, but he could hear the guy's voice breathing against his ear.

"It is finished," Angel Eyes whispered.

When Cole heard the automatic gunfire, the rain of bullets ricocheting off cars, *ping! ping! ping!*, glass shattering everywhere, people shouting orders and screaming for help, he knew a rescue operation was being staged. His men were here. Behind him Mr. Mark "the Elf" Alves engaged in a desperate struggle to free himself of his situation.

"Get it all out now, Mr. Alves," Cole said, calmly. "When I get you up north, I'll have you screaming for weeks."

The heavy thud of footsteps rushing up the stairs caused Cole to look toward the half-opened door. Outside in the dark hallway, he saw a flashlight zigzagging across the dirty floor and broken walls and ceiling.

"In here," Cole yelled.

The footsteps slowed to a walk. The beam of light hit the floor near the door, turned inside, and shone directly into Cole's eyes.

"They brought Owen Lee to the hospital," Cole said, squinting. "Conway just left via helicopter. He still has his Palm Pilot. We can listen to it, get his location. You need our van—get that goddamn light out of my face."

The light moved away. Cole blinked, his eyes readjusting to the darkness.

Standing before him was a man dressed in black combat gear, his face and head covered so Cole couldn't identify him. Then his eyes focused on the weird looking rifle the man carried. Wires ran from the butt of the rifle and fed directly into the base of the bulky backpack strapped across his back.

The scene from the bridge: his men stumbling about in a daze, screaming that they had been blinded. This one belonged to Angel Eyes.

The man reached down and grabbed the boxes of matches that had been left on the floor. He opened the box.

Cole, a man used to wielding terror, was not used to feeling it. In that quick moment, he tried to sum up the man standing before him, tried to figure out the key to disconnecting his present agenda in the only way he knew how: through greed.

"You let me go, you can name your price."

"Some men don't have a price." The man struck a match and tossed it into the air.

Cole watched it turn around in slow motion, like a baton, not believing what he was seeing until the small flame gently bounced on his lap.

It was like being swallowed inside a cone of fire. His clothes and hair went up first, and when the flames started to eat at his skin, the pain became unbearable, so searing in its intensity that he screamed and screamed for it to stop, screamed and screamed for help until his voice burned away. Inside the flames he saw his mother's smiling face come for him, her bony fingers forming a claw that reached out to drag him down into her world, a place where he would forever burn.

Major Dixon did not want to open his eyes. Every time he did he saw

(his two missing fingers, they're gone, Dix, GONE)

something that made him scream so loud he blacked out. He never thought such a thing was possible, but when the Russian guy who looked like a boiled ham in a bad suit raised the cleaver above his head, Dix's mind screamed out: *This isn't happening this is just a bad nightmare good God DON'T DO IT!* and the cleaver came down crashing down with a hard *clank* against the steel table and separated his fingers from his hand.

When he came to later—minutes, hours, he had no idea, time had no meaning here—he felt a warm stream of water hitting his face. Dixon opened his eyes and saw his torturer, the boiled ham, a big grin on his face as he finished urinating. Laughing, he zipped up his fly and walked out of the basement. Dixon was still lying horizontally, still naked and cold and wet and bound to the torture chair, but the pain was gone. A bad dream, that's all it was, just a bad dream, he told himself, and a bubble of hope built in his chest. He tilted his head to the side and saw the IV bag and the line hooked into his left arm, and when he raised his left hand up, his wrist still bound to the armrest, he saw the missing fingers, the stumps blackened, and the bubble burst.

It had happened. He was a prisoner in this gray dungeon and would be tortured an inch at a time until he delivered up the decryption code to the military suit—a code he didn't have.

He lost it later that night.

"You want the fucking code?" On and on until someone walked into the basement, a guy who had sleepy eyes and wore a bandanna and two gold hoop earrings. It was Chris Evans, Dixon's jump instructor and partner—the same guy who had sat in a chair in the corner and enjoyed a Twix candy bar while Dixon begged and screamed for the torturing to stop.

"Spill it," Evans said. He was dressed in some baggy jeans that showed off the stitched Calvin Klein band of his underwear. The guy was a spitting image of the steroid meatheads from Dixon's youth, guys who liked to kick him around because he was weak. Dude probably lifted weights without his shirt on in front of a mirror and then jerked off because he thought he looked so good.

"Conway knows the fucking code."

"What did you say?"

"I said Conway knows the code. You want him, not me. I've got nothing to do with this!"

"I can't believe you called me down here for this." Evans shook his head, agitated, turned and walked back up the stairs. Lights out, and Dixon was back alone in the dungeon of permanent midnight where time didn't exist.

Time passed.

Through his anger and pain, a voice came to him and said, *You can't change what happened, you can only go forward. Conserve your energy, eat the food they give you, and use this time you've got to think of a way out of this mess.*

"It's hopeless," Dixon said into the dark.

It's not hopeless.

"Yeah, easy for you to say. You didn't have two of your fingers hacked off."

You can indulge in a pity party, or you can think of a way out of here before they remove another body part. Like an arm or a leg.

Time passed and Dix tried to think of a way out. The Russian never came back down. No one did. In fact, it seemed like everyone had lost an interest in him. Only one time did anyone come down, and it was Evans. He set up a TV, turned it on loud to some annoying twenty-four-hour Southern gospel show, Evans saying he was sick and tired of listening to Dixon cry and yell and scream like a pussy and needed something to drown out the sound. It was keeping him up all night.

Then they brought the girl down, and it all went downhill from there.

Dixon had been awake the entire time that had happened. When that guy with those gentle blue eyes bit the girl's ear off and then picked up the circular saw, Dixon clamped his eyes and tried to ignore it, wanting to black out. But he couldn't shut off his hearing. He heard the whining bite of the saw as it caught skin and bone and the way that girl screamed—it wasn't like in the movies or on TV where they tortured someone, the way she screamed, it was like her soul was being ripped out of her an inch at a time, and when Dixon felt her blood rain down on him, he screamed along with her and plunged into a blackness that severed any permanent ties to reality.

And you know what? He didn't care. Dix was thankful for the void. Deep in the void, he had a companion, the one true friend left over from his childhood with that idiot slob of a father whose only talents lay in drinking and the kind of systematic verbal humiliation that if you weren't careful could strip you of your humanity. *This is the deal, Dix, straight up, no bullshit. No matter what your captors say or do, they can't touch your mind. Your imagination, its contents and powers, they all belong to you. You control them. Just like the Holodeck on* Star Trek, *you can program your imagination to take you wherever you want.*

As he lay in the pitch-black basement that bled with its awful smells, his missing fingers still twitching like phantom limbs, Major Dixon blocked out the sound of the fat hens singing their gospel songs on the TV and transported himself aboard the captain's chair of the best ship in the fleet, the USS *Voyager.* A dreaded Borg cube had entered the Delta quadrant again and had somehow found an opening in its shields and transported aboard a team of drones. The drones had destroyed several of *Voyager*'s power grids; the bridge was dark and so were the hallways. Battle in the darkness. Screams. *Human* screams; the Borg was assimilating members of the *Voyager* crew. Hurry. Dixon ran down the hallway, phaser rifle in hand as he led his strike team to overtake the Borg. Wait. There was a distinct, muffled sound of a suppressor masking the gunfire of some twentieth-century automatic weapon. The gunfire ended. Silence. Darkness.

"Dixon."

A woman's voice, and she was close, too damn close, he could feel her breath and her words strong and loud and sharp against his ear. *Had to be one of the Borg, maybe even the Borg queen. Phaser ready, lock and load, baby.*

Dix felt the distinct sensation of a cold blade sliding against his skin as it cut through the rope and tape that bound his hands, feet, and neck to the chair. Blood flowed back into his limbs. He moved his hands to his face and touched his nose and mouth and lips. He was free.

It's a trap, it's got to be a trap, keep your eyes shut and get back down here where it's safe.

The woman yanked back both of his eyelids and said, "Dixon, we need to get moving."

The woman *was* part of the Borg; she was dressed in black tactical combat clothing and carried the kind of submachine gun popular with the twentieth-century unit known as the Hostage Rescue Team, once a part of the now-defunct government agency called the Federal Bureau of Investigation. But this Borg drone also had a peculiar night vision device mounted across her face.

"I'm not going to hurt you, Dixon. You're safe."

Pasha Romanov flipped up the night vision and turned on the tactical flashlight mounted under the stock of her HK submachine gun. A bright beam of white light lit up the dark basement. She shined the light in Major Dixon's eyes. They didn't register. He was in shock, lost in his own world.

Pasha shut the light off and slung the weapon behind her back. The entire house was dark from the small explosive device she had planted on the electrical box. After that, she had tossed a smoke canister through the window and then blew her way through the back door. The five men who had been guarding the house came running downstairs, and when they did, it wasn't hard to put them down.

Pasha's cell phone rang. She knew who was calling.

"Stephen?"

"Dixon is being held at 27 Park Place in Lynn," Conway said. He was yelling above the thumping blades of a helicopter. "The house is guarded with a security system and—"

"I've got Dixon." Pasha moved her light to the corner of the room. "And the suit."

"How did you—"

"I can't get into it right now, I'm running out of time." The neighbors had heard the explosion; some of them had ventured out of their homes, wrapped in jackets, to investigate the commotion. No doubt the police had been summoned. "Where's Raymond?"

"Running for his life. Forget him. Angel Eyes is here. I think he's going to make a run for the suit."

"He can't get it if he can't see it. You know the decryption code?"

"Ralph Wiggim. Meet me at 100 Summer Street, on the roof. A helicopter will pick us up and fly us out to Logan. We're going to take a private jet to Virginia. I've already made the arrangements."

"I'll see you there," Pasha said and hung up. She shoved the phone back into her jacket.

A wool blanket was on the floor. Pasha picked it up and wrapped it around Dixon, and then with both hands picked up his thin, shaking body, and threw him across her shoulder. He was light, no more than a hundred pounds. Grabbing his legs and holding them close to her chest, Pasha Romanov walked over and picked up the long suitcase that held the military suit and moved into the backyard. As she ran down the driveway, her van parked across the street, she heard the sound of police sirens building in the frigid evening air, coming closer.

Steve Conway crouched low in the alcove on the roof of the thirty-four-floor skyscraper on 100 Summer Street, uncomfortably high off the ground with the wind whipping around him like an angry storm, and watched Booker's helicopter fly away in the night sky full of stars, on its way to refuel. Far below and out of his view was the city of Boston, its downtown lights rising up and washing over the edges of the building's roof.

The wind roared and whistled, roared and whistled. Conway still wore the headset, the phone clipped to his belt. He had traded his bank clothes for something warmer: jeans, sneakers, a sweatshirt, and a dark blue Columbia ski jacket. He backed farther into the alcove, out of the wind, and rested his back against the wall. The door next to him, according to Booker, led to a room full of electrical equipment. Near the opposite end of the roof, where the helicopter had made a tricky and uncomfortable landing, and in full view, was a similar alcove with a door, this one leading to the stairwell on the thirty-fourth floor.

Once Pasha arrived, Conway would destroy the military suit—dumping it inside an incinerator would probably be best—and then they would fly to Logan where they would take a private jet that would fly them back to Virginia. One of Booker's men had made a copy of the CD recovered from the safety deposit box. That CD, along with the copy of Dixon's torture video, would be handed to the CIA Director himself. Let him clean up the fallout.

And he will. It's going to be an ugly, dirty affair, it's going to be in the national spotlight. No matter which way you look at it, you've ruined your career.

It was true. The Agency wouldn't be so forgiving with his need to broadcast dirty laundry on television. Here, alone on the roof, Conway accepted the sad fact that his career, the life he had built within the CIA, was over.

Booker's voice crackled on the earpiece: "Six mean looking dudes just entered the lobby."

Book and his men were watching the main entrance to the Summer Street building. The lobby layout—a wide stretch of yellow and brown tile—had three entrances: north, east and west, all with revolving glass doors. The east and west entrances were locked; the only way inside was through the main entrance on Summer Street. Once you walked inside, you had to check in with the building security behind the ornate, marble desk. Booker had replaced the building's security guards with his own men.

"They belong to Angel Eyes?" Conway asked.

"No combat gear, no blinding rifles."

"Must be what's left of Cole's. The lobby lights dimmed?"

"They dimmed any more it would be dark."

The suit offered the optical illusion of invisibility; it didn't change the laws of physics. If Pasha walked inside a well-lit lobby, she would be invisible, but her shadow would be thrown against the floor. It would be harder to see her shadow if the lobby was near dark.

"What about the entrances?" Conway asked.

"All clear. Looks like everyone's inside—two dudes just went down. Direct shots to the head."

Pasha. She was already inside the lobby.

"The rest are running into the lobby."

Beats of silence, the wind howling above him.

"Number three down. Four. We got gunfire," Booker said. "Five and six are down."

"It's Pasha. She's here."

"Elevator door in bay one just chimed open, but I can't see anyone."

"She's on her way up. How long until the chopper makes it back here?"

"Fifteen, twenty minutes tops."

But where was Angel Eyes?

He's got to be close.

If it came to it, Conway could destroy the suit quickly, right here on the roof. The Palm Pilot Cole had given him contained enough Semtex to blow the working military suit to bits.

Conway removed his Palm Pilot and called up the program just as Cole had instructed him. The timer was defaulted at two minutes. Should be more than enough. Press the lower button on the left and he would have a small bomb. Rip the computer from the suit, fasten the Palm Pilot to it using the roll of electrical tape inside his jacket, fling it into the air and watch as the computer, this goddamn piece of hardware that had cost so many lives, exploded into hundreds of fragments. He slipped the Palm back inside his coat pocket and waited.

Across the roof, the alcove door opened. Even in the dim light, Conway could clearly see the door swing all the way open and then shut. It looked like nobody had stepped outside. He kept staring, not wanting to blink, knowing what was about to come.

And it did. The black-clad figure of Pasha Romanov suddenly materialized out of thin air.

Conway moved out of the alcove. The wind gusted past him, howling, and knocked the headset down around his neck. His eyes watering from the cold air, he jogged over to her. Out of nowhere a gust of wind kicked him. He tripped and fell against the roof. He turned onto his back, the wind swirling around him, strong and howling. He thought he heard something, a *thump-thump* of helicopter blades, very faint. He looked around. He saw the dark sky.

And then the sky was gone.

Out of the darkness came the Blackhawk attack helicopter, the one Angel Eyes had stolen, the one Booker had sighted in Roxbury. The chopper flew past him toward the other end of the building. From the belly of the chopper a searchlight kicked on.

Pasha came to him and helped him back up. They both scrambled back inside the alcove. His ears ringing from the wind, Conway looked over Pasha's shoulder and saw the bright beam of light searching the rooftop for them.

"Pasha?"

She didn't move, didn't talk, just stood there, looking like some sort of futuristic lethal warrior ripped from a science-fiction movie. The intimidating-looking figure pressed a button on the wrist-mounted computer and the helmet's face shield flipped open.

Pasha's blue eyes stared back at him.

"Where's Dixon?"

"He's safe," Pasha said, and looked out at the Blackhawk moving across the roof.

Conway grabbed her left wrist and started to pry off the paperback-book–size computer mounted against her forearm.

"What are you doing?" she asked, looking back at him.

"Angel Eyes is here. We've got to destroy this thing. Get out of the suit."

Conway felt something cold and hard press against his temple. He looked up and saw what looked like a nine-millimeter digging against the skin near his temple.

"Step back," Pasha said.

It took a few seconds for Conway's brain to register what was happening. He stared at her, dumbfounded, vaguely aware as her free hand quickly reached around his back and yanked the Glock from his waistband. She tossed it onto the roof and the nine skidded across the floor.

"Let go of the computer, Stephen."

"Pasha—"

"Step back. Now." Pasha's eyes were as cold as her voice.

Conway knew she meant it. He straightened up and took a measured step back. He stood there, wrapped in confusion and anger and panic, and stared at her. For a moment there was only the whistle and roar of the wind.

"Relax. Everything will be explained," Pasha said. Like she was talking to a child.

This . . . it felt surreal. This woman—he had let her into his private world, had loved, shared secrets. She had saved his life twice and was now standing before him with a gun pointed at his chest. He stood in the cold air, his gaze moving between the Glock and the cold expression in Pasha's eyes, his brain struggling to find the hidden pieces and connect the larger picture.

"Stephen, I know you're confused, and you're angry.

After everything that's happened, I don't blame you. Don't do anything rash."

Conway stared at the Glock. He wanted to step forward and knock the gun out of Pasha's hand.

She can just as easily knock you to the ground. You've trained with her, she knows all of your moves. Don't underestimate her strength.

Over Pasha's shoulder, Conway saw the Blackhawk helicopter balancing itself in the strong winds, looking for a place to touch down. Pasha hadn't moved, hadn't reacted; she remained planted. Confident. Stoic.

The chopper's waiting for Pasha.

In that moment, the truth of what was happening, the truth of who Pasha Romanov really was, the mask she had worn all of these years—when they were alone, making love—all of it was a lie. In the span of four hours, he had been betrayed by two people he trusted and respected—one of whom he had loved deeply. He stared at her and thought, *Who are you?*

The picture came into sharper focus, and the answers he had sought all this time came bubbling to the surface. Conway had to force the words out.

"You're the leak. Not McFadden."

"He worked for us. All your questions—"

"You mean he was a traitor, like you."

"Don't be so willing to condemn what you don't understand yet."

"You sound like Angel Eyes." His voice sounded hoarse, outside of himself.

"He's an impressive man, Stephen."

"Obviously. He's programmed you well."

"The ideals that you live by, the things you and I fought for—to keep people safe, to keep this world safe—we can still do it, together. Only we'll be doing it on the right side, with the right people. We want you to be a part of this, Stephen. A part of us."

"Destroy the suit and I'll come with you."

"I can't do that."

"Angel Eyes told me he wanted it destroyed. To keep it out of the hands of people like Raymond Bouchard and Misha."

"The suit . . . it's too important to our work."

"So he lied."

"No, he didn't lie. *I* had a change of heart. This is my decision. Like coming here to get you."

"He has the laser rifle."

"I know."

"So that day, that was a setup too?"

"No. That was an accident. Armand's computer expert, Blake Mattenson, escaped with the rifle but wasn't good at hiding. We relieved him of it."

"And produced several more rifles."

"Again, my idea. We have to protect ourselves from the Raymond Bouchards of the world."

"Sounds to me like you're going to war."

"Everything Angel Eyes told you was true, Stephen. The man doesn't lie. All the weapons are hidden. Only the laser rifle was manufactured. And the name Angel Eyes? It belongs to Raymond. I didn't make the connection until after I discovered he sold us out. He's the one who killed Jonathan King—not us."

"You killed the other inventor, Matthews."

"He's the only one. The rest are safe. You can meet with them."

"All this . . . the whole time in Austin, all that work, it was all bullshit. You were going to help Angel Eyes retrieve the suit that day."

"Only Raymond betrayed us."

"The same way you're betraying me right now."

"I saved you at the Aquarium. I didn't have to. And after I saved Dixon, I had the suit. I didn't have to come here. I could have just left without you, but I decided to come here. To save you. Again."

"To save me," Conway repeated.

"Raymond has more friends like Cole. If you stay here, I won't be able to protect you."

"Where's Dixon?"

"With us. He's safe. We protect our own, Stephen."

We protect our own. The words summoned the scene from the Tobin Bridge, and the words Angel Eyes had said: *Right now, the suit is a one-of-a-kind item. It isn't a mass-produced weapon of destruction—yet.*

Angel Eyes mass-produced the laser rifle. What's to keep him from doing the same with the suit? He has Dixon.

Conway thought about the Palm Pilot in his pocket.

You have to destroy the suit, a voice said.

I'll end up killing her.

Then he recalled Angel Eyes that morning at the Holocaust Memorial, the way the man had his bare hand pressed against the glass. No grief on his face, no regret, no look of mourning, it was almost like . . . rapture.

Wearing that suit, you would be a god. A man would go to great lengths to have that kind of power. You said those words to Bouchard, remember?

Conway looked into her eyes and remembered them making love that last morning in Austin. *"I'll be watching you,"* Pasha whispered, her words sounding like a low, drowsy hum against his ear. *"I'll keep you safe, Stephen. I'll always be here for you. I promise."*

The woman in that moment and the woman standing before him with the gun were two different people.

Pasha made her decision and now you have to make yours.

The Blackhawk had landed near the back corner of the roof.

"Come with me and meet the man," Pasha said. "Give him a chance to explain."

"And if I don't like what he has to say, he's going to, what, just let me walk away?"

"I want you to be a part of my life. That's why I came back for you. Give this a chance." Pasha stared at him. "Please."

Conway placed his hands in his pockets. He felt the Palm Pilot. Pasha's eyes were on his hands.

"What's your decision, Stephen?"

I don't like the path the world has taken, Angel Eyes had said. *I often wonder what it would be like if the whole planet started over. I think it could happen. If the right person came into power.*

"Lead the way," Conway said.

The face shield on Pasha's helmet slid down and covered her eyes. She stepped out of the alcove first; the wind was strong and almost knocked her down. His heart heavy with the finality of his choice, Conway stepped out of the alcove and jogged toward the helicopter, his eyes on the opened bay door.

I'm doing the right thing. I'm doing the right thing. I'm doing the right thing.

Conway could see the face of the man in the lighted cockpit. The Austin Detective, Lenny Rombardo.

Another man who worked for Angel Eyes.

The wind blowing around him, Conway stepped up into the dark bay, Pasha still several feet behind him. Rombardo couldn't see him. Conway removed the Palm Pilot from his pocket. The program was already loaded. A two-minute countdown. All he had to do was press the button.

May God forgive me. Conway pressed the button and the timer started ticking down. He slid the Palm across the floor toward Rombardo and then turned around. Pasha was about to step up into the chopper. She still had the gun aimed at him.

"I've changed my mind," he yelled over the wind. "I'm not going."

Pasha's voice boomed over the helmet's speakers. "This is your last chance, Stephen. I'm not going to ask you again."

"I've made my decision and you've made yours. Good-bye, Pasha. Please forgive me."

Conway jogged away from her. When he turned around, he saw that she had climbed in beside Rombardo. She had taken off her helmet. Her eyes were locked on Conway's as the Blackhawk lifted into the air. The searchlight clicked off.

You did the right thing, Stephen. Whatever happens after this, know you did the right thing.

The Blackhawk had just sailed past the roof when the bomb went off. The attack chopper turned around and kept spinning. Conway ran toward the edge of the roof, not knowing why. The cockpit was still lit. Blood was on the glass. He saw Pasha. She was alive. She had blood on her face and was trying to take control of the Blackhawk. Rombardo's dead body, broken and twisted, was still buckled in his seat. But the chopper kept spinning, out of control now, sinking, the bomb having destroyed the navigation system. A final pass and Pasha looked at him, frightened.

Forgive me, Pasha.

The Blackhawk sank below the roof and Pasha was gone.

AFFLICTION

If you have been kicked around by life at an early age, or if your upbringing is defined by being bounced around foster homes and group homes for the troubled and unwanted and the forgettable, you learn the importance of not placing roots because nothing in life is permanent. The pleasing sight of a backyard pool from your bedroom window, or the thrill you get from playing baseball with a group of boys at a favorite playground, are temporary at best, special moments that can be taken away from you as quick and as easy as blinking your eyes.

Steve Conway had lived with Booker that first month. To escape when the media attention got bad, he would run an errand for Book but didn't want to work full time. What he wanted was some stillness, some time alone to reflect and process everything that had happened. Silly, childish demands when you're the dead center of a media storm.

But all storms pass, and when it did, life got real quiet. Conway rented an apartment on Hancock Street in Beacon Hill, a five-minute walk from Booker's place and just around the corner from where Riley used to live. *Used to*. The word was like a haunted echo in his heart. John Riley used to live here. John Riley used to be alive. Conway *used to* work for the CIA. He *used to* be in love with a woman named Pasha Romanov. She was dead now and so was John Riley. Life moved on.

It seemed easier to confront the truth here in the city, during early spring, surrounded by people. The weather was warm for April, and the college students at Suffolk were wrapping up their courses for the year. He would walk among them on the streets, see them in the coffeeshops, bump into them at the bars at night, and sometimes would listen in on their conversations about their problems, feel their ridiculous, almost childish angst and anger at why the world behaved the way it did. Sometimes he would talk with them. Mainly he just wanted to be near them, to soak up their innocence and youth.

In the dreams he would be out on a boat in the middle of the ocean, the night sky painted black above him, and whispered in the wind he would hear Pasha's voice calling out to him to come closer, come closer, Stephen, I have so much to tell you. So many secrets to share.

Sometimes he would wake up. Sometimes he would stay with the dream and keep searching for her. All he ever heard was her voice. Other times he would get up and walk through Beacon Hill's dark, cool streets until he found Riley's condo. Standing across the street, he would lean his back against the cool brick and stare at the dark window where John Riley used to live.

I did the right thing, right?
Answer: Yes, you did.
I did the right thing, right?
Answer: Yes, you did.

Knowing the truth offered little comfort. The truth required a high price and left a bitter taste in his mouth and a cavernous feeling in the pit of his stomach. The truth, he had found, did not have a place in the day-to-day business of life.

At night, Pasha kept calling out for him.

One vital lesson he had learned early and learned hard in his education in the group homes is that you don't take people at their word; you cannot count on others or their promises. If you decide to ignore these facts and invest emotionally in the truth, if you decide to believe in the illusory comfort of a safe and warm home—or, more recently, the whispered promises of a woman who loved you deeply—then you have only yourself to blame when it all comes crashing down.

Five years? Was that how long he had been with her? Inch-by-inch he had given himself to love and blind trust in another person, and within the span of a few seconds, she robbed him of every thought and emotion he had for her, wrapped it up neatly inside a balloon and sent it sailing away.

All this time both enemies had been so close to his skin.

All this time and he couldn't see it.

He had been used—twice.

Betrayed—twice.

Angel Eyes was right. Conway had been nothing more than a means to an end.

At night, alone in the darkness of his bedroom, he would listen to the sounds of the city. A Swiss clock, a housewarming gift from Booker's wife, ticked in the darkness. Time moving forward. The world owes you nothing. Time moves forward and you have to fight to find the ways in which to heal.

Summer arrived on the first Saturday in May. Before the sun had risen, Conway went out for a long run in the Boston Common. Drenched in sweat, he trotted up the flight of stairs, and then showered, changed into jeans and a white T-shirt. Coffee in hand, he walked out onto the roof deck that overlooked the city.

The sun had just started to rise. He watched the neighborhood come alive and in the air felt the springtime magic of hope and the promise of good things to come. He wanted to freeze this moment, to store it in a vial, use it when the next wave of anger and grief hit him.

Inside the apartment, the phone rang.

It's Booker, calling to check up on me again. Booker had assumed the role of big brother; he called early in the morning on the weekends to check in and chat, see what was happening, but what he really wanted was to get a sense of when Conway was going to come to work. He went back inside and picked up the cordless phone in the living room.

"Hello, Stephen."

It had been months since Conway had last heard the cold, monotone voice. He glanced down at his watch, his eyes tracking the second hand.

"I won't be on long enough for your few remaining friends at the CIA to track me," Angel Eyes said.

"I don't work for the CIA anymore." Conway moved back outside and stared down from the roof. The streets below him were quiet, empty.

"I was told the Director wasn't happy about your media stunt. Nobody likes their secrets played on television."

It was true. Conway had placed the truth before the needs of the Agency and had exposed the slick underbelly of an enterprise that thrived on keeping secrets. Add that to the fact that he had been in the national spotlight, his face too well known for any undercover work, and he was looking at a desk job. No thank you. Conway took his severance package and, with a few conditions, went home.

"I was also told that as part of your departure you agreed to have your phone tapped in case I called," Angel Eyes said. "I understand I'm a wanted man now."

"Where's Dixon?" Major Dixon's body had not turned up.

"I assure you that the Major is quite alive and quite safe. He's made a remarkable recovery, Stephen. Doesn't hold any ill will toward you. I wish I could say the same about your other friend." Angel Eyes laughed quietly.

Raymond Bouchard had disappeared. Conway had not thought of the man and didn't want to think about the man now. Or ever.

"Would you like to know about Raymond?" Angel Eyes asked.

"No."

"I rescued Pasha when she was a young girl. So full of venom. Not that I blame her feelings. After the horror she endured at the hands of Misha inside her father's kitchen, I was often surprised by her transformation. All things are possible if you have the right guide."

Conway stared out at the rooftops, the hum of traffic in the distance.

"You're the first man she loved deeply," Angel Eyes said.

Conway said nothing. His heart felt like it was beating inside his throat, stuck, struggling to break free.

"Pasha didn't have to die, Stephen. You could have come with her—could have become a part of us and lived that vision that struggles inside your breast."

"And if I didn't, you would kill me."

"I would never hurt you, Stephen."

"I saw you that day at the Holocaust Memorial. I saw your hand pressed against the glass, your eyes closed." Conway thought he heard a moan coming from the other end. "That's why you wanted the suit. You needed it to carry out your secret wish, the one you hid away from Gunther and Pasha because if they had ever found out, they would have left you."

"I'd love to chat, Stephen, but I'm afraid I'm pressed for time. Remember to mind your place."

"That sounds like a threat."

"Be sure to make use of the gift I left for you on your doorstep." As gentle as a whisper, Angel Eyes hung up.

Conway ran down the stairs and opened the front door. A brown-wrapped, 8-by-11 envelope leaned against the stairs. He picked it up, felt it. No name and no postage; it had the weight of a stack of papers. A bomb? He didn't feel a watch battery.

I would never hurt you, Stephen.

Back on the patio roof, Conway sat down in his chair

and opened the package. Attached to the front of the file folder was a neatly written note:

Dear Stephen,

We dedicate much of our life wondering why we've been treated unfairly; why we've been victimized and used; discarded; passed by. It is on our deathbeds, about to draw in our last breath, that we finally come to the realization of how much time we've wasted on these petty transgressions that in their collective sum are worthless; how we took for granted the gifts that had always lain beneath our feet or next to our hearts, or how we failed to see the joy and beauty and splendor that offer themselves to our eyes every day.

Claire Arlington, like yourself, is a survivor. A cunning warrior. I won't tell you much here; it will spoil the wonder of the discovery.

Icarus was warned by his father not to fly too close to the sun. The boy didn't heed his father's warning and plummeted into the sea. Enter your mother's life free of judgment. If you can do that, you may finally begin the process of exorcising those demons of doubt and curiosity that torment you deep in the night.

I think of you often.

Steve Conway leaned back in his chair, and in the blood-red early-morning light, met his mother for the first time.

Working with blood in this age of disease called for multiple layers. One had to be careful.

Raymond Bouchard was disease free. His blood had been tested for all the known lethal viruses—hepatitis and HIV—and had come up negative. It was safe to play.

A man in Amon Faust's position couldn't risk even the smallest chance of infection. Before venturing down into the basement, Faust would scrub his hairless skin under the hot water until it turned pink. After air drying, he applied the iso-foam alcohol, and when that had dried, he would apply the first layer: the Tyvek sterile garb. Next came the surgical suit and booties, and the two sets of sterile latex gloves.

The biohazard suit, the final layer, was critical. It allowed Faust to be close to the action when it got messy, as it often did down in the basement. The suit had its own respirator and air-flow supply. As a matter of personal taste, he refused to share the same air with a man like Raymond.

Faust hovered above the same surgical chair in which Major Dixon had been bound. Taking the boy's place was Raymond Bouchard, nude, his pale body sweating and shaking as the painkillers wore off. Raymond had become quite the addict—would, in fact, cry for another shot of morphine before another finger was taken. Only three left before moving on to the toes.

Raymond blinked with fear at what fresh new terror awaited him. He opened his dry mouth, his cracked lips quivering as he started in with another request for mercy.

"Please . . . no more . . . I can't . . . please, I'll do whatever you want."

Faust tilted his domed head to the side. Through the shield that covered his eyes, he looked at Major Dixon, who stood next to the same chair in which he had been tortured. The tray of torture instruments lay close to his mutilated hand.

"What shall it be, Major?" Faust asked, his voice amplified by the suit's speaker system.

Major Dixon looked down at the man who had orchestrated all of his pain. He wiggled the remaining fingers on his left hand, thinking. Under Faust's guidance, the boy had come far in the past few months. The mental conditioning had helped him erase the memories of what he had endured in the basement; Faust had helped shape the boy's rage, helped him channel it to more satisfying alternatives.

Major Dixon stopped wiggling his fingers. "Remove his tongue," he said.

"Novocain or not? Your choice, Major."

The boy didn't hesitate. "Like me, he gets nothing."

Faust turned back to the white-faced Raymond. "You've been charged with the crime of blasphemy, Raymond. Personally, I think you're getting off lightly. Now be a good boy and hold still. This won't take but a minute."

Few men have born witness to Faust's strength. With the agility and power of a snapping turtle, Faust pinned Raymond's head against the headrest and held it firmly, his right hand already on the jaw and pushing it open. Raymond's tongue wiggled like an exposed worm searching for a place to crawl away and hide.

Major Dixon fished around for the instrument of choice and settled on a scalpel. He looked up at Faust and smiled. Progress.

Major Dixon held the scalpel above Raymond's wild, terrorized eyes. Raymond started screaming.

"That's the spirit," Faust said. "Go ahead and scream, Raymond. Scream as loud as you want."

There's a saying in New England that if you don't like the weather, wait until tomorrow. On Monday, the week of Memorial Day, summer booted spring out of the way and flooded Boston with a heat wave. By Wednesday the heat was gone and spring was back, the air cool and dry, but by Friday morning, the start of the holiday weekend, the heat and humidity was so intense Conway wanted to shut himself inside a meat locker. He leaned back in the driver's seat of Booker's BMW, the windows down, parked across the street from the old two-story white Colonial home that sat directly across from the dormitory building at Framingham State College. He was sweating and miserable, but he wanted to keep watching.

The woman working the garden looked as frail as her tulips. She was dressed in jeans and a plain gray T-shirt spotted with dirt. It was ten o'clock; she had been out here since seven this morning, digging up dirt and planting with a feverish intensity, only pausing long enough to push her glasses back up her nose. Her husband, dressed in chinos and a crisp white shirt, came out every hour or so to give her a fresh glass of water.

Conway's phone rang. The woman looked up from her work and stared in his direction. He picked the phone up from the seat and answered it by the third ring.

"I'm at your place, and you're not answering your door," Booker said. "Where are you?"

"Out doing errands."

"Why you whispering?"

"I'm trying not to be one of those cell-phone ass-holes who feels the need to broadcast their conversations to the rest of the world. What's up?"

"Me and the family are going down to Falmouth this weekend."

Falmouth was part of Cape Cod. Booker's family owned a house near the water. During college summers, Booker would invite Conway and Riley to this place on weekends, and when Booker was older and more established, he bought the house from his parents and then purchased a boat, a cabin cruiser that slept four comfortably. Sun and water and good food and drinking. Lots of drinking.

"Sounds like a good time," Conway said. The woman had stood up. She was brushing off her jeans with her hands, walking toward him.

"That's what I'm saying. Get back here and pack your bags."

"I'll see you in an hour."

Conway hung up. The woman stood at the car window. She was maybe five-five, razor thin, and had the delicate bones of a bird. Her blond hair was tied behind her head.

"Good morning," she said brightly.

Conway cleared his throat. "Hello."

"I heard your phone ring and when I looked up, I thought I recognized your face. Were you at the school yesterday?"

"Briefly." He knew she was the director of a nursery school that was half a mile down the road. Yesterday, and the two days before that, he had been parked out in the lot, watching her play with the toddlers at lunch, and at night, around six, the time she left work, he watched her climb into a beat-up red Honda and drive back here to her home. A wedding band and an engagement ring were on her left hand. She was married.

"I didn't mean to startle you. I'm new to this area," Conway said, not wanting her to think he was stalking her or the kids at the school. "I'm thinking of having kids. I heard a lot of good things about this neighborhood and about your school, so yesterday, I thought I'd stop there and, you know, check it out on my own."

"Sometimes that's the best way to do it."

"And then this morning, I was driving by here, checking out houses for sale, and saw you working—"

"You stopped and have been sitting here this entire time, wanting to come up and ask me some questions."

"Something like that. I hope I didn't spook you."

"No, of course not. My name is Claire Arlington."

"Stephen," he said, and stuck out his hand. She shook it. It felt like a crackle of electricity hit him. His mouth went dry.

"Why don't you stop by the school Tuesday morning around nine and I'll give you the official tour."

"Sounds good."

"I look forward to seeing you then."

"Yes. Likewise."

"Enjoy your holiday weekend. Try to stay cool."

"Yes. You too. Thank you."

She smiled, accenting the tiny web of lines near the corners of her eyes, turned and walked back toward her home where her husband was standing outside waiting for her with a glass of ice water clutched in his hand.

They decided to do it Saturday morning, early, when the world lay quiet and still. Just before five, Conway and Booker crept away from the sleeping house, went down to the dock and climbed aboard the boat. The sky was a dark blue and the sun was up, peeking over the horizon, its red and gold colors washing over the bellies of the rolling clouds, the air cool and sweet. It would turn colder once they got out in the water. Conway was dressed in jeans and a beat-up gray UNH sweatshirt and wore his dark blue Red Sox baseball cap, a birthday gift from John Riley. Booker drove. Conway sat in the back in a padded white-leather chair, holding the urn tight against his hip.

The ocean makes you reflect on things. What Conway thought about in that peaceful, early-morning stillness was religion. Growing up at St. Anthony's, Catholicism had been drilled into him hard. He could recite any prayer on command; knew when to sit and kneel and stand; knew when to give thanks. He had performed the rituals with the manufactured, robotic joy of a toy dog programmed to bark and sit.

Conway didn't believe in the great Catholic watchdog God who followed you around twenty-four-seven and marked your activities and transgressions on a clipboard. And he didn't know if he believed in another world that existed beyond this one, some island paradise of blue skies and clouds and the sort of eternal joy that could send you to the kind of great heights of pleasure that only existed in dreams. What he did believe in was the power of nature. His time spent in Colorado had showed him how the simple act of taking a moment to give yourself to the view of a snow-capped mountain, or to watch a sunset, could bring you a sense of eternal peace that couldn't be found in pills or booze or listening to the worn-out sermon of a white-collared man who didn't know how to stir the joys or settle the fears that moved through your soul. When he looked out at the color of the sky, when he heard the water splashing hard against the boat and smelled the salty air in the cool wind, Conway felt a sense of peace, an acceptance and serenity that couldn't be forged from a store-bought Bible or recycled sermon.

Booker turned the boat around so that it was facing in the direction it had just traveled. They were far away from the bay, out in the water, but not far enough so that Conway couldn't see Booker's home. Booker cut the engine and turned around and leaned back against the wheel, his face hidden by his sunglasses. Conway stood up. His stomach was knotted. He went to hand the urn to Booker.

"No," Book said. "You need to do it."

John Riley's will asked Booker to spread his ashes across the sea in full view of Booker's home. Conway knew that Booker's change of heart was an invitation for Conway to share a final moment with a close friend, to start the process of grieving and, hopefully, closure. Conway navigated his way to the bow with the urn tucked under his arm.

The wind had a solid push to it; it swirled around

him, whistling past his ears. His feet firmly planted, the bow rocking up and down against the water's current, he looked down at the urn he held in both hands and thought about family. Conway only had two people in his life he could call family. One was behind him, and the other he held in his hands. John Riley, the essence of his short life, all the memories, everything he stood for and loved, was now compressed into black ash and resting inside this urn.

Conway placed his hand on the urn's lid. The images he had seen in the video, images that haunted his sleep every night, banged from behind their locked doors. Conway didn't want to remember Riley this way, not here, not now. But the memory was strong, and what Conway saw in his mind was

The two of them sitting in an outdoor bar in downtown Vail in the middle of winter after a long morning of skiing. It was early afternoon, and the sky was a bright blue, the sun warm on their faces, fresh powder everywhere you looked. John Riley had just kicked back in his chair, propped his boots up on the railing and smiled as he watched the good-looking people who lived off of trust funds walk the streets in their top-of-the-line ski wear. A Jimmy Buffet song was being pumped over the outdoor speakers.

"This place is heaven," John Riley said. He turned his baseball cap backward—the sure sign that he was shitfaced. "When we die, you think you and I will go to a place like this?"

"I doubt heaven is a ski lodge with blond chicks with big plastic tits."

"Of course it is. Why do you think I go to church every Sunday?" Riley laughed, drank some of his beer. "Where do you think we go?"

"Into the ground."

"And?"

"And that's it."

Riley laughed. "You're one morbid son of a bitch, you know that?"

"What can I tell you, I was raised a Catholic."

Riley laughed again. Then his eyes, shining with alcohol, turned serious. "It's all about choices, Steve."

Riley put on his sunglasses and stared out at the sunshine, at the people parading in front of him, his life limitless, his smile wide and genuine.

Here, alone with the water and sea air and a lifetime away from that memory, Conway made the choice to remember the good times. This is the power we have.

Steve Conway lifted up the lid on the urn. The wind kicked the ashes into the air. They swirled up into his face, into his nose and lungs, and when he looked up, the ashes danced around him and sparkled like diamonds in the sunlight. He closed his eyes and dove deep within himself, to those locked places where we hide and protect what we love and treasure. This is where we remember. This is where we live.

AUTHOR'S NOTE

This book is a work of fiction; the story and characters are products of my imagination. I made some minor changes to areas surrounding Austin and took some liberties on the roof design for the building located at 100 Summer Street in Boston. While the technology in this book does exist in one form or another, I decided to use some authorial license, given the rapid manner at which technology develops.

An article titled "Future Soldier" in *Popular Science* (July 2000) gave me the basis for certain aspects of the military suit mentioned in the novel. Robert I. Friedman's excellent book, *Red Mafiya: How the Russian Mob Has Invaded America* (Little, Brown), was not only a fantastic read, it also provided me with a fascinating look into the world of Russian organized crime.

World Without End wouldn't exist if it weren't for my good friend Jack Wentz. Jack was right there in the beginning and let me pick his brain for the past two years (and managed not to laugh too hard in the process). Chances are if you liked something in the book, the idea came from Jack. Fellow writer Lisa Dingle helped me to understand the hearts and minds of strangers and kept me on track. I couldn't do this without the valuable feedback of my reading crew:

Ron Gondek, Randy Scott, Neal Sonnenberg, and Mark Alves. All mistakes are mine.

The publication of *Deviant Ways* put me in touch with great people like Jeanne Dery of Postal Center USA in Tyngsboro, Massachusetts. Jeanne became a one-woman publicity machine, and thanks to her efforts, put the book in the hands of lots of readers. Thanks, Jeanne. Thanks are also in order for my good friend Barbara Gondek, who helped spread the word and introduced me to new readers all over New Hampshire. And thanks to all of the new fans I've met in person and over the Internet. I wouldn't be able to do this without you.

For reading, answering all of my questions, giving great advice, and being a great publishing guide and person, thanks are in order to my agent Pam Bernstein. Thanks to her assistant, Jonette Suiter, for all her work on my behalf.

I couldn't ask for a better group of people than the ones at Pocket. Emily Bestler, my editor, provided valuable input, support, and enthusiasm. Sarah Branham also provided great insight on the novel and answered what were probably lots of stupid questions. Thank you, Sarah. Cathy Gruhn, my publicist, I can't thank you enough for all your hard work. Thanks are also in order to art director Paolo Pepe for his hard work on the great jacket covers, and thanks to the Pocket sales force for their dedication and commitment.

Of course, none of this would be possible without the patience and commitment of my wife, Jen. I love you.

ATRIA HARDCOVER
PROUDLY PRESENTS

REMEMBERING SARAH

CHRIS MOONEY

Coming in hardcover
from Atria Books

Turn the page for a preview of
Remembering Sarah. . . .

The official name was Roby Park, named after Dan
Roby, the city's first mayor, but everyone who lived in
Pine Grove called it The Hill. Back when Mike was
growing up, the Hill had been nothing more than a
long, wide stretch of grass. At the top, sitting on a parking lot that overlooked the hill, you had Buzzy's, the
only place in town where three bucks bought you a
large Coke and a burger on a paper plate stacked high
with either fries or the world's greatest onion rings,
your choice. Twenty odd years later, Buzzy's was still
there, along with a liquor store and video store, and
now The Hill had one of those fancy jungle gyms and
a new baseball diamond with stands. The real attraction
was the floodlight. Winters in New England meant the
sky was pitch black by four, so the town splurged and
installed a telephone poll with a floodlight that lit up
every inch of the hill so you could go sledding any hour
you wanted.

The wide hill was divided into two parts: the left
area for the older kids, mostly snowboarders, and on
the right, the less bumpy area for the kids Sarah's age
and younger. The place was packed. Mike found a spot
in the lot that abutted the new baseball diamond,
parked his truck and got out. When he went around

and opened the door for Sarah, Mike picked her up and Sarah immediately launched into her protest about being picked up or carried—"I'm not a baby, Daddy, only babies get carried."—so he put her down. Sarah, naturally, refused to hold his hand.

Mike tucked the sled under his arm, and as he trucked slowly through the snow, Sarah walking beside him, lost in her own world and singing some made-up song about dragons living in Barbie's Dream House, Mike thought about all the times his mother had driven him here. When her face wasn't bruised too badly, she would come outside and smoke her Kools with the other mothers, all of them watching their boys play the winter version of Demolition Derby. Mike would no sooner jump on his cheap red plastic sled from Woolworth's than Bill's sled would come charging into him from the side, Bill pushing him off the sled and sending Mike tumbling across the snow, Mike laughing his ass off the entire time. And the thing was, the mothers laughed too. Kids fell. Kids got bumped and bruised and cut and got themselves back up and then got bumped and bruised and cut all over again.

Those days were gone. A lot of parents now had Jess's plastic-bubble mentality to childcare. Sarah couldn't slip and fall without Jess being right next to her, scooping her up, Mommy's here, everything's going to be okay. Right. Mike was all too well aware how much the world loved to kick you in the ass, and when it did, it sure as hell didn't offer you an apology or a helping hand. Sometimes it kicked you again. Harder.

"DADDY!"

Mike stopped walking. He turned around and saw Sarah standing a few feet behind him, her head craned, looking up at him. The pink snowsuit's hood was wrapped tightly around her head, the imitation white fur lining it blowing in the wind as snowflakes melted against her glasses.

"What's wrong, peanut?"

"I *told* you I don't like that name."

Oh boy, she's in a mood. "You're right, I'm sorry," Mike said.

"You were looking at the kids sledding and you looked like you were sad and I asked you why and you *ignored* me."

Mike was often amazed by the way little kids came with some innate, hidden tool that constantly measured the slightest fluctuation in your mood, the tone of your voice, your facial expressions. It was as if they came equipped with invisible antennae that alerted them the second something was off.

"Now how could I ignore you?" Mike said. He dropped the sled on the ground and then got down on one knee so he was eye level with his daughter. "You look like a big pink marshmallow."

"What were you thinking about?"

"I was thinking about my mother."

"Was it happy thoughts?"

"Always," Mike said, forcing a smile.

"Your mother's name is Nana Mary."

"That's right."

"Nana Mary went to heaven before I was born. She's in heaven with Mommy's daddy, Grandpa Jack. He went to heaven before I was born too."

It went back to the antennae thing. Jess had pictures of her parents, pictures of her two sisters, Sarah's aunts, Ruth and Jean, in framed pictures that hung on the walls all over the house and in the small, decorative photo albums that were scattered on the coffee table.

When Sarah was about three, she went through this phase where she was drawn to the photo albums and would want you to sit with her as she went through each picture and told you, like you were learning this for the first time, the name of each person, who they were related to, where they lived. Mike didn't own any pictures of his parents. His old man had destroyed the few pictures of Mike and his mother years ago, burning them in the backyard. No pictures of his parents anywhere in the house and Sarah asking questions, Mike had to tell her something, so he said his mother had died—and for all practical purposes, she had—and as for his father, well, he just lived far away, too far away to call.

But Sarah, she had those antennae up and working, and while she sensed that it was okay to talk and ask questions about Nana Mary, she didn't ask questions about Grandpa Lou. Mike had to give his old man some credit. The son of a bitch had done one thing right in his life: he had promised to stay away and he had.

Sarah started jumping up and down, squealing, *"There's Paula, Daddy, there's Paula, look, here she comes!"*

Mike looked at the bottom of the hill. It was packed with so many parents and kids, Christ, it was almost impossible to pick out anyone, but Sarah kept jumping and pointing. Finally, Mike zeroed in on the familiar blue snow tube just as it hit a ramp and went airborne maybe a foot. Paula O'Malley wasn't prepared for the landing. She lost her balance and fell off her snow tube, tumbling hard across the snow. Paula sat up, snow in her hair and mouth, and, tears ready, looked over at her father standing a few feet away.

"Turn off the waterworks, Paula, ya just bumped your bum is all," Wild Bill said, his black Harley

Davidson baseball hat pulled low over his shaved head, a wad of chewing tobacco bulging against his bottom lip. A small gold loop earring dangled from each ear.

Satisfied by her father's tone, Paula reached down, grabbed her hat and started shaking out the snow.

Sarah said, "I want to go sledding with Paula."

Mike held out his hand and Sarah swatted it away.

"No, Daddy, just with Paula."

"Sweetie, Paula's eight."

"So?"

"So you're six."

"And a *half*, Daddy. I'm six *and a half*."

"What I mean is Paula's bigger than you. The big kid's hill is very bumpy, and some of the kids have set up ramps." Mike pointed to where Paula just wiped out. "If you hit one of those ramps, you'll go flying in the air."

"Like a bird?" Sarah looked very excited by the possibility.

"Last time you went down by yourself, you fell off the sled and hit a patch of ice. You got your big bump on your head, remember?"

"Oh yeah. That hurt. And Mommy was mad at me."

Not at you, sweetie. Mommy was mad at me because I let the world hurt you.

"Come on, we'll go down together," Mike said and stuck out his hand.

Sarah swatted his hand away. The stubbornness she had inherited from him was set hard in her blue eyes, and it took Mike back to last summer, when he was teaching Sarah how to swim, Sarah not wanting to wear her floaties and wanting to learn to swim on her own—not with a helping hand from him, on her own. Mike let her try it, and Sarah sank right to the bottom (Jess was there, of course, hovering around them the entire time, nearly screaming at him to pick her up, Jesus Christ, hurry). No sooner did Mike bring Sarah up for air than Sarah would want to try it again, on her own. He was so in love with this part of his daughter, her stubborn, almost unbendable need to fight to do things in her own way and time that he had to do everything in his power to keep from smiling.

Don't you dare let her go down that hill by herself, Jess's voice warned him. *What if she falls again and hurts herself bad this time? What if she breaks a leg or cracks her head open—Jesus Christ, Michael, look at how small she is. What if—*

Your mother never spoke up, another voice added. *You want to raise a girl to become a woman who's terrified to speak her mind? You let Jess kill off this part of her, Sarah will end up marrying a prize like your old man. That the life you want for her?*

"Daddy, Paula's getting ready to go back up the hill."

"Sarah—"

"Can I go, *pleeeease, pleeeease*—"

"Sarah, look at me."

She knew that tone. The pleading stopped and she snapped her attention to him.

"You go up the hill with Paula, you come back down with Paula, understand?"

"I understand."

"What did I say?"

"Up and down with Paula."

"Right. I'll be standing over there next to your godfather, okay?"

Sarah grinned, her top teeth crooked, the bottom two missing. She gripped the rope for the sled and trudged through the snow, screaming for Paula to wait up, and as

Mike stood up, he felt that smile of hers fill him and warm him deep into his bones.

You realize what you've done.

He had committed the worst of parental sins, siding with the child, and he didn't care. Fuck it. You get to be six—excuse me, six and half—once in this life, so fuck it.

'Course, that wasn't going to stop what would happen tomorrow.

Jess's moods were as constant and predictable as the tides. Tomorrow morning, shortly after he left to head to Wellesley to work on the addition, Jess would pack Sarah and the dog into the Explorer and head north to her mother's house in Rowley. Mike would come home to an empty house and find Jess's message waiting for him on the voice mail, Jess saying that they were going to stay the night, blaming it on the snow or, if it didn't snow (and it might not; you couldn't trust New England weathermen, they dropped the ball so many times) she'd offer up some lame excuse about not feeling well or being tired. Either way, his punishment would be losing the only day he had to spend with his daughter, Sunday. And he was fine with that. The important thing here was that Sarah got to be a kid. Collecting these fun moments from her childhood, snapshots she could look back on and smile at—that was the stuff that mattered in life. Real life, with all of its sucker punches and bone-weary bullshit, would always be there, but that time you had when you're six, believing that life was just this big merry-go-round of fun full of parties and visits from Santa Claus and the Easter Bunny and the Tooth Fairy, shit, you only had a small period of time when that sort of magic actually seemed real, why take it away?

Wild Bill stood alone, a good amount of space

between him and the people who had formed small groups, talking among themselves and, Mike noticed, occasionally cutting sideways glances in Bill's direction. Bill saw the familiar pink snowsuit and turned around just as Mike walked up to him.

"Seriously, does Jess get jealous when you wear her jacket?"

The jacket in question, a Christmas gift from Sarah, was made of black wool and cashmere. More importantly, it was clean and new—unlike Bill's faded blue Patriots jacket that dated back to the early eighties, Bill refusing to give up the old, ratty jacket with its grease stains and torn pocket until the Pats won the Super Bowl.

Mike said, "You don't like it?"

"No, it's great. If I had a vagina, I'd wear one too."

"You're right. I should probably trade it in, get myself some tats and earrings and go for that nasty hobo look you got going on." Mike removed his pack of Marlboros from his trendy black jacket, his eyes watching Sarah chugging up the hill.

Bill said, "This snow's too good to waste. Glad Jess had a change of heart."

Mike lit a cigarette with his lighter, and then took a long, satisfying drag. "One of us did," he said, thinking about the note *he* left for her on the island table, written in black marker on a sheet of paper and not a Post-It note, the words as big as a sign so she wouldn't miss it.

Bill spit into a large Dunkin Donuts coffee cup and Mike smoked, the two of them standing quiet as they watched their girls moving up to the top of the hill now, their shapes disappearing behind the floodlight and the snow, shit, it had really started to pick up.

"Bumped into Bamford on the way home," Bill said.

"And how is that fat bastard doing?"

"Getting a divorce."

Mike whipped his head to Bill. "You're shitting me."

"That's what you get for marrying a broad with a terminal case of PMS."

"But the kids—"

"Sully, the guy was fucking miserable. Just because someone leaves it doesn't make them a bad person."

Mike took a final drag and flicked the cigarette butt into the wind. The three glasses of Crown on an empty stomach had made him a little drunk and filled him with the need to talk. He could feel it building in him right now, begging him to just open his mouth and let it all out. He fished out another cigarette from his pack and looked out to his left, at East Dunstable Road where cars were piled up on both sides. A taxi was crawling west toward the connection for Route 128 and seeing it made him think about the day his mother left. Mike could picture her sitting so quietly in the back of the cab, her twelve years of marriage packed up in the suitcase beside her, the driver asking, "Where you headed? North or South?" And for the first time his mother would make a decision and a man would listen. When she picked her new direction, Mike wondered if that scream trapped inside her skull had finally died.

Paula's snow tube slid over to them. She didn't get up. She sat there, sulking.

"What's with the puss?" Bill asked.

"Jimmy Mac," Paula said.

Everyone in town knew about Jimmy Mac, Bobby MacDonald's youngest, supposedly. Bobby Mac was the kind of guy who liked to spread his love around and have litters of kids with different mothers in the Mission Hill projects. Rumor was Jimmy Mac had stabbed a fifteen-year-old drug dealer down at the Common, Jimmy taking business lessons from his old man.

"He's up at the top, pushing everyone out of the way," Paula said, and then in rapid fire added, "He's always picking on us, like last week, we were walking home from Stacy's house and Jimmy Mac saw us and blew his nose all over Joanne Chambers and made her cry. I told him to stop it and he called me a dink and pushed me down. He's mean."

"I couldn't agree more. Come on, baby girl, we'll go have a chat with Mr. MacDonald," Bill said, and Mike saw in his friend's eyes that wild shine, the look Bill got as he entertained the different ways he could redecorate your face.

Mike said, "Let's go to Buzzy's. Paula, you want a cheeseburger?"

"I want french fries and mayo."

Bill's face twisted into a grimace, his lips puckering—the same face he made at last summer's Fourth of July barbecue when his wife, Patty, slipped him a soy dog instead of a real hotdog. ("Jesus Christ," he said after spitting out a half-chewed wad onto the grass. "This hotdog tastes like feet!")

"Go load the snow tube on the truck and I'll meet you up top," Mike said to Bill. "Sarah should be down any second."

Bill lumbered off with Paula and Mike lit his cigarette, his eyes sweeping the bottom of the hill for Sarah's pink snowsuit. Heading to Buzzy's was a good idea. The snow had picked up, and so had the wind. Some people, Mike saw, were packing it up, going home.

Mike had smoked half his cigarette and Sarah still

hadn't come down yet. Come to think of it, only a handful of kids had sledded down.

Jimmy Mac.

Mike stuck his hands in his jacket pocket and brushed his way past the parents and kids slowly trekking their way up the walking path. Sleds and snow tubes whisked by both sides of him, the air charged with giggles and shrieks and laughs, Mike kept his eye out for Sarah's sled. He reached the top of the hill and stepped out of the glare of the floodlight.

In the span of time it had taken him to get up here, the visibility had gone from bad to worse. Now he could barely see six feet in front of him. Headlights coming from the cars parked along the road next to him, along with the headlights from the parking lot above, were buried behind the snow. Mike could make out the shapes of bodies crowding the top, all of them bumping into each other, shouting for people to get out of their way.

"Sarah, it's Dad. I'm at the top."

Out of nowhere a group of kids rushed past Mike as if being chased—or chasing someone. Mike looked over his shoulder and watched as they bolted down the road, disappearing behind the snow. Mike turned back to the hill, moving as he yelled.

"Sarah, it's Dad. Wave to me."

The hood.

Right, he had had wrapped her hood so tight around her head she probably couldn't hear him. Not with wind and all those different voices up here laughing and yelling and screaming at the top of their lungs, the horns honking from East Dunstable Road. Mike felt a flutter in his heart that made him move a bit quicker, put some urgency in his voice.

"Sarah."

"Sarah, I'm up here, up on top of the hill. Wave to me."

"Sarah, where are you?"

On and on Mike kept saying her name as he moved his way through the crowd. The bodies disappeared, and now Mike was standing closer to part of the hill with steep embankments that rolled into the woods and trails. Where the hell was she?

"Bill?" Mike yelled down the hill. "Bill?"

"Yeah?" Bill yelled back.

"Sarah down there?"

"No. Why?"

I can't find her.

Mike turned around, faced the direction where voices shouted and laughed.

Calm down. She's here.

Bill yelled, "You okay?"

"Yeah. Take a look down there, will ya?"

Mike started walking back, about to call out Sarah's name again when his boots kicked something hard. He looked down and saw what looked like Sarah's sled.

Bending down, Mike brushed off the snow covering the seat. SARAH SULLIVAN printed in black block letters, in his handwriting.

"Sully, she's not down here," Bill yelled out. "You got her?"

Sticking out next to the snow was what looked like the end of an expensive pen. Mike leaned in and saw that it wasn't a pen, it was something else, and when he reached down and lifted it out of the snow, he saw that he was holding Sarah's glasses.

"*SARAH?*"

She was here, had to be, Sarah wouldn't leave without him or Bill.

"SARAH? SARAH, IT'S DAD, WHERE ARE YOU?"
Please God, please answer me.

All around him cars were starting, leaving the parking lots and waiting in the traffic for their turn to pull onto East Dunstable and head home.

Mike stumbled out onto the road, almost slipping on the snow, and ran up to a Honda Accord in the lead, the car about to make a turn when Mike banged on the guy's window. The guy's son, four or five, jumped in his seat and Mike kept pounding on the glass until the guy rolled the window down.

"My daughter, Sarah Sullivan, is six, six and a half," Mike said, breathless. "Goes to St. Pius."

"Sorry, man, I'm from Chelsea."

"Would you get out of your car and help me look? She's wearing a pink snowsuit."

The guy nodded and pulled over. Mike attacked the next car, pounding on the window until the driver rolled down the window, Mike checking the back seats and underneath the car on the off chance Sarah got hit. The parking lot for the packy and convenience store was backed-up with traffic, the cold air blaring with car horns, people out of their cars and swearing for Mike to get the hell out of the road.

Bill appeared out from a curtain of snow, Paula cradled in his massive, tree-trunk arms.

"Sully, what the hell—"

"Her glasses, I found her glasses next to her sled. Paula, what happened up here? Tell me what happened."

Paula flinched at the sound of Mike's voice.

"Sully, it's okay, calm— "

"Sarah can't see without her glasses, she—"

"I'm sure someone saw her all worked up and had the good sense to bring her inside Buzzy's. She's probably in there right now pigging out on a burger and rings." Bill put his meaty hand on Mike's neck and squeezed it. "Relax. Everything's going to be okay."

Visit the
Simon & Schuster Web site:
www.SimonSays.com

and sign up for our
mystery e-mail updates!

Keep up on the latest
new releases, author appearances,
news, chats, special offers, and more!
We'll deliver the information
right to your inbox — if it's new,
you'll know about it.